Power

Stone

— Light & Shadow —

This is a work of fiction. Similarities to real people, places, or events are entirely coincidental. Some aspects of this story are inspired by personal experiences and emotions, particularly around the theme of resilience against adversity.

POWER STONE - LIGHT & SHADOW
First edition. November 3, 2024.
Copyright © 2024 T. Ben Talion.
Written by T. Ben Talion.

PROLOGUE

A tall, youthful figure stumbled up the snow-covered hill, only stopping when it reached the old oak at the edge of the spring. Its movements were sluggish, every fiber of its body screaming for rest, but the danger left no room for such a luxury. The cold wind tugged at the thick, soaked coat that offered little protection, and deep breaths sent waves of pain through its chest. The figure leaned one arm against the rough trunk, the other hand shakily reaching for its hood. With a quick tug, it pulled it back, revealing a blood-smeared, dirty face in the moonlight — young, yet scarred by battle and escape. The adolescent's breath came in gasps, the metallic sheen of the blood reflecting the pale light that fell upon him.

Trembling fingers traced his wounds. Across the bridge of his nose, beneath the small bump, ran a deep gash, while warm liquid trickled down from his forehead into his eyes. He raised a hand to find the source. A gaping tear cut through the dark, damp hair on the left side of his head. The pain burned like fire, but it was the least of his worries.

He clenched his teeth and cursed quietly. "Damn." It was more of a whisper, an exhausted word lost in the wind. A curse at himself, at the moment the plan had failed, and they had discovered him. They had seen what he was and what he was capable of. How long would it be before they found him up here? Their shouts echoed through the trees, filled with determination to hunt him down.

From here, he could see the lights of the monastery he had fled just ten minutes ago — but there was no sign of those who were supposed to meet him here. Alone, his chances of making it out of this alive were slim. "Where are you?" he muttered to himself, his eyes nervously scanning in all directions. With great effort, he pushed himself away from the oak and limped toward another tree on the opposite side of the spring.

There, they had stashed their packs, and he quickly found them again. He pulled out some dried fruit and a linen cloth — the wounds had to be tended to first, and something had to be done about his waning strength before he could continue. In his current state, neither fleeing nor fighting was an option.

With trembling hands, he reached under his coat for the small leather pouch attached to his belt. Even opening it was difficult, but he managed, and his left hand slid inside. Only a brief moment passed before he pulled out a needle, thread, and a small vial.

The youth soaked the linen cloth in the liquid from the vial and pressed it to the wound on his head. The burning pain was intense, but he had expected it and gritted his teeth. Stitching the wound, however, was a different matter entirely. "Two stitches should do it... hopefully." His hand trembled even more as he brought the thick needle closer to his head. He closed his eyes and took a few deep breaths. He had stitched up countless wounds before; it had become second nature. Eventually, the pressure was great enough that the flesh gave way.

He kept his eyes closed during the procedure, cursing internally at the pain and the fact that none of the others had made it here yet. After ten minutes, it was finally done — the wound was stitched, and he exhaled in relief. His pursuers seemed to still be searching the area, and to his fortune, they hadn't seen him flee up the hill.

Once more, he soaked the linen cloth in the liquid and pressed it to his head again. With trembling fingers, he pulled a narrow band from his pouch and tied the cloth in place. He leaned heavily against the tree, as if trying to anchor himself to its stability. A part of the tension drained from his body. "At least that's one less thing to worry about," he murmured softly. But a new question burned in his mind: "What next?"

They would hunt him down. The Church of Light now knew he had resurfaced after they had thought him dead. Too many Clerics and Magisters had witnessed his abilities — there was no undoing that. He could flee, hide in the southern wildlands where the Church had not set foot in years. But between him and the wildlands lay a hundred kilometers of unforgiving cold, and it was far from certain that the mountain tribes there would welcome him.

As he thought, he mechanically reached for his waterskin and opened it. Not much was left inside, but he drank greedily until the last drop quenched his parched throat. The skin was empty. With shaky hands, he stowed it back, his movements slow and clumsy. For a moment, he leaned against the tree again, trying to organize his thoughts. The storm had passed, the air was clear and cold, and the snow sparkled in the moonlight. In the distance, he could make out the faint lights of the city. The watchtowers on the city walls stood bright and menacing in the darkness. No matter which path he chose, this might be the last time he would see them.

Should he fight? His condition argued against it, as did the strength of those pursuing him. He had seen what the Magister was capable of. A second encounter would be far shorter than the first. And yet — the youth came to the bitter realization that luck had finally abandoned him. Nothing forced him to take the risk and stay at the monastery longer than necessary — but he didn't want to pass up the chance to make his tormentors pay for what they had done to him.

Lost in thought, he reached for his chest, feeling the power stone beneath his linen shirt. "Today, you'll have full control, I promise," he whispered in his mind to the stone. But there was no response — no reaction. A wave of disappointment washed over him.

He was torn. On one hand, he felt a strange indifference toward his fate. Whatever was to come, he could accept it. He found a grim peace in knowing that none of those who had once tried to kill him were still alive. His life should have ended back then, and everything that followed was, to him, merely a bonus.

On the other hand, he thought of the last few months — of everything he had achieved. The friendships he had made. The control he had gained over the power stones that were meant to kill him. The changes that had occurred because of him. The thought of having to give all that up hurt more than the gaping wound on his head.

Voices were drawing nearer. One of the search parties seemed to be climbing the hill. Arik peeked out from behind the tree and saw a larger gathering of white lights. His expression fell as he realized this was no ordinary search party — it was everyone who had been at the monastery. "At least they're attacking openly, not treacherously," he murmured as he stepped out of the shadows and threw off his cloak. The cold night air filled his lungs, and he exhaled calmly. Spirals of light and shadow unfurled from his shoulders down to his arms. The same pattern repeated from his waist to his legs. For his torso and head, he chose thinner threads, as fine and interwoven as he could manage. Within half a minute, his armor was complete.

He recalled with gratitude how the shadow-walkers had taught him the use of various combat techniques and weapon styles. His talent for arm claws had become second nature to him. He focused and formed them: a one-meter-long claw for his right arm and a shorter one for his left. For his final battle, he wanted to bring out the best he had to offer. The voices and sounds grew louder with every passing second. They were now only a hundred meters away.

He looked up at the sky and saw the clear stars above. Tears streamed down his cheeks, and he closed his eyes. Back then, his will had kept him alive. Was it justice or vengeance that had fueled that will? He had never asked himself that question before... But now, on the brink of his final fight, the answer seemed unimportant.

His stone began to glow. It released energy that coursed through his body. The youth felt it from his toes to the tips of his hair and allowed it to flow. The armor he had created was reinforced without any effort on his part; he seemed to grow taller, stronger, and the exhaustion melted away.

Freed from all burdens, he moved forward. He effortlessly entered the realm of Unlight and turned inward. "I'm ready," he whispered to his power stone. A smile crossed his lips.

A cascade of impressions flooded his mind, and he thought his brain was playing tricks on him. Out of the corner of his eye, he saw a familiar face grinning broadly at him. But the blow from the club that struck the back of his head — he recognized as real, just before he lost consciousness.

CHAPTER 1

From the depths of the underground complex came the sound of massive, old wooden boards splintering. The noise echoed off the cold stone walls, creeping through the dark passageways. Each crack was like a blow to the silence, reverberating until it finally reached Teto, pulling the entire common room into its spell. He sat there with the others, the group's faces lit by flickering torchlight, as he inevitably began to wonder whether he had made the right decision. Teto crossed his arms behind his head, leaning back as his expression grew more thoughtful. The shadows cast by the many torches along the walls had a calming effect, helping him gather his thoughts. But with each dull snap of the boards, the uncertainty within him seemed to grow.

Had his "guest" recovered so quickly? Or was there another explanation? The question gnawed at him. When he had found the young man on the street a day and a half ago, the youngster had been on death's doorstep. He looked no older than 16 or 17, and his build suggested he was more scholar than fighter. The color of the cord on his robe supported that assumption. Physically, it was unlikely that he would even survive the first night. And yet, he had. "Our guest has quite a strong will," Teto murmured, drawing that conclusion from the distant sound. His forehead furrowed, the creases deepening over his already weathered face.

It had to be the stones in the youngster's body. Teto wouldn't have survived so long in this world if he hadn't learned a thing or two about power stones. In his 42 years, he had witnessed a few times how the stones could take over a person's body once their willpower was extinguished. But he'd never stayed around long enough to see what happened afterward. Like many others, he believed it was far healthier to run as fast as possible. No one considered it cowardice to flee from such a situation — even the instructors once recommended it.

Teto closed his eyes, took a deep breath, and sighed. Many of those he led didn't have the same experience as him. They were at risk if they crossed paths with the youngster. With a calm, low voice, still leaning his head back, he spoke: "Diemo, go and get everyone to safety. Don't fight the newcomer. In his current state, he's unpredictable, and you'd all be risking your lives."

Teto finally brought his head forward again, locking eyes with the young man seated across from him at the table. Diemo was in his mid-twenties, his eyes dark and cold, his scarred, clean-shaven face as unmoving as stone. Diemo remained unfazed.

He stood, kicking his chair back with his right foot. The fingers on his left hand twitched like those of a puppeteer, and within three seconds, he had disappeared into the shadows below. Teto turned his head to the left, looking at a small woman in her late twenties with waist-length blonde hair. In contrast to Diemo's imposing muscles, which could intimidate by presence alone, she seemed delicate and fragile. Before Teto could say a word, she cut him off with her almost squeaky voice. "Don't even think about it!"

Teto feigned innocence, and she continued. "You know perfectly well that there's too little space down here in the tunnels for me to fight properly."

"We'll have to discuss that again soon, Fenna," Teto responded dryly. "At some point, you won't be able to avoid a fight. An opportunity like this won't come around again soon."

The complex shook, and the screams of several people echoed down the tunnels. Teto's face grew more serious, and he corrected himself with a sigh: "On second thought, I'd better handle this myself before our newcomer destroys the entire complex."

Had he underestimated the urgency? Should he have gone with Diemo after all? These questions raced through his mind as he bolted upright, grabbed his staff, and rushed off.

Shortly after he left, a rough voice rang out. "Why didn't he send us?" It came from a man seated across from Fenna, about 10 years older than Teto. The older woman next to him replied, "Because Teto doesn't want us to snuff out that light of his." She snickered, her raspy voice cutting through the room, before the man responded, "That wouldn't have been a problem. I could've just promised to break a few small bones." Both immediately caught Fenna's glare, making it clear they shouldn't push their luck.

Teto reached the well-lit corridor where the youngster had been. From a distance, he could see the damage to the stone wall. Splintered oak fibers were scattered across the passage. To his relief, the unconscious fighters had already been pulled from the danger zone and were being treated by healers. Those who had managed to flee or had only sustained minor injuries noticed their leader's arrival. Their faces were etched with fear.

"Te... Te... Teto... we tried to stop him," one of them stammered. Teto looked at her, noticing the thin red line of blood slowly trickling down her forehead, across her nose, and dripping onto the ground. She clearly had a head injury. He raised his right hand to stop her. "This wasn't a fight you should've been involved in. When facing someone like that, the only option is to flee if you want to live to see another day." Teto paused, looking her directly in the face, though his words were loud enough for everyone to hear. "There's no shame in that. This will be the first time I face him myself." His shoulders tensed, the staff in his hand trembling slightly.

Despite his nerves, he smiled gently, exuding confidence. He had to conceal his doubts, as he had done so many times before. It was the burden of leadership. Then he pointed at the wound beneath her red-blonde hair. "Get that treated quickly, Ostara. I have to move before things get worse. Did you see the color of his eyes?"

Ostara hesitated, unsure why it mattered. "White and black… Why?"

"Good," Teto replied. "That means it hasn't happened yet. If the stone colors merge, we'll have even more trouble. I assume our guest is just around that corner?"

"Yes, Diemo and Romilda are holding him off. Diemo immediately pushed him back when he arrived and covered our retreat."

"He shouldn't have fought him… why can't he ever listen to me," Teto muttered, leaving Ostara behind as he rushed ahead. Small black spheres appeared out of nowhere and began to orbit him. They were no larger than plums. At first, only a few; then dozens, then hundreds of them.

As he turned the corner, a flash of white light blinded him. Teto saw Diemo being thrown against the stone wall. Like a sack of potatoes, Diemo slumped forward and fell onto the cold stone, motionless. Teto sprinted forward, liquid shadow already covering his body. Just before he reached the corner, he raised his staff with both hands, swinging it like a sword. "Romilda, down!" he bellowed as he swung. The orbs that had been circling him shot toward Romilda. She dove forward, barely dodging them. The landing wasn't smooth, but she managed to cushion most of the fall. Her arms ached, but there was no time to think about it. She had to get up quickly.

Not all the orbs hit the youngster. But enough struck him to knock him off his feet and send him flying several meters back. Romilda was already on her feet again, knowing the attack was over. "Grab Diemo and get to safety!" Teto ordered. She complied, and moments later, Teto was alone in the hallway with the youngster. The youngster stood once more. Except for his head, one half of his body was bathed in light, the other in shadow.

"You've caused enough damage. Time to end this." With those words, Teto acted, and a shadow wall shot from his body, filling the entire hallway. The youngster stood still, seemingly unbothered that the intensity of his light was diminishing. He stood for a moment, as if trying to summon something. When nothing happened, he charged at Teto, throwing a basic punch. Teto dodged effortlessly. The youngster repeated his attacks a few times, then switched to kicks. These missed their mark as well.

Their eyes met. The youngster's face twisted into a broad grin, mocking his opponent. Then Teto saw it happen. The colors of the youngster's eyes merged into one — if it could even still be called a color. It was Unlight, the realm between light and shadow.

"That… is unexpected," Teto muttered, surprised, but it didn't faze him. He hadn't anticipated it happening so soon.

The youngster attacked again. This time, he was faster, more precise. More dangerous. Each strike came like a whirlwind, but Teto dodged effortlessly, his movements fluid and controlled. The youngster's light seemed to tear through the surrounding shadows, but Teto remained unshaken. 'You're fast,' Teto thought, 'but not fast enough.' With a single, precise movement, he thrust his staff into the youngster's abdomen, snuffing out his power in an instant. The youngster was thrown backward, spitting blood. Teto had amplified his strike just enough to ensure the youngster wouldn't get back up. Light and shadow peeled away from the youngster's body.

Teto let his shadow dome dissolve and approached the unconscious body, grabbing him by the collar and dragging him down the corridor to the others. There, he dropped the youngster to the floor and ordered them to chain him up. Before returning to the common room, Teto made a quick stop at his quarters. He needed a few moments alone. After closing the door behind him, he exhaled deeply, the tension draining from him. "Strong mind, weak body… we really got lucky there."

CHAPTER 2

Teto entered the common room, deep in thought, the same room he had left about twenty minutes earlier. Fenna and the other two were still seated at the table. The light from the torches reflected off one man's bald head. Teto headed toward the table, but had to stop for a moment. His left leg ached again, as it often did in the eight years since the last battle. He took a deep breath and swallowed the pain.

"Did you kill him?" the old woman at the table asked mockingly, looking up at him. She grinned widely, revealing poorly maintained teeth beneath her wild gray curls. A short giggle followed her question.

Teto didn't respond with words. He snapped his right hand, and a small black orb struck the old woman's forehead, causing her to tumble backward along with her chair. Instead of getting up, she stayed lying down, laughing uproariously. Teto sat down on his wooden chair and reached for his cup. Resting his left elbow on the table and swirling his drink in his right hand, he waited for her laughter to subside.

"Are you done?" he asked irritably, the words escaping his lips. "I find nothing funny about this. Our 'guest' has seriously injured two of us, and seven others were lucky to get away with lesser wounds. Diemo is among them."

The old woman sat up and cleared her throat before replying, "They'll be fine. Especially Diemo — he's tough as nails. Reminds me a bit of good old Raban here in his younger years." She nudged the burly man with the bald head and wild beard beside her. His stout arms were visible beneath a dark green woolen vest, and on both upper arms were uneven oval, matte black stones embedded into his skin.

"And quit looking so grim. No one died."

"No, thank the gods, we were spared that much. When we're done here, go and assist the healers. Make sure Diemo is back on his feet as soon as possible. I wouldn't rule out this happening again in the coming days."

"How bad is it?" Fenna's high-pitched voice came from beside Teto. She sounded uncertain.

"The stones had taken control of him." Teto clenched his fist beneath the table, his eyes gleaming with tension. "His attacks were powerful, but completely uncoordinated." He grimaced. "It happened while we were inside the shadow dome. The stones' powers merged. But I was able to subdue him pretty quickly. It's surprising how fast it all happened. He's only had the stones for two or three days."

"Next time, you'll go immediately — before we actually lose people!" Fenna shouted, her face flushed with anger. "Take these situations more seriously! It's bad enough that Vanadis and Raban are joking around here. I always thought that with age, you'd get wiser! Instead, you're acting like spoiled little brats!" As she aimed to pound the table with her fist, her hand turned black and swelled to about three times its size. The moment it touched the table, it splintered and broke in half. Mugs shattered with a loud crash, and shards scattered among the broken wood. The bowls of food also spilled across the cold stones. Even Vanadis toppled backward in her chair again.

The once-bustling common room fell into sudden silence. Fenna stared at her hand, her face turning pale. "S-sorry… seems like I lost my temper." Her cheeks were still flushed, though now from embarrassment.

The two old folks exchanged a brief glance before bursting into raspy laughter, their voices creaking like old wood. Raban's shoulders shook gently, while Vanadis's laugh resembled more of a cackling giggle. Raban went to fetch a new table while Vanadis lazily kicked aside the broken pieces within her reach. Once they had a new table in front of them, they resumed their conversation.

Teto spoke first. "We're keeping him here."

"What?" the other three exclaimed in unison. Fenna snapped at him directly. "Have you lost your mind? Even if we manage to stop him from tearing apart our entire complex and killing most of us — if the Church of Light finds out, they'll destroy us. They'll do what he failed to do." She calmed herself slightly. "Not even those two," she gestured toward Vanadis and Raban, "could handle the number of paladins the Church would send to Aregelia."

"I rarely agree with Fenna," Raban chimed in with his calm, deep voice, "but that would be too much. Back when they took the city, enough of us managed to escape and build this place. It was close, but we did it. Now they control the city, and they'll hunt us to the last shadow." He shook his head. "No, Teto, it's too great a risk for all of us."

"WHAT are we risking, really? Our slow and steady decline, which we've been living through for the past twenty damn years?" Teto's voice was rough, years of pent-up frustration spilling out. Thoughts he had suppressed for so long now surged forth. "Our community gets smaller every year. Even after our defeat, we were twice as many as we are now. I'm tired of constantly fighting against decay. We've become so insignificant that the Church doesn't even bother hunting us anymore." His hands clenched into fists.

Teto let his gaze sweep over the three. "We've been given an opportunity, one I don't know if we'll ever get again — and you want to let it slip by?" With a wave of his hand, he signaled Fenna not to interrupt him. "No, with him, the situation changes, and we're already at an advantage because we're the only ones who know. We need to bring him under control. Train him and teach him how to wield his powers. Fenna?"

"Yes?" she asked, her voice still tinged with uncertainty.

"You said he was wearing the robe of an Extractor when Diemo found him?"

"Yes. He must have been one of those who finished their apprenticeship a few days ago."

"We should keep that in mind." Teto's voice was firm. "That youngster likely has knowledge that could prove useful to us. Fenna, grab Diemo — once he's up again — and a few others. You need to gain his trust. Help him with whatever he needs and intends to do."

Teto turned to Vanadis. "You," he pointed a finger at her, "will take him down if he loses control. Quickly, painlessly, permanently."

Vanadis grinned widely, her eyes gleaming with anticipation. "Ohhh… I like it when you're so cold and calculating."

"A simple yes would've sufficed, old hag."

"Raban… there are preparations to be made. Twenty years ago, you were in your element and accomplished things I'm still grateful for. Can you do it again?"

Deep lines creased Raban's face, but after a brief hesitation, he answered Teto. "I'm a bit rusty, but yes, I will. It'll take time and some of the men and women, but I'll let you know when everything's ready."

"I'm not sure how this will all play out, but let's make the best of it." Teto raised his cup. "To an uncertain future!"

"Not so fast, Teto," Fenna interrupted, grabbing his arm and pushing it back down. "Do you really think, just because you've dreamed this up in your head, that we'll immediately agree?"

Teto smirked crookedly. "That was part of the plan, so yes. Why do you ask?" He tested her patience, casually sitting back with the cup in one hand and a plate in the other. But he could feel the tension rising in the room.

"Has it occurred to you that you need to share more information with us and can't make this decision alone?" Fenna retorted sharply, her eyes narrowing as she scrutinized him.

"Yes and yes." Teto tilted his head slightly, locking eyes with her. Out of habit, he tried to run his fingers through his graying hair, only to realize too late that he still had the cup in his hand. Awkwardly, he spilled half its contents. With an annoyed sigh, he set the cup back down on the table. Fenna raised a hand to her face, shaking her head slightly. The other two held back, though it was clear they were stifling laughter.

Teto shook his head, dismissing his clumsiness, and composed himself again. "Good old Vanadis here," he gestured toward her, "has always been content whenever there was a chance to make members of the Church of Light bite the dust. Our youngster still counts as one of them to her. I bet she's already hoping for the next opportunity."

Fenna shot Vanadis a quick look, and in that moment, Teto's words were confirmed: the murderous gleam in Vanadis's eyes spoke louder than words. A wide, almost smug grin spread across her face.

"As for Raban…" Teto paused, letting his gaze rest on the older man. Raban returned the look with a barely perceptible nod. "He knows exactly what my plan is. After all, he's already helped me put it into action once before. There will be a few adjustments, but he's with me. I know that." Teto waited, giving Fenna a moment to realize that this time, she wouldn't be able to win against him.

"Information has been shared, and the two of them agree with me. Even if Diemo were here and we held a vote — it wouldn't change a thing."

Fenna remained silent, though her eyes betrayed her inner resistance. Finally, she sighed and relented. "I accept it. But that doesn't mean I approve."

Teto raised his cup again, this time with a knowing smile. "To an uncertain future!"

CHAPTER 3

He woke up in a dimly lit room. His upper body shot up as if he had suddenly awoken from a nightmare. Slowly, he turned his head left, then right, his eyes scanning the room. A handful of thoughts rushed into his mind, all demanding answers at once. But first, he needed to regain his bearings and assess any danger.

In one corner stood a shabby wooden table with a candle and a pitcher. The walls, floor, and ceiling were made of unevenly shaped stones in various shades of gray. The ceiling formed an arch. The walls were bare, and there were no windows. Yet he felt a faint draft in the room, and the flickering torches seemed to move with it. A door reinforced with iron was in another corner. The room was no more than four, perhaps four and a half meters long and three meters wide, he estimated.

"Where am I?" he asked himself, understandably so. Then he felt the pain. It came from his abdomen, but "pain" wasn't quite the right word. It was more like an echo of pain, as if the worst had already passed, but the aftershock still tormented him.

Carefully, the young man lifted the gray, slightly tattered linen shirt. Something wasn't right. He couldn't recall ever putting on a gray linen shirt. As he pondered this, he realized he couldn't remember anything — not how he had gotten here, nor what had happened the last time he was conscious. Nor could he recall why he was in chains.

The only reason he remained calm was that his brain was desperately trying to make sense of the situation. The rusty chains felt heavy, but they hadn't yet triggered the panic they should have.

He let go of the linen shirt, which he had grabbed almost absentmindedly, and ran a hand through his short-cropped hair. As he searched his memory, three things kept surfacing — light, shadow, and a name. Whether it was his own name, how could he know?

Then he lifted the linen shirt again, this time higher. His usually nondescript features contorted, and an uncontrolled, panicked scream escaped his lips. The mere sight of a jagged black stone, about the size of a thumbnail, embedded in his navel would have been enough to make him scream. Scars radiated from the stone, spreading across his abdomen, further intensifying his panic. "What in the world happened?" he shouted, his voice full of alarm, not caring that he was alone in the room.

Suddenly, the sound of keys clattering, followed by the creak of a door opening, reached his ears. Paralyzed with fear, he had no choice but to wait and see what would happen next. The door swung open, and a slender woman, about one and a half meters tall, stood in the doorway. In the faint candlelight, he could make out her long, dark blonde hair and the freckles dotting her narrow face. The woman, whom he estimated to be in her late twenties, was dressed in a long, ornate tunic in shades of dark blue. Several pouches hung from her belt, along with a knife sheath and a dagger. In a slightly higher, though not unpleasant voice, she greeted him: "Well, had a good sleep?"

When a minute passed with no response from him, she continued, "Oh dear. I suppose the stone has robbed you of the ability to speak." He wasn't sure whether she was serious, as her tone carried no hint of sarcasm.

"I'm Fenna. I'm glad to see you're conscious. We weren't sure if you'd wake up at all. It's been almost three days since Diemo found you in the alley."

At the word "alley," time seemed to stop for him, and fleeting images flashed in his mind. Three faces that felt oddly familiar. Hands pinning him to the ground. Then darkness. A voice. Deep and ominous, unfamiliar to him. "NO, YOU LITTLE WORM!" it shouted at him. Then he was back in the present moment. Fenna seemed unaware of his inner turmoil; apparently, not much time had passed.

"I..." His vacant gaze drifted to the wall next to the door. Fenna smiled in relief. "So, you can speak after all. That makes things easier. But for now, just take it easy. Are you thirsty?" He nodded. His mouth was bone dry, and as soon as she mentioned it, it felt as though he could drink an entire barrel. She walked over to the table, grabbed the pitcher, and hesitated for a moment. It was only a brief pause. Then she handed it to him. He almost snatched it from her hand. The drink tasted mildly sweet. It was watered-down mead. About twelve seconds later, the pitcher was empty. The parched feeling in his mouth was washed away, and he sighed in relief.

"Do you know your name?" she asked, her voice a blend of gentleness and urgency. Arik gathered his thoughts. He knew he could speak — after all, he had asked questions aloud in the empty room just minutes before. "I... I think so. Not entirely sure. I think... Arik?" His uncertainty was palpable, as though he were discovering the words for the first time.

Fenna gave a slight nod, but her expression grew more serious. "What happened?" Arik finally asked, his voice barely more than a whisper.

The lightness in Fenna's voice faded, replaced by a more somber tone. "We were hoping you could shed some light on that." She paused briefly before continuing. "Three days ago, some of us were attending the annual consecration, as usual. One of our people noticed something unusual during his patrol — and found you unconscious in an alley." Her gaze drifted to his body, her eyes lingering on the scars.

"Consecration?" Arik interrupted, his curiosity piqued. "What's a consecration?"

She pondered how to explain it simply. "At the end of their apprenticeship, initiates receive a light power stone. We believe your scars are connected to such a stone — and the black one underneath it."

"Light power stone?" Arik furrowed his brow, and panic surged within him as he lifted his shirt higher.

There it was — a perfectly round, white stone, about the same size as the black one, embedded in the center of his chest, emitting a faint glow. From the black stone, a snaking scar stretched upward to meet the white stone, touching it. Arik felt himself being overwhelmed by the situation, his lungs growing heavy with each breath.

But before Fenna could say anything, Arik collapsed back, losing consciousness. Fenna huffed quietly and rolled her eyes. "Teto was right, he's definitely not a fighter. Why did I expect anything different?" Then, raising her voice, she called out: "Diemo? Get a plate of food ready!"

It took a few minutes for Arik to regain consciousness. When his eyes fluttered open, he felt groggy, but he was determined to get answers. Out of caution, Fenna offered him an out: "If you want, I can leave you alone and — "

"No," Arik interrupted quietly. "What does all this mean? What are these stones? Where am I?"

Fenna let out a deep sigh. "You're in a small, tight-knit community that looks after people who — like you — carry a black stone." She pushed her tunic aside to reveal her left shoulder. There, a black stone was also embedded in her skin, though without the scar tissue that tormented Arik.

"This isn't my only stone. But you won't know how many I have. Trust me, it's better that way." She paused, her expression turning serious, her voice taking on a conspiratorial tone. "If I can offer you some advice, don't tell others how many stones you carry. It could cost you your life."

After a brief silence, she continued. "You're the only one here who carries two different stones. That's something you should know. We believe you're safe here — at least from those who gave you the stones." She looked into his confused face and added, "At least safe from the people who implanted the light power stone in you."

"Most of those who carry such a stone in their chest are consecrated members of the Church of Light. We suspect… no… we're pretty certain you're one of those who were consecrated just a few days ago."

Once again, time seemed to freeze for Arik. In his mind's eye, he saw a sacred building, illuminated by blinding light. People in white robes with red overlays. A radiant light surrounding him. The voice returned, more menacing than before: "NO. BEGONE!" Then he snapped back to the present, the image fading.

This time, Fenna noticed. "Are you okay, Arik? You looked like you were completely out of it for a moment." Arik composed himself, struggling to find his words. "Yeah, I think so… Thank you for doing all this for me." Fenna sighed again, her voice still serious. "I'm not sure you should be thanking us. We don't expect thanks. And once I've told you everything, you might reconsider whether you want to thank us at all."

Arik felt the confusion pulling him deeper. He was overwhelmed, helpless. "Everything? What do you mean? Isn't this enough?" he asked hesitantly, his voice soft. Fenna grabbed a stool from under the table, sat down next to his bed, and looked at him.

"Well, if you didn't have a stone inside you, we would've left you there. It's not uncommon to find people unconscious in the alleys of this city. We don't have many rooms down here. And if you only had the light stone, we would've left you for the Church. But you have a shadow power stone — and that changes everything. Especially since that stone was likely implanted on the same day as the other one." She paused, letting the words sink in as she considered how best to explain the next part.

"Even though we don't have all the knowledge the Church does, we're not completely in the dark. The rule of thumb is that you should wait a certain amount of time before implanting another stone — and that time corresponds to the number of stones you already have, in years. For you, that would've meant waiting at least a year." Fenna paused again, taking a deep breath in and out. Arik could see the worry lines etched into her face.

"You're probably wondering what happens when you ignore that rule." Arik nodded silently, too afraid to break the silence. "Permanent physical damage, unbearable pain, and, in the worst case, death. Those would be the consequences." She looked him straight in the eye, her gaze piercing. "Arik, someone wanted you dead."

CHAPTER 4

Silence.

Minutes passed without either of them speaking. From other rooms, faint voices and sounds drifted in.

"If...," Arik finally broke the silence, "if this was supposed to kill me, then why am I still alive?" Fenna frowned. "We don't know. It's quite possible that the Church of Light might have an answer for that. But I strongly advise you not to go looking for them." She stood up and walked toward the door. "Excuse me for a moment. I'll refill the pitcher and bring you something to eat." The door closed behind her. Slightly bewildered, Arik sat upright in the bed, staring at the opposite wall, wondering when everything would start making sense.

Shortly after, the door opened again, and behind Fenna, Arik saw a broad-shouldered figure carrying a tray. He watched closely as the candlelight revealed more of the person. They were much taller than Fenna, by at least two or three heads. The most striking feature was the dark, spiked hair that abruptly ended at the sides. Several scars marked the still youthful face, though the dim lighting made it difficult to see clearly. Muscular arms extended from a sleeveless, dark gray linen shirt, and like Fenna, the stranger wore a belt with various pouches and a dagger.

The hulking figure eyed Arik with a suspicious gaze but silently handed him the tray. Arik thanked him and took a strong drink from the pitcher. On the tray were two wooden bowls — one held two apple slices and three shriveled, black fruits Arik couldn't identify. The other bowl contained an undefined, porridge-like mass with a wooden spoon stuck in it. "Is this... porridge?" Arik asked hesitantly. The giant nodded silently.

Fenna admonished him, "You can speak, you know. Your menacing looks are just scaring him, and he doesn't even know where he is yet." "It doesn't bother me that he's quiet," Arik replied. "But I feel like he's about to steal something from my bowl with the way he's glaring at me." With that, he grabbed one of the black fruits, which turned out to be a dried plum — definitely not one of his favorite foods, but at that moment, he didn't care. He bit into the fruit and turned to the rest of the fruit bowl.

Fenna nudged the hulking man lightly with her elbow. "Come on, big guy, say something, or he's going to think you're mute." The man grumbled, "I go by Diemo. I found you in the alley and brought you here." Grimly, he turned to Fenna. "Satisfied?" he growled, to which she responded with a mischievous, "Never."

"Do you still need me here? If not, I'll head to my watch shift." Fenna looked puzzled. "But your shift doesn't start until sundown?" "Exactly. See you later." Diemo left the room, slamming the door behind him. "A real ray of sunshine, as you've probably already noticed," Fenna remarked with an ironic smile.

Arik looked up from his tray, the spoon of porridge in his mouth. "Hm?" He pulled the spoon out and swallowed. "Sorry, I got distracted for a moment."

Fenna sat back down on the stool and took the tray from him once the bowls were empty. "It's not that important, Arik. Diemo isn't the only one here who will be... let's say... reserved toward you. It's because of your power stones."

"Shall I take a guess?" Arik asked, slowly starting to piece together the bigger picture. Without waiting for a response, he continued, "You said I'm the only one here with both a light and a shadow power stone. His behavior, along with what you've said, suggests that this combination is either very rare or that those who carry it tend to meet a grim end. I'm guessing it's both — and that the Church of Light makes sure people like me are 'freed' from our 'burden'."

His words surprised even himself. They just poured out. The stunned look on Fenna's face told him he had hit the nail on the head.

"The Church," Fenna added, "doesn't think highly of those who carry shadow stones. But they don't actively hunt us because it wouldn't make a difference. Sooner or later, more people would find new stones in the dark corners of the city, bringing chaos with them." She paused briefly, sighing, giving Arik a chance to interject: "So you stay here and try to gather people as best you can?"

"As best we can," she confirmed. "Often... I mean, when we're lucky, we find new ones during our nightly patrols through the city. One of our craftsmen, Alvar, had wandered into the shadow realm and didn't know how to get back. If Hatto and Gunder hadn't passed by that particular path that night, they would have missed him. What I'm trying to make clear," she continued, hoping Arik wouldn't jump in again during her pause for breath, "is that for the Church, nothing is more dangerous than a power stone bearer who can't control the power of the stone. It becomes especially dangerous when the bearer's will isn't strong enough, and the stones take over."

Arik noticed that Fenna's expression shifted with that last sentence. It seemed as though she had just remembered something not too long ago. Instead of prying, he latched onto the other part of her statement: "So that's why they leave it to you to handle people like me — and as long as you keep a low profile, they won't come after you?"

"I don't remember us ever making an agreement with the Church. Maybe Teto knows more. He's been leading the shadow-walkers since Aregelia was taken twenty years ago." A cold shiver ran down Fenna's spine as she recalled the events of that time.

"The siege… it lasted for months, and the city's supplies ran low. Eventually, the army and the power stone bearers had to surrender — the overwhelming force was just too much. But those who were bonded to power stones weren't simply executed in the marketplace." Fenna paused, taking a deep breath before continuing. "The soldiers rounded up all the remaining city inhabitants in the marketplace, forcing them to watch as the consecrated ones — more specifically, the Extractors — cut the power stones out of the bearers' bodies. Their screams…" Fenna's breathing grew heavier, "I'll never forget them. It took hours for the Extractors to finish their work."

Her gaze wandered to the ceiling, lost in thought, while Arik listened, entranced. "It was all about making an example — showing what happens when someone carries power stones other than those of the light. In our community, there are some who fought against the Church back then and witnessed many of their comrades die. Especially those people harbor a deep hatred for the consecrated ones, particularly the Extractors. Not even Teto can stop them from acting on their hatred." Arik felt compelled to ask, "Do you mean they attack the consecrated ones?" Fenna nodded, her words cool. "Especially the young ones. The ones who've just completed their initiation. For the older ones here, they're easy prey. Since they make the bodies disappear quickly, the Church hardly bothers investigating the disappearances. They rarely put in the time or effort to send the consecrated ones to search for them. We've seen it happen often."

Arik recoiled slightly, pressing his back against the cold stone wall. "It sounds like you've personally taken part in some of those attacks..." Fenna rolled her eyes and snorted angrily. "If it makes you feel better — if I'd wanted you dead, you would be, and we wouldn't be having this conversation." "No!" Arik raised his voice, his heart starting to race, a fear-driven anger rising within him. "That doesn't make me feel better at all! It just scares me even more, especially since you've chained me up." He lifted his right arm and pointed at the chains with his finger.

"Those...," Arik's voice softened as the realization dawned on him, "you put those on me because my body was taken over by the stones..." He felt ashamed, but he didn't know how to continue. His anger subsided as he calmed down.

"Listen," Fenna began, trying to soothe him, "yes, there were injuries because of you — but you didn't kill anyone, partly because Teto intervened in time. We all make mistakes, but what happened wasn't something you could control."

A brief silence followed before Fenna continued, "For me, it was different back then. I took part in attacks often in my youth. But Teto brought me to my senses and got those foolish ideas out of my head." "I'd feel more comfortable with Teto right now," Arik murmured uncertainly. "I'd rather talk to him." Fenna nodded understandingly, but she calmly explained that Teto wasn't available at the moment. "He'll talk to you when the time is right."

With a serious tone, Fenna summarized her warning: "I just want to make it clear that you need to be careful here. Not everyone is well-disposed toward you — especially the older ones. Up until three days ago, you were part of the Church, and many here saw you in your robes." Arik looked at her in shock as the realization hit him. "Please don't tell me that I..." He couldn't finish the thought. Fenna completed the sentence for him: "... that you were an Extractor? Yes, you were."

Arik stared at the floor in shame, a feeling of deep embarrassment washing over him. After everything Fenna had told him — what kind of person must he have been to belong to such an institution? Had he, too, ripped power stones from someone's body and killed them in the process? These thoughts overwhelmed him with sudden nausea, and he vomited. It was too much for him. Too many emotions, too many conflicting feelings. His mind decided to take a break. Arik passed out once again.

Fenna wasn't sure what had just happened, but she remained alert. A growing sense of unease spread through her. She shifted nervously on her stool. "I need one of the old ones in here!" she called out into the hallway. A trained ear might have caught the faint hint of panic in her voice. "And fast! This could get ugly in here any minute."

She felt her heart pounding, hearing it in her ears. And then she saw the first sparks.

CHAPTER 5

The Lightstone began to glow. At first weakly, barely noticeable, then stronger and stronger, until the entire room was bathed in pure light. Then the Shadowstone awakened. Instead of sparks, a dark cloud poured from the stone and slowly spread throughout the room. Fenna jumped up from her stool and moved back a few meters. Her heart began to race, but she wasn't frozen in fear. The hairs on the back of her neck stood on end, blood pumping rapidly through her veins. Unsure of how to react, she readied herself for a fight, not wanting to be caught off guard.

In several spots on her dark blue tunic, dark wisps of mist appeared, eerily similar to the cloud hovering over Arik. Within seconds, these shadows enveloped Fenna completely, transforming her into a two-meter-tall shadow golem. "Damn, that's the best I can do down here!" cursed the golem, its lips unmoving. Fenna's voice was deeper and rougher, but still unmistakably hers. Meanwhile, sparks were still shooting out from Arik. Fenna wasn't sure how much time had passed.

Fenna heard footsteps approaching but didn't dare take her eyes off Arik. Moments later, Diemo and Romilda entered the room, the door banging loudly against the stone wall. "Vanadis isn't coming," Romilda reported with a mix of concern and frustration. "Did the old hag spend minutes laughing again because she refuses to take anything seriously?" the shadow golem asked irritably.

"Pretty much. How do you know?" Romilda answered with her usual monotone voice.

"Because she's always laughing and never takes anything seriously. She probably wants to see if we can keep him in check and only step in herself if we fail." "Three guesses," Romilda retorted. "You should spend less time with her. She only listens to Teto, anyway." Fenna wanted to continue the conversation, but she didn't get the chance.

As abruptly as the light had begun, it stopped. The room instantly darkened, and the black cloud vanished. Arik began to move his limbs spasmodically. The hairs on the back of everyone's neck stood up once again. Carefully, Fenna called his name, "Arik... Arik, are you awake?" Arik lay still for a moment, then weakly answered, "Yes." A wave of relief washed over Fenna, Diemo, and Romilda, though the tension in their bodies didn't fully fade. Arik lifted his head, but something was different. "However," he added, his voice noticeably distorted as though something else was speaking through him, "not completely."

Diemo audibly swallowed, Romilda let out a short scream, and Fenna stood frozen. All three stared at Arik's face: one eye was completely white, the other entirely black. "He's still resisting, refusing to let us take full control."

The entity inhabiting Arik's body calmly surveyed the three shadow-walkers. "Two of you seem familiar, but the third figure I have not seen before. Where is the old figure who so rudely interrupted my existence?"

"We're not telling you anything!" Diemo had regained his composure, and anger flared up inside him. He clutched his cudgels tightly, ready to strike. Romilda, who had also recovered, let her black hair grow longer and longer until it reached the floor. With a venomous remark — "Damn Lightstone scum!" — she rushed toward Arik, but a large black hand from the shadow golem blocked her path. "STOP.

That's exactly what it wants," Fenna said calmly but firmly. "Why are you still here? You know what Teto said."

"I want revenge!" Diemo growled. "I won't let it end like last time!"

The chains binding Arik suddenly rattled as black and white threads shot out from his power stones, wrapped around the chains, and effortlessly shattered them. Arik stood up, tore off his linen shirt, and examined the scar on his stomach. A black and white shimmer slowly crept toward each other. A grim smile spread across his face. "What are you waiting for?" the entity inside Arik taunted. "It won't be long before they merge."

Romilda and Diemo exchanged a glance, then nodded to each other. Together, they charged forward, past Fenna. Diemo launched a frontal assault, a series of practiced cudgel strikes rained down on Arik, but the entity blocked them effortlessly. "That didn't work last time either," it mocked. An apple-sized sphere with a black-and-white spiral pattern formed in its right hand, ready to be hurled at Diemo. But suddenly, its arm couldn't move. It realized that its hand was being held by a bundle of black threads. Diemo's attack had only been a distraction to give Romilda time to slip out of its sight and incapacitate the entity.

The entity wasn't yet ready to unleash its full potential. That's why Romilda was able to restrain it with her shadowy hair. Fenna seized the opportunity immediately, before the entity could find a way out. The shadow golem charged forward and struck with precision and force. Arik collapsed instantly, falling to the ground.

"Stay alert," Fenna commanded the others in the room. "Let's wait a moment, see if he moves again." But Arik remained motionless, blood slowly trickling from his mouth, his breathing labored. "Diemo, go get a healer. We'll keep an eye on him." Diemo nodded and left. Fenna, still in her golem form, gently lifted Arik and placed him back on the bed.

Suddenly, she heard a faint clearing of the throat behind her. The rough voice immediately gave away that it was Vanadis. Fenna didn't turn around — this was no time to deal with the eccentric, wiry old woman with the long gray locks and her hideous dark green woolen dress. "If you've come to kill him, you're out of luck, Vanadis," Fenna made no effort to hide the contempt in her voice. "We've got him subdued."

"For how long this time?" Vanadis shot back provocatively. "It didn't take long for the stones to take over that flesh bag again. Sure, you beat him this time with your little tactic, but how long do you think it'll be before he figures you out?" She paused for effect. "I'm offering you a quick way out of this mess."

"But Teto..." Fenna began, trying to establish a boundary, but Vanadis cut her off sharply. "TETO isn't here, young shadow. Even if I end it now, he'll accept it." The air seemed to crackle as they locked eyes in a silent battle of wills. Diemo and Romilda stood tense beside them, ready to intervene at any moment.

Fenna clenched her teeth. "Damn old hag!" she thought bitterly. She couldn't win against Vanadis, not even with Romilda's help. She didn't even know how many power stones Vanadis had — or what fighting style she preferred. Most who had seen her fight didn't live to tell the tale, and those who did kept silent, fearing they'd meet the same fate.

"Why did Teto have to leave me alone with her?" Fenna sighed and let her golem form dissolve, returning to her smaller, more delicate shape. She turned around, walked determinedly toward Vanadis, grabbed her by the collar, and pulled her down to eye level.

"If you think you can boss me around, you've got another thing coming." Fenna's voice was still rough and intimidating, a tactic she had perfected over the years. "Oho, now I'm really scared," Vanadis retorted, unfazed. "Those little parlor tricks won't work on me."

Suddenly, the room plunged into darkness. Romilda called out for Fenna, but she remained silent, trying to adjust to the new situation.

The darkness lasted only a few seconds before the torches reignited, illuminating the room once more. Vanadis now stood behind Fenna, a dagger in hand, ready for combat. "Any more questions, young shadow?" she taunted. "Yes, one," Fenna replied dryly.

"And what might that be?" Vanadis asked with a broad grin. "Are you sure you want me to tell Teto?" "I already told you earlier — Teto won't care," Vanadis replied confidently.

"That's not what I'm talking about," Fenna said calmly. "I mean the other thing." The atmosphere in the room shifted immediately. The grin disappeared from Vanadis' face, and without a word, she sheathed the dagger. She tied her wild hair back into a braid. "If you tell him THAT, you should leave the city and never come back."

Vanadis took a step forward and knelt by Arik's bed. In a serious tone, she asked, "Have you ever done this before?" "What exactly do you mean?" Fenna asked, still confused by the sudden change in topic and the shift in Vanadis' demeanor. It was as if a switch had been flipped.

"I mean a stone suppression," Vanadis explained. "It should give him time until he can control the first stone." Fenna hesitated briefly, then answered, "No, not yet." Vanadis nodded. "Then pay close attention. You too, Romilda. You'll need this when you get your fourth stone — and bring your sunshine along."

Both Fenna and Romilda knelt next to the bed, and Vanadis began the procedure, while Diemo stood behind them, observing everything.

CHAPTER 6

Arik woke up. His head throbbed, and his body felt like it had been put through a wringer. Slowly, he raised his arms and felt his body. He quickly realized he was no longer chained. Did that mean he was no longer a threat? He could feel both stones under his skin, but when he touched the Shadowstone, he grimaced in pain. "Why is it always the stomach...?" he murmured softly, not really expecting an answer.

"If that's where you want it," croaked Vanadis' raspy voice, "we can aim higher next time and break your ribs."

Normally, he would've been startled, but he was slowly getting used to these strange occurrences. He didn't even flinch at the fact that he couldn't see where the voice was coming from. Instead, he asked, concerned that he might have hurt her, where Fenna was.

"She's probably asleep. She can't watch over you all the time. Can you sit up, little one?"

"I don't think so. Did it happen again? Are...," Arik hesitated. Had Fenna ever mentioned the name of the group that had taken him in? "Are your people hurt again? What do you even call yourselves?"

"Shadow-walkers. And no, this time you were the only one who took a beating." She added reassuringly, "It won't happen again anytime soon. I've seen to that."

Arik briefly considered whether he wanted to know what exactly she had done. He couldn't quite read her. Caring and cold at the same time, her signals seemed contradictory. "Who in the world is she?" he wondered. Should he ask?

"So, shadow-walkers, because you all carry Shadowstones inside you?"

"Is it that obvious? I still think 'Royal Stone Corps' would've been better, but that's long gone."

Arik caught the sarcasm, and he dared a retort. "Then I fit in perfectly. You don't happen to have some black paint or tar, do you? My Lightstone still needs to be colored." He tried to laugh, but instantly regretted it when the pain in his abdomen warned him that it was a bad idea.

"You could remove it yourself. You already know how."

"Alright, alright, I surrender," Arik said, sensing that his conversation partner always had a ready answer. "Who are you, anyway?"

"Vanadis. Or 'Old Hag'. Sometimes 'Witch' or 'Mist Crow'. My favorite title is 'Crazy Old Woman'. I've got so many names around here. But for now, I'll be the one taking a closer look at you."

"Excuse me?" Arik blurted out, followed by a startled "Whoa!" when Vanadis suddenly appeared out of nowhere, leaning over him, allowing him to see her up close for the first time.

"Well, well, well... haven't you got any manners?" She shook her head. "Let's see what we have here..." She focused her attention on Arik's head.

"Short brown hair. Classic church haircut, but terribly unkempt. Last cut about ten days ago..." Vanadis began, as Arik felt time briefly stand still, and fleeting memories flashed before his eyes. But before he could see the images clearly, he suddenly felt a warm sting on his cheek. Vanadis had slapped him.

"Stay with me, little one. You can daydream later!"

"But those weren't..." Arik began to protest, but Vanadis immediately cut him off, with the help of another slap.

"I don't care what you call it. As long as I'm here, you stop that nonsense." She refocused on his head. "Right, I was at your head."

With her left hand, she grabbed Arik's jaw and gently turned his head from side to side. "Slight nose bump. Slim face. Dark brown eyes. Unshaven stubble. Slight brow ridge. A few freckles. Based on your face alone, I'd say you're almost seventeen and from one of the villages north of Aregelia. Am I right?"

Arik felt overwhelmed. "Um... yeah? If Fenna didn't tell you, I still don't have my memory back..."

Vanadis immediately grinned broadly, and the sight of her crooked teeth made Arik flinch again.

"Well, good thing I'm here. I can tell you even more." She hummed quietly as she continued her unusual yet precise examination. Her fingers glided almost playfully over Arik's arms, as if she were searching for a hidden secret within his muscles. About three minutes later, she finished her inspection with a satisfied grunt. "There's no doubt you were trained as an Extractor. You don't have the muscular build of an Executor, nor the agility required for an Explorer. You have calluses on your hands, but only to the extent of occasional hard work. And from what I can hear coming out of your mouth, I'd almost think there's something going on in that head of yours."

At first, Arik was impressed by her precision and eye for detail. But then it dawned on him that these skills were likely acquired in questionable ways. "How do you know all this?" he asked, though inwardly he feared hearing the answer.

Vanadis hesitated for a moment, as if searching for the right words to downplay the truth. "Well," she began cautiously, "I've had a lot of dealings with the church's recruits over the years. You learn a few things." She tried to make the statement sound insignificant, but Arik picked up on the undertone.

"And... were those recruits still alive after crossing paths with you?" he asked, his tone sharper than he intended.

Vanadis put on an almost innocent expression, as if she were oblivious to any wrongdoing. "Well... let's just say not all of them made it. But recruits disappearing in this area is nothing new, is it? There was a year when it got all of them. Even the Paladins who were supposed to investigate had trouble figuring out why." Her eyes gleamed as she continued. "They almost didn't make it back themselves. After that, the church didn't send anyone for three years."

"And the night Diemo found me... could it be he saved me from a similar fate?" Arik sensed he was on the right track, but Vanadis didn't seem willing to reveal more details.

"Interesting question," she said with a slight smile that didn't reach her eyes. "But I wonder if you're asking me on Fenna's orders? That would be just like her." She let the thought hang in the air, then abruptly changed the subject. "Back to what I started. Agreed?" She didn't wait for an answer and simply continued. "Let's move on."

Her fingers glided further over his body, inch by inch. It was as if she were trying to read his history from his skin. Arik watched her silently, his body twitching whenever she pressed on painful spots. She discovered scars Arik had long forgotten, commenting on them with quiet remarks like "Interesting..." or "That must have hurt..."

When she finally reached his left leg, Vanadis traced the long, narrow scar that ran along his calf. "That one wasn't fun, was it?" she asked quietly, examining the scar as if it were a relic from a distant past. "But don't worry, it probably won't get worse than what you've already been through."

"Turn over, kid," she suddenly ordered in a rough but almost motherly voice. Arik obeyed without resistance and let her continue. Vanadis pushed the gray linen shirt up to his neck and felt along his upper body, increasing the pressure in certain areas. Arik gritted his teeth as she hit his sore spots, but he endured it. Vanadis seemed satisfied with her examination and then focused on his neck and head before finally allowing him to sit up again.

"You can turn back around. Or sit up, whatever's more comfortable." Arik sat up, the pain in his stomach now reduced to a dull ache, which he tried to ignore. He looked at Vanadis expectantly. She seemed to be searching for words, deep in thought, as if piecing together a complicated puzzle. Worry lines had formed on her face, and for a moment she seemed lost in another world.

After minutes of silence, Arik snapped his fingers, though the attempt failed. The sound he made was barely more than a soft rustle, and Vanadis didn't react until he cleared his throat loudly.

She blinked a few times, as if waking from a dream. "Sorry, kid," she said slowly, as she organized her thoughts. "I was just trying to put the pieces of your puzzle together. But one thing at a time." She pointed to his left leg. "You probably have siblings, don't you? Maybe a brother or a sister. That scar there looks like it came from an accident. Nothing serious, but you probably got it when you were still a child."

Arik nodded slowly. That sounded logical to him, even though he couldn't remember the details. "Yeah... that sounds about right."

"Very good." Vanadis flashed her wide, crooked grin, a sight Arik doubted he would ever fully get used to. "There are also several small scars on your arm. Not very noticeable, but at a second glance, you can tell it was more than just a simple cut. It looks like someone tried to carve a letter into your skin."

Arik raised his eyebrows skeptically, unsure whether he should take this comment seriously or not. Vanadis noticed his questioning look and continued. "Your sister — or brother — must have been pretty curious. They were probably a few years older than you too, maybe a bit more experimental. And their name starts with an I, am I right?"

"Do you often meet recruits with scars from siblings?" Arik snorted, half mockingly. He tried to provoke Vanadis, but her eyes sparkled with enthusiasm, as if she'd just found a great toy.

"You need to spend more time working on your wit, boy." She waited to see if Arik had another sharp remark ready, but he remained silent. "No, I just had the pleasure of having an older brother myself. Believe me, you learn what siblings can do to each other to satisfy their curiosity."

Arik nodded, unsure whether to respond to the comment. The mood between them kept shifting between seriousness and humor, and he couldn't find a clear cue on how to handle Vanadis.

She continued to scrutinize him with her piercing gaze before abruptly changing the subject. "What definitely can't be blamed on your brother or sister are the broken bones and bruises I've noticed. They've healed, but there's clearly more behind them than childish games. You can't blame Fenna or Teto for that either. We only break bones of enemies — or, if necessary, take their lives altogether. Sometimes both."

"Got it," Arik muttered, slightly annoyed. "If you want to get rid of someone, you don't do things halfway."

Vanadis chuckled softly, letting the satisfaction linger in her voice. "You're learning quickly, I'll give you that. But apparently, you didn't learn back then to avoid those dullards — I mean, Executor recruits."

Arik was confused. "You mean other people from the church beat me up?"

Vanadis' tone became sharper. "Among others."
"What do you mean by that?" he pressed, unsure where she was going with this.

"I've seen this often enough with Extractor recruits. I mean, I've heard about it. Your kind becomes quite talkative when they're properly motivated."

"Thanks for that," Arik replied with a sarcastic smile. Vanadis scratched her forehead thoughtfully and studied him again. "The way the church handles such matters is simple — they prefer blunt force. It's easier to make Executors out of thugs who don't ask questions. And when they go after people like you, the Magisters are long gone. They don't care."

"Charming. So why would anyone want to join the church in the first place?" Arik wondered, struggling to grasp the absurdity of this system.

"That's a valid question," Vanadis acknowledged, taking a few seconds to think through her answer. "There are reasons some people join the church. Sometimes it's conviction, sometimes it's family pressure."

A brief silence fell between them before Vanadis quietly added, "But do you really want to know everything? Sometimes it's better not to find out." Arik thought for a moment before he quietly replied, "Why not?"

Vanadis lowered her gaze as she calmly responded, "Because your memory loss might actually be a blessing. Many people would give anything to rid themselves of their darkest memories."

A heavy silence settled over the room as Arik leaned against the cold stone wall, his head tilted back. He crossed his hands behind his head and stared thoughtfully at the ceiling, as if the answers to his questions might be hidden there. "Even you, Vanadis?" he finally asked quietly.

"Maybe." The monotone reply revealed no emotion, giving him no insight into her true thoughts. Arik realized there was little point in probing further. It would have been easier to get a rock to talk.

"Even if I never get my memory back, fragments will keep coming up." He looked directly at Vanadis. "It's already happened, but it was nothing really important." Vanadis raised an eyebrow. "Was that one of those moments earlier?"

"Probably," Arik admitted, "but before I could make anything out, you interrupted it."

"I see." Vanadis showed no remorse. "It was just the wrong moment. And I'd do it again." "But you can't always be there when it happens. Or slap me every time."

"I didn't plan to, kid," she replied dryly, "others will have to take care of that."

Arik let out a deep sigh. "I'll have to decide. Either I hope that the bad memories never come back..." His voice trailed off as he struggled to finish the sentence. Vanadis stepped closer to him, her voice softening. "Or you face the memories when they come. And we'll help you deal with them when the time comes."

Arik felt a lump in his throat and could only manage a quiet "Yeah," before lowering his head. A soft sob escaped him. Vanadis placed a hand on his shoulder. "Sleep on it for a night. Or two." Arik just nodded. Both knew the conversation had to end here.

They sat quietly in the room for a while longer, time passing slowly until eventually, Vanadis was relieved by someone else.

CHAPTER 7

The torches lit the room as best they could. Teto wished he could look out of a window, but there wasn't one. One of the many circumstances he regretted day after day. So all he could do was stare into the fire of the torch with his crystal-blue eyes. Suddenly, his pupils shifted color. Blue gave way to black, and Teto closed his eyes. He effortlessly felt into the room, searching for any unwanted presences. It was as if thousands of invisible threads extended from him, able to sense everything down to the smallest speck of dust, whether hidden in the shadow realm or not.

Teto had not chosen this room without reason for this kind of meeting. It measured only five by three meters. Large enough to avoid feeling cramped and to accommodate a table and enough chairs suitable for the purpose — but small enough not to expend too much energy scanning it. As Teto routinely checked the room, Vanadis, Fenna, and Raban were already seated at the large wooden table.

Unlike Fenna, Vanadis noticed when she was being scanned. Intrigued, she admired how Teto's muscular contours were highlighted by the flickering flames, making him seem even larger than he already was. "Oh, Teto, if only I were twelve years younger..." she muttered unconsciously, loud enough for the others to hear.

Raban struggled to stifle his laughter, while Fenna slapped her forehead with her left hand. "I'd still call you a crazy old woman," responded Teto, who hadn't missed Vanadis' comment. He didn't feel flattered in the slightest. "But I would definitely take the opportunity to inspect all your stones more closely."

"You wouldn't find them all anyway," she replied with a wink, even though he still had his back to her. "Even my late husband couldn't, and he knew me inside out."

"Come on, sister," Raban scolded Vanadis with feigned indignation, a mischievous grin on his face. "You know how easily impressed the younger ones are." He glanced pointedly at Fenna and handed her a mug of mead. She took it and drained it in one go.

"Are we here to talk about Vanadis' desires and her dead husband? If this keeps up, I'll be so drunk in half an hour that you won't understand me anymore." Teto turned around. "No, we're here to discuss our next steps. What else do you think we're using this room for?" He turned to Fenna. "How's Arik?"

"He's under control and making progress since the incident a few days ago. He sleeps a lot, but I think that's helping him gradually recover his memories." Vanadis chimed in, continuing her previous point. "If he even wants that. He seems scared of it."

"Then take away his fear," Teto stated in a cold tone. "Convince him that he wants it." He looked at Vanadis and Fenna intently. "I'm aware of your position. His abilities will open up new possibilities for us, and I'm not going to miss out on that. And Fenna?"

"Yes?"

"Watch him from the shadow realm." She nodded. "Now that that's settled…" His expression lightened slightly, and the stern tone gave way to curiosity. "Raban, how are things progressing with you?"

"Slowly but steadily. My contacts haven't grown over the years." He pulled out a map and spread it on the table. Teto sat down and let his second-in-command take the lead. "Luckily, not much has changed in the area over the last 20 years. The old training camp about eight kilometers to the north has been converted into a monastery by the church, but none of us have ever been there."

Teto leaned forward, his eyebrows raised with curiosity. "How quickly can you send someone there to gather information?" His curiosity was palpable, but Raban met his gaze without wavering. Raban shook his head slightly. "The monastery isn't important right now," he replied. "Neither the northwest forest nor the northern forest are suitable for your plan, as they're too close to the monastery, and it would cut off our route to the south almost entirely."

He ran his finger over the map. "If we settle in either of those forests, we'll have to reach this ford in case of emergency. The southwest forest, on the other hand, is vast and has two confirmed fresh water sources." Raban tapped on two points. "We wouldn't need to cross the river or pass through Aregelia. We'd also avoid the southern marsh, and we have options to move in these directions…" He traced his finger clockwise from the southeast to the northwest on the map.

To Raban's right, Fenna folded her arms, trying to picture the landscape Raban was describing. Her brow furrowed as she considered the potential consequences of his plans. She shot a quick glance at Vanadis, wondering if she shared the same concerns.

Raban looked up at Teto. "Diemo, Romilda, and I would set out tonight with your approval to begin preparations in the forest." Teto paused briefly. "Vanadis, send two of the old shadows to support Raban." She nodded. Teto turned to Fenna. "Do you have any objections to Diemo and Romilda being assigned to this task?"

"No," Fenna answered in her high voice. "I'll inform them right away. I'll assign Ostara to guard Arik instead. Since he currently only has one active stone, she should at least be able to keep him in check." A silent nod of agreement.

"Can you estimate how long it will take to finish everything in the forest?" Teto shifted the focus back to the planning.

"That depends on who will help me," Raban thought for a moment. "And much of it will only become clear once we begin preparations. I don't expect we'll be done in under three months." He drew two lines on the map, both leading from the southwest of the city to the surrounding area. "Back then, we still had the builders who helped us construct the hideout and the tunnel. Since one of the tunnels leads to the harbor district outside the city walls, the only option left is the tunnel leading towards the southern marsh if we want to enter and leave the city unnoticed." He pointed to the southern line. "From here, we head southwest and establish a way to cross the river without relying on the path through the southern marsh."

Raban raised his head and looked at Fenna. With all seriousness, he asked her, "How far can you jump?" Despite the occasional banter, she knew how meticulous Raban could be when it came to planning. "I don't know…" Fenna admitted, embarrassed. "The river here is between 15 and 20 meters wide. The crossing should be ready in a few weeks. A boat would be too conspicuous, if I could even procure one." Raban paused, gathering his thoughts. "Swimming is too risky. That's why I'm asking you."

"Give me some time to figure out an answer to your question," Fenna requested. Raban nodded. She continued. "Teto, when are you going to share your plan with us?" Addressing this point, Teto smiled slyly. "You and Vanadis are already catching bits and pieces… so why not: I want to relocate the hideout. Everything here," he circled his right index finger in the air, "will remain available to us, but primarily just to maintain access to the city."

He hesitated, unsure whether to reveal the other part of the plan. Vanadis and Fenna would piece it all together sooner or later. "Soon, I'll be leaving Aregelia for a while to visit the surrounding towns and villages." Vanadis flashed her widest grin, resembling a cat that had caught the canary. "I like the direction your thoughts are heading."

"Don't tell me…" Fenna sensed trouble whenever Vanadis bared so many of her crooked teeth, "…you're planning to take over the city."

"I was thinking more along the lines of three or four." Teto looked directly at Fenna's open mouth. "For about six years now, the church's realm has stopped expanding. They've hit their limits and need to consolidate. The Alliance of Free Cities, which formed as a counterweight to the church out of necessity, still stands. I'm heading to Sydrik to seek support." He stood up. "I should be back in five or six days, and on the way, I'll also pass through Tarsk. Haven't been there in a while…" Teto radiated a kind of anticipation that Fenna had never seen in him before.

It was all too much for her, everything that seemed to be crashing down on the shadow-walkers. "And you're doing all this because we now have an inexperienced unlight-walker here in the hideout?" Teto was about to respond, but she made it clear with her gaze that she wasn't finished yet. "You're risking the lives of hundreds, or even thousands, of people because of Arik?" She began to subconsciously wrap herself in the black veil, growing larger by the second. "Has it ever occurred to you that you can't just make such a decision for several cities without a second thought?" Her voice grew raspier, deeper, and more threatening. At the same moment, Teto's eye color changed again, though Fenna didn't notice. Raban and Vanadis sat calmly, nodding slightly in Teto's direction.

"I'm not ready to give my life for such madness!" Her chair toppled backward as her shadow golem form reached over 2.5 meters in height. She was nearly tall enough for her head to touch the ceiling. "And some of the young shadows here will feel the same." The noise coming from the room had caused a stir throughout the hideout, and now there was a flurry of activity just outside the door. "You all know how many of us lost our parents in that stupid war. How many had to watch as their parents had their stones ripped out in agony." She couldn't grow any larger without causing the room to collapse. Each word thundered out of her, making the walls tremble. Then, the room's walls were enveloped in darkness — Teto had created a shadow dome. "Let it all out, Fenna," Teto spoke calmly to her. As if Raban had been waiting for this signal, he sprang into action. His eyes turned pitch-black, and he effortlessly slid his right arm into the shadow golem. He immediately found the pouch at Fenna's belt, where a small bag was stored. He wanted to secure the shadow stones inside.

She didn't even notice what Raban was doing. She let out the loudest scream she was capable of, and her shadow was streaked with red lightning. Unperturbed by all this, Raban stood up, positioned himself behind her, and reached into her shadow again, this time aiming directly at her head. The shadow golem froze, and the shadows began to dissipate, first slowly, then faster and faster. Fenna reappeared, tears streaming down her face. Raban released her head, pulled her close, and held her in his arms.

In the bag on the table, something began to move. Vanadis opened the pouch, and one of the stones twitched back and forth, prompting her to take it into her hand. She briefly examined the oval, smooth stone, then closed it back in her hand and let herself be guided. Vanadis had to stand and walk toward Fenna. The stone led her to Fenna's right shoulder. Vanadis carefully pulled down the dark blue tunic at that spot, revealing one of her stones. It was just as irregularly circular as Arik's.

She held one stone to the other, and the two merged, forming an asymmetrical rod. The shadows on the walls dissolved, and Teto's eye color returned to normal. "Anyone who doesn't want to fight will be taken to the free cities. Any citizens who don't wish to stay can leave Aregelia, no matter which direction they choose. No one will be forced to stay." The tension subsided, and Teto took a deep breath. "And I'm glad that another one of your parents' stones has now bonded with one of yours." He collapsed into the chair.

"I think that's enough for today. Raban?" Raban nodded and placed Fenna in one of the chairs. She was exhausted and used her remaining energy to keep from falling off the seat. Meanwhile, Raban went to the door and opened it. The shadow-walkers, who had been ready for battle due to the commotion inside, instinctively backed away as the door swung open. But as soon as they felt Raban's gaze, their instincts kicked in again, and they took off running. Raban then helped Fenna back to her feet. He nodded once more to Teto before guiding Fenna into the corridor. Her steps were unsteady, and the emotional weight of the meeting bore heavily on her — but at the same time, Raban's strong arm and calming presence gave her the support she needed. They walked through the hideout's halls, drawing worried glances from the shadow-walkers they passed.

"Thank you, Raban," Fenna whispered, her voice barely more than a breath. "It's nothing," Raban replied gently as he led her to her quarters.

They reached a simple wooden door, with Fenna's name written in faded letters. Raban carefully opened it and guided her inside, mindful not to disturb the quiet peace of the room. He helped her sit on the narrow bed and pulled the worn blanket over her shoulders. Fenna stirred slightly, her eyelids fluttering open.

"Raban…" she murmured, blinking in the dim light. Raban knelt beside the bed, his hand resting on the edge. "How are you feeling?" he asked, his voice a deep rumble that seemed to ground her. Fenna took a moment to gather her thoughts. The room was her refuge from the chaos outside, a place where she could let down her guard. "Exhausted," she admitted, meeting Raban's gaze. "Can you… can you…" Her body and mind desperately needed rest. "…Ostara…"

Her eyes closed again, and she couldn't finish the sentence. Raban stayed for a moment longer, watching over her until her breathing became steady, and she drifted into a peaceful sleep. He stood quietly and made sure the blanket was snug around her before turning to leave. As he closed the door behind him, he thought about the responsibility that rested on his shoulders. But for now, Fenna was safe.

CHAPTER 8

The horse-drawn cart began to move.

The last harvest had been brought in, and the time to say goodbye had come. Arik's mother waved to him and Bero in farewell; her eyes were filled with tears. Not only because she had to say goodbye to her son and his best friend. The two of them were all the family she had left, and now they were being taken from her for a long time. Even though Arik was still quite young, he understood the meaning behind her tears. He tried to smile — to give her one last joyful look to remember him by — but he couldn't. Instead, tears welled up in his own eyes. Bero put his arm around him.

The ride was anything but comfortable, but it was still better than walking the autumn rain-soaked roads to Aregelia. It was also safer, as an Executor and an Explorer of the Church of Light were on the cart, making an attack less appealing. Arik had heard rumors that in the twelve years since the conquest of Aregelia's region, there had been repeated attacks on the carts that collected children from the villages and brought them to the school.

The landscape passed slowly by them, and none of them spoke. The explorer had strictly forbidden it, as he needed to focus his attention on monitoring the surroundings. A group of chattering children would be anything but helpful. So Arik decided to take pleasure in the colorful leaves of the trees — and not fall asleep from boredom.

After a while, they arrived at the next village. Here, a thin, lanky boy was waiting on a bench in front of a house with his parents. They hugged him tightly one last time and then sent him toward the cart. The Explorer pulled out a scroll and stood up. He unrolled it, looked at the boy, and asked in a stern voice, "Are you Alexander?" to which the boy nodded. "Then get on!"

For a moment, it seemed like something was turning in Alexander's head before he followed the command. Arik remembered Alexander's ferret-like face when he saw him up close. He'd run into him once or twice at the Aregelia market in the past, and Alexander had left the lasting impression of being as dumb as a loaf of bread.

The cart set off again, heading for the next village. In total, there were supposed to be five stops before they would pass through Aregelia's gates. The sight wasn't new to Arik, Bero, Alexander, or the other four children — though Arik wasn't entirely sure about Alexander. After all, they were all eight years old and had been to the market with their parents or farmers at least once or twice.

The carriage rolled down the main street, over the wet cobblestones, slowly heading toward the market square. It would take them ten minutes to reach it and pass by the large church. Arik noted in passing that the construction was still not finished. His mother had often told him bedtime stories about the temple that had once stood in place of the church — and had voiced her displeasure about the new building more than once.

The carriage turned left onto a narrower street behind the church and stopped after about three minutes in front of an old, three-story building. It was the old guardhouse, which had been converted into a boarding school after the city's conquest. After passing through the gatehouse, the carriage moved toward the courtyard entrance. Upon arrival, they were instructed to disembark — and follow the Explorer through the tunnel.

The courtyard seemed huge and strange to Arik, as he had never seen anything like it before. "Alright, stand over there and line up!" barked the Explorer, pointing to an area where about twelve other children had already gathered and formed a line. They did as they were told. The rain, which had started a while ago, was getting heavier.

It felt like they waited an eternity until all the children from the city and the surrounding area had arrived. Bero's and Arik's clothes were soaked through, but they didn't mind — they had often had to help in the fields in the rain. Arik's gaze wandered, looking for familiar faces among the crowd. He recognized a few, and rolled his eyes at two — Michael, a chubby boy with closely cropped, dirty blond hair and a simple-minded face, and Thomas, a small, normally built boy with short blond hair, whom Arik knew to be sly and sneaky. The other children, if he knew them at all, left him mostly indifferent.

Three men in beige robes with red cords around their waists and red vestments on their sleeves and hems climbed the steps to the podium that had been set up before the children. The one in the middle, the shortest Magister, took a step forward and removed his hood. He let his gaze sweep over the disorganized group of children and sighed. "It's the same sight every year," he murmured resignedly to himself, acknowledging that some of the children couldn't even manage to line up properly.

"It's not the same for us, Helder," came the voice of the Magister on his left, with a baritone tone. He also removed his hood, ran his right hand through his thick hair, and continued coolly, "Your head, after all, gets balder every year." Helder ignored the comment — just as he had in previous years. From his right, however, came a deep, dry, and calculating voice, as the third Magister remarked that he considered it a blessing to be able to determine early on which child was more suited to strengthening the mind — and which to strengthening the body. It was moments like these that made Helder wonder why his fellow Magister even held this position instead of putting his skills to better use elsewhere.

Helder composed himself for a moment, then took a deep breath — followed by a cough. He was practiced at speaking in a loud, bright, and penetrating voice.

"Welcome!"
Some of the children flinched as Helder let his first word reverberate with full effect, giving the other two Magisters the opportunity to study their reactions. A few moments later, all eyes were locked on the Magister as if mesmerized. "Today marks the beginning of a new chapter in all of your lives!"
"Can't he come up with a new speech? If I have to hear that again next year, I'll push him off this podium — in front of these brats."

Arik was confused. Why could he hear the Magister's thoughts? When he had stood on this square eight years ago, he hadn't been able to. Something was different. He organized his thoughts — and let Magister Helder continue speaking.

"Exactly twelve years ago, the Church of Light saved this wonderful place from the chaos of the power stones, and in all its greatness and kindness, it wishes to provide the new generation — you," he stretched both arms forward, "with the foundations for a safe and better life. Before you lie four years of learning, in which we — Magister Hariolf," he gestured with his left arm toward the Magister who had removed his hood, "Magister Erlolf," his right arm swung in the direction of the Magister who still had his face hidden under his hood, "and I, Magister Helder, will teach you everything important."

"What wise words, dear Helder," flattered Magister Hariolf, "As every year." Helder turned toward him and shot him a dirty look.

The dissonance hit Arik again. He couldn't have heard the snide remarks — the Magisters had been too far away from him at the time. Also, it hadn't rained back then. He tried to pursue the thought further, but it felt as if something was pulling him back into his memory. The images of the past began to overlay his thoughts. He entered the building with the other children, where they were divided and followed another Magister who hadn't been present during the introduction. He wore the same beige robe as Magister Helder, but his vestments and cord were blue. Arik couldn't recall the Magister's name, but he did remember that he ranked below Helder.

They entered one of the dormitories, though "large room" would have been a more fitting description. The wall of smells they passed through was, to put it mildly, hard to get used to — and could make an unsuspecting person gasp for air. Arik wasn't the only one affected. The walls of the dormitory had absorbed the smell of sweaty boys aged eight to sixteen over the years — and had now become an inseparable part of the place, against which even the largest amount of fresh air was powerless.

In the dimly lit room, eight old beds were crammed closely together, each with a wooden chest underneath. The walls had three hooks opposite the beds, but there was no sign of tables or chairs. The Magister told them to make themselves comfortable and wait for the bell — that would announce dinner. Bero and Arik managed to snag two beds next to each other, and both were relieved that they wouldn't have to share a room with Thomas, Alexander, and Michael. Curiously, both of them pulled their chests out from under their beds to see if there was anything inside. Bero was quicker than Arik and, upon opening his chest, let out a "Hmm," a mix of disappointment and satisfaction. Satisfaction because there was something inside, and disappointment because it was only clothing. A pair of pants, underwear, a shirt, and a robe — all in a cheerful uniform gray and placed in the chest with the utmost care, the kind of care a person who didn't care about anything might muster.

Arik opened his chest and found the same sight. He felt there was something else inside, so he rummaged through the clothes. Nothing. He closed the chest — only to open it again. Still nothing. He closed it once more and concentrated. "Show yourself!" he demanded of the unknown thing, surprised that his voice sounded like it did now — not like a child's. He opened the chest — and saw the black stone.

"You weren't in here back then," Arik dryly remarked. The room darkened, and everything — except the chest — disappeared around him. He picked up the stone. "LET! ME! GO!" a dark voice suddenly echoed, and Arik was too stunned to comply.

"LET! ME! GO!" the dark voice boomed again, even more threatening this time, but Arik was now more present in his reaction.
"No!" he retorted sharply, "You're in my memory, in my mind!"
"SO WHAT. I HAVE ALREADY ENTERED YOUR..."

"STOP!" Frustration and anger at being at the mercy of these events finally burst out of Arik, giving him the strength to push back against the stone. "I may not be able to face both of you at once, but I can certainly keep you under control on your own. And if you don't like it, I couldn't care less."

"DON'T EVEN THINK..." the stone growled, more menacing than before, but Arik was not intimidated. "BE! QUIET!" Arik shouted, his face growing redder with each word. "Just be quiet, or I'll remove you as soon as I regain the knowledge of how to do it."
"THAT WOULD BE YOUR DEATH!"

Arik paused for a moment, considering his options, then calmly responded, "So be it. Then I'll finish what the others couldn't." He waited briefly for a response from the stone, but none came. "It's still better than living in constant fear that I might lose control over you." Arik closed his eyes and smiled. "And you forgot to mention that I'd also have to remove the white stone."

The stone made one more attempt to regain control. A black veil spread over Arik's hand, slowly creeping up his arm. Amused, Arik watched the sight and reached for the veil with his other hand as it neared his elbow. Effortlessly, he pulled it off, stuffed it into his mouth, and swallowed it. Then, he lifted his shirt and looked down at his stomach.

The sight stirred something within him, because here, in his memory, his stomach looked just as it had for most of his life — normal. Arik brought the stone to his belly button and placed it there. Resolutely, he spoke to the stone, "I accept you as part of me, but the control stays with me. Do you understand?"

"YES!" came the immediate reply, but without the menacing tone.

As the stone began to bond with Arik, thin black threads extended from it, penetrating the skin around his navel. It took several minutes for the process to complete. During the procedure, Arik had closed his eyes and took a deep breath once it was over. He exhaled, opened his eyes, and found himself back in the dormitory. His pupils were now pitch-black. His perception had changed. It was as if someone had laid a thin black film over everything that existed. He studied his hands and arms, as if noticing them for the first time. They, too, were covered by this thin layer.

The memories began to rewind, back to the moment when the Magister left the room. Behind him, Arik sensed something. A figure made of shadows.
"Was she really there back then, or have you been tampering with my memory again?"

"YES. THE FIGURE WAS TRULY THERE. SHE ALSO HID HER THOUGHTS, WHICH IS WHY I CAN'T SHOW OR TELL YOU ANY MORE ABOUT HER."

"Thank you for showing me," Arik said sincerely. "I think it's time to wake up. But one more question."
"YES?"
"Will every stone be as difficult to handle as you?"

Before he could hear the answer, Arik woke up and sat up. He closed his eyes for a moment, concentrated, and opened them again. His pupils were once again pitch-black. Arik glanced around the room and noticed a shadowy figure in the corner by the door. Instinctively, he grabbed the plate from the table, aimed, and threw it. While the plate didn't hit the figure — Arik was far from having a skilled throwing arm — the figure was startled and dropped its camouflage.

It was Fenna. "Stay calm, Fenna, it's me," Arik tried to reassure her. "The stone and I... we've come to an understanding."

CHAPTER 9

Fenna stared at him, perplexed.

She had known that it would happen sooner or later, but the timing still surprised her. Due to her condition, it was also difficult for her to show any other reaction. Arik noticed that he was gradually developing a finer sense for changes in his surroundings. Something was wrong with her; he could feel it clearly.

"Are you okay, Fenna?" he asked, with genuine concern in his voice.

Fenna had taken nearly an entire day to recover enough for her body to allow her to stand again. Now, she had been in Arik's room for less than two hours when he woke up. Although even a blind person could see how exhausted she was, Arik sensed something else about her — something different. Deep down, he knew that this change wasn't a threat. It felt as if there were two Fennas — the one sitting across from him, and another, foreign presence that was flowing through her, throwing her off balance. She interrupted his train of thought. "You can feel it, can't you?" Even though her voice sounded weaker than usual, she managed to surprise him. He didn't know what to say for a moment, so it was up to her to break the silence again. "That something has changed with my stones."

"Yeah... but I can't quite put it into words," Arik admitted, uncertain. He scratched his head as the words circled in his mind. "When I look at you, it's like I'm seeing double, but I know the other person isn't you. Do you understand what I mean?"

"Better than you might think. It gets more challenging every time." She sat down on a chair and took a deep breath. "It's like a stranger takes a seat in your head every time and makes themselves comfortable."

"And then they want to tell you what to do, right?" Arik saw an opportunity to dig a little deeper, though he felt a twinge of guilt, given how worn out she looked.

Fenna was momentarily thrown off by his comment, realizing what he had just said. "Most people don't notice it until they get their third stone. It's as if the stones encourage each other to take control over you." She looked at him. "You know what happens when they succeed."

The memory made Arik uncomfortable, and a feeling of unease spread through him. He instinctively turned away from her, which she noticed immediately.

"That wasn't…"

"…what I meant?" Arik finished for her, his voice heavy. "I get it. I'd be more surprised if you didn't hold that over me for a long time." She wanted to respond, but he raised his hand to stop her. The discomfort gave way to resignation, and he stared at the floor. "I'll do you all a favor and not have any more stones implanted." Arik paused and took a deep breath. "And if… if someone else forces another stone into me… then… then…"

"Then we'll lock you down here again until you can control it." This time, Fenna didn't let him finish. "Just survive the next three years without a new stone, and we'll be fine." She tried to smile, attempting to give him some hope. "Maybe we'll even manage to help you achieve a fusion."

"Fusion?" Arik asked, confused.

"When one stone merges with another." She rubbed her temples. Though the headaches had subsided, they were still present. "It's not pleasant, but it's easier to control. It's like the two stones fight over who's in charge, like old washerwomen bickering." She closed her eyes, massaging her temples. "And even though you'd rather rest your head on an anvil while a blacksmith is hammering away — you have to adapt during that time."

"One voice was already more than enough..." Arik mumbled, overwhelmed by the memory of the insistent voice. He lost his train of thought for a moment, unsure where he had intended to go with it. It had felt so real. Like he was an eight-year-old boy again.

It came back to him. "Do they mess with your memories too?"

Fenna let out a soft groan. "Every time. But don't ask me why they do it." She stared at the ceiling, lost in thought as she watched the flickering candlelight dance on the walls. "There comes a point where they start creating random memories. I thought..." Fenna hesitated, unsure whether she should tell him. But he needed to be prepared, just as she hadn't been. "I thought the others were exaggerating — trying to make sure we young shadows didn't make the same mistakes some of them did." Arik lay on the bed, listening intently, watching the dancing flames on the ceiling, which had a calming, almost hypnotic effect on him. "In the years after Aregelia fell to the Church, many wanted to drive them out. They implanted new stones too soon." Her voice grew weaker, and Arik had the impression that it was hard for her to get the words out.

Sensing why, he pressed gently. "The stones took control, didn't they?"

"Yes." A tear rolled down her cheek, disappearing into her ear, leaving a faintly unpleasant sensation that she barely noticed amidst the heavy thoughts weighing on her. "Later, Teto told me that out of sixteen shadow-walkers, only two were strong enough. I knew the stones could mess with your mind... but that they could give you new memories too..." Fenna shuddered at the thought. "That was the first time the stones did that to me. If it gets stronger each time... why did they take the risk back then?"

"Do you know who the two survivors were?" Arik asked, his curiosity piqued. But Fenna couldn't satisfy it. "No. No one likes to talk about what happened back then. Normally, the new ones here aren't told about it either." Before he could dig any further, Fenna changed the subject. She turned her head to Arik and locked eyes with him. "What did the stone show you?"

He hesitated, and Fenna remained silent.

After a while, the first words tumbled from his mouth. "It... it was... the day the Church took me from my village." Fenna was grateful that Arik hadn't interrupted her earlier and now returned the favor. "I saw... Bero and me, riding in a cart through several villages, picking up more kids along the way." He concentrated on recalling everything clearly, feeling Fenna's gaze on him. "Eventually, we arrived in the city and stood in a courtyard where Magister Helder gave his old speech. And under my bed, in a box, was my stone." "The black one or the white one?" Fenna asked, careful not to interrupt him.

"The black one," Arik replied quickly. "But it only appeared after I called for it."

Fenna was taken aback by the revelation, nodding in agreement as her assessment of Arik was further confirmed.

He went on to reveal that he had seen a shadow in the memory.

"A shadow?"

"Yes."

"Like me?"

"Yes."

"At the boarding school?"

"Yes."

"Vanadis."

"Yes." The words tumbled out of Arik's mouth more quickly now as the realization hit him. "Wait... what?" Fenna rubbed her temples. "Why isn't that crazy old hag just as open with her?" she thought, frustrated. "I only know because I caught her once during one of her 'walks,' as she calls them. She said she was just stretching her old bones to stay in shape." She let out a derisive noise and glanced toward the door. "As if. Sometimes I really think she went overboard with the stones, as bizarre as she acts at times." As she spoke, Fenna made a circular motion with her right index finger near her temple, indicating that she thought Vanadis was crazy. "And yet, I'm glad she's not our enemy."

"I believe you," Arik agreed.

Fenna stood up and briefly steadied herself with her left hand against the wall. "Get up," she said, motioning for Arik to stand. "It's time for you to get out of this room. But first, one more question."

"Yes?"

"Can you support me when we leave?" Her voice no longer sounded as weak as it had at the beginning of their conversation, Arik noted in passing. He stood up as well and left the bed. He paused and instinctively closed his eyes, trying to sense the room.

"One moment, please." Silence fell around him. A new feeling welled up inside him, a new sense of awareness. Something he couldn't quite name. The sensation grew within him, surged through his limbs, flooded his torso, and reached his head. "What now?" The thought of uncertainty flashed through his mind.

"THIS IS IT!" echoed the voice from deep within. Like a pulse, the sensation flowed out of Arik's head, spreading across the room, bouncing off the walls, and returning to him. In an instant, he sensed everything. The chair, the table, the bed. The dresser with the plate and cup. The bucket for his needs. The iron fittings on the door, the keyhole. Fenna. And the figure standing outside the door.

"YOU'RE WELCOME!" the voice echoed again.

"What? ... How? ... Huh?" was all he could say in response. "DEEP WITHIN YOU," the voice continued, "ARE DESIRES. HOPES. YOUR WISH TO NEVER BE CAUGHT OFF GUARD AGAIN HAS BURNED INTO YOU OVER YEARS."

Arik understood. He had been given a new way to see. For the first time in a long while, he smiled. "Thank you."

"YOU'RE WELCOME."

He opened his eyes. He couldn't tell how much time had passed. They both looked at each other, and Arik expected a reprimand for making Fenna wait. But instead of scolding him, she smiled back. This time, it wasn't forced to cheer him up. The smile was genuine — it came from the heart. She understood what had happened and was happy for him.

Slowly, he walked over to Fenna and supported her. Together, they began to move.

"Who's standing outside the door?" he asked cautiously, prompting a soft laugh from her. "Just Diemo. How did you do that?" They were at the door, but he didn't open it yet. "The voice helped me. It was like I spread my thoughts around the room, and they came back to me. Why does that matter?"

"You've just used an ability for the first time, and now I know who can help you train it." There was something positive in her tone. She knocked on the door three times, as if they had arranged it beforehand. "But first, let's go see if we can find Raban."

Keys rattled. The door was unlocked from the outside. It opened, and Diemo stood before them.

CHAPTER 10

Diemo stood directly in front of Arik, his expression as dark as a gathering storm. His spiky hair, which had caught Arik's attention during their first encounter, looked unchanged — but Arik wondered if Diemo had gained new scars, or if they simply appeared different now. Why did this guy always wear sleeveless shirts anyway?

"I'm glad to see you too, Diemo," Arik teased, trying to keep a straight face, as his counterpart's scowl deepened. "Fenna, I'm afraid he's going to eat me alive." Fenna and Arik couldn't help but giggle, managing to suppress the urge to burst out laughing.

"Funny," came the dry response. Diemo considered it a waste of energy to come up with a sharp comeback here. "What are you planning to do with him, Fenna?" It felt to Arik as if Diemo were speaking right through him, as though he were nothing but air.

"I wanted to fetch Raban and bring Arik to the briefing room with him. We're making progress, and it's time Arik meets him."

"Should I take him over while you fetch Raban?" Diemo asked gruffly.

"Follow me!" he ordered Arik once Fenna had nodded her approval and another shadow-walker had been summoned to accompany them to Raban. Diemo didn't bother to adjust his pace to see if Arik could keep up — he just marched ahead. The short corridor, barely ten meters long and a meter and a half wide, opened into a much longer hallway. Arik felt a noticeable draft, but couldn't pinpoint its source.

Half under his breath, Arik muttered a comment. "I can see the decor here is just as colorful as the room I've spent the last few weeks in." Diemo stopped abruptly, and Arik instantly regretted saying it — followed by the thought, *Damn, how does he have such good hearing?* He was referring to the unmistakable noise behind them, probably coming from a common area. Ahead of them was another room where several shadow-walkers were sparring against each other.

"If you don't like it here, then just leave. I'd be more than happy to show you the door!" Even though it was as dry as everything else Diemo said — like a sandstorm in midsummer — it was a rare emotional outburst. Arik misunderstood the seriousness of the situation as he imagined what Diemo would look like with a bright red face. But his thoughts were interrupted when he noticed the shadow-walkers had abruptly stopped their fighting. They gathered in the short hallway, and more appeared from around the corner, all with confused and alarmed expressions.

Diemo was standing directly in front of Arik again, staring him in the eyes. "Is all of this just a joke to you?" The situation grew more threatening, and it seemed to Arik that Diemo was getting bigger. His pupils suddenly turned black, and he started moving his hands like a puppeteer. "I can be funny too." Arik had no doubt about that — but he knew he wouldn't like the punchline. The ground beneath him turned black, and he fell.

In a matter of moments, Arik lost his sense of direction. He was falling, but a second later, he was back where he had started falling from. Yet he didn't stop — he kept falling, faster and faster. He looked up and saw that the ceiling was as black as the floor. It was a fall without end. A familiar feeling rose inside Arik. Not the one he had felt just minutes ago in the room. No, this was the feeling of being powerless, unable to do anything about it. Every fiber of his being hated that feeling.

"Stop…"
"…it…"
"…now!"

It took him three rounds to get the sentence out. His navel pulsed, he took a deep breath, and he addressed something within himself with a single word: *"Go!"* It worked a little faster than last time. Multiple paths unfolded before his mind's eye. Each one represented a different approach to dealing with the situation. "You wanted control, so it's up to you to choose." The voice radiated a growing sense of confidence and security, and Arik was almost happy to hear it again.

What should he choose? There were so many ways to end this situation. What he really wanted was simply to stop falling and stand on his own two feet again. Disabling Diemo was an option, but what would the consequences be?

He needed firm footing. "Where should I focus my energy?"
He needed stability. "In my feet? No..."
He needed balance. "In my arms and hands? Yes..."
He wanted to make it impossible for anyone to throw him off balance.

The energy gathered where he wanted it. Without overthinking it, still with his eyes closed, Arik angled his arms downward. The moment had come.

"STOP!" he shouted at the top of his lungs, releasing the energy he had stored in his hands all at once. He was no longer falling.

"WELL DONE KID." Arik felt a surge of pride, especially because the voice had praised him. "Thanks… again." He opened his eyes and looked at his right arm. His forearm was completely black — and longer than he remembered it being. He also didn't remember it being strong enough to ram his fist into the ground. The same sight greeted him when he looked at his left arm.

Diemo stood unfazed in front of him. "That was just the warm-up, now for the final touch." He held both hands in front of him, palms parallel, his right hand above his head and his left below his waist. Slowly, he brought his palms together, and the two black portals began closing in on Arik. "What's your damn problem, Scarface?" Arik's patience had snapped, and he was ready to do whatever it took to give Diemo more than just a headache.

"Enough!" a voice boomed from behind Arik down the hallway, and plum-sized black spheres shot past him on either side, arcing slightly before slamming into Diemo's torso. The impact lifted him off his feet, and he was thrown several meters backward. He managed to regain control mid-air, landing in a roll. He knelt.

"Stay out of this, Gunder! You have no authority over me!" Diemo snapped back sharply."

"And you have no authority over me, hothead. It wouldn't kill you to crack a joke or laugh once in a while." Gunder stepped in front of Arik. Only now could Arik see that Gunder wore a robe in what must have been fifty shades of gray, with the hood pulled over his face. Ignoring Diemo, he spoke to Arik in a friendly and reassuring manner: "You can undo it now. There's no more danger." Feeling his face flush with embarrassment, Arik whispered, unsure of himself, that he had no idea how to do that.

Gunder didn't acknowledge Diemo getting back to his feet and preparing to sprint again. His focus was on guiding Arik.

"Close your eyes, boy, and relax," he continued in the same calm tone, noticing the concern on Arik's face. "But..." Arik tried to warn him, but Gunder merely raised his right hand to interrupt him. "I know. Your expression gave it away." In a split second, Gunder spun around and used the momentum to swing his right arm. He struck.

But Diemo was still out of reach, and the blow seemed to hit nothing but air. Then, a circular black void appeared in mid-air, and Gunder's fist disappeared into it. Diemo was only five meters away when a hook to the chin stopped him in his tracks. In the middle of the hallway, where Diemo had just been running, a second circular black void had appeared, from which an arm with a clenched fist extended.

With an irritated snort, Gunder withdrew his fist from the void in front of him, while simultaneously the arm and fist sank back into the other void. Both voids then dissolved, and Gunder turned back to Arik.

"This won't be the last time he tries, trust me," Gunder explained, his tone calm once again, which made Arik want to know the reason.

"Because I messed him up so badly that one time?" he asked directly.

"Exactly. When you lost control, some people here got hurt. But more than anything, his pride took the biggest hit." Gunder's words only raised more questions. Most notably, they both seemed to forget that they were still being watched by the other shadow-walkers and that Arik was still in the same form he had been in minutes ago. Their conversation was abruptly interrupted by Fenna, who was walking down the wide hallway with Raban. A few of the shadow-walkers had brought them over.

She first looked down the hallway to her left, where Diemo was still lying on the floor. Then she turned her head to the right, where Gunder and Arik stood. But it was Raban who spoke first.

"Fenna, pick Diemo up and give him a good talking-to." She saw a familiar twitch in his eye, a sign that he was furious and barely restraining the urge to shout. They were interrupted in their own conversation by the situation. "I'll handle Gunder and Arik." Fenna nodded and gestured to two other young shadows, who grabbed Diemo by the shoulders and carried him past Arik. They moved down the same hallway that led to Arik's room, but they entered a room one door earlier. The two young shadows quickly reemerged and took up positions at the entrance of the hallway.

Meanwhile, Raban spoke to Gunder, though it was more of a command that he gave gruffly. "Get him down and take him straight to the briefing room."

"Understood, Raban," Gunder confirmed, short and to the point, as Raban was already walking away.

"Can I ask you something, Gunder?" Arik cautiously approached.
"'Course."
"How do I get down from here — and are there any more cheerful characters like him that I need to watch out for around here?" He was clearly frustrated now, so Gunder tried to defuse the situation. "Take a deep breath first, Arik." He waited a few moments, giving Arik time to follow his instructions. "Now close your eyes."

"Good. Try to feel the energy flowing from your arms into the shadows." Circling Arik, he waited for a reaction. About a minute passed, during which nothing happened. The others around them began to whisper. "Don't let them distract you,"

Gunder encouraged Arik, taking the time to assess who was watching them. "I've guided enough of these people through their first steps to know that some of them struggled a lot more than you are right now." Some of the shadow-walkers chuckled awkwardly, while others laughed as they remembered their own first time.

It's there, Arik thought. *I know it.* He took another deep breath. *I just have to grab hold somehow.* He inhaled deeply again and exhaled. *I know how it feels, so I should be able to...* One finger at a time, he searched for it. His hands grew cold. *Are these really my hands?* He felt the coldness of the stones at the ends of his rods.

Since when do I have rods? Something clicked. *How do I control this now that it's in this form?* He didn't feel pressured to rush — he had time and could focus. *Tuck tuck tuck ... Come on, energy, come back to me...* He knew it was ridiculous to treat his powers like chickens on a farm, which was why his attempt failed.

"Find the point where you can pull!" Gunder's voice rang out.
The point I can pull? Should I ask him what he means, or... wait... hold on... Arik's face showed his concentration. He reached for the inner surface of his rods again.

Got you! He exhaled in relief as he mentally grabbed hold of what felt like a thread. Out of sheer curiosity about what would happen, he tugged on it. The rods shrank with each passing moment, retreating into his body. His hands no longer felt cold.

What felt like an eternity to him happened in less than a second. The shadows were gone, and gravity returned to its rightful place. Since Arik was only about half a meter off the ground, he landed more or less safely on the stone floor and opened his eyes. A smattering of applause followed. "Everything okay?" Gunder asked him.

"Yeah... somehow," Arik replied, a little uncertain. Why couldn't he be as proud in that moment as he wanted to be? "Can you answer my other question now, please?" Gunder put an arm around his shoulder.

"Of course, on the way to the briefing room." It was less than 20 meters away, so Gunder kept his answer short. "Yes, there are people you should avoid for now. All of the old shadows, for instance. Well, except for Vanadis, Raban, and me. Among the younger ones... Romilda, for example — you messed her up pretty badly, but her grudge also stems from the fact that you threw her boyfriend into a wall."

After turning right once, they stood in front of a door. It looked the same as all the others in this place. "Diemo?" Arik asked.

"Correct. Good guess," Gunder replied just as he knocked on the door. "Great."

After the door opened, both of them stepped inside.

CHAPTER 11

"Ready?"

Teto looked at Romilda expectantly. A whole day had passed since they had performed the merging on Fennas, and she still wasn't in the right frame of mind to make decisions. That's why he hadn't bothered asking for her permission when he decided to involve Romilda in his endeavor. Even though he was the leader of the shadow-walkers, it would have been unwise in the long run to bypass his officers — but going alone on such an important mission would have been even more foolish. Was he getting reckless?

They had adjusted their clothing accordingly, as they were about to begin their journey in broad daylight. Now, both of them stood in the backyard of an old building in the city's harbor district, next to a horse-drawn cart loaded with several barrels and a cage with three ravens. A trusted associate had provided both. Teto could no longer rely on the same level of trust he once had, but for this purpose, it was more than enough. An autumn breeze blew through the courtyard.

"Do I really have to wear this, Teto?" Romilda complained in her signature, deep alto voice. She eyed the clothes she was wearing skeptically — a simple brown over-dress over a light gray under-dress, with a brown belt around her slim waist. Romilda hated having to tie her black hair back into a ponytail, but being forced by Teto to wear a braided braid under a white cloth cap was just too much. It made her narrow face look strange. Inside, she toyed with the idea of literally "knocking the bottom out of the barrel" — or simply cutting her hair off.

Teto eyed her for a moment. "I don't see the problem. Everything looks perfectly normal on you. Diemo would certainly agree." Romilda snorted softly, clearly uncomfortable in the clothes. Too much fabric that could get in the way during a fight.

"Easy for you to say. You don't look like a maid either — more like a failed merchant in that plain tunic and those brown pants. Do they at least itch?" There was a sharpness in her voice that puzzled Teto. Had he missed something, or was she alluding to something he didn't understand?

Slightly confused, he climbed up onto the cart. "Come on, we don't have all day. I'm just glad it's sunny today and I didn't see any clouds on the horizon." It was best to focus on the essentials again. Maybe she'd explain what was bothering her along the way. They had plenty of time. He took the reins in his right hand and waved her up with his left, and she climbed up, annoyed. With a "Hyah!" the cart began to move. Turning his head toward her and looking into her blue eyes, he gave a command: "Until we're out of the city, I don't want to hear a word from you. Understood?" She responded with a dismissive "Hmpf," so Teto repeated firmly, "Understood??"

Reluctantly, she replied, "Understood!"

When this was over, he'd have to have a serious word with Fenna. It irritated him that one of his lieutenants seemed to be forgetting who she was dealing with. The cart rolled out through a narrow gate onto one of the side streets. He adjusted his wool cap.

The cart rolled leisurely toward the main street. Teto didn't regret for a moment that he'd brought two feather pillows for Romilda. The cobblestone streets were notorious for giving carriage drivers sore backsides. After about ten minutes, they turned right, just a few hundred meters away from one of the four city gates. As long as they didn't raise suspicion, the city guards didn't care which carts passed through — only occasionally would the church's priests inspect them more closely. If luck wasn't on their side, Teto had planned ahead, as the barrels were filled with honey mead they were supposedly taking to Tarsk.

They passed through the first gate. Teto glanced around discreetly, satisfied that they didn't stand out among the other carts. After another fifteen minutes, they turned right again, heading toward the marketplace and the church. Twenty more minutes on the broad avenue, and they'd pass through the second gate and leave the city behind. He noticed that the streets were much quieter than usual. Likely because many of the farmers were busy harvesting crops from the fields. "Nothing unusual, then," he murmured to himself, earning a questioning look from Romilda.

The timber-framed houses of varying sizes, the marketplace, and the church passed by at a leisurely pace. He hadn't missed the fact that two groups of four priests had crossed their path by now. The church was sending its newly consecrated ones on their first missions, which was customary about six days after the consecration. As in previous years, he could tell from the robes that each group consisted of three Executors and one Explorer. They were meant to gain their first experiences before being sent to the borderlands. From what Teto had heard, the church used this process to separate the wheat from the chaff.

The last ten minutes within the city passed without incident. The only real danger so far had been the overzealous mothers who let their children collect chestnuts from the street, giving any cart driver who got too close to their children a deadly glare. His own mother would probably have done the same if

Teto hadn't been 25 years old when the chestnut trees first bore fruit. They drove through the south gate and could already see the southern marsh in the distance. As far back as he could remember, these places had always borne their names, and he admired the ingenuity of the city's former inhabitants.

He heard whistling beside him. Romilda had started whistling shortly after they left the city, and he sensed a tension between them in the air. Once they were far enough from the city, he turned to her, keeping his eyes on the road. "Romilda, I don't know what your problem is, but I need your full attention." She kept whistling.

"We have to pass through the borderlands." Her whistling stopped abruptly. "Why?" she asked seriously.

"I'm heading to Sydrik, and it doesn't help me one bit," Teto explained, "if you keep acting like a stubborn child." His words were firm. "Does this have something to do with Arik?"

"Is it that obvious?" Every syllable dripped with sarcasm. Teto had had enough. "Get a grip, or I'll send you back." They sat in silence for the next few minutes. The occasional crunch of the wheels on the road was the only sound breaking the silence between them. Teto sensed that Romilda was wrestling with herself. He knew she wasn't the type to give up easily or back down, and that was exactly what he needed from her right now — the determined lieutenant she always was. If Teto had been looking at Romilda, he would have noticed her opening her mouth several times as if she wanted to say something.

The sunlight was broken by the trees lining the roadside. The occasional gusts of wind that swept across the land also lost their strength because of them. After a while, Romilda seemed to have sorted out her thoughts. Without looking at him, she said quietly,

"Why has so much been happening since he arrived?" Teto waited to see if she would elaborate. "Diemo picks him up, and ever since, it feels like everything revolves around him. Like you see him as some kind of savior." Teto couldn't deny that accusation, and he knew it.

Speaking in a calm voice, he explained, "I don't see him as a savior. I never have, and I never will." Romilda listened closely to his words. Just hearing that calmed her down considerably.
"We took him in because we take in anyone who carries a shadowstone. Just like Diemo, just like Ostara, and just like you. Just like most of the young shadows who are with us." He closed his eyes briefly and took a deep breath.

"Then why are you making such a fuss about him?" Romilda pressed.
"Am I making such a fuss?" He didn't seem to agree at all. "As long as he doesn't have control over his stones, he's a danger, and I have to respond to that." The marsh was now directly in front of them, and the road wound through it. They were now exposed to the sun, as there were no more trees along the roadside.

Not backing down, she continued, "And that's why you're sending Raban into the forest and embarking on a journey through the borderlands. How great a danger must he pose for you to put yourself in even more danger because of him?"
As usual, Romilda had hit the nail on the head. The land around them became flat and marshy, dotted here and there with dead tree stumps. "My plans aren't based on Arik. At least, not directly," Teto said, still searching for the right

words. "It's... he... This is the first time we've found someone like him. And it may seem strange to you, but I see it as a sign that times are changing."

They let the words sink in for a few minutes. To their right, far off in the distance, Romilda could see four figures struggling through the marsh. Their white robes and the fact that no one in their right mind would choose such a difficult path left no doubt: they were priests of the church. Pointing with her left index finger in their direction, she alerted Teto. "Keep an eye on them, please," he asked, and Romilda nodded briefly.

"Arik will never become a great fighter, but he has a very strong will, especially when it comes to his mind. And the combination of lightstone and shadowstone will certainly open up some possibilities for us." He now looked directly at her.

"Just see him as someone who makes achieving my goals more likely." With these words, Teto managed to noticeably ease the tension between them, though Romilda's doubts still gnawed at her. It would likely take some time before they were fully resolved.

The priests were getting closer to the road, and Romilda tried to gauge whether their paths would cross. She couldn't help but notice that the lead priest moved more lightly over the terrain. He must be the group's Explorer. If the Executors could keep up the pace, the group would soon reach the road. But as things stood, an encounter seemed inevitable. With this realization, she turned to Teto. "In ten to fifteen minutes, we'll run into them. What's the plan?"

The gears in his head turned. What could happen? He went through every possible scenario. *Best case, they leave us alone and head toward the city,* he thought. *If they go the other way, we remain inconspicuous. An attack is out of the question in broad daylight. If we're unlucky, they'll climb aboard, ride with us, and start asking questions.*

"No attack, and we stay inconspicuous. Above all, we stay calm. We'll put on the cloaks too," he said in a calm, almost analytical tone. Romilda reached behind her into the cart and pulled out two brown cloaks.

It was like a snail's race as the shadow-walkers and the consecrated ones drew closer to each other. "Romilda?" Teto asked, still keeping his eyes on the road.

"Yes?"
"Put on a facial expression like life is a burden you have to bear."
"What?" she replied, confused.

"I just need to remind myself of how many headaches Vanadis has caused me over the years," he explained dryly, "then it comes naturally."

"I see." She took a moment to compose herself. "How about this?"
They glanced at each other for a moment before turning their heads back to the road. "Can I ask..." Teto couldn't finish his sentence, because Romilda's "No!" came like a shot.

The first thing the four consecrated ones saw as they reached the road was a cart approaching, with a driver who looked like he hadn't relieved himself in days, and a maid who seemed to suffer from the same problem. The Executor, distinguished by his gaunt frame and prominent ferret-like face, stepped up to the cart and signaled with a hand gesture for them to stop.

"Halt. In the name of the Holy Church of Light, we command you to take us with you!"

CHAPTER 12

Teto stopped the cart, annoyed that the consecrated ones had chosen the most inconvenient situation for him. The fact that they had to be young, arrogant Executors made the situation even more unpredictable. Now, he had to put on a good face for a bad game. He was about to greet them, but he hesitated too long.

"It's the Church of the Holy Light, you idiot." The Explorer — a seemingly well-trained youth about Arik's age, with the standard haircut of the Church — appeared visibly irritated. He gave the ferret-faced Executor a smack on the back of the head, then walked past him. Standing before Teto and Romilda, he gave a slight bow, and the two of them discreetly but thoroughly studied him. A green cord around his waist, no insignias on his shoulders — and unlike the other consecrated ones, the lower part of his robe, blowing in the autumn wind, wasn't dirtied by mud. Without exchanging a word, both of them immediately knew due to their experience: Despite his young age, this Explorer could be a serious threat.

He stepped closer, making the contours of the pockmarks on his face more visible. They could now better estimate his height: just under six feet, so slightly shorter than Teto, but a hand's breadth taller than Romilda.

"Greetings, travelers. My name is Bero, and I am an Explorer in the service of the Church." The Explorer had adjusted his tone and now sounded much friendlier than he had toward the other consecrated ones. "I sincerely apologize for the behavior of consecrated one Alexander just now. But tell me, would you be willing to transport us across the southern marsh on your cart?" His choice of words was remarkably polite, even for an Explorer. Neither Teto nor Romilda had expected such a silver tongue.

To appear more simple-minded, Teto deliberately took his time before responding to Bero's question with a mumbled, "Sure, hop on." He nudged Romilda. "Make some room back there so everyone can fit." Romilda clumsily climbed onto the back of the cart and pretended to struggle as she rearranged the barrels. All of a sudden, Bero leaped up and began to help her. "Thank you so much, but please, let me handle this," he said politely as he pushed a barrel to a different spot. Romilda shot him a shy glance, noticing his dirty-blond hair and blue-gray eyes up close, and thanked him as well. She grabbed the cage with the ravens and sat back down next to Teto.

The heavier consecrated one with the dull expression, the consecrated one with the devious look, and Alexander walked past the cart and waited for Bero to finish with the barrels. They briefly considered helping him but purposely refrained from doing so.

"And don't you dare touch the contents of those barrels," Teto mumbled again, intentionally keeping his gruff tone. "Maybe we should teach this peasant to speak only when spoken to," the heavier one sneered as he climbed onto the cart. Teto and Romilda heard only a dull thud, and they turned around in disbelief. Bero had spun around in an instant and kicked his fellow companion in the chest, sending him to the ground.

"And you, my dear Michael" — Bero's tone turned cold again — "should be reminded that we owe the people a certain amount of respect!" The third, greasy-haired Executor with a devious look jumped onto the cart from the side, tackling

Bero from behind and knocking him off his feet. They both flew off the cart and landed right on top of Michael, who screamed in pain. Of all the possibilities Teto had run through in his mind, it had never occurred to him that the consecrated ones might start fighting each other.

"If they keep this up, the Church won't last another year," he muttered quietly, to which Romilda responded with an equally quiet, "Mhm."

Bero was dazed. Although he had landed softly, he had also served as a cushion for the impact of his attacker. This allowed the devious one to get back on his feet first. He grabbed Bero by the robe and yanked him up. The commotion caused the birds to become restless, and some other travelers had already stopped to watch the strange scene.

"Get lost, filthy rabble," Alexander snarled at the onlookers, firing a flash of light from his right palm to blind them. They had no choice but to flee. Pleased with himself and his actions, he sprinted over to the devious one. Upon reaching him, Alexander grabbed the still-dazed Bero in a hold from behind.

"Have fun, Thomas," he cackled with a wide, sadistic grin on his face. Thomas didn't hesitate, punching Bero hard in the gut, causing him to groan in pain.

Things weren't going well for Bero, and his chances were getting worse by the minute. His intelligence, clearly superior to that of the Executors, was no longer enough to make up for his numerical disadvantage — especially since he could barely think straight. He could still recognize rhetorical questions, but only if they were accompanied by a physical component, such as Thomas's taunting question: "Want another one?" followed by another brutal punch to the gut.

Carefully, Teto climbed off the cart, grabbing his staff and using it to steady himself with every other step as he moved toward Thomas. He could hardly believe what he was about to do. Alexander seemed not to understand why the cart driver was suddenly approaching them. But when Teto brought the staff down hard on Thomas's head, it triggered a brief mental block in Alexander. He stood motionless as Thomas collapsed, unconscious.

Now finding some amusement in his mumbling, Teto ordered Alexander directly, "That's enough! Let him go." The dazed Bero fell half-unconscious to the ground, and Teto supported him. "Pack the others onto the cart and hurry up." Teto took advantage of the fact that the last Executor wasn't exactly blessed with an excess of intelligence and seemed particularly susceptible to orders. Without protest, Alexander did as he was told.

Teto carefully grabbed Bero under the arms and slowly dragged him to the front of the cart. With a mix of gentleness and the necessary resolve, he laid him down on the rough boards, so Bero could lean his head against the sidewall. Bero groaned softly when he felt the contact, but otherwise remained still.

Meanwhile, Alexander had begun loading Michael and Thomas onto the cart, though he was doing so rather clumsily. First, he grabbed Michael's arm, pulling him up, only to give him a half-hearted kick that was more awkward than effective. Michael nearly slid off the cart again, prompting Alexander to mutter a disgruntled curse. After several more feeble attempts, he finally managed to heave Michael onto the cart. Thomas fared no better; his weight and Alexander's clumsy movements made the task a laborious ordeal, giving the whole scene a near-tragicomic quality. Eventually, Thomas lay next to Michael, both of them breathing heavily, while Alexander himself was sweating.

Alexander was almost left behind on the road, as Teto had forgotten to tell him to get back on. It wasn't until Romilda's sharp look caught his attention in time that Alexander jogged the rest of the way behind the cart.

"This has to be a dream, right?" Romilda was visibly struggling to comprehend what had just unfolded. But Teto didn't respond, pressing a finger to his lips to prevent any unintended slip-up that might reveal their cover. A moment later, Teto mumbled to her, "Check on the Explorer, girlie." Romilda's sharp glance suggested he probably shouldn't use that word in this context again. The inner realization was reinforced by the unpleasant feeling as if she had stabbed him in the back.

Romilda climbed into the back of the cart and gave Bero a few gentle slaps on the cheek. "Hey!" she called out softly and hesitantly. She didn't like this situation at all and wasn't sure how much longer she could keep up this amateur acting. She was tempted to ask Teto if they could just throw the priests into the river they'd reach in about forty minutes. A cool autumn breeze blew across her face, as if delivering an answer. But since she didn't speak the "language of breezes," — or commonly known as „breezian" — she couldn't decipher its message.

There was no reaction. Romilda leaned forward to Teto and grabbed the water skin. She turned back to Bero, removed the stopper, and poured a little water over him. Another slap wouldn't hurt, she thought. This time, it should be a bit stronger. She drew her hand back and swung. But before her hand could reach Bero, his arm shot up out of nowhere, grabbing her wrist.

"Please..." he managed to say before a coughing fit shook him. Bero gasped heavily, his face contorted with pain. Dark spots appeared on his robe as small drops of blood splattered onto the fabric. Romilda instinctively pulled back, the smell of iron and sweat hanging in the air. Teto glanced over his shoulder as the ravens in the cage briefly cawed and flapped their wings in agitation.

When no more blood came, Romilda held the water skin to Bero's mouth. Bero drank greedily, gradually clearing his head again.

"Please... no more... hitting." His voice was still weak, but he was able to string together coherent sentences. "Forgive me, dear consecrated one." Romilda cooed softly, biting her lip briefly. "I meant no harm." Inside, a part of her died with those words. If it had been night, the four consecrated ones would never have left the marsh alive. She prayed silently that she wouldn't break character, knowing it would only get harder from here.

"Please, allow me to tend to your wounds and clean them," she said, raising her head toward Teto. "Father!" she began, catching Teto completely off guard. His face froze for a moment. His mind was racing in a wild jumble of thoughts — *Father?* He had prepared for everything, but this? The veins in his neck throbbed as his frustration rose. Neither did he realize that he had turned to face her, nor could Romilda fully process the movement when Teto whipped his head and part of his upper body around in a flash to stare at her. His gaze met Romilda's, and for a fraction of a second, uncertainty flashed in her eyes. But she stood firm, leaving no doubt that she was going to stick to her improvised role.

His gaze spoke volumes, and his words sounded like he was on the verge of skinning her alive.

"Mah... dearest daughter?" There was a reason Teto preferred to plan everything thoroughly: he hated improvising, as he was usually bad at it. But the situation they were in, and how he was reacting to it, was a rare exception. At least until this moment.

"Maybe I went a bit overboard just now," she admitted to herself inwardly, but there was no turning back now. "Be so kind and give me a clean cloth." Without taking his eyes off her, Teto reached for a cloth and handed it to her. "Clean" would only have been true in the dark. Then he turned back around and fixed his gaze on the road.

"Thank you, Father," she muttered in mock humility, knowing full well that things couldn't get worse for her now.

She then focused on Bero. The dirty cloth quickly soaked up the water, and she carefully wiped it over the bloody spots. The skin underneath was rough and torn, with a few scrapes starting to crust over in dark red. Bero didn't move, his eyes staring as if through a fog, while Romilda dabbed the painful areas. It was almost eerie how little he reacted to the pain — as if he had experienced far worse too many times before. He turned his head and, for the first time, noticed that Thomas and Michael were also unconscious on the cart.

Looking at the two of them, he asked, "Why are they lying here?" In her feigned, shy manner, Romilda recounted what had happened.

"Well, the fat one here..." — she paused and pretended to catch herself — "Forgive me, that was..." "...not your intention to speak ill of consecrated ones." Bero coughed again, and she handed him the water skin. "That one," he said, pointing at Michael, "is the consecrated one Michael. Or, as I call him — the Extractor of Food." As he laughed, Romilda joined in awkwardly.

"And the other one is... the consecrated one Thomas... the human embodiment of a greasy rat." His expression darkened.

"But now, please tell me what happened." His speaking difficulties would likely persist for a while, Romilda figured. "Well... After you kicked consecrated one Michael off the cart, consecrated one Thomas ambushed you from behind, which is why you flew off the cart." She paused for a moment, pretending to think.

"Then consecrated one Alexander ran over to you and held you down so that consecrated one Thomas could strike you unhindered." Bero listened attentively as Teto followed every word, ready to intervene if necessary.

"If it weren't for my father" — she patted him firmly on the back — "and him knocking Thomas unconscious, you'd be dead by now." Romilda turned her face away as if on the verge of tears.

"Thank you. To you as well, driver. I owe you both!" As he tried to deliver these words with strength, Bero fell into another coughing fit that lasted for a while. "Can you..." — another cough — "...please..." — yet another cough — "...take me to Sydrik?"

Teto was happy to mumble again. "'Course. We will," he responded gruffly, immediately following up, as he was curious about Bero's answer: "And what about the others?" "Give me a minute, I'll handle it," Bero replied.

Teto was increasingly having trouble figuring out this boy. "What exactly does he plan to handle?" he wondered in response to Bero's words. Romilda also remained uncertain, just as she was about Teto's decision to keep the consecrated one on the cart. She felt that he was playing a dangerous game.

CHAPTER 13

"When was the last time you guys used this room so often in such a short period?" Gunder asked into the room as he shut the door behind him. Raban, receiving the question, seemed to think about it for a moment but left it unanswered. Sometimes Gunder was hard to figure out, and there was no value in getting caught up in this triviality — especially because his mind was still on Diemo, whom he would have liked to drive straight into the ground. Instead, he got straight to the point: "Sit down," he commanded, with a brief nod toward the chairs.

Arik's gaze wandered around the meeting room as he sat down. The room was small, barely three by five meters, and deep inside the hideout, as the cool, dry air indicated. The flickering light of three torches on the walls bathed the room in warm orange tones, making the gray of the stone walls appear more alive. But the light barely illuminated the outline of the worn wooden table in the middle and the four plain chairs. The rest of the room hovered between darkness and twilight, creating an almost oppressive atmosphere.

Arik had expected the air down here to be stuffy and heavy, filled with soot and the heat of the torches, but to his surprise, a cool breeze flowed through the room. Exactly where it came from, he couldn't say. He furrowed his brow and gave Gunder a questioning look, which was only met with a slight grin. Even directly illuminated by the torches, Gunder still managed to keep his face shrouded in darkness, making it impossible for Arik to notice the grin.

Already seated at the table, Raban drummed his fingers quietly on the worn surface. His eyes were alert and flashed in the restless torchlight, shifting his gaze between Arik and Gunder. He seemed to be sorting out the right words in his mind but took his time. Everyone who knew him knew that he rarely acted hastily. A few minutes earlier, he had carefully checked the room — for any signs that they might be overheard. No one spoke a word as a silence settled, interrupted only by the occasional crackling of the fire.

"All right," Raban finally began, leaning back. "Now that you're here, Arik, we need to clarify a few things before we move on." His tone was calm, and his voice rough, but with a sharp edge that made it clear this was not a place for jokes or sarcasm. He studied Arik for a few moments to gauge his reaction. Arik looked somewhat worn out, sitting quietly and composed.

Still, his mind seemed alert and trained on observing. As Raban sized Arik up, Arik was doing the same to him. This made Raban feel as though Arik was counting every hair in his wild beard and searching for hidden patterns in the reflections of the flames on his bald head. "Is he trying to challenge me for control of the situation?" crossed Raban's mind as he noticed how meticulously Arik's eyes traced the contours of his body, the two visible stones he wore openly, and his dark green vest. "How did Fenna and Vanadis miss this aspect of him?" he couldn't help but wonder.

Raban collected his thoughts briefly and retraced them. "All right," Raban repeated, his gaze now firmly resting on Arik. "I assume you have questions, and that's fine. But before we get to that, let me explain how things work here." He leaned forward slightly, placing his hands flat on the table, letting a brief pause hang in the air. "My name is Raban. I'm Teto's deputy, which means I'm in charge when he's not around. But even when he's here, most things will go through me sooner or later."

Arik nodded hesitantly. "Nice to meet you," he replied, with a hint of irony in his voice that Raban completely ignored.

"That over there," Raban continued, nodding toward Gunder, "is Gunder. He was already a trainer before Aregelia was taken over by the Church. When the shadow-walkers formed after the fall of the city, he took over this role. Your training will be under his supervision. You can take that as a threat or a promise, depending on how you see it." Raban noticed that Arik relaxed slightly — not realizing that Arik was secretly grateful for his first encounter with Gunder.

Gunder, who had been sitting silently until now, let out a quiet growl and twisted his face into a crooked grin beneath the hood of his cloak, which came in every shade of gray imaginable. "Let me put it this way: I'm not here to make your life difficult, but it won't be easy either."

Arik couldn't help but react with a faint smile. "Well, that sounds like I can look forward to some joyful training sessions." Raban's expression remained unchanged. "You shouldn't take this lightly. Vanadis warned me that you have a tendency toward sarcasm. That can be useful at times, but not in this situation. This is about more than you realize right now."

Arik opened his mouth to respond, but then thought better of it. Something in Raban's tone made it clear that it was better to listen. "You have a choice here, Arik," Raban continued. "No one will force you to stay with us. You can leave anytime. But that would mean you're on your own out there. And in your current state, you won't last long. That's not a threat, it's just a fact."

An uncomfortable silence settled over the room, broken only by the restless crackling of the torches. Arik let the words sink in for a moment before shaking his head slightly. "You guys are really good at taking away any hope, I'll give you that."

Raban raised an eyebrow. "Hope? Hope is a strange thing. It can save you or lead you to ruin. But this isn't about hope, it's about survival. And part of that is making yourself useful." Arik felt his shoulders tense slightly. "And how exactly do you see that happening? I can barely remember what I used to be capable of."

"That may be," Raban replied calmly, "but Vanadis believes that your knowledge as a former Extractor recruit will come back once you have time to stabilize. Until then, we'll figure out where you fit best. The shadow-walkers aren't just made up of fighters. We have healers, craftsmen, and suppliers. We need more than just those who fight on the front lines. But no matter what you end up doing, you will be trained. Simply to increase your chances of not getting taken down at the first opportunity."

Arik shot a quick glance at Gunder, who merely nodded silently. Apparently, there was nothing to argue about regarding what Raban had said. "I assume you've already planned everything out," Arik said with a hint of resignation.

Raban leaned back and crossed his arms over his chest. "Not everything. Since you arrived, things have started moving in ways no one can predict. We're observing, and we're adapting. The same goes for you. It's up to you which path you take." Arik lifted his head and studied Raban, rubbing his forehead. "What exactly do you mean by 'things have started moving'?"

Raban crossed his arms over his chest, his face taking on a more serious expression. "Since you came here, Teto has made some decisions that will inevitably lead us into conflict with the Church. It's not just about your survival, Arik — it's about the fate of all the shadow-walkers."

Arik opened his mouth to press for more information, but Raban's hardened expression cut him off. "That's all you need to know for now. Let's focus on what's right in front of us." A tense silence filled the room before Raban finally continued: "Show me what you can do so far. Fenna told me you've already shown some control over your abilities."

Arik hesitated, then took a deep breath and tried to concentrate. He closed his eyes, feeling the energy of the powerstone within his body — a familiar sensation that slipped away as soon as he tried to grasp it. A minute passed without progress. Another minute went by, and Arik kept trying to gather the energy and channel it into his hands.

Slowly, frustration set in, as he had already managed to do it twice that day. He tried again, this time using a more creative approach. "Tuck, tuck, tuck... energy, come back here... ." The absurdity of the attempt hadn't changed since the first time, and Arik knew it. So, predictably, this method didn't work either. "Maybe another time," he thought, trying to stay positive. He kept at it, but after another minute, the realization dawned that it was leading nowhere. Finally, he opened his eyes and stared down at his hands in frustration. "I... I can't do it again," he admitted.

Gunder, who had remained silent until then, leaned forward slightly. "Have you used your powers in any way other than during the conflict with Diemo? Anything else come to mind?" Arik thought for a moment, then nodded. "Yes, I was able to... sense shadows. Somehow, I just knew where they were."

Gunder stroked his beard thoughtfully, which, like his face, was hidden beneath his hood. "Interesting." His gaze swept over Arik, as if he were seeing through him. "Your body and the stone need time to recover. For a first conscious use, that was already impressive."

Gunder's deep, calm voice echoed through the room as his cloak, in various shades of gray, seemed to come alive in the flickering torchlight. "What you've experienced, Arik, is not failure. Your body needs time to stabilize — and the shadowstone needs to adjust to you." Gunder leaned back and crossed his arms. "With the right guidance, we'll make progress."

"Very well," Raban grumbled to himself. "I did see earlier that you were already able to do something with your stone." He propped both arms on the table, clasped his hands together, and rested his chin on them. "Otherwise, your encounter with Diemo would have ended differently. It won't happen again that someone attacks you here, by the way." His voice took on an extra level of seriousness. "Fenna, Vanadis, and I will make sure of that."

Briefly searching his thoughts, Raban considered how to proceed. "For now, we're done here." It wasn't just a suggestion; it was a decision. "Gunder will show you around and explain everything you need to know. Including your new quarters. If you have any questions, ask him. He's in charge of you now. Understood?"

Arik nodded. "Good. I have other things to take care of. And Gunder?" His gaze shifted to Gunder, who remained silent. "I'll be gone this evening until tomorrow morning. Vanadis and Fenna will be in charge until then." Gunder nodded as well, and Raban left the room without further ado.

Gunder then stood up and stepped toward the wall beside the door. What Arik observed confirmed his suspicion. If he didn't know exactly where Gunder was standing, he wouldn't have noticed him. His cloak served as camouflage, and in

Arik's mind, the question of why began to take shape. But in this place, enough questions already swirled around to be answered, so he pushed it far to the back of his mind — aware that it would find its answer at the right time.

"Coming?" Gunder finally asked, sensing Arik's gaze on him. Pulled from his thoughts, Arik got up and stepped through the door that Gunder had just opened.

CHAPTER 14

Gunder opened the heavy wooden door and stepped out into the hallway, followed closely by Arik. Their footsteps echoed dully off the stone floor, blending with the muffled sounds drifting from the more distant parts of the hideout. The corridor was bathed in dim light, flickering from a few torches along the smooth stone walls. Though the flames burned steadily, they made the shadows on the walls dance like living figures. A cool breeze blew through the hallway, refreshing yet strange in this underground environment.

"Follow me," Gunder grumbled, turning left. After a few steps, they reached a massive wooden door. Without a word, he placed his hand on the handle and opened it with a soft creak. "This is one of our four storage rooms," he explained, gesturing for Arik to enter.

The room was twice the size of the meeting room they had just left. Shelves lined with dried fruits, meats, sacks of grain, and containers filled the walls. The sharp scent of preserved foods mixed with the dry smell of old wood. In one corner of the room, stacks of wine barrels stood, their worn lids telling stories of many years in storage.

Gunder reached for a wooden bowl sitting on one of the shelves and filled it with dried fruit in a practiced manner. "Here, take this," he said, handing it to Arik. "It's going to be a long tour. You could use a bite to eat."

Arik gratefully took the bowl, slipped a dried apricot into his mouth, and savored the concentrated sweetness — a pleasant contrast to the dryness in his throat. Gunder nodded in satisfaction as he watched Arik start emptying the bowl while they left the room and headed back down the corridor.

"Good," Gunder said as Arik finished the last of the fruit. Both of them approached the doorframe, their eyes fixed on the corridor. "Before we move on" — he pointed to the gap in the wall across from the storage room — "that's one of the exits leading upward. Don't even think about going up there alone." He turned to Arik. "At least not for the time being. Understood?"

"Understood," Arik confirmed, and Gunder continued speaking. "Let's keep going." They left the storage room and turned right into the main corridor. The hallway stretched about seven meters ahead before opening into a larger passage. "Down to the right, you'll find the washrooms and the latrine," Gunder explained briefly, pointing to the narrow hallway. "There's another set on the other side. Always good not to have to walk too far."

Arik nodded silently, following Gunder. Ahead was a wooden door that led into the next quarters. Gunder gestured toward the door. "One of our quarters," he said curtly, pointing to the other doors on both sides. "The next four doors you see on the left and right lead to the other quarters."

Their tour continued, moving down the hallway for about fifteen meters until Gunder stopped in front of a particularly wide door. "Here," he said, opening it. The room beyond was significantly larger than the meeting room. It was a training hall, which also served as a meeting space. The floor was made of smooth stone, and the walls were lined with weapons and training dummies, showing clear signs of wear from many strikes.

"This room is four times the size of the meeting room," Gunder explained, letting Arik step inside. The six shadow-walkers who were training with various weapons and techniques briefly glanced up to see who had entered the room. But upon seeing Gunder, they quickly turned their attention back to their sparring partners.

"You'll start working on your abilities here tomorrow," Gunder said firmly but kindly. Arik let his gaze wander through the room, observing the shadow-walkers for a moment. They were all fighting with wooden staffs, and some had already cloaked their weapons in shadow. He was astonished at the precision they displayed, a testament to years of training.

Arik felt Gunder's hand on his shoulder. "I regularly have everyone under my guidance fight without their abilities," he said.

"Why?" Arik asked, genuinely curious.

Gunder's response was calm and understanding: "Your abilities are one thing. But if you rely on them too much, you risk being defenseless if you can't access them. So always see them as an extension, not the foundation, of your combat skills."

That made sense to Arik, though he certainly wasn't looking forward to that part of his training. His eyes wandered further through the room, spotting another door at the far end. "What's in there?" he asked, intrigued.

"A mixed storage for weapons and supplies," Gunder replied matter-of-factly. "You can also access it from the corridor if you want."

Arik raised an eyebrow. "You really have everything here in doubles or triples, don't you?"

Gunder gave a small grin, one that Arik was starting to recognize. "Actually, we have many things in fours," he corrected. "This facility was designed so that if one storage or exit becomes unusable, we're not left stranded. Plus, the complex is large enough to accommodate up to 64 people."

They left the training room, and Gunder was about to continue the tour when Arik gestured toward the storage room. "Can I grab some more food?" he asked innocently.

Shaking his hooded head, Gunder replied, "Not yet. We'll pass another storage room soon." After this brief exchange, they continued their tour, heading west this time. Arik noticed that Gunder was leading him counterclockwise through the facility. Seven meters later, Gunder paused briefly, pointing right at a narrow corridor. "Over there is a staircase leading up, the second exit. Fenna and Vanadis have their rooms there too."

Arik nodded again as they moved on. Nine meters further, they reached another narrow hallway, this time without a staircase. "Here are Teto and Raban's quarters," Gunder explained, grinning mischievously. "We could take a peek inside Raban's room, if you like."

Arik snorted quietly but chose not to engage. They continued walking and eventually turned into a wider corridor. "This way," Gunder said, as they proceeded down the hallway. After about fourteen meters, they reached another right-hand turn.

Gunder listed off the rooms. "Down to the right is a dedicated armory," he explained, "and next to it is another storage room. Across from that are another washroom and latrine. Straight ahead is the workshop."

Gunder paused and grinned. "The advantage of having so many latrines is that you never have to wait for one to be free — unless, of course, all the quarters here are fully occupied." Arik nodded thoughtfully. "How many of you actually live down here?" he asked.

Gunder hesitated for a moment. "Currently, 31. We used to be more. A lot more. But the years and the Church have taken their toll. Sixteen years ago, we lost so many in a single day… ." Gunder abruptly stopped, his words hanging heavy in the air.

Trusting his gut, Arik decided not to ask further questions. He let the moment pass unnoticed, allowing Gunder to continue speaking. "Faster than we could find new shadowstone bearers. And often we weren't quick enough to beat the Church to them."

Before Gunder could move on, Arik cut in. "Can I please grab something to eat now?" He couldn't see Gunder roll his eyes, but he knew that he did. "Fine. Come on." Gunder quickly stomped to the storage room door after taking the bowl from Arik. He yanked it open and disappeared inside for a few moments before returning with a chunk of bread, a piece of cheese, and some dried meat. He handed the bowl back to Arik. "As you can see, our suppliers do a decent job."

"Thanks!" Arik said gratefully, grabbing the piece of meat.

Gunder led Arik further along, back to the wide hallway, and they turned left. They passed two more barracks on the right-hand side. After they passed both doors, Arik recognized the area — it was where his altercation with Diemo had taken place about half an hour earlier. "Diagonal left from here is the access to the South Tunnel," Gunder explained, leading Arik right, past the training room. Arik could still hear the sounds of shadow-walkers sparring inside. Unlike the first training room, they didn't enter this one.

Six meters past the training room entrance, they walked by the communal room. Gunder didn't stop. "You should avoid that place for now. It can be overwhelming to meet everyone at once," he said dryly.

Arik noted that they had passed a corridor on the right that led to his own quarters. "That room there is actually meant for a sergeant," Gunder explained, "but it's currently empty because a sergeant from the old shadows recently went missing on a mission."

They continued their route, eventually turning right, where Gunder opened a door. "This is the well room. This is where we get our fresh water. Make sure someone shows you how the system works before you try to get water for the first time."

Noticing Arik's confused look, Gunder added, "We don't have the time or patience for that now." Shrugging, Arik went back to eating his cheese.

They didn't walk the rest of the corridor, as it only led to the West Tunnel, another storage room, and the kitchen, which could also be accessed from the communal room. Arik used the opportunity to ask Gunder a question that had been on his mind since the start of the tour. "Why is the air so fresh down here?"

Gunder nodded. "The builders of the complex designed an extensive ventilation system. It brings fresh air into most of the rooms from outside. They were very thorough when they designed the place, so even if we were fully occupied, we could withstand a siege for two months without running out of water or food, or being threatened by a buildup of waste."

After Gunder explained this, they made their way back past the training and meeting rooms, directly toward another wooden door. Gunder stopped and gestured toward the door. "Here's your quarters."

Arik stepped inside and let his gaze wander. The room was larger than he had expected. Torches burned on either side, hanging between the beds. On both sides, there were four beds, each with a wooden chest underneath, and above each bed, there were three hooks for clothing. Arik remembered the dream he'd had about the boarding school and found this room to be a larger, better version of the dormitories — larger, because it was around eight by six meters, and better, because the usual smell of sweat wasn't present, and there were also tables and chairs.

Taking the opportunity, he placed the bowl — now containing only bread — on the table. He continued to survey the room, noticing several holes in the wall — some at knee height and others near the ceiling — all along the wall opposite the entrance. In the center of the room was a stone pillar, from which stone arches extended left and right to support the ceiling and provide stability.

"Pick a bed and rest up for a while," Gunder said in his deep voice, adding, "You'll have three roommates soon so that you're not alone in here, and so you can start getting to know some of the others." Gunder then left the room, leaving Arik alone.

Arik returned to the table and grabbed the bread. It seemed only a few days old — at least fresher than the bread at the boarding school. "Fresher than at the boarding school?" he questioned his own thought. He fell onto a bed without consciously choosing it. "Just like back then — farthest from the door, an advantage in case you need to react." This time, he had spoken the words half aloud and was immediately glad he was alone. "That wasn't part of your dream," he continued, tapping the black stone embedded in his navel.

"CORRECT!" the voice suddenly echoed in his head again.

CHAPTER 15

Gnarled willows and dead bushes lined the road, their roots partially exposed by the constant dampness. Here and there, old tree stumps jutted out of the swampy ground, as if they were the last remnants of a forest swallowed by the water. The flat land surrounding the road tended to flood completely on particularly rainy days, turning the marsh into a shallow lake. The cobblestones, while well-set, were damp at the edges, the grass in many places muddy and sodden. As they rode on the cart along this wide, paved road that wound through the marsh, an oppressive silence hung over the surroundings. The moisture crept in from all sides, and even on a sunny autumn day, the air was heavy and cool, further deepening the gloomy mood.

The hair on the back of her neck stood up instinctively as Bero released the power of his lightstone. It took him a few moments longer than usual to activate his power, but given his condition, that made sense. He raised his left arm toward Michael, with his index and middle fingers extended. Romilda watched as threads of light began to emerge from beneath the sleeve of Bero's robe, coiling around his arm. When they reached his hand, the threads merged and completely enveloped both fingers.

A long, two-finger-wide light rod began to grow from where his fingers ended. After about 15 seconds, the rod touched both the wood of the cart and Michael's back — and it stayed there. Curious about how Bero would proceed, she alternated her gaze between Michael and him. His eyes glowed with an intense white light, but his expression remained calm and focused. "Don't be startled," he warned Romilda before sending a pulse through the rod, which ended with a soft yet distinct pop. A clear groan echoed, and Romilda concluded it must have been far from pleasant. Despite the low volume of the detonation, it caught the attention of some passersby. They cast uncertain glances in their direction before identifying the source of the noise. Upon spotting the consecrated one, they quickly averted their gazes and returned to their own business.

Michael's left side was lifted by the pressure wave, causing his body to roll onto his stomach. Now, half of him lay on the cart while the other half rested on Thomas. "What do you think…" Bero coughed again, interrupting himself. "…how many more times I'll have to do that?" His voice carried a certain satisfaction over the quick chance to get some payback. Romilda, unsure of what kind of response he was expecting, kept it vague. "I... I don't know, Your Reverence," she stammered, secretly hoping, *but I hope it's many*.

As Bero spoke, pebbles and loose branches crunched under the cart's wheels. It swayed slightly as it crossed another dip in the road. "I estimate two more times…" — another cough — "… should be enough. As an Explorer, it's my duty…" — he paused briefly to suppress the cough — "…to constantly explore new things and expand my knowledge." The long sentence took its toll, and Bero had to take another deep breath. A cold wind swept through the marshes, carrying the smell of decaying mud and rot.

"But Your Reverence," Romilda pressed on, determined to uncover why there was so much discord among the consecrated ones — even if it pained her to keep up this act. "Why is there so much discord between you and the other consecrated ones?" In her thoughts, she added, *Please explain, so I can plant this seed of discord more deliberately*.

Bero closed his eyes for a moment. About a minute later, he opened them again and said, "Alright, I'm ready for another round." He repositioned the rod. "I'll explain it to you in a moment, just let me..." — another pressure wave shook the cart, this time a bit louder — "...finish this first." Those travelers, coachmen, and merchants who hadn't been nearby for the first explosion tried to figure out the source of the noise. But the reactions followed the same pattern as the first time.

The second pressure wave tossed Michael's body more violently, and now he landed with the left side of his back on the right side of Thomas. The rest of him once again made hard contact with the wooden cart. His left arm dangled off the end of the wagon. This time, Thomas groaned as well, feeling the impact. Michael, however, seemed to have finally lost consciousness after the first hit, as Romilda detected no further reactions from him. "What about Alex? Is he showing signs of suspicion?" Bero asked hoarsely, while Romilda glanced over at the Executor. "How would I know?" she replied hesitantly, trying to detect any uncertainty in his eyes.

"If he looks more confused than usual and has the expression of someone trying to..." — another cough interrupted him — "...pass stones." Given the clear enjoyment Bero seemed to derive from this situation, Romilda couldn't help but wonder if he might fit in well among the shadow-walkers. He'd surely get along with Vanadis. "No, Your Reverence, Alex looks normal," she finally answered.

"Thank you." Bero's gaze now rested on Romilda. "To your earlier question... Let me put it this way: Under normal circumstances, I would agree with you." His expression grew heavier. "But these aren't normal circumstances." He sighed deeply. "Maybe I'm still too young to..." — he fought off another coughing fit and took a deep breath — "… understand why the Church keeps people like these three around. I mean, beyond the first four years."

Romilda thought back to the day she was taken from her village at age eight and sent to the boarding school. Even back then, there were children like Alex, Thomas, and Michael, who caused more trouble than they were worth. "I understand that well, Your Reverence," she agreed. Bero, quick to switch gears, asked, "Why didn't you choose to stay with the Church after those four years?" Teto's ears perked up, and inwardly, he prayed that Romilda wouldn't find herself talking her way into trouble.

Romilda struggled to keep her emotions in check. At eleven, she and some other children had found a shadowstone in a dark basement corner. As a shy girl, she had been an easy target for teasing and ridicule. Why she had been taken along with the group, she couldn't quite remember. Suddenly, someone had shoved the shadowstone into her hand. "Come on, you're not too scared to use it, are you?" Whoever had said that was long forgotten — and didn't matter.

She had wanted to prove herself brave, just this once. So, she used the stone — and was promptly betrayed by the same children. As soon as they left the basement, they sought out Magister Helder and snitched on Romilda. She ran for her life, dashing through narrow alleys, always feeling like someone was hot on her heels. Suddenly, someone grabbed her and pulled her into a dark doorway, a hand clamped over her mouth. When she looked up, she saw the tousled hair and strange smile of a middle-aged woman — Vanadis.

In the distance, the river bend loomed, its slow-moving waters exuding a menacing calm. The cart slowly rolled closer to it. Some things were inevitable, some weren't — a realization Teto had only come to over the years. Just like the bridge that allowed the cart to cross the river, he wanted to prevent Romilda's response from throwing everything into the water. Playing his role as the concerned "father," he mumbled into the conversation: "She wasneededathome. Ibroughtherback." He left it to Bero to continue the conversation and smoothly deflected: "Andwhyare youstillthere?"

Bero sensed something stirring in Romilda and took a wild guess. "Bad experiences with these types?" He gestured toward the other consecrated ones. A tear rolled down her left cheek as she nodded. "It helps me to let it out," he grinned slightly, making a gesture with his head as he spoke: "You're welcome to do the same."

Relieved, she laughed softly, stood up, and kicked Thomas hard in the side. She took a step back and did it again. Michael slowly slipped off Thomas and the cart. On her third kick, she let out a scream, long-suppressed emotions from years ago finally breaking through. Under Teto's cloak, the first black spheres began to form. The fourth kick followed, accompanied by an even louder scream. Michael tumbled off the cart.

Half-laughing hoarsely, Bero asked her to step back from Thomas. "We'll see you in Tarsk, if you manage to make it there." A bang followed, and Thomas flew off the cart in a slightly larger arc, the cart jolting once again from the explosion. "Alex, stay here and keep an eye on them," Bero called to the consecrated one still following them, though by now they were already 20 meters away from Michael. The consecrated one stopped, turned, and walked back to the other two Executors. Glancing briefly over his shoulder, Teto wondered if the day could get any stranger. Shaking his head, he thought again, *Some things are inevitable, some aren't.*

Romilda sat back down. She sighed in relief. "Do you feel better now?" Bero asked her, having dispersed his power in the meantime. She nodded more firmly this time, and Bero continued: "Why did I stay with the Church?" He paused to think about how to best explain it. Absentmindedly, he reached for the waterskin and took another hearty drink. The urge to cough had subsided, though the hoarseness remained. "Because of a friend. Or rather, because of his mother."

"In our fourth year at the boarding school, she was taken by an illness." Talking about the memories wasn't easy for him. "She had taken me in many years ago and had a hard time with the fact that we both weren't there anymore." Romilda had closed her eyes in the meantime and was relaxing. Bero didn't mind; he took it as an opportunity to pause between his words.

Briefly, she opened her eyes and looked up at the sky. "What about your friend? How did he take it?"

"Not well. It really hit him hard. I think it would've cheered him up if he'd seen what just happened," he continued, his gaze drifting over the southern marshlands.

Romilda had a sense of why: "Did those three..." she began to ask, but Bero finished her sentence: "...make his life hard? Yes, quite a bit. Even before his mother passed, they made life tough for him. But after that..." he whistled through his teeth, "...they started beating him up too. He was reserved, withdrawn... made him an easy target. Even if he'd had more muscle, three against one isn't a fair fight."

"Sowhy didya stayanyway?" Teto chimed in again. It wasn't often that they got a consecrated one to talk, so even the smallest piece of information was valuable. The black spheres remained hidden beneath his cloak — a precaution in case the conversation took an unexpected turn.

Bero sighed. "Because he didn't know where else to go. He was familiar with the boarding school, and in a way, the Church offered some security. So we stayed. He became an Extractor, and I became an Explorer." Bero's gaze swept across the endless, gray marshland as if hoping to find answers to the questions that tormented him. But in the silence of the marsh, he found no comfort, only a suffocating emptiness that reminded him how lost he truly felt.

"Sooner or later, we'll have to go our separate ways, though. I'm just waiting for him to make it on his own." His voice carried a mix of resignation and a hint of bitterness, barely hidden beneath the polite facade. "I don't care what the Church thinks, I'm only staying because I hope he'll manage without me one day." Running a tired hand through his hair, he added, "That is... if he wasn't already gone."

Romilda and Teto perked up. "Has he been gone for long?" she inquired.

Bero shook his head. "Yes... no... about seven days, shortly after our consecration. I could swear those three empty-heads had something to do with it."

It carried some risk, but she had to ask: "What was his name?"

"Arik, why?"

CHAPTER 16

- 10 -

Darkness overcame Arik once more.

"Please, not again... I haven't even processed the last time," he muttered, half to himself. If sarcasm were a weapon, he would have been quite skilled at wielding it — and he had no shortage of worthy opponents.

"OH. MY DEEPEST APOLOGIES. SHALL I COME BACK LATER?"

"If it's not too much trouble," he thought back dryly. The shadowstone responded without missing a beat: "AS YOU WISH, SEE YOU LATER." Silence followed. Moments passed in a blur. Yet the darkness around Arik did not disappear. "You're still here, aren't you?" he asked, slightly irritated.
"I'M ALWAYS HERE."

Shouldn't he be learning how to control this by now? As if it had sniffed out his thoughts like a bloodhound on a scent, the stone responded with an almost menacing, "I CAN HEAR THAT TOO."

"Of course you can, what else did I expect? As much as I could marvel at what you've done with the place, could you please turn on the lights?" he asked, not hiding his annoyance.

The darkness vanished, and he was back in his quarters. "Thanks. I'm not a big fan of complete darkness." This was his first genuinely serious statement in the entire conversation.

"HOW IRONIC. WE ARE — " the stone began, but Arik interrupted: "And could you maybe tone it down a bit? Less booming, less echoing? You wouldn't believe the headache I had after the last time." Arik meant it. The low-frequency rumble of the shadowstone's voice definitely had its downsides.

"As I Was About To Explain To You… You're Welcome…" the voice added to Arik's mental "thanks," "… You Are Still In The Place Where Darkness Resides. No, Not There." Arik would take it to his grave, what he thought in that moment.

"This Room Is Merely A Replica Of Your Memory."
"And why are you 'showing up' right now?" Arik growled mentally at the voice. "Can't I just have a moment of peace before the next annoyance comes along?"

"I Thought It Was A Good Time Since Your Memory Has Been Triggered Again," the voice explained. "Let Me Just Show You And Stop Complaining."

The scene changed, and he found himself standing in the marketplace. It was a sunny autumn day, and he was standing in a line with others, all of them wearing the life-affirming gray robes. He quickly oriented himself. He seemed to be at the back corner of five rows, and based on the blue cord around his waist and those of the people in front of him, it became clear where he was.

With every bump in the road and every stone the wheels rolled over, Teto became more aware of the wisdom of his decision. He grabbed Romilda's cushion and handed it to her in the back of the wagon. Behind him, still gazing up at the sky, Bero continued talking. "I still don't quite understand why you want to know this in such detail." He scratched the few chin stubble he had at seventeen. "But I guess it can't hurt to have a few more people on the lookout for him." The few clouds in the sky were very good listeners, just like the young woman he had met with Romilda about an hour ago.

"The Magisters had ordered us to line up in rows of four in front of the church in the marketplace. First, there were the three rows of Executors — some of them were repeating their final year — then us four Explorers, with me in the lead, and then the Extractors. Arik stood all the way at the back." Bero couldn't help but grin as he remembered. "He was always the type to stay in the background, out of sight. When I turned to look at him, it was the first time in years I saw him looking... almost happy."

"Like a plant that, after a long time in darkness, finally gets hit by the first beam of sunlight breaking through the clouds." Proud of his phrasing, which would have made even his rhetoric teacher smile, he continued, "But we didn't have much time to exchange glances, because the Magisters stepped in front of us and demanded our attention. Lucky for me, I got to avoid them for a while longer."

"Is Magister Helder still at the boarding school?" Romilda asked cautiously. "I remember well when he introduced himself as the head during my time there." "Yes, he is," Bero confirmed. "The school is still under his thumb... sorry, I mean, his *leadership*. Was he bald back then too?"

Romilda smiled faintly, as there was something they shared. "Did he ever have hair? I certainly can't remember any." It felt good to joke about Helder with someone outside the shadow-walkers. "Does his consecration speech differ from the one he gives at the start of term?"

They had reached the bridge over the river, and the two horses suddenly changed their behavior. The southern marsh had made them nervous, and now they had the chance to gradually relax. About ten kilometers as the crow flies separated them from Aregelia, which grew smaller behind them with each passing minute. As if they had planned it, all three of them turned almost simultaneously to catch one last glimpse of the city.

- 8 -

He watched the Magisters step in front of them, and just like back then, Arik felt the urge to exchange glances with Bero once more. It could very well be the last time he saw him. Extractors, unlike Explorers, were rarely sent on missions and spent most of their time in monasteries built on the outskirts of every town. "Do you miss him?" the voice asked Arik.

"I... I hadn't really...," Arik had a lump in his throat. "...hadn't had the chance to think about it." Magister Helder cleared his throat, about to begin his speech, but Arik didn't care. "But since you ask... of course, I miss him. We grew up like brothers." Regret began to rise in him. Helder started addressing the students assembled before him.

Helder didn't matter. Not seven days ago, and not now. He had held Bero back all these years, been a burden on him. How many times had Bero had to make sacrifices because of him? How many times had Bero had to defend him? Bero had lost friendships because of him.

Nothing could change the fact that Bero and he were now going separate ways. Not Helder's words about how much they had all achieved, nor his speech about accepting them into the Church with the pride of a father. Arik barely registered the words, like distant, meaningless noise. Even if his life hadn't taken the turn it did that day, the Magister's well-chosen words would have rung true: "Today marks the beginning of a new chapter in your lives!"

Bero would finally be free from Arik.

"Don't Be So Hard On Yourself, Kid." Arik sensed that the stone could feel sympathy. So this was his new normal for the past week — "Empathetic stones, fused to my body." It wasn't new for him to feel anger because of the stone — what was new, though, was the disgust now welling up within him. "I never asked for you to become a part of me, so spare me your pity!"

"That Makes Two Of Us." the stone's voice grumbled, though it maintained its demeanor toward Arik. "From What I've Seen, I Can Confirm You Were A Burden To Him." "Then why shouldn't I be hard on myself?" Arik didn't understand why the stone was sparing him now, nor what it was getting at.

"Given The Circumstances — You Were Just Children, And It Would've Been Too Much To Expect Bero To Be Mature Enough." Arik tried to grasp the fact that the stone could access his memories, but he couldn't. It could have made him furious, but lacking any better alternatives, he restrained himself. "Bero Had The Ability To Help You More Permanently. He Didn't, And Perhaps He Even Enjoyed Having Someone Who Needed Him." The scene froze. Arik needed time to digest these words.

Once they crossed the bridge, the wide plain stretched out before them, fields that seemed to go on forever — although most of them had already been harvested. The cottages of the next village came into view, and to their right, they could now see the sprawling Southwest Forest. They had finally shaken off the oppressive veil of the swamp.

"No. It was one of his standard speeches." For some reason, Bero took a long time to answer. "He used the same line he'd said after the first four years." Bero struck a pompous pose, mimicking Magister Helder — even down to the throat-clearing. "I am utterly delighted by your progress. You, who have become like my children — let me put it this way." Gesturing toward Romilda, he implicitly asked her to finish the sentence. Her gaze conveyed that she had no idea what he was expecting from her.

He repeated the gesture.

"Forgive me, consecrated one, but I'm not sure what it is you want from me," Romilda tried to excuse herself innocently. Bero gave a dismissive smile, brushing it off. "No matter. It's probably been a while for you. When did you say you left the boarding school?"

"Thirtn yearsago." Like a lynx, Teto had been listening closely to the conversation. He had a bad feeling that Bero was starting to catch on. Now more than ever, they had to be as cautious as possible with their words. "Forgive me, I didn't mean to interrupt my story like that." As skillful as Bero was with words, Teto saw through him — he was used to dealing with smooth talkers.

"Where was I…." Just as easily as he mimicked Helder, Bero pretended to search for the right words. "…right. After his sermon, Magister Helder instructed the first row to enter the church. Since the first three rows were just meatheads… sorry, Executors, I'll skip the details." His tone was more pompous than what Teto and Romilda were used to by now, but it was hard to place because this attitude was rather normal when referring to Executors.

"Then," — a wave of pride swept from the wagon onto the cobblestones of the road — "it was time. My row was called to follow Magister Erlolf into the church." A strong gust of wind blew over them. It was as if Bero had summoned the wind himself, just for this moment. "The splendor of the church unfolded before our eyes. All the Magisters had lined up on either side of the altar, where Magister Helder awaited us."

Romilda and Teto, independently of one another, wondered how Bero managed to balance pride and indifference when it came to the Church. "We lined up in front of the altar and knelt. Then we were granted the great honor of repeating the oath." A clearing of the throat followed these words, and in his still-raspy voice, he directed his declaration to the world: "Yes, I swear to serve the Church of Light from this day forward!"

- 6 -

Arik watched as Bero and the other Explorers were led into the church. Soon it would be his turn — the last row. Minutes passed before Magister Erlolf emerged one final time and beckoned the Extractors inside. They started moving. Does it make any difference if I remember who the three gray robes ahead of me are? Arik wondered. "What Does Your Gut Tell You?" came the voice in his head.

"Have you forgotten where in my body you were placed?" Arik thought sarcastically. When no response came, he grinned in satisfaction, only for the voice to immediately snap back, "Don't Get Too Full Of Yourself."

They ascended the steps and entered the church through the grand portal. Arik had never cared much for this building — it was too plain and pompous for his taste. He followed the three students ahead of him hesitantly, letting his gaze wander around the room. All the Magisters were present. Helder and Hariolf stood solemnly by the altar, waiting for Erlolf. The Extractors, out of habit, lined up before Helder and knelt. The oath was recited, but Arik remained silent. He couldn't remember whether he had spoken the words back then.

"No, You Didn't," the voice whispered, straight from his thoughts. An inexplicable sense of relief washed over Arik.

"You Were Ready To Serve The Church." "Only out of lack of alternatives. Who takes in two orphans?" Slowly but steadily, memories began rising from the depths of his mind — fragmented images, like small bubbles floating up from the bottom of a dark lake.

The first Extractor student was now instructed to stand and remove his gray robe. He did as told, then lay down on the altar — a rectangular slab of white marble adorned with golden patterns that wound around the lightstones embedded in the stone. As the student lay there, Magister Helder stepped up to the head of the altar and spoke a few meaningless words that might as well have been left unsaid. The stone would bond with the body regardless.

A few more minutes passed before it was Arik's turn. As he rose, he saw that the Extractor students were now wearing white robes, waiting patiently for him to receive his stone. Arik removed his gray robe, bowed to Magister Helder, and lay down on the table. As he lay there, Helder leaned over him. From this angle, the Magister looked even more unsettling than usual. Then, Arik saw the stone.

The moment froze. "Are You Sure You Want To See This?" the shadowstone asked. "Yes. I think so." Arik was aware of the possible consequences, but he knew it would prepare him for what was yet to come. "But I have a question for you first." "I Can't Answer With Just Yes Or No. This Memory Of Yours Is… Complicated." It wasn't the answer Arik had hoped for, but he had no choice but to accept it — for now.

Magister Helder received the stone from Hariolf and placed it on Arik's chest. At first, nothing happened, then Arik felt a strange sensation. It was as if a thousand tiny needles were piercing his body, followed by a wave of energy. Time seemed to slow down, and an eternity passed. Then it happened — energy from the lightstone streamed out of Arik's mouth and eyes, brightening the already well-lit room even more. It was over, and he exhaled.

- 5 -

The first merchants from Tarsk were coming toward them on the wide road. After crossing the bridge, the roadsides were lined with trees again. Among the larger trees, smaller ones had sprung up. It was rare for builders from Aregelia to make it out here to maintain the road. Where the road in the swamp was uneven due to moisture, here the cause lay in the lack of care. The carts rumbled over roots that pushed through the pavement, and in some places, the path was so bumpy that it felt as though the wheels might break at any moment.

Bero took a deep breath, shaking off the last traces of his pride, and resumed his story. "After we all received our consecration, Magister Erlolf led us to the side room, where the other newly consecrated ones were already waiting. I can still remember the crowd — everyone in their new robes, each with a new stone in their chest." A slight smile crept across his face before he continued. "When Arik entered the room with the other Extractors, he gave me a quick wink when we finally saw each other again. I had tried to speak with him, but there were simply too many people wanting something from me. So he spent most of the time just standing quietly in a corner."

Romilda listened attentively, while Teto occasionally made a low humming sound to signal that he was still listening. They gave the consecrated one the time he needed to sort his thoughts.

"Well, we were told that we had the rest of the day to ourselves," Bero went on. "At least until evening. The Magisters gave us... free time — for the first time in years. Of course, that time was limited, but it still felt... strange."

Bero leaned back in the cart, letting his gaze wander through the rows of trees lining the road. "It was a strange day. The city was full of life, everyone celebrating the newly consecrated, yet I had this feeling that something wasn't right. Arik was quieter than usual, maybe he already sensed that our paths would soon part." He paused, as if recalling how that moment had felt.

"In the evening, there was a small banquet as part of the celebrations," Bero continued. "Nothing grand, but for us — who were hardly accustomed to such luxuries — it was a welcome change. I remember exactly how Arik and I sat down at one of the tables, a little away from the others. We barely spoke, but there was no need to. He didn't want to wait until it was all over — he wanted to leave early so he could get back to the boarding school. The last look he gave me as he left the banquet is burned into my memory. It was the last time I saw him."

Bero fell silent for a moment. The sound of rolling wheels and the crunch of uneven stones broke the quiet. Then he added softly, "I never got the chance to tell him that I miss him."

The scene shifted again. After a brief glimpse of the room filled with the newly consecrated, Arik found himself at the evening banquet. He was sitting at a table with Bero, and they had already helped themselves to food. "At least it's not porridge this time," Arik said as he peeled an egg.

Bero didn't reply immediately, seemingly too focused on swallowing a whole chicken leg. Finally, he managed to clear his mouth. "It's a shame we didn't get this more often, but I hope that as consecrated ones, we'll eat better than we did the past eight years."

"We'll see... we'll see..." A smile flickered across Arik's face. "I'm just glad I won't have to put up with them for a while." His voice sounded light and carefree. He gestured toward a group that included Alexander. "True enough," Bero replied, relieved. "Although I do wonder how some of them managed not to stab themselves with their own swords." Arik's mouth curled into a grin.

"I just hope I won't end up in the same group as them," Bero said after a moment of silence, though he could already see from Arik's face that his hope wasn't shared. "Odds are one in three. But I wish you luck that you don't end up as their Explorer," Arik replied. After a brief pause, he added with a mischievous smile, "But if you do, please do me a favor and make them march through the Southmoor as often as you can."

"Maybe I'll just leave them there and see what happens." The thought made Bero chuckle, and Arik joined in. "Just don't make it too obvious. And be careful — they're capable of anything." "Don't worry, I value my life too much." Those words reassured Arik, and he felt compelled to reply, "You know, despite the last eight years, I still value my life too. And now, they can't touch me anymore."

After a while, Arik excused himself and left the banquet early. The banquet hall was in the town hall, directly across from the church on the market square. The sun was already setting as he exited the building. A light gust of wind blew toward him. He closed his eyes and took a deep breath, savoring the feeling of freedom that briefly washed over him.

He decided to take the back entrance to the internat and cut across the market square, passing by the church on the left, and then through the narrow alleys that were so familiar to him.

- 3 -

They were heading toward the first intersection, a few hundred meters ahead. Clouds had begun to gather on the horizon, gradually obscuring the sun. Though the clouds were still scattered and small, it was clear that the gray wall in the sky was approaching. Teto suggested that they take shelter in the next village if the rain began.

Bero had been silent for several minutes, lost in thought after finishing his story. Almost casually, and without changing his expression, he brought something up. "You know what we Explorers had drilled into us during our training? Something we had to remember, because it was in every graduation and year-end speech?" He paused, enjoying the sudden tension that filled Romilda and Teto. "Every Magister, regardless of the boarding school, uses the same phrase: 'I am truly delighted by your progress.' That's the litmus test for all who walk this path."

A sly smile crept onto his lips. He leaned forward, his voice lowering, almost conspiratorial. "Anyone who doesn't know that phrase wasn't in the boarding school long enough for it to sink in — which, in most cases, can only mean one thing: you're a shadow-child." A moment of silence followed, heavy and oppressive. "You never finished boarding school, did you, Romilda? Show me what you're hiding."

Romilda froze as Bero gave her a pointed look. "Come on," he pressed, gesturing toward her cloak. "Just a quick peek. I just want to make sure you're not hiding a stone from me."

"LeavemyDaughteralone!" boomed Teto, his voice thundering without even turning around. His mind raced — he knew his plan had failed.

They couldn't use their shadow powers recklessly. There were too many innocent people around, and the sunlight exposed them too much. It was something he had already considered when he had created the orbs still hidden under his cloak. Additionally, it was impossible to predict how the other people on the road would react or if more consecrated ones might appear. Conflict was unavoidable, especially since Bero already knew their faces.

"Stay out of this, old man!" Despite his scratchy voice, Bero's words carried authority. "Or I'll take you into custody as well." None of them noticed as the lid of a barrel nearby creaked open just a fraction, and a sharp-eyed gaze peered out. Bero's confusion grew even more when something suddenly struck his head out of nowhere, causing him to lose his balance. At the same time, the cart hit another large stone, and Bero lost his grip entirely. He tumbled off the side of the cart, narrowly missing one of the nearby trees.

Arik hadn't noticed them.

Three figures left the town hall only moments after him, quietly following his steps. Excitement barely contained, they struggled to suppress their giggles and cackles. If the wind had blown from the other direction, their sounds would have reached him, and he might have noticed. But as it was, he walked on, oblivious, into the alley.

Then everything happened quickly. On what seemed like a signal, Alexander and Michael sprinted forward, while Thomas held something dark in his hand, tossing it into the air every now and then, whistling as he did. Arik turned just in time to see the two of them rushing toward him. He tried to make a run for it, but it was too late. Alexander and Michael closed in too fast and kicked him between the legs, sending him crashing to the ground.

As he fell, he scraped his hands and face on the cobblestones, landing flat on his stomach. Groaning in pain, Arik didn't dare move. Then a kick landed in his side, flipping him over onto his back. While Michael pinned him down, Alexander pulled out a knife and cut open Arik's robe at his navel. The two of them laughed and cackled like madmen.

"Why... won't you just leave me alone?" Arik managed to gasp, only to be immediately mocked by Alexander. "Because it's always been fun trying out our little pranks on you." In the darkness of his dream, Arik saw Thomas approaching, holding the shadowstone tightly in his hand. It was a mirror of the events that had occurred a week ago.

Before Romilda or Teto could react, a loud clatter suddenly echoed through the air. A barrel lid flew open, and Vanadis, hair disheveled and grinning broadly, appeared out of nowhere and leaped over the cart. After quickly assessing what had just happened, he too jumped down from the cart, drew a dagger, and rushed toward the unconscious Bero lying on the ground. Using the moment Vanadis wasted no time rifling through his robes.

After a few moments, she looked up at Teto, immediately sensing the anger in his eyes. "A simple 'thank you' will do, Teto." It was one of those rare moments where Vanadis made it absolutely clear, with her sheer presence, that she would not back down — Teto would have to choose his next words carefully.

Bero began to stir.

- 0 -

Both Bero and Arik lay on the ground, each gasping for breath. Standing over them were two figures — Teto, still holding his dagger, and Thomas, who held the shadowstone in his fingers like a dangerous trophy. The silence was oppressive, thick in the air.

Vanadis was the first to break the quiet, her voice cold and emotionless. "The game is over. Time to face reality." Her eyes swept over everyone present, a hint of disdain flickering in them. "Your life as an Explorer ends here, Bero."

Thomas leaned over Arik and pressed the stone against his navel. With a malicious grin, he asked, "So, are you as curious as we are to see what happens next?"

CHAPTER 17

The common room was bustling with activity. Shadow-walkers, young and old, sat at tables, engaged in quiet conversations or busy with maps and plans. The large room was bathed in warm, subdued light that emanated from candles and hearths. In one corner of the room, two large fireplaces crackled, their glowing embers creating a cozy, almost homely atmosphere. The air was filled with the soft sounds of murmured discussions, clinking dishes, and the rustling of fabrics. However, at a particular table, away from the general bustle — where usually only the leadership members sat — there was concentrated silence. Raban, Diemo, Ostara, and Fenna were gathered there.

Raban sat with his arms crossed, his serious gaze sweeping over those present. Next to him sat Fenna and Diemo, both deep in thought. The conversation they'd had earlier still lingered between them, casting a shadow over their mood. Across from Raban, Ostara sat quietly and composed, like a hunter lying in wait. Her slender, agile frame and reddish-blonde hair, which fell softly over her shoulders, made her look even more like a predator. Her freckles were gently highlighted by the flickering light of the room.

"Alright, let's get to the plan," Raban began, his deep, rough voice cutting through the general murmur in the room. "We'll leave the facility through the southern tunnel. From there, we'll head about a kilometer southwest. That's where we'll reach the river." He looked directly at Fenna. "Your task will be to do some practice jumps first. Once you're confident, you'll use the shadow golem to leap across the river."

Fenna raised an eyebrow and leaned back in her chair. "Why so complicated? It would be easier to use one of Diemo's portals. Or better yet, Ostara could just fly over." She nodded toward the silent figure next to her, who shyly lowered her gaze.

With his attention now on Fenna, Raban showed no surprise as he responded. "I know, Fenna. But I want you to try it with the shadow golem. It's important you become confident in that ability."

Diemo, who had been quiet until then, couldn't suppress a grin. He leaned back in his chair, his eyes gleaming with amusement. "Nice to know my portals are so appreciated," he murmured, half to himself, half to the group. But his remark only earned a frown from Raban and a shy smile from Ostara, who briefly looked down before glancing back up at Raban.

"Diemo's portals are impressive, no doubt," Raban continued, casting Diemo a brief, serious look. "But we need to make sure we're prepared for any situation. Using the shadow golem requires precision and control, and it's better for Fenna to practice now than in a situation where we have no choice."

Fenna nodded again, this time with more resolve. She knew Raban was right, even though the simplicity of Diemo's portals or Ostara's ability to fly over the river was tempting. Ostara, on the other hand, said nothing. She simply lowered her head slightly, her eyes fixed on the ground, clearly uncomfortable with the topic.

"Ostara," Raban now addressed the young woman, who still seemed somewhat lost in thought. "You'll be securing our way back. Once Fenna makes it across the river, we need to be ready to act quickly if something goes wrong." At this,

Ostara raised her head, her eyes clear and focused. "Understood, Raban," she replied softly but with a hint of determination in her voice.

Raban's thoughts seemed to pause for a moment, rearranging themselves. "You know, Fenna, you made a good point earlier. Diemo should also take the opportunity to practice his abilities." Almost bored, Diemo responded, "If you insist. Can we get going now?"

Raban stood up and gestured toward the door. "Yes, Diemo, we're leaving. But what's the rush? Romilda is with Teto right now." Fenna and Ostara giggled, while Diemo looked slightly embarrassed. A brief moment passed in which no one spoke. "Alright. Let's go," Raban said, signaling the start of their mission.

With these words, everyone rose from the table. The soft scraping of chairs was lost in the general noise of the common room. As they made their way to the door to leave the hideout, the other shadow-walkers cast them quick, knowing glances before returning to their own tasks. The four of them left the room together, passed through the corridors of the hideout, and headed toward the southern tunnel. Along the way, Diemo shot a playful glance at Fenna. "I hope your golem isn't afraid of heights today." Fenna responded with a mocking grin before focusing again on what lay ahead.

When they finally reached the exit of the hideout and entered the tunnel, the warm atmosphere of the common room gave way to the cool, damp air of the underground. The light from the torches danced on the stone walls as they moved forward, determined to complete the first step of their mission.

The four shadow-walkers entered the southern tunnel in an orderly line. Raban led the group, followed by Fenna, Diemo, and Ostara. The air was cool and damp, and the echo of their footsteps quietly bounced off the walls. The tunnel stretched ahead like an endless tube of cold stone, supported by a massive arch that loomed overhead. The light from the torches affixed to the walls cast long shadows that danced on the damp ground, enveloping the tunnel in a dim twilight.

Ostara, bringing up the rear, pulled her cloak tighter around herself. "It's colder than I expected," she muttered softly, more to herself than to the others. Diemo, walking in front of her, glanced back and grinned. "Too late to turn back and warm up now. You'll have to tough it out till the end."

Raban, who was half-listening to the conversation, shook his head slightly. "What's the matter? Already freezing? You'd better start moving faster."

"No problem for me," Fenna quipped, quickening her pace. "Maybe I'll jump ahead just to warm up."

Diemo chuckled lightly, teasing her. "Are you really going to bring out the golem just to cross the river? I'm sure my portal would be cozier."

Raban cut him off with a brief, "We're sticking to the plan."

The tunnel seemed endless, but eventually, they saw the exit in the distance — a faint light like a narrow crack on the horizon. As they approached the end, the air grew fresher, and a cool breeze brushed against their faces. After a while, they reached the exit — a narrow gap in the darkness leading outdoors. As they stepped out of the tunnel, they felt the cool evening wind, which had already teased them in the tunnel, now fully on their skin. The stone exit led onto an open field, concealed by a small, overgrown hill. The sky was already dark, the sun long set, and the chill of the night crept through their clothes.

"Well, here we are," Raban said as he took the last step out of the tunnel, feeling the cold wind against his skin. He had prudently put on an extra layer over his wool vest so that the stones on his shoulders wouldn't be immediately visible. "No turning back now; this is where it gets serious."

"What a perfect setting for a cozy night stroll," Fenna joked, rubbing her hands to warm them. "Next time, we're definitely bringing cloaks," Diemo said as they started toward the river. Ostara, following the conversation with a quiet smile, pulled her cloak tighter around herself without saying a word.

The path to the river was calm and uneventful. The group moved in unison through the tall grass, which rustled softly underfoot. The night had fully descended, and only the moon, partially veiled by a thin layer of clouds, offered a faint, silvery light. Behind them, the lights of the city watchtowers glimmered, though they barely illuminated the outer edges of the city walls.

Despite the pitch darkness of their night journey, the four shadow-walkers were undeterred. Each of them used the power of the shadowstone to pierce the darkness and see clearly, even in the blackest night. The world no longer appeared to them as an impenetrable void but rather a space filled with sharp contours and deeper shadows, providing them with a clear sense of orientation.

When they reached the river, the group halted at the bank, gazing at the water that flowed quietly yet powerfully before them. The river was about twenty meters wide, and its current appeared deceptively calm. Yet all of them knew better than to step into it. Anyone who fell into the water would be swept away without question. Even for experienced swimmers — none of them were, considering how exposing their shadowstones in public would cause quite a stir — it would be nearly impossible to escape the river's grasp. The strength of the water was a hidden danger, lurking beneath the smooth surface.

Ostara moved to the edge of the bank, leaning forward slightly to survey the surroundings. The moon's reflection flickered briefly on the water before the waves swallowed it again. Without a word, she gave Raban a brief nod, signaling that she would scout ahead. Her slender, agile form almost merged with the shadows of the trees as she slipped into the darkness. One final glance at the group, and then she vanished silently into the bushes and trees lining the riverbank.

Raban waited a moment, ensuring that Ostara was out of sight before turning to Fenna and Diemo. "Alright, time for you to start your exercises," he said calmly, but with a certain firmness that left no room for argument.

Diemo nodded curtly and immediately began gathering his energy. He took a few steps back, closed his eyes, and raised his hands. The shadows around him started to move, flowing like thick ink toward a single point in front of him. Diemo's face showed no sign of strain, but the intensity of the darkness around him increased. Suddenly, he pulled his hands apart, and a bright rift appeared in the air, quickly expanding into a circular portal. It was impressively large — nearly three meters in diameter, big enough for someone to easily walk through. The portal shimmered slightly, pulsating like a liquid mass of shadow and light.

"This is the largest I can manage right now," Diemo said with a hint of pride as he gazed at his work. The edges of the portal flickered and wavered as though they were struggling to maintain form, but it remained stable. "It could fit all of us if we need it on the return trip." Diemo kept the portal steady, though beads of sweat began to form on his forehead as he fought to maintain the immense power needed to sustain it.

Raban nodded approvingly. "Hold it as long as you can… let me know when you can't anymore!" He then turned his attention to Fenna, who had closed her eyes and was taking deep breaths. Her face was concentrated, her brow furrowed as she began to gather the shadows around her. The darkness crept toward her like living tendrils, enveloping her feet and slowly crawling up her body. The shadows formed a dense, black shell around her, gradually taking shape. The process was fluid but required immense mental effort.

Slowly, Fenna's form began to grow. The shadows around her continued to condense, forming massive, angular limbs. Her hands transformed into enormous claws with sharp-edged fingers, while her legs grew thicker and broader. Her outline blurred as she reached six meters in height — four times her normal size. The golem was now fully formed and would have dominated the scene had shadows been more visible in the darkness. The figure appeared raw and powerful, as if made of solid stone, blacker than the night itself. The surface of the golem was rough and irregular, almost like a crude stone sculpture, and it seemed to absorb the surrounding darkness.

Fenna's eyes were hidden behind the thick mass of shadows, but her vision was sharp and clear. She could see every stone on the riverbank, every ripple in the water, and every tiny branch lying on the ground. The golem moved sluggishly but with a deep strength that was felt in every step. Fenna could feel the energy of her stones coursing through her body, enhancing her muscles and sharpening her senses. It's easier than last time, she thought. The improvement in her stone's power was already making a difference.

Despite the river's deceptive calm, Fenna knew this attempt would be a great challenge — not only because of the distance but because of the precision required to control the golem. One wrong step could send her tumbling into the swift current.

Still holding the portal steady, Diemo watched Fenna's transformation with a grim smile. "Not bad," he muttered appreciatively. "But I think you were bigger last time."

Fenna didn't let his comment bother her. She took a deep breath, focused for a moment, and then took her first steps toward the river. She turned north, running parallel to the river. The ground trembled slightly under the mass of the golem as she gathered momentum and prepared for the jump.

She managed about 15 meters, but she knew she could go farther. The landing had been anything but smooth, but she had managed to roll through it. The shadow golem maintained its form, and she didn't feel her energy waning yet. She aimed her second jump toward Raban, taking care not to land on him. She took another running start and launched herself off the ground.

During the second jump, Fenna felt herself using her full strength and landed safely after more than 20 meters. She almost flew over Raban and Diemo, and the ground shook lightly under the force of her landing. But Fenna remained stable, while Raban and Diemo were caught off guard by the sudden tremor and stumbled. "One more try," she muttered to herself, getting back into position. Fully focused, she didn't hear Diemo cursing loudly as he struggled to maintain the portal's form.

He was running out of strength. The portal flickered, and the edges began to destabilize. "Raban!" he finally called out, holding the portal up with his last bit of energy. Raban stepped behind Diemo without hesitation, placing a firm hand on his back. "Close your eyes and focus only on the energy in your stones," Raban instructed, his voice calm and authoritative. "I'll guide your energy."

Diemo obeyed, closing his eyes and allowing Raban to take control. The energy flowing through his stones and body slowly stabilized as Raban took charge. It felt as if an invisible hand was channeling the power into organized streams rather than letting it flow wildly and uncontrollably. After a minute, the portal was stable again, and the flickering edges smoothed out.

"Well done," Raban said with a satisfied nod. "Now make it bigger." Diemo gritted his teeth and focused. He didn't notice that Raban had already removed his hand from his back. The dark mass of the portal slowly expanded, inch by inch, until it was half a meter wider in diameter. "Now hold it again, for as long as you can. When your strength fades, let it disappear in a controlled way," Raban instructed in his deep, gruff voice, feeling a sense of pride at the display of skill.

Meanwhile, Fenna felt her control over the golem improving. Her movements were more precise, and the distribution of strength came effortlessly. Satisfied with her exercises, she now focused on the final jump. She took a deep breath, tensed the shadow muscles, and fixed her gaze on the point across the river. "One more running start," she told herself.

The golem began to move in long strides.

Then she leaped.

CHAPTER 18

Fenna landed with a dull thud on the other side of the river, about five meters from the bank. The damp earth not only crunched under her weight but also broke sticks and branches that had failed to get out of the way.

She stood still for a moment, stabilizing her balance. It was a bit easier since her landing had pressed her several centimeters into the ground. Her breathing was heavy but controlled as she felt the energy of her stones continuing to pulse through her body. She had managed the jump better than she had hoped. Her eyes scanned the area, searching and alert, but the surroundings seemed calm. Only the soft sound of the river behind her filled the air.

Suddenly, she noticed movement out of the corner of her eye. Ostara emerged from the shadows, nearly silent and as graceful as the shadow of a cat. Her reddish-blonde hair shimmered faintly in the weak moonlight as she approached Fenna. "The area is secure," she reported quietly but precisely. "No patrols in sight, just some animals near the forest and in the fields. Nothing we need to worry about."

Now that they were sure there would be no disturbances, Fenna was ready to continue. "Good. Then I'll practice a few more jumps here. If I increase the pace and the distance, I can improve my control." She still had enough strength to maintain her form, and her plan should pose no problems. "In the meantime, could you please fly around and check on Raban's surroundings again? We don't want any nasty surprises."

Ostara hesitated briefly before nodding. "Understood. I'll be quick." Her sharp eyes briefly scanned the trees at the edge of the field, as if to ensure there was no hidden danger, before she turned and vanished back into the darkness.

Fenna watched as Ostara silently melted into the shadows that wrapped around her like a protective cloak. Then she turned back to her own task. She took a deep breath, letting the energy course through her body again, and prepared for the next jump. Once more, she took a running start and leaped.

She was starting to enjoy it, soaring several meters high over the water. Mid-flight, she decided to roll on landing, which she executed smoothly. The ground vibrated again under Fenna's impact, but this time she was far enough from Raban and Diemo that they weren't thrown off balance. A satisfied smile played across her lips as she maintained control over her shadow golem form.

Raban jogged over, giving her a critical look with his arms crossed. "Everything alright? You looked a bit shaky on the landing."

"Don't worry, I've got it under control," Fenna replied, taking a deep breath to gather her thoughts. "I'll do two more jumps. I think I've got the hang of it."

Diemo, who was now panting heavily, lifted his head and looked at her with exhausted eyes. Sweat gleamed on his forehead, and his gaze was slightly glazed from the effort. Noticing his state, Fenna grinned mischievously. "Come on, Diemo. Hang in there! If you give up now, you'll have to apologize to Arik. And we both know you don't want that."

"Before it... comes to that..." — he gritted his teeth and focused again — "... I'd rather... go through... a portal... to nowhere." The edges of the portal flickered slightly, but he kept it stable, though each breath became more laborious.

Raban kept a watchful eye on the surroundings, scanning the tall grass that swayed gently in the wind and the night sky, where he spotted a familiar figure. Ostara was back, silently circling above like a bird of prey, securing the area.

Meanwhile, Fenna prepared for her next jump. She tensed her muscles and made one final check to ensure her form was stable. Then she moved, her steps heavy and powerful. With a final, determined push, she leaped into the dark night.

Even before the jump, she had decided she would once again roll through the landing. But this time, she wanted to raise the challenge. As she came out of the roll, she immediately tensed her shadow muscles, forcing the golem to stand up straight. Without hesitation, she spun around, set her gaze on the opposite shore, and launched herself back for another jump.

Just before reaching the end of the bank, she propelled herself forcefully into the air again. She quickly realized that this jump didn't quite reach the height of the last one. Internally, she braced herself for a quick landing response. With every fraction of a second, she became aware that she wouldn't land on the shore.

The impact was even more intense this time, and Fenna landed just a few meters from the edge of the bank. The ground gave way beneath her feet due to the pressure, and the golem began to slide slightly. Cold river water splashed against her legs, and for a moment, she almost lost her balance. The slight pull of the water, which began to wrap around her massive feet and ankles, immediately alarmed her. She stood about half a meter deep in the water, continuing to slip further in.

Tensing her shadow muscles, she pushed back against the dangerous tug of the river, struggling to maintain her balance. Every moment counted, but she kept control and eventually managed to free herself from the water's grip, regaining solid ground under her feet.

Relieved and proud of her success, she decided to end the transformation. The shadows that had enveloped her body began to dissolve and sink back into her. The towering form of the golem shrank as the shadows retreated into her normal, human shape. In less than a minute, Fenna was back to her usual form — breathless, but satisfied.

No sooner had she reverted than she let herself fall onto the cool grass, savoring the moment of calm. Her breathing was rapid, but the sense of accomplishment left a faint smile on her face. She felt the cold ground beneath her and heard the river rushing beside her — the same river that had almost dragged her to a watery grave not five minutes earlier.

Diemo, who had been watching Fenna's jump through gritted teeth, couldn't suppress a weary chuckle when he felt the ground tremble from the impact. He barely managed to dissolve the portal in a controlled way. The shadows forming the portal dissipated like smoke, swallowed by the darkness. Diemo let go of the last remnants of his energy and collapsed backward with a deep sigh.

"Done," he murmured before exhaustion finally claimed him, and he tipped over, lying flat in the grass. He lay there, panting heavily, his chest rising and falling with each breath. He could barely move in his current state, but the feeling of having completed the challenge brought a tired smile to his face.

Fenna glanced over at him and shook her head slightly. "Not bad, Diemo," she muttered to herself, still lying in the grass and gazing up at the clear night sky. "But you can still apologize to Arik... ." The stars twinkled above them, and for a moment, the world seemed to be in perfect harmony.

Both of them lay, breathing heavily, several meters apart on the ground. It was a sight that made Raban smirk. "So, still cold?" he asked with a teasing tone in his voice. Both lifted their heads tiredly and cast him an exhausted look, but neither could muster a "yes." Their energy was clearly spent.

"Alright, we'll take a ten-minute break," Raban decided. "You've earned it." He sat down on the grass as well, his eyes scanning the surroundings vigilantly. The night was quiet, with only the chirping of crickets and the sound of the river breaking the silence.

Suddenly, Ostara appeared beside Raban, so quietly that even he was startled for a moment. She bowed her head respectfully and whispered, "Raban, may I have permission to investigate something further?" Her eyes were sharp and focused, her usually calm demeanor replaced by a hint of unease. Raban nodded and asked, "What's wrong?"

"Upstream, about half a kilometer away, I noticed something. It could be a threat or maybe just a trick of the light, but I want to be sure. I saw something unusual — maybe a person. It's better if I take a closer look," Ostara explained calmly, but there was a sense of urgency in her voice.

Raban considered for a moment and then looked over at Fenna and Diemo, who were just starting to shake off their exhaustion. "Alright, check it out. Be careful, and report back if you find anything." Ostara nodded, her eyes briefly scanning the others before she vanished silently into the darkness again.

The ten minutes flew by for Ostara, and just as Raban was getting ready to set off again, she reappeared. Her reddish-blonde hair was slightly tousled, and there was a mix of tension and concern in her eyes. "I found someone," she reported quietly. "There's a person lying unconscious on the bank. He's hypothermic, but I'm not entirely sure who he is. But it looks like it could be Helko." Diemo and Fenna perked up at the mention of the name.

Raban raised an eyebrow. "Helko, out here? Show us the way," he ordered, but Fenna intervened. "Wait… let me just… transform into my golem form, and we'll get there faster." Raban moved toward Fenna immediately. Moments later, she felt his hand on her back, followed by the familiar sensation of him guiding her energies. "Thank you… let me try something," she said.

Unexpectedly, Fenna let out a loud cry and instantly transformed into a three-meter-tall golem. It was as if a wall of shadows had flowed directly from her. Raban's hand was still on her back, though it became harder for him to keep it there. "You're doing this again, I assume?" His deep voice carried a note of discomfort, and he pulled his hand back when she confirmed it.

A second cry followed, and Fenna reached four and a half meters in height. The scream also sounded significantly deeper than the first. The other three watched with interest, curious about what Fenna intended to do, as none of them had seen her do this before — at least not on purpose. They all assumed she would stop after the third scream since that would match her training size, but she went one more step.

Now standing at seven and a half meters tall, Fenna's golem towered over them. "That worked well," she rumbled in her deep golem voice, which was even lower than before. "I'll carry you both on my shoulders." With that, she reached for Diemo, who looked anything but pleased, and did exactly what she had said. To his surprise, he found the seat surprisingly soft and quickly found his balance. "Now you, Raban."

Reluctantly, Raban let her lift him and place him on the other shoulder, unsure whether to feel irritated or proud in this situation. In the end, he decided on both. "Ostara, you can land on my head," Fenna offered. Ostara felt flattered, though Diemo couldn't resist taking a jab, which embarrassed her. "If you're not going to lift her like us, at least make sure she doesn't leave a mess on top of you."

Unhappy with Diemo's behavior, Fenna decided to reprimand him: "Diemo, you've already made one mistake today. Hold back, or I'll test how far I can throw you in this size!" Diemo sheepishly apologized to Ostara, but she ignored him, as he had just compared her to a bird and insulted her beloved gargoyle form.

Fenna then set off, and moments later, Ostara landed on her. Staring at Diemo, she cursed him under her breath. It took less than two minutes for them to cover the half-kilometer distance. Fenna lowered Raban and Diemo, who quickly rushed to the person lying on the ground.

The situation suddenly became serious. They didn't know how long he had been out here or how he had ended up in such a state. "He's still breathing," Raban said with relief. "Fenna, pick us both up again, and carry Helko in your hands." Raban quickly took charge, coordinating the group. "Ostara, fly ahead and make sure we don't run into any consecrated ones."

For ten days, they had received no sign of life from him, and now he was here, unconscious. All of them hoped that later, he would be able to answer their questions.

CHAPTER 19

It had only been six days since the consecration. Six days since they had found Arik half-dead on the street and taken him with them. He didn't deny that he had been a driving force behind some changes, but now those changes were beginning to overwhelm him. Never in his life had he expected Vanadis to be capable of something like this. She might have been a little off in the head, but this... Teto was at a loss for words, and he had been suffering from headaches ever since.

The one who suffered the most from Teto's mood was Romilda, who hadn't dared to sit near him since then. Something inside her warned her against it, as if she risked being skinned alive if she did. She had seen Teto in all kinds of states — he had been most upset when the provisioners had made his favorite meal and he hadn't gotten any. That evening, heads had rolled — luckily, only heads of cabbage.

Teto's aura was so intense that even the cobblestones of the street seemed to smooth themselves to avoid irritating him further. No crickets chirped, no birds sang, and every creature of nature had sought shelter in the face of the brewing storm. Romilda hadn't seen any other travelers since either — it was possible they had all hidden behind the trees along the roadside to avoid his scornful gaze.

The conversation between Vanadis and Teto had lasted a good hour. Romilda had spent the whole time sitting in the horse cart, which they had parked in the shade of the first village they had come to after crossing the river. She had only caught fragments of their discussion during the moments when they had yelled at each other. It wouldn't have taken much more for the frightened villagers to light the signal fire to summon the guards — even though it would have taken them an hour to cover the 17 kilometers to the village.

"Teto?" Romilda asked cautiously, as if she were trying to defuse a trap. She quickly realized she had triggered another.

"What?!" he hissed through his teeth, the sharpness in his tone making her uneasy.

"I... I..." — she tried to continue, but couldn't.

"Get to the point," he growled again.

"I... was just wondering... if we'll be setting up camp soon." It was already evening, the horses were exhausted, and the sun was beginning to set. Teto processed the thought in silence for a few minutes. Romilda had only the faintest idea of the torment the thought must have been causing in Teto's mind — and the fear that he wouldn't leave this place in one piece.

Then he spoke. In his words, Romilda heard the echo of her thoughts.

"There's a village a kilometer ahead. We'll rest there." She realized he was somewhat approachable again, and she felt the urge to test her luck.

"What did Vanadis tell you?"

Teto turned to face her, his gaze so icy that it made her blood freeze. She swallowed hard, preparing herself for the same fate as her earlier thought.

"Curiosity can be deadly, young shadow." With these words, Teto turned away again. Romilda seemed to shrink, while Teto grew larger with each passing second. She lay silently in the cart for another quarter of an hour, waiting for her blood to thaw and for her courage to return. She could have sworn she had heard ravens during that time.

Get up first, Romilda told herself, and immediately put her plan into action. "And not having important information can also be deadly!" The tension between them was not the usual playful banter, nor was it about establishing rank, as it had been at the beginning of the journey. Romilda wasn't willing to risk the mission just because Teto was enraged. She was a sergeant of the young shadows for a reason, and her words carried weight — even with Teto.

Teto snorted in irritation, cracking his neck, and prepared to lecture her.

"You'd better get used to the fact that I'm not going to talk about it!" But Romilda wouldn't let herself be intimidated again, leader or not.

"And you'd better realize that you're on the verge of jeopardizing our mission. If you can't think clearly, I'll temporarily relieve you of your command!" Her words were sharp, her resolve unshakable.

"Just try it!" Teto remained stubborn, ready to defend his position fiercely. Romilda had no choice but to increase the pressure.

"Then you'll have to finish the mission alone, and deal with the barrel yourself." She pointed to the barrel where Vanadis was hiding. "I'll stay with you in the next village for the night, but at sunrise, I'll ask the merchants if they'll take me back to Aregelia."

For a moment, time seemed to stand still, and it felt like an eternity before Teto reacted.

"Do what you want. Travelers shouldn't be held back." The indifference in his voice almost frightened her. How devastating could whatever Vanadis had told him really be? Romilda wasn't ready to give up yet, so she made one last attempt.

"Then I have no choice but to wait until you fall asleep."

At first, Teto was unsure of what she meant, but then he understood.

"As if you could stay awake longer than me." Teto was just as capable of playing this game. "Should I just tie your hands or bind your feet too?"

Romilda shot back. "You're a stubborn old mule. And I thought Vanadis was bad," she muttered, nearly out of options, but then another idea struck her. She could make sure she woke up before Teto and take the cart toward Aregelia. Without his cover as a merchant, even Teto would have to pull the plug. But unlike with her other arguments, she responded to his last comment with a simple, "Alright, do whatever you think is best. I'll head back tomorrow morning."

It didn't feel like a victory for him — quite the opposite. The shadow-walkers relied on trust and the ability to count on each other in any situation. The fact that Teto had to shut Romilda down so harshly pained him. But he didn't see another option, not yet. He needed time and peace to process what Vanadis had revealed and figure out how to respond. But he had neither, and that made his frustration all the worse.

Should he have Vanadis imprisoned when they arrived? Was that even possible? Imprison her? The old raven was as free as a bird and would do everything in her power to stay that way. Could he banish her from the community, or would the consequences be too severe? Regardless of her role as the leader of the old shadows, if she left, too many would follow. Raban, for sure, Helko — if he were still around — along with many of the old shadows. Even some of the young shadows might join her. By Teto's estimation, half the shadow-walkers would stay with him, and the other half would follow Vanadis. That would be the end of the community and make survival infinitely more difficult. That wasn't an option for Teto.

The village ahead had been in sight for some time. They still had about two kilometers of road to cover. The path was becoming increasingly bumpy and uncomfortable, and Teto's backside had been aching for hours, despite the cushion. They hadn't seen any other travelers in a while — many had likely already found shelter. Teto closed his eyes, tapped into the energy of his stone, and scanned the surroundings. He wasn't as comfortable in open spaces as he was in small, enclosed areas, but after two minutes, he had managed to extend his range to about 20 meters. He could manage it.

Thirteen years. That's how long it had been going on. Teto had always wondered where Vanadis disappeared to for days at a time. But even for her, it must have been a logistical challenge to pull this off year after year. The question now wasn't whether Raban was involved — it was how deeply. His influence was now unmistakable. Could Raban still serve as his deputy under these circumstances?

Every now and then, the cart passed an apple, plum, or pear tree — just like the three trees ahead of them. On the seat beside him, Teto conjured several pea-sized spheres and waited until they were almost beneath the first tree. The sun was already halfway hidden behind the distant forest to his left. Without any visible signal, the spheres shot upward at an angle. Branches creaked, leaves rustled. A moment later, as the cart passed directly under the tree, several apples fell onto the wooden planks. One apple landed right in Romilda's outstretched hand, which she had placed at just the right spot.

He would need to send another raven once they reached the village. Teto would keep Raban as his deputy — for now. Vanadis, however, would be relieved of her position as leader of the old shadows until further notice. The task of carrying out this decision, Teto thought, would fall to Raban. Should he refuse to follow the order, he would be demoted to sergeant. Since Gunder wasn't involved in Vanadis' schemes, he would take her place.

They approached the second tree — a plum tree, its branches heavy with fruit. Teto waited for the right moment but sensed something zip over his head. When he looked up, he saw something long, thin, and black wrapped around a branch. The cracking sound was louder than with the first tree. The branch, laden with plums, broke off and flew toward him, along with the black thing. Teto ducked, and both flew over him, though they grazed him slightly. Behind him, Romilda retracted her shadow hair and plucked the first plum from the branch.

The shadow-walkers would ask questions. Sooner or later, the truth would come out, and Teto wouldn't be able to stop it if Raban made a well-thought-out move. Everything Raban did was calculated, nothing was done on a whim — a fact that both reassured and worried Teto. Should he turn back and ensure nothing fell apart? Was his mission so important that it couldn't wait a few more days? Could they return to Aregelia so soon after the incident with the consecrated one without risking more?

They neared the third tree. They could not complain about a lack of variety, as plump, juicy pears were waiting for them there. Despite Romilda's actions at the last tree, Teto prepared himself again. The spheres shot out, hitting the branch loaded with pears. But he must have struck it at the wrong spot, tearing part of the wood. The branch splintered and broke, covering half the cart with wood, leaves, and pears. The tension between Teto and Romilda shattered soon after.

Romilda giggled first, followed by Teto. For both of them, it was a relief. The giggling turned into loud laughter. Romilda rearranged the branch on the cart to make it look somewhat intentional. After this spontaneous burst of joy, Teto felt a sense of relief. His thoughts were still there, but they weighed on him less in the present moment.

"Romilda?"

"Yes?"

"As soon as we've set up camp, I'll tell you everything."

"Thank you... I appreciate that."

"And... sorry about earlier."

"It's already forgotten."

A short time later, they reached the village.

CHAPTER 20

The next morning, Teto and Romilda continued their journey. Tarsk was only about five kilometers away. Knowing that their cart could only cover around 30 kilometers per day, they were in no rush and didn't wake at the crack of dawn. They had accepted the hospitality of a villager for the night and stayed in a small barn.

Both of them brushed the hay off their clothes and out of their hair. Romilda had decided not to undo her braided hair, so it took her little effort to remove the straw. Afterward, she threw on her brown overcoat and tied a white cloth cap over her head. Half aloud, she muttered, "I'll be so glad when I can wear my normal clothes again." Her deep, resonant voice carried clearly enough for Teto to hear.

"Wouldn't it be nice if that were our biggest concern right now?" he responded unprompted while pulling on his brown pants and boots. As he fastened the straps, he cast a skeptical glance her way. With a bit more force than necessary, Romilda tossed his tunic at him. "Are you sure we shouldn't head back to Aregelia?" she asked, a note of uncertainty in her voice. "That decision wouldn't be entirely wrong, but I can understand why it's not without risk."

Teto pulled on his tunic. "I trust Raban and Fenna to make the right moves. Especially Raban. He won't throw away the last 20 years just like that — especially since I'm not planning on exiling Vanadis from the shadow-walkers." He then walked over to the cage holding the two remaining ravens and began feeding them. "I'm just hoping Vanadis will leave on her own, though that would be a significant loss." Worry lines creased his forehead.

"As crazy as she might be, when it comes to her powers, she's more skilled than anyone else," he continued, speaking with a touch of admiration. "Back then, before the fall of Aregelia... I saw her true strength. With her five stones, she wiped out entire squads of Executors. Even Paladins struggled against her." Romilda chimed in with another point, "And let's not forget, it would also be a blow to morale." "That's true…"

They left the barn, Teto carrying the raven cage in his left hand. Outside, they were met with a gusty wind, filled with autumn leaves and raindrops. As Teto secured the cage onto the cart and went to thank their host for their hospitality, Romilda hurried to the stable to fetch the horse. She held her dress down to prevent it from being blown up, sparing her any embarrassment. Once everything was ready, the cart resumed its journey once again.

About an hour later, they reached the gates of Tarsk. The landscape, unlike that around Aregelia, was quite hilly, so they could only see the city once they were within two kilometers. Even from that distance, something about the sight of the city unsettled Teto. Had they taken a wrong turn? Should he have stopped to ask for directions? Something was different, but he couldn't put his finger on what it was. He was ready to curse inwardly if they ended up being delayed by another day because of him.

Tarsk, like Aregelia, was situated by a river, but it wasn't as wide, and there was no harbor district clinging to the city walls. Teto searched his memory until it clicked: "The outer walls weren't there the last time." Indeed, it seemed they hadn't been built all that long ago, but they now posed an additional obstacle for him.

The city wasn't as large as Aregelia, but it had once been a bustling trade hub where three major roads intersected, leading to neighboring kingdoms. As it appeared to them now, the church had slowly been transforming the city over the past 17 years. They could make out several training grounds outside the city walls, as well as regiments of regular troops and consecrated ones. Romilda even spotted a group of Paladins and quickly pointed them out to Teto. It was clear that Tarsk had become a garrison town for the church — a fact that displeased Teto greatly.

"If we get into trouble here, it won't be as easy as in the southern marshlands." Teto tried to make Romilda aware of the underlying danger, but she responded calmly: "I've noticed that too. At least they don't seem to be checking the carts." He was glad to have her with him — she had an excellent eye for details. Nodding in agreement, he added, "If we were still at war, we might have a real problem right now." "Well then, cheers to peace," Romilda replied with a subtle hint of sarcasm.

They passed through the first gate. The outer ring's walls were only five meters high and maintained a constant distance of about 100 meters from the inner walls. From what Teto could estimate, there was a ten-meter-high tower every 150 meters. Unlike the fewer, steeper towers of the inner ring, these had crenellations and flat rooftops. Two streets ran between the walls, hugging the inner wall. Countless identical buildings lined these streets — barrack after barrack after barrack.

The cart rumbled on, accompanied by the rhythmic clatter of hooves on the cobblestones. The soldiers they passed spared them only brief, uninterested glances. Teto and Romilda remained silent, each lost in their own thoughts as they made their way through the streets. The city was busier than expected, but the activity here was far from reassuring. The streets bustled with marching troops, barked orders, and the metallic clanging of weapons and armor. Teto could feel the tense atmosphere hanging over Tarsk like an invisible hand gripping the city in constant control.

As they approached the inner ring, the street narrowed. A wall stretched out from the gatehouse on either side, slightly taller than the outer ring's towers. Teto could see soldiers patrolling here and there. The guards at the gate were clearly more alert, scrutinizing everyone who passed with heightened vigilance. Teto forced himself to maintain a neutral expression, while Romilda slightly lowered her head to avoid drawing unnecessary attention.

"We need to get through here as inconspicuously as possible," he whispered as they passed the first checkpoint. "Stay calm and let me do the talking if it comes to that." Romilda gave a brief nod, keeping her eyes on the guards who were now dangerously close.

"Halt!" called one of the guards, a tall woman with short, dark hair and a stern expression. "Where are you headed?" Teto smiled politely, though inwardly he was tense. "We're simple travelers, on our way to Sydrik. We have goods to trade," he replied calmly, gesturing to the cart. The guard scrutinized them for a moment, then nodded and waved them on. "You're lucky, it's a slow day. Move along," she said curtly before turning back to her duties.

Teto exhaled in relief as they passed through the gate and moved deeper into the city. "That was close," he muttered under his breath. "We can't afford to make any mistakes here. This city is a powder keg, and the smallest spark could set everything ablaze." In his mind, he unconsciously pieced together the puzzle, and the incomplete picture forming in his mind made him uneasy. "Romilda, we need to send a raven as soon as we're out of the city."

Though Romilda didn't have the same keen sense as Teto, she still felt a gnawing unease. "I feel it too, but share your thoughts with me," she requested. "First, the new consecrated ones want to come here, then we find out that the city has been turned into a garrison town," he began, tapping his nose with his index finger as he organized his thoughts. After a brief pause, he continued, "We find the city teeming with soldiers so soon after harvest season, and then we get stopped like any other cart and questioned about our intentions."

"Don't tell me..." Romilda trailed off, struggling to piece it all together, so Teto finished the thought for her. "That the church has finished consolidating its power and is preparing to expand further?" It was all too much for him, and he let out an exasperated groan. "Here I finally decide to take action, and now this. It'll be so much fun continuing our plans with Raban." His voice had gotten a bit louder, causing some nearby soldiers to glance his way.

By now, Teto had become quite adept at deception, so the unwanted attention didn't faze him. He straightened his shoulders, feeling his muscles tense. A plan began to take shape in his mind. "Time for a distraction..." He shot Romilda a quick look and whispered, "Just play along... I'm about to put on a show."

Then, in an exaggerated and dramatic voice, he proclaimed loudly, "It's about my beehives. My beehives! Fortune finally smiled upon me, and I thought I'd finally be able to buy myself a new plot of land." Dramatically, he turned to Romilda and pointed at her with an outstretched arm. "And now, my daughter confesses that her fiancé ran off with all my money!" To make it more convincing, he focused on his genuine feelings of betrayal from Vanadis' actions — his outrage was anything but feigned.

"Please calm down, Father!" Romilda responded, regretting once again that she had referred to him as her father the day before. "You know it's not good for your poor, old heart when you get so worked up." His expression twisted slightly as he tried to silently ask her, *Did you just call me 'old'?* "I'll find him and get the money back, Father. Please calm down and forgive me!" At those words, Teto sat back down, placed a hand on his forehead, and shook his head. The soldiers seemed uninterested in getting involved in such a domestic matter and waved them off. With a "Hyah," the cart resumed its journey, and Teto breathed a sigh of relief.

"What now, Teto?" They had made a pact the night before that they would never speak of moments like this again. They let it happen and then pushed it out of their minds. "We need to find a specific tavern. It's off the main streets, about seven minutes from here." They continued deeper into the city.

The streets of Tarsk were narrow and bustling with life. Houses stood closely together, their mostly wooden facades adorned with small, hand-painted signs indicating craftsmen and merchants. Romilda had never been to this city before, and her gaze flitted over the various buildings. Here and there, she spotted soldiers in various postures — some leaned casually against walls, while others stood in groups, seemingly deep in conversation. A small group of five soldiers laughed loudly as they rolled dice on an overturned barrel.

"The tavern is just a few more streets away," Teto muttered, steering the cart carefully through the narrow alley. The noise of the city grew more muffled, and the houses clustered even more tightly together, with the streets winding like a maze. Eventually, they stopped in front of an unremarkable building. A simple wooden sign hung above the door, reading "The Grey Cask."

They halted, and Teto jumped down from the cart. "Here we are," he said quietly. "The only tavern in the city where only residents are allowed... or rather, *must* go if they want a drink." After a brief pause, he added, "This means we'll find the best information here... but also the hardest to obtain."

Romilda nodded and dismounted as well. She tied the horse securely and made sure the cart was safe. "What exactly are we looking for here?" she asked softly. "Allies," Teto replied curtly, his voice barely more than a whisper. "And maybe some information... if I can find the right person."

They approached the door of the tavern and gently pushed it open. The air inside was thick with smoke and the smell of beer. The conversations briefly halted as the two strangers entered. Out of habit and caution, Teto quickly scanned the room — city folk, ordinary people who looked nervous but carried a certain quiet vigilance in their eyes. "We'll have to be careful here," he whispered to Romilda before they stepped further into the room.

In one corner, there was a table with no occupants, so they sat down there. As if out of nowhere, a woman appeared beside them with two mugs, setting them down on the table. "Ten copper coins," she demanded in a raspy voice, eyeing Teto intently. He handed her eleven copper coins with a firm look. Just as quickly as she had appeared, the woman disappeared again. Scratching his head, Teto remarked, "They were friendlier last time."

Both took their first sip of the dark beer. They wisely chose not to ask if its murkiness was due to the brewing method or the water. The strong, almost sticky flavor coated their tongues and palates, as though it intended to linger there for days. Teto closed his eyes, reaching out with his senses. It would take a few minutes, but they had time. Four minutes later, he opened them again.

"Two tables to our left. All three of them. Watch their reactions," he instructed after another sip from his mug. Casually resting his head on his left palm, he discreetly closed his eyes again. A thin shadow line crept across the floor, nearly invisible, weaving through the shadows of tables and chairs. He aimed for the person with the most stones — likely shadowstones, judging by his assessmen — and tapped one of those stones three times with his shadow tendril.

The person, a stout bald man around Teto's age, turned and looked directly at them. Teto opened his eyes, raised his head, and grinned. Lifting his mug, he gave them a knowing nod. "Once we finish our drinks, Romilda, we'll meet our new friends."

CHAPTER 21

Was it day or night?
How long had he been asleep?
His mouth was dry, and he felt like he had been run over by a cart. The visions his shadowstone gave him were exhausting.

Arik stared at the ceiling. Shadows danced across it, cast by the flickering torches and the draft. The sounds around him slowly found their way to his eardrums. Someone was in the room. Was it Fenna — or perhaps Vanadis? At that moment, his brain signaled that he could solve the mystery quickly if he decided to sit up and look around. He agreed with himself that this was a good idea.

Two beds over, a wiry youth with dark, tousled hair stood, dressed almost exactly like Arik. They stared at each other, each adapting to the unforeseen situation. The boy, about Arik's age, had hair that fell into his forehead, half-covering his green eyes. He blew it out of his face, never losing his serious expression.

"We shaved your head while you slept," the wiry youth said, his light, almost cheerful voice adding to Arik's confusion. Before Arik could touch his head to check if there was any truth to the statement, another voice — deeper and more serious — came from his left: "Alvar, let him wake up first."

A young man stood, leaning against the stone archway, observing them. He had an athletic build, muscular and wiry, with piercing dark eyes, almost black. His short hair was perpetually tousled, as if he had just come from a fight. His clothing was functional and simple — and unlike Arik's and Alvar's gray attire, his was in dark tones. He carried a short sword on each side.

"Alvar borrowed one of my swords for that," he continued with a faint grin, much to Hatto's disapproval: "Keep my swords out of it, or I'll shave more than just your head with them." Hatto walked over to the bed next to Arik's and sat down.

Arik's thoughts slowly began to clear. He closed his eyes, and a familiar sensation rose within him, spreading through his limbs, flooding his torso, and finally reaching his head. A thought followed: *Wait a second, I know this.* He searched for the trigger, silently telling his stone: *Don't give it away, I'll find it... wait... yes, that feels... right.* As before, the feeling flowed from Arik's head, expanding throughout the room, reflecting off the walls, and then returning to him. Arik opened his eyes again.

"Well, my hair seems to still be there, as far as I can tell." He received puzzled looks from both Alvar and Hatto, as he hadn't even touched his head to check. Raising his right index finger to touch his nose, Arik formed his next thought: "And who's the third of you, hiding behind the pillar?"

Hatto and Alvar exchanged questioning glances. From behind the pillar, a low grunt replied: "Bruno," and another young man emerged.

He looked to be in his early twenties, the oldest of the three, with a sturdy frame, broad shoulders, and a kind, friendly face framed by a short beard. His brown eyes exuded a calmness and warmth that Arik imagined could bring comfort to many in troubled times. His movements were careful and deliberate, and he carried a bag that seemed to be filled with medicinal herbs.

Bruno looked Arik over as he slowly walked over and sat next to Hatto. "Hello there. We're the three who volunteered to share this room with you. You already know our names." His gentle manner was immediately apparent to Arik. "Would you like something to eat? You've been asleep for quite some time."

"I'd like that… how long was I out?" Arik asked, eager to have his most pressing question answered. Bruno decided to speak for the group from that point on: "Three days, give or take. But we weren't too worried, as this isn't the first time something like this has happened. Alvar?"

"Yes?" Alvar replied warily.

"Please go fetch him a decent meal from the storeroom — he needs to regain his strength. Also, let Raban know that Arik is awake. We'll take him to the washroom in the meantime."

With an "On it," Alvar left the room, closing the door behind him.

Arik nodded gratefully and rubbed his face. The feeling of exhaustion still weighed heavily on him. *Three days?* It had felt like only a few hours. The visions the shadowstone had shown him were more intense and confusing than ever. He could still feel the stone's presence vibrating within him, a faint hum pulsing through his veins.

"This way," Bruno said gently, motioning for him to stand. Hatto was already at the door, holding it open with his foot. Bruno led the way slowly, and Arik followed, while Hatto closed the door behind them.

They walked down the corridor to the left. The flickering torchlight illuminated their path, but a sense of oppressive darkness seemed to lurk in the hallways. As they passed a small wooden door, secured only by a simple latch, Arik hesitated briefly, clearing his throat softly. "Uh… I need to use the latrine, if that's alright," he murmured. Bruno nodded understandingly, gesturing toward the door. "We'll wait here," he said.

Arik opened the door, stepped into the large, windowless room, and closed it behind him. Inside, there were several small stalls made of wooden walls and doors. The room smelled heavily of aged wood and damp stone, but to his surprise, he found dried plant leaves instead of the coarse cloths usually provided at the boarding school. He sighed in relief. *At least some semblance of civilization*, he thought, quickly finishing his business. The fact that there was still a supply of fresh air even in here brightened his mood.

A short while later, he stepped out again, feeling much lighter and grinning at the two men. "Good choice with the leaves," he remarked dryly. Hatto merely grinned, while Bruno chuckled softly.

They continued down the hallway and soon reached the washroom. It was about the same size as the previous room and similarly utilitarian in its setup. Several low partitions separated smaller stone basins, and multiple buckets of cold water were lined up along one side. The air was cool and fresh, carrying a faint scent of soap. On a narrow shelf lay several pieces of soap, neatly arranged, along with some coarse cloths, likely meant to serve as washcloths.

Arik picked up one of the unused soaps, noting its clear, milky color, and grabbed a cloth. He began to undress, shivering slightly as the cold of the room seeped into his bones. Gritting his teeth, he started washing himself thoroughly. The cold water, which Hatto poured from a bucket into the stone basin, made him shudder, but it was a welcome refreshment after the exhausting visions and his long sleep.

Standing beside him, Hatto suddenly grinned and picked up one of the buckets. "Ready?" he asked with a mischievous smile, not waiting for an answer before dumping the entire bucket of cold water over Arik's head. The icy shock made Arik gasp for air, but then he broke into laughter. "Thanks, Hatto… really… thanks," he managed between laughs.

After drying himself off, Arik was handed a fresh set of clothes — clean versions of what he had been wearing before. He put them on and immediately felt much better. The new clothes fit well and were perfectly suited for his duties as a shadow-walker.

When they returned to the room where Arik had woken up, Alvar and Raban were already waiting for them. Arik was curious about what would happen next. "Please, take a seat, Arik," Raban said, gesturing to a chair. Arik grabbed the wooden plate of food and sat down as instructed, placing the plate in front of him. The aroma of the warm meal wafted up to his nose, but he pushed the plate aside for the moment as Raban began to speak.

"How are you feeling, Arik?" Raban asked, studying him intently. His eyes seemed to take in every detail of Arik's face, as if searching for signs of weakness or confusion.

"I'm alright," Arik replied with a slight shrug. "A bit off-balance, but it's manageable." He nervously ran a hand through his hair, grateful that it was still there. "These visions… they're very intense."

Raban nodded. "That's to be expected. The stones you now possess often push their bearers to the limit, especially in your case. That's why I want you to rest today and regain your strength. Tomorrow, you'll begin your training, as we discussed, under Gunder's supervision." Nodding slowly, Arik let the words sink in, remembering his last interaction with Gunder and Raban.

"Before we move on, I want you to try using your abilities again," Raban continued, leaning slightly forward. "See if you can sense if anyone else is in this room. Take your time and focus."

Arik took a deep breath and closed his eyes. The now-familiar sensation spread through his body, a faint hum vibrating in his veins. He murmured softly to himself as he focused on the stone's energy, trying to find the trigger. Time seemed to slow, and for Arik, several moments passed as he sharpened his concentration and organized his thoughts. Then it happened — he found the trigger in his mind and, moments later, located a shadow hiding behind one of the pillars. "There… behind the pillar," he said, opening his eyes, his pupils still as dark as night, his voice now steadier. "A shadow… someone's hiding there."

A faint smile played on Raban's lips, and he nodded in approval. Gunder slowly stepped out of the shadows, his footsteps barely audible as he approached Arik. "Well done," he praised in his deep voice. "You've made progress, Arik. I can feel it." He then added, kindly: "Your body is adjusting more and more, and I suspect you're getting the hang of your stone."

Turning his attention back to the young shadow-walker, Raban continued, "For now, when you're not training, you'll be assigned to work with the suppliers." He gestured toward Bruno. "Bruno will guide you and help you integrate into the community." Bruno nodded in confirmation. "Don't worry, we'll manage," he said kindly. "There's plenty to do, but I think you'll adjust quickly ."

Arik felt a sense of relief that he wouldn't be thrown directly into the hardest tasks. But then he noticed something was off with Raban. There was hesitation in his eyes, as though he was hiding something. "What's wrong, Raban?" Arik asked cautiously. "I sense there's something more."

Raban sighed softly and hesitated for a moment before reluctantly answering. "I've received information from Teto that concerns you. But it's best if Teto tells you himself." He paused briefly before adding, internally cursing Arik's intuition, "And… Vanadis hasn't been seen since last night. No one knows where she's gone."

Arik swallowed hard. The news about Vanadis left him with a sinking feeling. He had many questions, but he knew it wasn't the right time to ask them all.

"It's not the first time my little sister has disappeared, but this time is different." Worry lines creased Raban's forehead. Arik's gaze searched the room for someone who could explain why Raban referred to Vanadis as his little sister. Gunder caught his questioning look and nodded, prompting Raban to continue, to the surprise of everyone present, as it was very uncharacteristic of him to be so talkative.

"A few days ago, she tried to take advantage of an opportunity to travel incognito with Teto to Sydrik, but along the way, there was an incident with some consecrated ones, and she had to confess things to Teto that she'd rather have kept to herself." Gunder shrugged unknowingly as he noticed Arik's growing sense of being overwhelmed by the information. Meanwhile, Raban's flow of words continued: "Things she's been doing for a very long time, all because she lost both of her children to the church and because she lost her husband 16 years ago. She hasn't been the same since. And now, Teto has removed her from her position as leader of the old shadows, and I had to enforce it, and it's tearing me apart. I didn't want to do it. I didn't want to, and now my sister is gone. Do you understand, Arik?"

Gunder nodded vigorously behind Raban, prompting Arik to give a quick "Yes" in response. Recognizing the signs, Gunder took Raban by the arm and led him out of the room.

None of them spoke, the situation leaving them too bewildered to find words. In the silence, they all agreed that what had just transpired regarding Raban's breakdown must not leave this room.

Ten minutes later, Gunder returned, and for everyone except Arik, the exercises began, with him at least able to watch with interest.

CHAPTER 22

"If it becomes clear that you cannot defeat your opponent, run from him and find another way. Because fighting isn't everything." These words ran through Arik's mind as he jogged through the South Tunnel with the other shadow-walkers. Gunder had shared this wisdom with him the day before while everyone else was busy with their exercises. Running up and down the tunnels was part of the daily routine for all shadow-walkers, and Gunder insisted on it. Even Teto, Vanadis, and Raban couldn't escape it and had to run at the front of their groups.

The group Arik belonged to consisted of the suppliers, Healers, and Craftsmen. Without him and Gunder, who led the group, they were 13 men and women, though half of them were teens and children. Bruno and Alvar were also part of this group, while Hatto, as a fighter, was in the young shadow group led by Fenna.

Arik was only expected to complete one lap through the tunnel for now. Gunder knew that Arik's body needed time to adjust to the physical routine. Rushing things would be counterproductive. However, eventually, the time would come when he, like everyone else, would have to complete four laps, which covered a distance of about five kilometers.

Of course, Gunder had come up with something extra for the morning exercises to hone their abilities — the entire tunnel was pitch-black, so they all had to rely on their ability to see in the dark. Arik wasn't sure how far they had run, but they had not yet reached the halfway point. His concentration was fading by the minute, making it increasingly difficult to keep his dark vision active. Bruno, running beside him, noticed Arik falling behind.

"We're almost there. Gunder won't rip your head off if you take a short break while we do our next lap." Arik was starting to realize that despite his young age, Bruno was something like the heart and soul of the shadow-walkers. But instead of a complicated thought, Arik only managed to groan out, "... good ... idea… bruno…" even unable to press out the capital letters.

They all felt the increasing breeze. To lighten the mood, Alvar theatrically shouted from the group, "The end is near!" earning a few chuckles and a couple of exaggerated "Oh no!" After another minute, the group stopped and rearranged themselves. Bruno spoke briefly with Gunder, who then gave the order: "Alright, everyone back the way we came. You know the drill. Arik, wait here until we return." Then they set off again.

Arik leaned against the cold, damp tunnel wall, breathing deeply and feeling the rough stone under his fingers. The echo of many footsteps grew fainter and fainter until it was swallowed by the darkness. Soon, he couldn't see the group at all, even with his dark vision — only the faint light from a torch at the tunnel entrance remained. The chill of the autumn morning seeped into the tunnel, and he felt it creeping into his legs. His limbs were on the verge of shivering, and he fought to keep it under control.

The previous day, he had closely observed the reactions of the other shadow-walkers when they entered the training room and saw him waiting on Gunder's orders. Some had looked at him as if he were an intruder, a stranger who had stumbled into their familiar world. Others seemed cautious, their glances hard to interpret, as though they didn't know whether to welcome him or keep their distance. He felt the mistrust hanging in the air like an invisible barrier. He couldn't blame them. Just ten days ago, he had hurt some of them when the stones had taken control of him.

Bruno and Alvar had accepted him right away. They stuck by his side, helping to break the ice with some of the other shadow-walkers, enough that they at least acted normally around him. Still, there were those who chose to remain cold and suspicious. Arik remembered the looks he got when the two had joined him.

An older shadow-walker, whose name escaped Arik, had furrowed his brows and pursed his lips tightly. A young woman, maybe a few years older than him, had almost ignored him and would have struck him on the head during weapons training if Gunder hadn't stepped in. But then there were those small moments — like when Alvar stood next to him and whispered a few encouraging words, or when Bruno quietly took a shadow-walker aside and spoke a few convincing words to them. It was these small and larger gestures that helped Arik not feel entirely lost.

As he waited, he tried to sort through his thoughts, organizing the events of the previous day in his mind. Raban's breakdown, the sudden openness about Vanadis' past, and the fact that he was now truly part of the shadow-walkers — all of it swirled in his head like a storm.

He knew he had to prove himself. Only by doing that could he earn their respect. This world was so different from anything he had ever known. How long would it take for him to fit in? What if it was never enough? Doubts gnawed at him, but at the same time, he felt a spark of determination. He wanted to succeed. He had to.

The minutes dragged on. The cold in the tunnel was relentless, finally creeping into his bones, and he began to shiver slightly. Slowly, he could hear the echo of footsteps again and see shapes in the distance — the group was returning.

As the group neared him, Arik stood up and felt his muscles ache. Bruno, walking at the front with Gunder, waved him over. "Ready for the return trip?" he asked with a slight smile. "Or should we carry you?" Alvar teased, not giving Arik the same gentle treatment Gunder did.

Arik nodded to Bruno, even though he didn't feel ready at all. "Ready as I'll ever be," he replied, trying to hide the exhaustion in his voice. He had never been one for physical exercise, a fact he now regretted. Once they had reorganized, they set off, and much to Arik's relief, the return journey seemed shorter. After just a few minutes, they reached the other end of the tunnel.

"Arik, while we do our last lap, go fetch some water from the well and bring it to the training room. Understood?" Gunder didn't expect a reply, as his instruction was clear. To the rest, he added, "Alright, everyone, one last lap." The group set off again, and Arik climbed the stairs, letting his eyes return to normal.

Walking quickly, he passed the training room and the common room, arriving at the well within a minute. He entered the room, grabbed one of the buckets, and placed it next to the well. Bruno's words from the previous day echoed in his mind: "There are a few rules when it comes to the well. Rule number one: the only thing that should go into the well is an empty bucket attached to the rope." This rule had confused Arik, as it seemed obvious to him, but he had decided it was better not to ask for clarification at that moment.

He grabbed the crank and began turning it at a steady pace. The bucket descended into the well. "Rule number two: never place anything on the edge of the well, and never sit on it." That rule made more sense to Arik, and he had nodded at Bruno when he heard it. The bucket reached the water and began to fill. A few moments later, Arik turned the crank in the opposite direction, and the now-full bucket slowly rose.

"Rule number three: if anything breaks, no matter how small, go tell the craftsmen. Don't try to fix it yourself." Bruno's voice had carried a lot of emphasis when he had said this, and Arik couldn't help but wonder what had led to the introduction of these three rules. He removed the bucket from the well and poured the water into a container. Before leaving the room, he secured the winch so the bucket wouldn't accidentally drop into the water. Now that he thought about it, this last step could easily be added as a fourth rule. He made a mental note to suggest it to Bruno later.

Carrying the full bucket, he headed toward the training room. Behind him, he could hear the echo of many footsteps from another group coming out of the West Tunnel. Once inside the room, he set the bucket by the entrance and sat down on a wooden bench. It only took a few minutes before Gunder and the others entered the room, grabbed wooden cups, and helped themselves to the water. Gunder announced that they had ten minutes to rest before they would continue.

Arik had the option of participating in the next exercise. Bruno and Alvar encouraged him to give it a try, so he stood between them. The group formed a circle, and Gunder stood in the middle, ready to give instructions. "Alright. Even if you're bored because we do this every day, you know my stance on the basics. So, I want to see your Second Skin!" Arik had seen what Gunder meant by this the day before. Each of the shadow-walkers focused, and within seconds, he could see a black film spreading over their skin, gradually covering them entirely.

The night before, Arik had asked Alvar, Hatto, and Bruno how they summoned the Second Skin. He was glad they had taken the time to explain it to him and let him try it out. So now, in training, he felt confident enough to give it another go. He was familiar with the sensation of the stone's energy within his body, and now, he just had to concentrate that energy inside the stone. Seven seconds later, he had done that part and gently released the energy from the stone. He spread it over his scar on his abdomen and slowly sent it up to his neck.

Everyone else was already finished. From head to toe, they were covered in a black substance, even their clothing cloaked in darkness. They stared at Arik, some of them expecting the worst, which caused the tension in the room to rise by the second. When they saw the energy start to emerge under Arik's clothing, that tension spiked. Gunder remained calm but kept a close eye on him. "Very good, Arik, take your time. I heard you asked the others to explain the Second Skin to you," Gunder said, his voice filled with a hint of pride, which the others picked up on and used as a cue to relax a bit.

Finally, it was done. Arik had fully covered himself in darkness, though his clothes were still visible. A few of the shadow-walkers giggled at the sight, finding it rather amusing — even Gunder allowed himself a grin under his hood, though no one could see it. He cleared his throat. "We'll hold this state for ten minutes. Arik, if you feel your strength fading, pull it all back into your stone!" Six minutes later, Arik had to do just that.

The rest of the training, Arik spent sitting on the bench, watching as the others practiced their individual skills before moving on to weapons training. After an hour and a half in total, the daily exercises were over. Not everyone had made it to the end, so Arik wasn't alone on the bench the entire time.

Afterward, Bruno took him along to the suppliers' tasks. Like with the exercises, the tasks were all about mastering the basics. Together with the other five suppliers, they took care of distributing water to the washrooms and privies. Afterward, they headed to the kitchen to help prepare food for everyone — stews made from root vegetables, porridge, and fresh bread. The meals were simple but filling, and no one dared complain to the suppliers. Occasionally, some of the fighters would go into the southwest woods at night and bring back various game — a welcome treat for everyone in the complex.

Life at the shadow-walkers' base wasn't too different from his time at the boarding school, except that here, everyone looked out for each other, and no one made life unnecessarily difficult for him. With each passing day, Arik felt more accepted, starting with the suppliers, who were beginning to appreciate his effort.

CHAPTER 23

The last week had been exhausting for him. His daily duties as a supplier were physically demanding, and Gunder had also raised his expectations. By now, Arik was already expected to run his second South Corridor round and maintain the first shadowstone exercise for the full duration.

There were always bright spots that helped him keep going. Not only did Bruno and Alvar keep an eye on him to ensure he didn't overexert himself, but others were also starting to warm up to him, lending a hand when things got tight.

The other shadow-walkers had also grown accustomed to him sitting in the common room in the evenings with Hatto, Alvar, and Bruno, chatting away cheerfully. Diemo's behavior toward him had changed, too, in the sense that he simply left him alone. Diemo still hadn't apologized, and Arik thought about whether he should take the first step — even though it wasn't his fault, he had hurt Diemo, Romilda, and a few others on his first day.

Arik sat with the other three from his room, as well as two of the suppliers — Fara, a woman in her early 30s, and Ricke, a woman in her mid-50s — at one of the back tables in the common room. The corridor to the kitchen was right next to them, so their table choice was no coincidence. Some had taken the chance to grab the last of the soup and were slurping it — like Bruno — enjoying every drop.

Teto entered the room. Everything went quiet, and only the slurping sounds remained.

Except for the leaders, none of them had seen Teto much recently. The gray hairs on his head had increased significantly, and it seemed like he hadn't had a proper night's sleep in days. He scanned the room and everyone in it before speaking loudly and seriously: "Everyone, to the meeting room, immediately."

The words were absorbed by the group. They dropped everything and followed him.

A few minutes later, everyone had gathered. Not all were standing — Helko and a few of the old shadows had taken seats on the wooden benches. Gunder, Raban, and Fenna flanked Teto, waiting for him to give them the floor. A loud clearing of the throat filled the room — Teto was ready to begin.

"Hello, everyone. It's been quite a while since we last gathered here, and for some, this is their first time at such a meeting." He scanned the faces of the group, many of them looking expectant. "The purpose of these meetings is to inform all shadow-walkers of major upcoming changes and to address any uncertainties that might arise."

Even Alvar, known throughout the complex for his witty remarks, held back during this serious moment. "To get straight to the point: Over the past two weeks, Raban and I have been preparing something that, with your help, will advance tonight." The tension in the room grew. "We are going to establish a new camp in the Southwest Forest." After this statement, a wave of murmuring spread through the room, bouncing off the stone walls until it almost turned into a loud hum.

"SILENCE!" Raban bellowed, causing everyone to fall silent. No one dared to make another sound. Teto continued: "For what's to come, we need space — and this underground complex can only offer us so much. The stone-bearers from Tarsk alone make up 50 men and women, and more groups from other cities will join us over time." His gaze dropped briefly, and he took a deep breath. The next part would be harder to convey.

"The Church is gathering its troops in Tarsk. They've turned the city into a garrison and are planning an attack on Sydrik. We expect the attack in about three months." Worry and confusion appeared on many faces. Some of the shadow-walkers began to suspect where this was heading. "We are not in a position to intervene directly in the conflict, nevertheless I've made an agreement in Sydrik: Our task is to disrupt the Church's supply routes to the south for as long as possible, until we're strong enough to take Aregelia."

He let this information sink in for about a minute before continuing.
"My original plan was different, but given the new circumstances, this is the best course of action. I will be traveling frequently in the coming weeks, as it's essential to involve the stone-bearers from other cities. It's crucial that Sydrik does not fall into the Church's hands, or at least that they suffer enough losses to delay their expansion by several months."

Any attempt to whisper or mutter was quickly quashed by Raban's piercing gaze, ensuring Teto could continue his speech without interruption.

"I don't expect all of you to follow this path, and once we unite with the group from Tarsk, you will all be free to either leave or stay here in the complex. Due to its strategic importance, I have no intention of giving this place up — this remains our gateway to the city." A sense of relief spread among the group, mixed with the lingering concern in the air.

"We can't do nothing and slowly decay as a group down here — or we can take matters into our own hands and fight to end the Church's rule over this city. I've made my decision, and in the coming months, you should make yours as well." He exhaled loudly. Though he had only been carrying this burden for a short time, he was glad to finally set it down, at least partially. Unsure if he had ignited a fire among the shadow-walkers, he stepped back. Perhaps it would take time, he thought — it wasn't easy to spark change after 20 years of stagnation.

Next, Raban stepped forward and took charge. "Any questions?"

The shadow-walkers were still processing everything Teto had just told them, and this delayed any immediate questions — but Raban's intimidating presence convinced most that it was better to remain silent for now.

"No? Alright, then the questions will probably come up when it matters the most." It was nothing new for Raban to receive no questions, so he wasn't thrown off and kept going. "You'll now be divided — one group will come with me to build the camp, the other will stay here with Gunder and Fenna to maintain the complex."

Raban pulled out a list and began calling out names of those who would accompany him to the forest. Arik didn't know everyone yet, as some hadn't introduced themselves to him, but a few names were familiar. Fara and three other suppliers were assigned to Raban, along with Romilda, Diemo, and Ostara. Two craftsmen, whom Arik thought Alvar had mentioned before, were also named. The group was rounded out by six fighters and two healers, bringing the total number of shadow-walkers to 18. Arik was relieved that Fenna, Gunder, Hatto, Alvar, and Bruno would be staying in the complex, so he would have familiar faces around.

The meeting was over. Those going with Raban were instructed to gather everything important within the next two hours, as their departure was planned for then. Arik remembered the thought he had back in the common room, realizing he needed to hurry if he wanted to apologize. Pushing past a few shadow-walkers, he managed to catch Romilda and Diemo just in time.

"Can…" Arik had a lump in his throat; the situation was clearly uncomfortable for him. "…do you have a moment?"
"Just because I've been leaving you alone," Diemo's face took on that familiar expression of barely contained fury, "doesn't mean you can annoy me now."

Romilda stepped in before the situation could escalate. "Diemo, hold yourself back. You don't have to be friendly, but nastiness doesn't help anyone. What is it, Arik?" It was clear to Arik that Diemo would rather bite into a lemon than even remotely show him kindness, but he gritted his teeth and summoned all his courage. "Romilda, Diemo — I'm sorry."

Even Diemo seemed taken aback, caught off guard. "Excuse me, what?" he muttered, confused.

"I'm sorry," Arik repeated, "for the fact that you were hurt because of me back then."

"Uh…" Diemo stammered, clearly confused, "…uh… alright. Thanks?"
Romilda was also surprised, but not as off-balance as Diemo. "Thank you for apologizing, even though it wasn't your fault." To Arik's surprise, she hugged him, catching him off guard as well. He glanced over at Diemo, who returned a bewildered look. After the hug, Diemo swallowed his pride. "It… uh… I'm sorry too. For what I did to you that one time." Romilda gave him a playful nudge.

"But don't expect me to hug you too," Diemo quickly added. "Fair point. Thanks," Arik replied. They all felt a weight lift from their shoulders.

"I'm not asking us to become friends, but I'd appreciate it if we didn't make each other's lives harder," Arik said, fighting back tears — a battle he was clearly losing. Romilda hugged him again, offering comfort. A thought crossed Arik's mind — that she knew something — but he couldn't quite put his finger on it.

Just then, he heard Teto calling from the room: "Arik, come in for a moment." Romilda let him go, and they said their goodbyes. Except for Teto, the room was empty. Arik stepped inside and closed the door behind him. It was only then that he noticed how warm the room had gotten. The air was stuffy, and it would take a while to air it out again. Teto dragged one of the benches to the middle of the room, sat down at one end, and gestured for Arik to take the other.

Once they were seated, they looked each other in the eye. "Our last meeting was over two weeks ago, wasn't it?" Teto said, attempting to break the ice. "Even though you probably won't remember it for obvious reasons. I'm just glad we can have a normal conversation this time." Arik was still trying to figure out why Teto wanted to talk to him. "What can I do for you, Teto?"

"It's not about your duties or your training — I'm up to speed on those. Gunder gives me regular updates, and I have to say, I'm pleased with how things are progressing for you." Teto's calm words reached Arik as if through a fog. What did Teto really want? The silence that followed felt like an eternity. Arik's heart started racing, his breathing quickened. "Romilda and I had an encounter with four consecrated ones on our way to Sydrik," Teto finally said, "and it went… let's just say… 'differently' than we expected."

Arik's ears perked up. "You know I have nothing to do with them anymore, right?"

"Of course," Teto replied, maintaining his calm tone. "It's possible that we've figured out what happened to you, and I want to apologize for not addressing this with you sooner." Arik waved it off, trying to sound nonchalant. "It's fine — I've been busy anyway. I haven't even had time to talk to Fenna lately. Speaking of which — where is she, by the way?"

He had hit a sensitive spot. Teto let out a brief sigh. "I sent her to look for Vanadis. She should be back tomorrow. But that's not the point." His face showed the weight of the past few days, and Arik, looking into his ice-blue eyes, saw just how tired they seemed. "The point is that based on the information Romilda and I gathered, we suspect that three young Executors — Alexander, Thomas, and Michael — ambushed you after your consecration and implanted the stone in you." At this point, Teto wanted to share more, but Arik interrupted him.

"I know. It was Thomas who implanted it." The names — Alexander, Thomas, Michael — triggered a storm in Arik's mind. Images and fragments, blurred faces, screams. He felt his stomach clench as a wave of fear washed over him. "My memory…" His voice wavered slightly, "…isn't fully back yet. But the stone has… shown me some things."

Hearing this made Teto pause. "Since when… why didn't you tell us…?" "For about a week. It happened during my long nap," Arik explained nervously. "And I just hadn't gotten around to telling anyone… like Fenna or Vanadis."

It was an unintended jab that Teto took in stride, allowing him to continue. "These three Executors are quite... particular. But they're exactly the kind of people the Church likes to recruit for its purposes." Arik nodded in agreement, thinking to himself, *If only you knew, if only you knew.*

"Are they really that bad?" Apparently, Arik had said that out loud, prompting a response from Teto. Arik nodded again, and Teto pressed on: "Do you know who Bero is?" "Bero..." Arik was taken by surprise. This conversation was turning into a contest of who could throw the other off-balance.

"You met him?" Regret etched itself onto Teto's face. "To his misfortune... yes. Unlike the other three, Bero possesses an intelligence, an understanding that should not be underestimated. And that was his downfall."

Arik's heart skipped a beat, then began racing. A chill ran down his spine as cold, paralyzing fear gripped him. The words echoed in his mind, and for a moment, all he could think was: *Bero.* The hope of seeing him again felt as fragile as a young plant, about to be crushed underfoot. "What... what... did you do to him?" His voice cracked, almost pleading.

Teto chose his next words carefully. "He figured out what we are, and then Vanadis showed up out of nowhere. She overpowered him with ease." They looked into each other's eyes. "He's not returning to Aregelia, Arik."

This time, Arik fought back tears. "But there was something else he said to us."

"What was it?" "He wondered what had happened to you, and..." Teto's voice softened.

"He misses you."

CHAPTER 24

Two weeks had passed since the group under Raban's command had left the complex, and for the first time in a month, the moment had arrived for Arik to return to the surface. Fenna, Hatto, and Bruno wanted him to accompany them on a patrol through the harbor district, as they believed he was ready.

The silence that now frequently fell over the common room had become almost palpable, like a heavy veil settling over the remaining shadow-walkers. For the twelve shadow-walkers left behind, it was an adjustment to feel the complex so deserted at times. Although the changed situation meant less work for the suppliers, the workload remained the same, as only three of them remained.

Hatto, Bruno, and Arik were sitting in the common room with Ricke and Alvar, at their usual spot near the hallway that led to the kitchen. They had packed provisions for the patrol, since such an outing typically lasted two hours and could be quite exhausting. Arik was already helping himself to the bag of dried fruit and received a critical look from Ricke.

Arik grinned innocently while stuffing the dried fruit into his mouth. "What? The fruit is delicious, and I'll need the energy soon," he said with mock innocence, his mouth still half-full. But Ricke wasn't fooled. With a stern look, she tried to grab the bag — but Arik was quicker.

"The fruit is for those going on patrol, Ricke." He swallowed the food. Ricke watched him with narrowed eyes as he stuffed another handful of dried fruit into his mouth. "At this rate, you'll run out of your provisions before we even leave," she remarked dryly, crossing her arms over her chest.

Alvar chimed in to lighten the mood: "You shouldn't just have him prepare the food, you should let him have some too. That way, he wouldn't look so skinny. His face is all gaunt."

"No one told us that," Bruno responded innocently. "I thought a carrot and some water was enough for a whole day." His comment made everyone at the table laugh.

"Ah, let the boy eat," Hatto joined in, leaning back comfortably in his chair. "If he has enough strength, he can carry us." Taking advantage of the surprise, he quickly grabbed the bag of fruit. This time, Arik reacted too late and let out an indignant, "Hey, I wasn't done yet!"

Ricke adjusted her headscarf, which covered her graying hair. "Yes, you were," Ricke replied with a mischievous grin. "We don't want the others having to roll you through the streets." Alvar enthusiastically picked up the idea and ran with it: "The day we can do that with Arik, I wouldn't miss it for the world. Maybe we can find a hill to roll him down."

Bruno glanced toward the door, his forehead creased with concern. "Where's Fenna, anyway? She's usually not this late."

"Maybe she got lost?" Hatto joked, popping a handful of nuts into his mouth.

Ricke shook her head. "If anyone could get lost in this old place, it definitely wouldn't be Fenna." Just then, the door opened, and Fenna entered, slightly out of breath. "Hope I didn't keep you waiting too long," she said, seeing the group greet her with expectant smiles.

"There you are, finally! We were about to go search for you," Bruno teased, giving her a nod. "I was just about to suggest we throw Alvar down the well so he could check for you down there." Alvar shot Bruno a glare, but his messy hair fell into his eyes, softening the effect. Instead, he playfully nudged Bruno in the shoulder.

"Don't worry, I haven't lost any of my old habits," Fenna replied with a sly smile. "Let's get going. We have a lot to do." The group, except for Alvar and Ricke, stood up and followed Fenna out of the common room. They passed by the well room, where they could hear the soft trickle of water echoing in the darkness. Ricke gave a quick glance at the buckets, lined up neatly, and nodded in satisfaction.

They continued on their way and descended the stairs to the west tunnel. According to the others, it was slightly shorter than the south tunnel and led to the harbor district outside the city walls. The cool stone walls almost felt calming as they made their way down the stairs. A tingly feeling of anticipation spread through Arik's chest, like the excitement before a jump into the unknown, as they descended deeper into the tunnel. They had chosen not to bring torches, relying instead on their abilities.

The daily training was paying off, as using his abilities no longer drained his energy as much. "We should be there in a few minutes. Bruno's with me, and Arik goes with Hatto. Stay in the shadow-realm the whole time," Fenna instructed. For about a week, Arik had been practicing how to enter the layer of reality the shadow-walkers called the shadow-realm.

No one could explain exactly what this in-between world was, but they had taught him the rules of it. The shadow-realm swallowed sounds and words like a hungry abyss but let everything from outside seep in, like the whisper of a ghost that knows no boundaries. In the shadow-realm, one was invisible to outsiders, but everything could still touch them. Lightstone bearers were to be avoided, as they had the ability to pull someone out of this in-between world — or, as others put it, to unmask them.

Shadowstone bearers had long been favored as spies, slipping through the darkness like silent shadows. They were also masters of ambush and hiding, their presence often only noticed when their enemies vanished. Rarely did they seek open conflict — but anyone who underestimated them would soon regret it. Arik had also learned why he was different — because he carried a lightstone, he could enter another in-between world — the Unlight.

In the Unlight, there was no place for touch or revelation; it was a realm beyond the shadows, untouched by light — a domain of silent assassins where every step was a whispered promise of death. Anyone who walked in the Unlight could only be seen by their own kind. For centuries, many kingdoms had no choice but to fight fire with fire.

While shadowstone bearers were spies, Unlight-walkers were assassins, capable of ending entire wars with a single stab — or starting them. If the Church of Light ever discovered that an Unlight-walker was lurking in their territory, a hunt would begin — merciless as a storm bent on destruction.

They were almost at their destination, and Arik could already make out the vague outline of a staircase in the darkness. He had noticed earlier that the tunnel sloped slightly — a detail confirmed by the short flight of stairs ahead. Later, he would learn that this slope was intentionally designed to prevent nearby groundwater from seeping into the tunnel and destabilizing it — after all, they were only 200 meters from the river.

Fenna pushed open the door at the top of the stairs, stepping into the backyard of an old, run-down building. Arik followed her and the others, his chest filling with a mix of excitement and anticipation — until the smell hit him. The air was thick with the foul stench of dead fish and stagnant water. He felt his stomach clench and knelt beside the shed they had just exited, giving in to the urge to retch, adding his own note to the disgusting symphony of smells.

Fenna's eyebrows furrowed as she stepped closer to Arik, peering over his shoulder. "Don't tell me you stuffed yourself with dried fruit?" She turned to Hatto and Bruno, her voice taking on a sharper edge. "And you didn't stop him? All that fruit, gone to waste... such a waste." Her nostrils flared slightly as she planted her hands on her hips.

"We couldn't have known he was going to throw up," Hatto tried to soothe, with Bruno quickly agreeing. "True, Hatto. But then again... would we have done anything differently?"

After a few minutes, Fenna, now composed, returned from the tunnel — she didn't want to draw attention. Back with the group, she gave the order to shift into the shadow-realm. Arik, now more practiced in using his abilities, felt the energy flow through his veins in gentle waves, gathering in his hands. There were many ways to enter the shadow-realm, but he preferred to imagine pulling aside the veils of reality like a heavy curtain, stepping through to the other side.

Now Arik saw it again: the transparent black film that had settled over everything. Glancing left and right, he saw the others, who had also just arrived in the shadow-realm. "Not bad, Arik," Fenna encouraged him. "That's coming along well, I'd say."

"Thanks," Arik replied, accepting the praise. "The others help me with my training — it saves time and energy."

Fenna nodded in approval, a small smile playing on her lips. Like many others, she was relieved and proud that Arik was becoming more of a full-fledged member of the shadow-walkers. The worries that had plagued her on his first day seemed long gone. His apology — even though he had only expressed it to Diemo and Romilda — had been well-received by the rest of the shadow-walkers, further increasing his acceptance within the group.

After passing through the archway, they split up. Fenna and Bruno went right, while Arik and Hatto turned left. Over the years, they had developed a system to make their patrols as efficient as possible. "What exactly is the purpose of all this?" Arik asked. Hatto tried to give a satisfactory answer: "We're looking for shadowstones and for people who've bonded with a shadowstone. And we keep an eye out for anything unusual."

They walked cautiously through the harbor district, the narrow alleyways stretching out like a tangled web before them. The smell from earlier began to mix with that of damp wood and the smoke rising from the chimneys of the taverns. Hatto explained that the harbor was mostly bustling in the early morning hours and that now was the time for shady characters to come out. Arik watched as the few people who were still out hurried by with their heads down.

"Stay close to me," Hatto whispered without looking at Arik. "If anyone notices or touches us, things could get messy. The consecrated ones in the gatehouses can show up faster than you'd like."

Arik nodded and followed Hatto's lead. They kept to the middle of the path, careful not to slip on the wet, slippery cobblestones. Every now and then, they spotted a patrol, but they managed to stay well out of sight.

Rounding a corner, Hatto suddenly stopped and raised his hand, signaling Arik to halt as well. A group of consecrated ones was walking down the alley, lighting the nearby area with a glowing light orb. "Let them pass… or better yet, let's move back to the previous alley." They quickly retreated to the side alley and waited until the consecrated ones were far enough away. Arik had caught a glimpse of their faces in the light but didn't recognize anyone.

"Now," Hatto murmured, and they continued on until they reached a narrow side street off the main road. "You're doing well," Hatto praised, "but don't get distracted. Things can change fast here in the harbor district."

"Are there always consecrated ones around here?" Arik asked.

"Yeah, we usually count two to three groups," Hatto replied, ready to share his knowledge as well. "The two at the back — I know them from the academy. One was a year ahead of me, the other shared a room with me."

Hatto nodded. "We figured the new ones would be paired with the experienced ones. Thanks for confirming that. But let's keep moving."

They ventured deeper into the district. The gentle lapping of water and the creaking of ships in the wind blended with the shouts of sailors finishing up their last tasks of the day or gathering for card games. Arik felt his senses sharpen as adrenaline coursed through his veins.

"Do you see that shed up ahead?" Hatto asked, pointing to a run-down building whose wooden door hung on a single hinge. "That's one of our collection points. Let's go inside and take a look around." Moments later, they reached the shed and slipped through the narrow entrance. Inside, it was dark and damp, with dusty lanterns hanging from the wooden walls.

"Keep your eyes open," Hatto muttered. "For anything suspicious — even just a mark in the dust. We don't secure this place very well." Carefully, they began searching the room. The cold crept through Arik's clothing, and he had to force himself to breathe steadily. When footsteps suddenly echoed, he froze and glanced over at Hatto, who signaled him to stay calm. "Remember, they can't hear or see you."

Through the cracks in the wooden wall, Arik saw another group pass by — it was just guards. "They're usually not a threat, but don't take them lightly," Hatto explained, trying to give Arik a sense of the outside world. "Have you chosen a weapon to fight with yet?"

Arik's heart raced, but he remained completely still, just to be safe. "No, not yet." "Then try arm claws," Hatto suggested. "They're great for blocking attacks, and you can't be easily disarmed."

"Thanks, I'll keep that in mind."

Hatto knelt in the center of the room and carefully lifted one of the floorboards. With sharp eyes, he inspected the hidden space beneath. "Good, everything's still here." After replacing the board, he turned to Arik. "This is for emergencies. Some bandages, well-wrapped dried meat, and water. If something happens to you here in the harbor district and you need a place to retreat to."

Then he moved to the door. "We've only been out for 15 minutes — let's keep going. We still have two other places to check. We do this every other day." He grinned widely. "You'll get used to it — it'll come with time." With that, Hatto opened the door just a crack. "Maybe we'll even find a shadowstone today."

Together, they stepped back into the alleyways.

CHAPTER 25

They stared at each other, weapons drawn. The silence in the room was palpable; none of the onlookers dared to speak a word.

"Are you scared of me?" Gunder asked provocatively, aiming to rile up his opponent. "And yet, I'm down an arm-claw compared to you."

"I've often wondered if you hide your face under that hood so no one can see your buck teeth." Some of the bystanders couldn't help but snicker at Arik's comeback. Arik felt a draft around his legs. They were shaking. Not from the cold — this was his first serious weapons fight, and it filled him with more than just unease. "If your weapon skills are even half as sharp as your tongue…" Gunder seemed amused by their verbal exchange, "…then I have nothing to worry about."

Arik knew Gunder was right. For over a month now, he had been taking part in the daily exercises, and his body had changed. He had gotten rid of his church-mandated haircut, and growing stubble now dotted his head. It was undeniable that he had gained muscle mass and stamina. He could now run the South Tunnel circuits with ease, and the basic exercises with his powers no longer challenged him. Still, he maintained the necessary respect for the fundamentals, agreeing with Gunder that mastering and practicing them was essential. Otherwise, sooner or later, he would run into trouble during a raid.

Gunder firmly believed that pain was an important teacher. To him, it wasn't just about the shadow-walkers being able to defend themselves; they also had to understand the reality of a painful attack. Arik knew this, and it was precisely what made him so nervous in this moment.

Out of nowhere, Gunder charged at him, closing the seven-meter distance between them in less than a second. Arik knew that weapon training was not one of his strengths, and ten days of practice weren't enough to hold his own in a fight like this. Nonetheless, as Gunder attacked from the right, swinging his arm upward with his arm-claw, Arik instinctively attempted to block it. He positioned his own left arm-claw and braced his legs. The claws clashed, but Gunder's body was still in motion — he used this momentum to knock Arik off his feet. Gunder barreled into him, sending Arik flying back about a meter. He hit the ground with a thud, feeling the pain from the impact. Arik let out a groan. After a few moments, he got back up. Hatto had helped him to his feet and patted him on the shoulder.

Gunder grinned under his hood and returned to the spot where he had launched his attack. "Had enough already?" Provocation was a core part of Gunder's fighting style — it was meant to throw his opponent off balance. Arik wiped his mouth and decided to play along. "Unlike you, I've still got plenty of energy, old man."

This time, he was the one who initiated the attack. Like Gunder before him, he swung his right arm-claw upward. Gunder, with far better reflexes, was already in a defensive stance before the attack came and easily deflected Arik's blow. Still in motion, Arik leapt to the side, knowing full well that the impact would be anything but pleasant.

As he jumped, he swung his left arm. Out of the corner of his eye, Gunder noticed Arik had cloaked his arm-claw in shadows. What he couldn't see, however, was that the shadows extended along the blades, lengthening them — and as Arik moved, they lashed out like a whip, landing a direct hit on Gunder's back. Although Arik ended up on the ground again, he grinned with satisfaction. Murmurs spread through the room as Gunder turned his back to him and began to laugh. He had cloaked his torso in shadows as well, negating the effect of Arik's attack. Then he turned back to Arik and signaled for the onlookers to help him up.

"Good, good, good," Gunder muttered with satisfaction before switching back to his loud voice. "Good. A well-executed surprise attack using your abilities. Have you been practicing in secret?" he asked Arik.

Shifting awkwardly in place, Arik replied, a bit hesitantly, "Well… I had some time in the evenings when I wasn't on a raid."

"A wise use of your time," Gunder remarked, though the comment seemed more for himself. "Maybe you should become one of our fighters after all — your creativity can make up for a lot of weaknesses."

Arik blushed, feeling his embarrassment settle in. "I'd better stick to being a supplier and follow Bruno's path, supporting the healers. I learned a few useful things at the boarding school." Arik didn't know how else to phrase it. Everyone among the shadow-walkers knew how the Church used its knowledge of human anatomy, so Arik refrained from making a big deal out of it.

"All right, you can think it over," Gunder replied, fully aware that Arik shouldn't elaborate on the subject, and tried to steer the conversation in a different direction. "Everyone, find a partner now and continue weapons training on your own. Feel free to use the other room, too." He waited for everyone to confirm before continuing. "I'll be leading the raid tonight.

Hatto, Helko, Arik — we'll meet in the common room after dinner." The three of them nodded.

"And don't eat so much dried fruit beforehand again," Alvar called out, prompting a round of laughter. "Looks like the embarrassment isn't going away anytime soon," Arik thought, "Are they going to hold that over my head forever?" Amidst the laughter, Gunder shouted, "Great parting words, everyone. Enjoy your training."

The rest of the day flew by. Arik and the other suppliers had a lot of work to do, but for a while now, Hatto and the other fighters had been helping out to lighten the load. Evening approached, and with it, the raid.

Helko, Hatto, and Arik were already sitting at one of the tables near the entrance to the common room. They listened to Bruno's lute playing, and Fenna quietly hummed along to the song's lyrics. Alvar kept the beat on a self-made drum. He had built it himself, as he had the workshop to himself all day to "test" things. Little by little, more shadow-walkers joined in, though none were louder than Fenna. With the interplay of torchlight and shadows, a nearly mystical atmosphere formed. No one noticed when Gunder appeared in the doorway, leaning against the frame. No one saw how deeply the music moved him, how he shed a tear. They all sat in a trance, even after they stopped singing.

It took a while for them to return to the present moment. The conversations resumed quietly, and when Hatto spotted Gunder, he nudged the other two, and they left. They turned right, passed the South Tunnel, and made their way to the camp near the briefing room. There, they climbed the stairs that led up to the city.

At the end of the staircase, they unlocked a hatch and opened it. They found themselves in a small shed in the southwestern part of the city. Everyone stepped out, and Helko closed the hatch behind them. He reached through a hole to the left of the hatch in the wood. There was a click. He had activated the lock.

"Arik, you're with me today. Helko and Hatto, you head west, we'll go north. You know the meeting point?" Gunder's orders were short and clear, and the two nodded. "See you in the shadow realm." With those words, they entered it. Arik had stuck to entering this liminal space as if parting a curtain and saw no reason to do it differently now. The groups set off.

The first fifteen minutes passed uneventfully. The streets were dry, and no consecrated ones were in sight. Arik decided to address a thought that had been nagging him for days: "Why am I never paired with Helko? Is he avoiding me?" Gunder kept his eyes on the street ahead, answering seriously, "Maybe it's because you shared a bed once?" "Is he not taking me seriously?" flashed through Arik's mind, but he rephrased it before speaking aloud: "Please, Gunder, be honest with me. He's open and helpful with all the other young shadows, but not with me."

After nearly a month, Arik had gotten used to everything in the complex — except for Helko, who remained an enigma to him. One day, Arik had rounded a corner and found Helko standing before him. Muscular but not overly broad. His piercing green eyes looked slightly down at Arik, though it was due to his height. They were so close that Arik could see the fine lines of crow's feet and scars on his face, in addition to his well-groomed short beard. After a few seconds, Helko had walked away without a word.

"He doesn't know you, and he's always taken some time to warm up to newcomers," Gunder sighed. "He's also still dealing with memory loss and hasn't been able to tell us what happened to him. Please be patient with him." Arik felt bad after hearing this explanation, as if he had just wronged Helko, so he fell silent for a while.

They were only a few hundred meters from the main street leading to the harbor district when screams echoed through the alleyways. Gunder and Arik quickly moved to find the source. They paused for a moment. "That way." Gunder pointed west and took off running, with Arik right behind him, effortlessly keeping pace. For the first time, the boots, specially made for these raids, gave him excellent traction. They sprinted through the alleys. The screams moved south, and they adjusted their route.

Both of them noticed the light emanating from a light orb at the same time. It came from the consecrated ones who were chasing someone down a nearby alley. "We've almost got him," one of them shouted, while another cackled with glee. "Don't let him escape!" A third, equally enthusiastic, added, "He's in for it when we catch him!" Arik's stomach clenched. He recognized the voices. The voices that had haunted him for years.

"Don't Let The Feeling Overwhelm You!" his shadowstone called out in his mind. A month had passed since Arik had last heard its voice. Adrenaline surged, overriding the feeling in his gut. Consecrated ones and shadow-walkers were now running parallel to each other, and with long strides, Arik overtook Gunder, who was still unclear about what was happening. "Those three are mine!"

Gunder grasped the seriousness of the situation and picked up speed. "I Know What You're Planning. Let Me Please Have Some Freedom!" the stone offered, though Arik wasn't sure if it was truly an offer or more of a demand. Nevertheless, he relented. "Fine!"

The movements were still his. At least, partially. He felt what the stone wanted and jumped. Black pillars shot out from under his boots, giving Arik enough momentum to land on the roof of the low house that separated the two alleys. The landing didn't slow him down, and he sprinted diagonally across the roof, not sparing a thought for whether he might slip on the tiles.

Then he saw them. The three consecrated ones were chasing a girl, no older than 12 or 13. They were nearly upon her. His Second Skin enveloped him, unconsciously summoned. He jumped again and landed behind Alexander, Thomas, and Michael. The light pulled him out of the shadow realm, but the Second Skin remained. "HEY, BRAINLESS MORONS!" he yelled. The consecrated ones stopped and turned around. "Why don't you pick on someone your own size?"

The three grinned at each other and charged at him, their fists glowing with light. Shadows formed arm-claws on Arik's hands. "They're Not Sharp, But They'll Get The Job Done." Alex reached him first, swinging a punch. With some difficulty, Arik dodged by stepping his left foot back, causing the punch to miss its target. Alexander couldn't stop his forward momentum in time. The short shadow claw dug a centimeter into Alex's stomach. He looked at Arik in disbelief, who would have liked to follow up with his right hand but saw out of the corner of his eye that Thomas and Michael were flanking him.

He pulled the claw out of Alex's stomach and ran against the direction of his attackers. Alex dropped to his knees, screaming in pain. After about ten meters, Arik spun around, arms outstretched. The arm-claws extended to the same length; they were now a meter long. Pushing off the ground with his right foot, he gained speed and sprinted through the gap between Thomas and Michael. Both had formed batons of light, ready to take Arik down.

His plan failed. They hit him first.

Arik hit the ground, and they continued beating him. He broke into laughter. They hadn't broken him back then — and today wasn't the day they would succeed. Time stood still. "I'M READY!" the voice thundered in his head. "So am I!" he thundered back. "Let me break Vanadis' seal. If you want to take over my body, I'll accept it. Just promise me you'll kill these three." "SO BE IT."

In a vision-like state, he stood before a massive white gate, covered by a web of shadows. A black figure stood next to him. "All You Need To Do Is Place Your Hand On It." Arik stepped closer.

"Arik!" He heard a distant voice and wondered where it was coming from.

"Arik!" It drew closer, but he still couldn't pinpoint its origin.

His hand was almost at the web of shadows.

"Arik!" The voice was now right next to him.

Suddenly, he was lifted up and found himself back in the alley. Confused, he looked around. The light of the consecrated ones had disappeared, and Thomas and Michael lay unconscious on the ground.

"What in the world was that?" Gunder yelled at him, pulling him back into the shadow realm. It felt strange for Arik when someone else did it. "Let me kill them!" Arik snapped back, only to receive a sharp slap across the face.

"No. Or do you want the Church to start hunting us again? Because three consecrated ones were killed at once?" Arik had never seen Gunder so angry before, and there was nothing left for him to do but give in. While they argued, the girl emerged from her hiding spot, holding something in her hand. She walked up to Thomas and kicked him between the legs. Arik and Gunder exchanged bewildered looks. "Can I do that too?" Arik asked Gunder with an innocent expression.

"You're not supposed to kick someone when they're down," Gunder began, but Arik had expected this. "Those three never had a problem with it," he shot back, pointing to his stomach.

"All right, but don't overdo it." Gunder rolled his eyes before noticing something. Arik began enthusiastically pounding on Alexander, clearly enjoying himself. Meanwhile, Gunder approached the girl, who had leaned against a wall to catch her breath. He placed a hand on her shoulder and pulled her into the shadow realm as well. She froze like a statue when she saw Gunder standing before her in his gray robe.

"If I were you, I'd wait until you get your next stone."

CHAPTER 26

On the way back, Gunder didn't say a word to Arik.

They re-entered the complex through the entrance in the shed, and Gunder headed straight for the common room. He instructed Arik to wait outside with the girl. The common room lay quietly before them, with only muffled voices and the creaking of the old wooden door audible. Arik felt the cool, stuffy air flowing out as Gunder closed the door behind him.

"Are you in trouble now?" she asked, worried. He smiled, trying to ease her concern. "And if I am, so what? It won't be anything I can't handle." He attempted a confident smile, but for a moment, a flicker of unease flashed in his eyes. His hand, resting on her head, trembled slightly, as if he wasn't as calm as he seemed. He patted her head, tangled with black hair, steering the conversation away: "Are you nervous? I imagine this must all feel overwhelming for you."

The girl smiled hesitantly. Her lips twitched slightly, as if she was struggling to hold the smile. A faint tremble ran through her body, and her fingers played nervously with a strand of her messy hair. With her large brown eyes and freckles, she might have looked very innocent to Arik, if it weren't for the fact that, fifteen minutes earlier, she had kicked a consecrated one between the legs. Since she didn't know what to say, she remained silent, and Arik spoke again: "Just think of this as an improvement over the boarding school: bigger rooms and more variety in the food." She couldn't help but grin at that, understanding what he meant.

A moment later, seven fighters burst out of the common room and rushed past them. Ostara followed at a more leisurely pace, heading toward Arik and the girl. Arik was surprised to see Ostara, as she was part of the group that was supposed to help set up the new camp. But since four more from that group emerged from the common room ahead of her, he figured they must have returned.

"This is Ostara, and I think she's going to take you to your room now." It was clear Ostara didn't feel comfortable in this role. Awkwardly, she addressed the girl: "Arik's right. Come with me, please. What's your name, by the way?" Arik noticed the look for reassurance in those large brown eyes and nodded. "Tialda," she answered shyly. "Well, come on, Tialda. Let's get you something to eat first," Ostara said, leading her away.

Gunder seemed to be taking his time, as Arik had been standing outside the common room for what felt like an eternity. Minutes dragged on, as slow as honey. Arik could feel his heart pounding in his ears, nervously tapping his foot on the floor. He inhaled the smell of old wood and metal, mixed with the faint hum of voices behind the door.

He could make out an animated discussion inside, though only in fragments. Then they emerged: first, Teto, with fury written all over his face. "Training room!" he ordered sharply. Before Arik could react, Raban and Fenna also appeared. Teto opened the door to the training room, which was right next to them. "Get in there and sit down!"

Silently, Arik entered the room and sat on a bench. Diemo and Romilda sat next to him, while the others, including Gunder, stood in a semicircle a few meters away. Teto strode toward him, his eyes blazing with anger, the veins on his neck bulging. The rage in his voice made the walls of the room tremble, and Arik felt a shiver run down his spine, as if he had been struck by a cold gust of wind. "HAVE YOU

COMPLETELY LOST YOUR MIND?" In that moment, Arik desperately wished that he only heard this shouting in his head and that it wasn't Teto screaming at him. Arik wanted to respond, but Teto interrupted him firmly: "YOU SPEAK WHEN I TELL YOU TO, UNDERSTOOD?" With a nod, Arik signaled that he understood.

"The only reason the Church isn't hunting us down anymore is because we always stay hidden and don't attack consecrated ones in broad daylight." Closing his eyes, Teto rubbed his forehead. He exhaled. "Gunder would have resolved the situation without a fight. What you did was irresponsible!" His left hand touched his nose, eyes still closed. His fingers massaged the bridge of his nose, as if trying to dispel a pain. For a moment, his face seemed frozen in deep concentration, then he took a heavy breath, the tension in his shoulders visible. "It's one thing if you put yourself in danger — we won't stop you from doing that. But when it comes to the shadow-walkers, it's not your decision to make. Do you understand?"

Arik nodded again. There was a pause. Then Fenna's high-pitched voice broke the silence. "He's only 17, Teto. Given the circumstances, none of us would have acted differently." "He could have been killed," Teto replied, in no mood to tolerate objections.

"Did you at least get one of them?" Romilda asked curiously. A vein began to throb on Teto's forehead, and even Arik hadn't expected such a question. "Unfortunately, the shadow arm-claws weren't sharp enough, or I would have," Arik said. Diemo chimed in with his usual gruffness: "Then I'll show you how to make them sharp enough when we have the time."

Arik's mind couldn't keep up. Why were Diemo and Romilda taking his side? Especially Diemo? And how many people knew about the events of his past? "ENOUGH!" Raban's roar snapped Arik out of his thoughts. "We're not here to discuss Arik's fighting skills. We're here to knock some sense into him before he gets himself killed doing something this reckless again."

"Then you don't understand who I am, Raban!" Suddenly, Arik was on his feet, staring Raban down. "I would do it again — just like those three fools will keep tormenting the weak. Tialda told Gunder and me that those three often wander that district, chasing children." His feet carried him forward, and he took a step toward Raban. "And just so you know — I let my power stone take over a bit."

Another step. Now Arik stood directly in front of Raban. No one interfered with what was happening. It was becoming increasingly difficult for Raban to resist Arik's intimidation. For the first time, the boy had an aura Raban had never seen in him before. It was sheer willpower. He felt like a rabbit ensnared by a snake, unable to tear his gaze away from Arik's piercing eyes. A cold shiver ran down his spine, his hands clenched into fists, his breathing heavy and uneven. "If Gunder hadn't intervened, I would have broken the seal and let both stones take full control. This time, I wouldn't have fought back."

Raban's stony facade began to crack, so he prepared to strike back: "That would have been your death. Not immediately, but eventually." "How many times have I heard that now? My fate was sealed the moment the second stone was implanted in me. This now is just a bonus, something I can use to hold those responsible accountable for what they did to me!" Arik's eyes widened slightly, and he bit his lower lip, as if trying to suppress an inner tremble. The lines on his forehead deepened, while a shadow of unrest crossed his face. With that, Arik had broken through Raban's defenses; fear crawled into the creases of his expression.

"Romilda and I will gladly help you with that," Diemo's words grounded Arik again. Everyone stared at the bench where Arik sat — disbelief written on their faces at having heard those words. Arik wondered what could have happened that made Diemo and Romilda want to support him. Before anyone else could speak, Diemo continued: "But promise us you'll be patient and won't do anything reckless again." On the verge of tears, Arik nodded. His eyes glistened with moisture, and he swallowed hard, trying to push back the rising emotions. His jaw quivered slightly, and his hands clutched his linen shirt tightly, as if it were the last thread of his self-control.

Gunder, Raban, and Teto exchanged confused glances, unable to dissuade Romilda and Diemo. But Fenna had one more surprise: "I'll help you too, Arik. The time will come." Her voice was calm but firm, and her eyes glowed with a coldness that stood in stark contrast to her usually gentle nature. There was an enigmatic glimmer in her gaze, as if she knew something the others hadn't yet guessed. The three old shadows felt as though Fenna was suddenly surrounded by an icy wind.

She turned to Teto, mustering all the conviction she could in her next words: "We'll suspend patrols for a week until things calm down. Yes, Arik made a mistake — but like I said, he's only 17. Vanadis, on the other hand, has been causing havoc in the city for 13 years, letting young consecrated ones disappear. It's a miracle we haven't been blamed for it." She now directed her gaze at Raban. "Diemo and Romilda should go back to the new camp to train with Arik. We'll manage without them for a while, right, Raban?"

Through everything that had just happened, tears were quietly running down Arik's cheeks. His hands lay limp in his lap, and he felt his body grow heavy and cold. The tears fell slowly, like hesitant droplets, tracing wet paths across his skin. He turned around and sank back down onto the bench.

Teto snorted loudly. He crossed his arms over his chest, his expression dark, as though caught in an internal struggle. His shoulders were tense, and his nostrils flared slightly as he suppressed his frustration. The way the conversation had turned was not to his liking. It was as if the younger generation had challenged the old guard, questioning their authority. He reminded himself that he bore some responsibility for this shift. His breathing was heavy, and a hint of resignation crossed his features. He felt the weight of the years on his shoulders as he looked into the faces of the younger generation standing before him. Slowly, it dawned on him that it would be impossible to prevent these changes in the long run. So, he saw only one path forward — to steer it as best he could.

Teto cleared his throat. He relaxed his shoulders slightly and spoke with a voice that carried both sternness and determination. His gaze traveled from one face to another, as though weighing their reactions. "Well, it seems you're all quite convinced of what you want to do." For a moment, he had lost his edge, so he chose a different approach. A faint smile tugged at the corners of his mouth as he formed his next sentence, though his eyes still glimmered with the vigilance of a leader who always wanted to maintain control. "We'll surely find a way to integrate your… desire… into our plans. Or do you see it differently, Arik?"

Through his tears, Arik looked up at Teto. His mind couldn't comprehend whether he had won or lost. His thoughts raced as he tried to grasp the meaning of the words. A faint tremor ran through his body as he felt the uncertainty spread like a coldness within him. He had never been in a situation like this before, so he was at a loss for words. "Just nod," Diemo whispered to him, and Arik did exactly that, then slumped slightly, as if all the tension had drained out of him.

"Does anyone else have something to add?" Teto surveyed the group for a few seconds, but no one spoke up. "Good. Then let's put this behind us. We have other matters to discuss." Everyone looked at him, though some faces showed they knew what was coming. "We're here to relieve everyone from the old camp — that's what we call this place now — although Romilda and Diemo will be returning with us, against the original plan."

"I'll be sending two fighters from the new camp as replacements shortly." By now, his tone had returned to a calmer pitch. "In general, Raban and I have decided to rotate personell between camps regularly."

There was a knock on the door. "Come in!" Teto commanded in a firm voice, and the door opened. Ostara stepped into the room and hesitated, waiting to be given permission to speak. Her eyes were slightly downcast, and she seemed nervous, as if unsure how her words would be received. Her hands trembled slightly as she tried to find her voice. "What can we do for you, Ostara?" Teto asked her immediately.

"The new girl… Tiara… the one Gunder and Arik found," she began, somewhat uncertainly. Teto helped her along: "What about her?"

"There's nothing wrong with her directly. She told me there are more like her." All the attendees raised their eyebrows, curious about how many there were. A murmur spread through the group, and suddenly the tension in the room became palpable. The eyes of those gathered glowed with both interest and concern.

"With her, there are 15. They've been hiding in that district from the Church for quite some time." Surprised by the high number of shadowstone carriers they didn't know about, a few jaws dropped. Teto asked incredulously, "15? All around her age? And how did they get the stones?" After a brief moment of reflection, Ostara replied, "Some are children and teenagers, others are the parents. They've specialized in searching for power stones, and they seem to be very good at it."

Teto took a few moments to better assess the situation. "Raban, for now, we'll stick to the plan. Tomorrow evening, you'll go with Tiara to her group and assess the situation. Take all the fighters, but make sure Tiara doesn't notice." He took a deep breath. "At the first sign that something's wrong, return immediately. Take the North Staircase and blindfold her. We need to minimize the risk."

Raban nodded his agreement, grunting, "I'll send you a raven." His voice was deep and rough, like the growl of an animal that wasn't entirely satisfied but was following its instincts. His eyes stayed firmly on Teto, and a barely perceptible nod accompanied his words.

"She wanted to return to her parents anyway and wouldn't want to stay here without them," Ostara added after Teto finished speaking. He responded, "We won't force anyone to stay here. But given the situation, the girl should remain here until tomorrow, and you can tell her that, Ostara." "I'll do that," Ostara confirmed. "I'll go to her right away unless you have more questions." "No, thank you for the information, Ostara. We'll see you later. Dismissed." He waited briefly for Ostara to leave the room. He watched her until the door quietly closed, and a look of weariness crossed his face as he briefly rubbed his forehead before continuing to speak.

"Alright, everyone moving to the new camp will depart before sunrise so we can cross the river under the cover of darkness. So, it's best if you pack up your things and get some rest, or you'll struggle with the eight kilometers ahead. Now, dismissed."

Conversations like these stirred in him the longing to return to the old days. He sighed deeply, his gaze drifting into the distance, as though he could see the shadows of the past. A bitter smile played on his lips as he remembered the simpler times, when his decisions were clear and accepted without resistance. It was easier then, and he didn't have to look after so many at once — but the price for that would be stagnation and decay. A price he was no longer willing to pay.

CHAPTER 27

Winter had descended upon the new camp. Snow blew between the dense trees in the forest, slowly covering the ground, millimeter by millimeter. The sunlight broke through onto the clearing, which had been carved out of the woods to create a space for the camp. The snow-covered ground gleamed white under the light. Initially, the clearing was much smaller, but as more shelters were needed, it expanded.

To reduce their use of wood, the shadow-walkers built their dwellings by digging large, deep pits, coating the walls with clay, and creating roofs from logs and earth. Each of these dwellings had a small fireplace and a kind of chimney to let the smoke escape. Numerous shelters were built this way, providing warmth and protection for over 100 people from the wind and weather.

The first few months had been tough for all the shadow-walkers, but with support from Tarsk and the ten new arrivals who had joined a month and a half earlier, they made it through. The camp was always busy, with no fewer than seventy stone bearers at any given time, except for the days when personell rotated between camps. They quickly got used to the constant coming and going, and due to the proximity to Aregelia, the old camp was also used by the shadow-walkers from Tarsk. In an effort to foster unity, both groups agreed to share the same name from now on.

Not long ago, the group had started building an earthen wall to protect the camp from unwanted visitors. This wall was already halfway finished before winter hit, freezing the ground. Some of the shadow-walkers from Tarsk began reinforcing the existing wall with a permanent layer of shadows. Many others paused their work to witness this spectacle, as they had never seen anything like it before.

Meanwhile, others were tasked with monitoring the trade road between the cities, keeping an eye on the church's troop movements. It had become clear that the Church of Light planned to launch its assault in the winter, just as they had done during the war that had ended fifteen years ago.

Arik had been to the new camp several times but never got the chance to form new connections. The constant rotation between camps, the exhausting work, and daily training made that impossible. He was simply glad to regularly see Hatto, Bruno, and Alvar. The only constants were Romilda and Diemo, who continued preparing him for the inevitable confrontation with his tormentors. After three months with the shadow-walkers, Arik had reached a level of skill that would allow him to face off against an experienced Executor, no longer so reliant on the element of surprise.

Around noon on the sixth day of Ariks stay, a raven arrived at the new camp, landing on one of the chimneys. A burly man with broad shoulders and muscular arms, hardened by years of physical labor and battle, approached the bird and removed the message tied to its leg. As he opened the scroll and began to read, snow fell on his bald head, melting instantly. The water droplets slid down his forehead, tracing the deep lines of his face before falling to the ground. His sharp, dark eyes scanned the message, and unconsciously, he raised his right eyebrow, making the old, small scar there shift slightly.

Arik had crossed paths with this man a few times but never exchanged words with him. During a conversation with Teto, Arik learned that this was Jelto, the leader of the shadow-walkers from Tarsk, and that he was known for his reserved nature. Teto had also shared that it wasn't easy to get Jelto to open up or trust anyone. It took a drinking contest — one that Teto won — before Jelto finally warmed to him, and even then, it was only on Teto's second visit to Tarsk that he was allowed to enter their camp.

Jelto trudged through the snow, now ankle-deep for many, with the raven perched on his shoulder. He made his way to Teto's quarters, descended the stairs, and knocked on the door before stepping inside.

The ceiling was low, like in all the shelters at the new camp. Jelto wasn't particularly tall, but he was close to hitting his head. Teto was sitting on his bunk, studying maps and reports when Jelto entered. He looked up briefly. "Come in, sit down." Jelto glanced around, confused. There was nowhere to sit except the bunk, and the birdcage didn't seem like an option. Noticing this, Teto apologized, "Sorry, old habit." He cleared some papers to make room.

"What can I do for you?" Teto asked, still somewhat distracted. Jelto sat down beside him and handed him the message the raven had brought. As soon as he entered, the raven flew from Jelto's shoulder to the ground and began pecking at something. "The message is from Tarsk. The troops have set out for the south. My... I mean, our comrades in Tarsk have already sent a raven to Sydrik. In two days at most, they'll be at the city walls."

Jelto reached under his worn leather jerkin, his posture relaxed and slightly hunched forward. In the flickering candlelight, Teto thought Jelto looked exhausted. Jelto pulled out a flask and opened it. Teto frowned at what Jelto was about to do and intervened. "Put that away, Jelto. Think of our crew. You're responsible for my lot too." Jelto hesitated for a few seconds, giving Teto a critical look before putting the flask away without a word. He took a moment to collect himself. "Have you heard anything from the other cities?" he asked.

Teto nervously rubbed the bridge of his nose. His eyes flickered momentarily as he thought, glancing around the wooden walls of the shelter as if searching for the right words. "Mersouion and Kalaigia... the groups there are considering whether to wait and see if we survive the winter. And, much to my delight, we're holding up fairly well, though it's not always easy to transport supplies from the old camp here."

Jelto snorted derisively. His eyes narrowed, and his jaw clenched as he tried to suppress his rising anger. The response Teto gave reminded Jelto of old times. "I still don't understand why you sought allies in those two cities of all places." He slammed his fist onto the bunk. The wood groaned under the pressure, and a dull echo filled the room. Jelto exhaled heavily, his fingers trembling slightly with suppressed rage. "Or have you forgotten that those cities surrendered without a fight when the Church's troops arrived at their gates? Aregelia and Tarsk could still be part of the alliance and free today!" He muttered curses under his breath, his face twisting, a deep crease forming between his brows. His lips moved in silent words, recalling long-lost battles and old grievances.

"No, I haven't forgotten. I had to try anyway." As Teto spoke, he placed his right hand on Jelto's left shoulder. "Then we'll do it without them. I'll assign some of my people to you, ones who know the area well. That should help with cutting off their supply routes." He grabbed a map and unfolded it in front of Jelto. "Here," he said, pointing to a village. "This is the first village after the bridge. Position yourselves in the village and behind it, so you can catch them in a pincer. How does that sound?"

Jelto studied the map intently. "Hmm... we can retreat into the forest if needed... that shouldn't be underestimated. For a first ambush, it's a pretty good position." He raised his head and gave Teto a sideways glance. His eyes locked on Teto's face, sharp and appraising, as if trying to read every expression. "You should start making some church patrols disappear within Aregelia, but first, stage some diversionary attacks and wait for their reaction." "That'll stoke fear and uncertainty among the consecrated ones. They'll start moving in larger groups, and then you can set a trap. When ten of them disappear at once, the church will have to pull troops from other cities."

"You've done this before, haven't you?" Teto had heard stories about how much resistance Tarsk had put up to stop the Church's advance. For a year and a half, they had laid siege to the city, and one day, the gates were opened, and not a single resident could be found. No stone bearers were found either. After the city was taken, it was said that Jelto had remained, along with his most loyal comrades — General Jelto and his shadows of the underworld.

Jelto's grin turned into a mischievous smile. "I never got to tell you how much I would have loved to have Vanadis in my ranks at that time, but she said she couldn't do that to her brother. Do you know how many consecrated ones she..."

"ENOUGH!" Teto's voice cracked through the shelter like a whip. The muscles in his neck tensed, and his hands balled into fists. For a moment, his face was a mask of fury. Vanadis was still a sore subject for Teto, one that could send him into a rage. He sounded irritated, a vein pulsing on his forehead. "Anyway... I've got a particularly motivated group for your plan. But I'll also take some of your people along, so mine can learn a thing or two about your... conflict resolution methods."

Unfazed by Teto's outburst, Jelto resumed planning. His face remained calm, but his eyes gleamed with a challenging spark. A brief, almost imperceptible movement of his eyebrows indicated that he recognized and relished the power play. "How many of our fighters should we deploy?"

"Will fifteen be enough for the ambush, plus two healers?" Teto seemed to have regained his composure, though it wasn't easy. "For our operation in Aregelia, I'd plan for about twenty... that leaves us with..."

"Seven fighters to defend the camp," Jelto calculated coolly.

"Make that eight — I'm staying here and leaving Raban in charge," Teto corrected him.

"That should be more than enough," Jelto continued his planning. "I just need to make sure that during our ambush, the carts stay intact and that we can safely transport the seized supplies back to the camp. Otherwise, it won't be worth it."

"Station fighters where the field road leads into the forest on the way back," Teto advised, earning a bored look from Jelto. "Do you think I'm a complete novice?" Jelto tossed the folded map into Teto's lap.

Teto's response was stern, "No, but it's better I say it explicitly so you don't forget. And try to keep the consecrated ones alive — I have a special use for them." Blood rushed through Jelto's veins; his heartbeat quickened as he sensed that Teto was about to propose something unexpected and unconventional. "I'm listening," he said, unable to suppress the excitement in his voice.

"Forgive me for keeping quiet about this matter until now," Teto began, his voice calm, almost cold. "But we have someone very special in our ranks who could greatly facilitate our plans." Jelto edged closer, gripping the bunk with both hands, signaling Teto to continue. "One of my crew has both a lightstone and a shadowstone and has also been trained as an Extractor."

Jelto took a few minutes to process this information. Silence hung in the shelter, broken only by the sounds of the bustling camp outside. In the meantime, he reached for his flask again but stashed it away once more when he felt Teto's gaze on his back. Finally, he managed to speak: "Now that's something. I know a few in my ranks who'd be thrilled to get their hands on a lightstone. I can already think of a few names..."

"Thanks for immediately grasping my thoughts... but I think we should gather everyone for a briefing. Hand me the signal horn over there." As Jelto fetched the horn, Teto secured the raven, who was still pecking at the floor, in the empty cage. Together, they left the shelter, and Teto blew the horn for an assembly.

It took a few minutes, but soon everyone in the camp had gathered around them. The sound of boots crunching through the snow mixed with the murmurs of the shadow-walkers, who curiously eyed their leaders. Out of habit, Teto scanned the crowd, still unsettled by the number of faces he now had to look at.

"Shadow-walkers of Tarsk and Aregelia — thank you for gathering so quickly." Teto exuded a confidence that spread to the crowd. Jelto, by convention, took over the speech. His voice was loud and clear, cutting through the cold air as if to drive away the chill with the power of his words. "Half an hour ago, we received news that the attack on Sydrik is imminent." A wave of murmurs and whispers rippled through the crowd, causing the two to pause briefly.

Teto continued, "That's why Jelto and I have discussed our next steps." Seizing the pause, Jelto chimed in again. "Some of you will accompany me to a village not far from here, where we will lie in wait to ambush the Church's next convoy."

The two exchanged annoyed glances. Each wanted to lead the address but had never agreed on who would speak when.

"Some will go to Aregelia," Teto began again, his tone tinged with irritation, "and carry out a series of attacks to force the Church to pull troops from elsewhere."

"The rest of you," Jelto, convinced it was his turn to speak again, "will stay here at the camp with Teto and keep everything running. It'll be a bit emptier here for a few days." The crowd was still processing the back-and-forth, which was why they failed to react adequately to what had been said.

Finally, Teto turned directly to Arik. "Arik, in a few days, it'll be your turn to join in!"

CHAPTER 28

Later that same day, the group under Jelto's leadership set out, accompanied by all the healers, suppliers, and craftsmen. Their mission was to establish a small camp at the forest's edge, providing Jelto and his fighters with a fallback point for a few days. The journey from the forest's edge to the new camp was five kilometers — some parts through dense undergrowth, others along the narrow hunter's and woodcutter's path used during the season.

Together, they managed to build small shelters made of thick branches and leaves within a few hours, and they gathered enough wood for a campfire. Along with the supplies brought from the new camp, this created a foundation that would allow Jelto — accompanied by Gunder, Helko, another fighter from Aregelia, twelve of his own men, and two healers — to launch attacks on the supply routes for about a week.

Late in the evening, even before Jelto's support crew returned to the new camp, Raban's group set out. Besides seven fighters, only Teto remained at the camp. Although Raban and the others followed much of the same trail as Jelto, their journey would be much longer. Eleven kilometers of dense forest and the river separated them from the old camp — but thanks to the regular rotation, the route had become deeply ingrained in everyone's memory.

After nearly two hours, they stood on the riverbank. The sky was clear, and the stars shone in all their glory, but the wind whipped against them, as if determined to prevent them from crossing the water. The shadow-walkers stood like bundled pillars, unaffected by wind and weather. Only

Diemo's hands moved, as if he were a puppeteer manipulating invisible strings. Over the past few months, he had performed the task he was about to do countless times.

Directly before them, a portal began to form from a tiny point, as shadows spread like living tendrils and shaped themselves into a half-circle. The edges flickered as if competing with the surrounding reality, and a faint hum filled the silence, like distant, whispered voices. Diemo gave the command, "Go!" and they all ran through the portal, leaving only him on this side of the river.

As the shadow-walkers stepped through the portal, they felt a slight pull, as if the air around them was thickening. A cold breath, like that of an ancient creature, brushed their skin, leaving a tingling sensation down their spines. The darkness of the portal seemed to swallow them, and for a moment, the world felt still and boundless.

A satisfied smile flickered across Diemo's face as he held the portal steady without much difficulty or help from Raban — though he knew he could never have come this far without Raban. Then he stepped through himself.

Upon arriving on the other side, he immediately closed the portal again. Raban nodded to him approvingly and gave the order for them to continue. Diemo, filled with pride, was about to follow the group when Romilda stepped in front of him, wrapping her arms around him. She stood on her tiptoes and kissed him passionately.

As Romilda embraced Diemo and their lips met, time seemed to stand still for a moment. Her heartbeat synchronized with his, and in that brief, intense moment, nothing else existed — no darkness, no fear, only the beating of their hearts and the warmth of their touch. They might have continued gazing deeply into each other's eyes forever if Raban's loud clearing of his throat hadn't snapped them out of the moment.

It wasn't long before they reached the South Tunnel and entered it. The air became noticeably warmer, and several members of the group sighed with relief. In Arik's mind, he wondered if now was the time to try. It had taken him a long time to even come close to matching the tone, but recently, he had finally managed it. He cleared his throat and mimicked Gunder's voice as best he could: "Alright, everyone, last lap."

For a moment, there was confusion and silence. Hatto was the first to start laughing, as he was one of those responsible for the idea. The ice was broken, and the entire group joined in the laughter — even the shadow-walkers from Tarsk, who were by now well-acquainted with Gunder's daily exercise routine and recognized the phrase.

A few minutes later, they reached their destination, and Raban headed straight for the common room. It filled quickly, and everyone removed their coats to be warmed by the fire and torches. Among the shadow-walkers already seated, there was confusion, as the next rotation wasn't scheduled until the following week. Arik and Hatto sat with Ricke and Fara, who had taken their usual seats at their table. As soon as Arik and Hatto entered, Fara eagerly waved them over, clearly happy to see them again.

Raban couldn't help but notice that the sudden appearance of his group had caused some unease. Clearing his throat, he stood up and finally spoke in his deep, gruff voice: "There's been a change of plans. The Church started marching on Sydrik today, and now we're going to stir things up in the city. Tomorrow morning, there will be no exercises; instead, we'll hold a meeting."

A restless murmur spread through the crowd like a wave. Some leaned toward their neighbors, whispering hurriedly, while others shook their heads or furrowed their brows, trying to grasp the significance of the news. Despite Raban's announcement, curiosity got the better of those who hadn't been present for Teto and Jelto's briefing, and they began bombarding the new arrivals with questions.

After a while, Arik and Hatto said goodbye to the two suppliers and made their way to their quarters. Although Arik had only spent a week at the new camp this time, he was still glad to be back in his own bed. His legs felt heavy, as if stones were tied to his ankles, and his eyes burned with exhaustion. The feeling of the soft, scratchy blanket against his skin as he finally lay down was like a warm, comforting cloak wrapping around him.

The next morning, everyone in the old camp was awakened by Raban's gentle and melodic voice as he made his morning rounds through the complex. "EVERYONE UP NOW!" Raban's voice boomed through the stone corridors like the deep rumble of thunder, startling even the deepest sleepers awake. Like a mantra, echoing off the stone walls, Raban repeated the sentence over and over until the last shadow-walker finally made their way to the washrooms.

One by one, the assembly hall filled up until nearly forty shadow-walkers sat on benches, leaned against the walls, or took seats on the floor. Raban, Fenna, Romilda, Diemo, and one of the fighters from Tarsk sat facing the others, overseeing the room. The air was thick with a mix of curiosity and quiet tension as the old and new shadow-walkers crowded into the assembly hall. It was an unfamiliar sight for the four of them, seeing so many new faces, as the hall was now filled not only with shadow-walkers from Tarsk but also those who had joined under Tialda. When Tialda spotted Arik, she waved wildly and cheerfully at him.

"Your new girlfriend, huh?" Hatto teased, having noticed the interaction. Arik didn't find it amusing, especially since Tialda was only twelve years old. "Very funny," he retorted dryly. "If anything, there's someone else I'd rather get closer to."

Hatto raised an eyebrow, intrigued. "Since when, and who?" he asked with interest. "The one on the left of the two girls from Tarsk," Arik whispered, trying not to draw too much attention to himself. "You mean Gunda?" Hatto responded, loud enough for Gunda to hear her name and look up. With a big grin, he raised his hand in greeting and pointed directly at Arik. Gunda's face turned bright red, and Arik wished he could sink into the ground.

"Sometimes I hate you, Hatto," Arik muttered under his breath, earning a quick, "I know," in return. Arik crossed his arms over his chest and shot Hatto a sharp side-glance, his lips pressed tightly together in discomfort. Hatto, unfazed, grinned and winked at Gunda, who blushed even more and hastily looked away. Arik's heart pounded in his chest as if it was trying to leap out of his throat.

Finally, the room quieted down, and Raban was able to begin the meeting. "Nice that I don't have to clear my throat or yell this time. But first things first: good morning, everyone!" With those words, he began his speech, gradually finding his rhythm. "For those who missed it yesterday: The Church's forces are marching toward Sydrik, which means we shadow-walkers must fulfill our part of the agreement with the free cities."

A restless murmur spread like a wave through the crowd again. Some leaned toward their neighbors, whispering hastily, while others shook their heads or furrowed their brows, trying to comprehend the gravity of the news. Raban waited for the room to quiet down. "Teto never explained to you what this agreement was that he made. I think it's time to remedy that." He paused, scanning the crowd for their reactions, then continued.

"In Sydrik, they knew an attack by the Church was imminent, so they made an agreement with Teto that, once the attack began, we — together with our brothers and sisters from Tarsk — would intercept the supply lines through Aregelia and, at the same time, reduce the number of consecrated ones within the city." The murmuring broke out again, primarily among those who hadn't been aware of the agreement. "In return, they will help us liberate Aregelia, Tarsk, and eventually Mersouion and Kalaigia — and defend these cities afterward. This would be the first time in fifteen years that the Church of Light is pushed back."

He paused for a few moments, taking a deep breath. The noise level in the room swelled, a chaotic mix of whispers, skeptical glances, and nervous fidgeting. The air felt thick, almost oppressive, as if it had absorbed the shadow-walkers' nervous energy and rising questions.

"We will create unrest among the patrols for a few days, launching attacks — and then, in broad daylight, we will strike a larger patrol and, if possible, take prisoners." Uncertainty now fully gripped the crowd, and Hatto stood up. "Does … does that mean…" he began hesitantly, his voice growing louder as the noise in the room rose, "… we're going to have consecrated ones down here? I mean, besides Arik?"

A web of shadows formed around Fenna's throat, followed by a deep, smoky, "SILENCE!" As the room fell quiet, she worked up the nerve to answer, after exchanging glances with

Raban. "Yes, that's the plan," she continued in her golem voice, but then dissolved the web and resumed her usual high pitch. "The quarters next door will be converted later today so we can keep them there. We'll suppress the lightstones and shackle them." Fenna's hands trembled slightly as she spoke, and she kept her gaze lowered, as if unwilling to see the shadow-walkers' reactions.

She remained calm throughout, but just as with Raban, there was a trace of uncertainty in her voice — and Hatto picked up on it. "What exactly are we going to do with them?" he pressed. The murmurs flared up again, like a hornet's nest that had been struck. To spare Fenna from the reaction, Raban stepped forward, positioning himself like an immovable, indestructible rock before her. He was the one who had convinced Teto of this idea — it was his responsibility to drop the bombshell.

Raban's eyes gleamed with determination as he stepped forward. The room seemed to hold its breath. "To extract their power stones." His voice was like a sharp blade cutting through the stillness. A collective, sharp intake of breath swept through the crowd, as if every single person could feel the weight of his words in their bones.

Silence.

Arik's mind buzzed. "Kid, Stay With Me." His shadowstone spoke again, clearly concerned for its bearer. "I Get That This Is A Lot, But You Gotta Stay Present."

Arik was paralyzed, except for his eye, which blinked wildly. In an attempt to snap him out of it, Hatto snapped his fingers in front of his face. "Arik, are you still with us?" Fear gripped Hatto, and he turned to Raban. "I think this was too much for him."

Something was in the air, and every fighter present donned their Second Skin, some drawing their weapons. The ground beneath their feet trembled slightly, as if something massive was waiting to be unleashed. In the next moment, Raban bellowed, "All non-fighters, get out! Get to safety!" There was a hint of fear in his voice.

"Kid, This Isn't What You Want To Do."

The shadow covering Arik's lightstone began to crumble.

"What Happened A Few Weeks Ago Was Different."

More and more of the stone's glow broke through.

"Sure, It's In Our Nature To Take Control."

A third of the shadow was gone.

"But What You're Doing Isn't Helping Any Of Us."

Fenna let out a loud, piercing scream and transformed into her golem form in an instant. Her head reached the ceiling. As she moved, the floor groaned under her massive weight, and dust trickled down from above. "I'm sorry, Arik." Her voice was rough and deep. She charged and swung her massive arm. The blow caught him completely, sending Arik flying against the wall. A thick shadow cushion formed between him and the stones just before impact. Arik got back on his feet, his eyes pitch black. He shook himself off.

More than half of the shadow was gone.

"Was it always their plan to use me for this?"

"Could Be, Kid. Are You Sure You Want To Go Through With It?"

"I don't know. It was always about those three bastards. I don't know. If I can do this. To Others."

"Does It Make You Angry That You Have To Do It, Or That They Just Expect You To?"

"The second one, yeah. The first... I don't know."

"Wanna Let The Big Guy Know How You Feel?"

"Yeah."

Arik relinquished control to the stone. In an instant, a carpet of shadows spread across the floor and over Arik. None of the fighters could react as Arik disappeared into the ground. Everyone was tense, each taking a combat stance. Suddenly, a black fist shot out of the floor, landing an uppercut on Raban that sent him flying into the air and crashing back down. Then a disembodied voice echoed through the room: "This Is A Warning. Remember It!"

At the spot where Arik had disappeared, he slowly reemerged from the ground. The shadows gradually receded from his skin, and finally, his black eyes faded. He was calm, the anger gone. Nothing about him trembled, not even as he registered all twenty fighters in the room, their focus entirely on him. Sometimes, it helped him to talk to the stone.

"Anything else you'd like to tell me or have me do for you?" His voice was neutral, without edge or sarcasm. By now, Raban was back on his feet, and apart from his pride, he appeared unscathed. It was clear to him that Arik wouldn't let himself be pushed around anymore, not even through his control over the stone. He also realized that this time, he'd gone too far with his plans.

"No, that's all," Raban finally said, visibly shaken. Would it have been better if Teto were here instead? "You're dismissed from the meeting."

Arik turned and walked toward the door. Before opening it, he said, "Let me know when I should do the first extraction." Then he glanced back over his shoulder at Raban. "I'm always ready to practice on you."

He left the room, not even bothering to close the door behind him. Ostara followed him first, then Hatto. When Fenna left as well, Romilda and Diemo followed. Another young shadow-walker joined them — and to everyone's surprise, so did Gunda and two other fighters from Tarsk.

Raban had lost the younger generation.

CHAPTER 29

- 1 -

"Arik, wait!"

Shortly after him, Ostara stepped out of the room and saw him running down the hallway. Arik turned around and looked at her skeptically as she nervously tucked her red-blonde hair behind her left ear. She walked toward him, not noticing that other young shadows were also leaving the room and approaching him. They all gathered around him. Ostara nearly jumped in surprise when Hatto suddenly ran past her.

"Yes?" Arik wasn't quite sure what was happening; after all, he had just made his point and then left. The first to speak was Fenna. "Are you okay?" she asked, concerned, her voice tense. "What are you going to do now?" She struggled to keep calm, as her anger from the situation boiled inside her. The way both Raban and seemingly Teto, too, had handled things, and what they expected, made her blood boil. She didn't even notice how her hands had clenched into fists.

"Yes, I'm fine." His tone remained unchanged; it was still emotionless. "I'm just going to get something to eat. Why do you ask?" His response baffled everyone standing around him. It was hard for them to understand how someone who had just used his abilities in such a way, to show an authority figure his limits, could remain so calm. A soft murmur rippled through the group, like a low hum, as everyone tried to find their own explanation for Arik's behavior.

Fenna, who was the least shaken by his statement, finally reacted. "You... you just knocked Raban to the ground...

Did you lose control of your stones?" There was a quiver in her voice; she was still trying to process what had just happened.

"You taught me one thing very early on." Arik's words sounded almost mechanical as they left his lips. "Never talk about your stones." Some of those around him felt a cold shiver down their spines. They had never seen him so cold and calculating before, and what he said in that moment was revealing. Most of them instinctively understood that what he had done in the meeting room was far from a loss of control. It all pointed to the opposite. "If you want to talk more, we can do it in the common room over a bowl of oatmeal." Without waiting for a response, he started walking.

They followed him, moving like an excited yet determined unit, their eyes fixed on Arik. Some quickened their pace, as if they wanted to force an answer, while others hesitated, seemingly afraid of what they might hear next. The air was heavy with unspoken questions and the electric tension of a looming conflict.

In the common room, they pushed the tables together, and all those who considered themselves young shadows took a seat. The room suddenly felt smaller, as if the walls were closing in, while the young shadows gathered around the tables. The silence was stifling, broken only by the crackling of the fire and the faint rustling of clothing as they found their seats. The room was warm from the fire, but there was a noticeable coldness that had nothing to do with the temperature.

Everyone watched Arik intently, who sat at one end of the table. Arik returned their gazes and saw a range of emotions — uncertainty, concern, fear, but also confidence and calm.

"Are you all just going to watch me eat?" Arik asked the group, signaling that they shouldn't wait too long to answer.

"What just happened?" Hatto blurted out, unable to contain his curiosity.

"I took some time to think and came to the conclusion that this will be the last time Raban or Teto gives me orders." Several jaws dropped at the table, and some gasped for air. "And from what I understand, I've just been assigned to the healers." The healers, including Bruno, exchanged uncertain glances. Fenna then cleared her throat. "I understood Raban's words the same way."

Her voice became steadier, as she seemed to have collected herself by now. "From now on, all orders from Raban or Teto will go through me. The only people who can give you orders from now on are Romilda, Diemo, and me. Bruno, I need more support — can I count on you?" Bruno nodded, and Fenna turned back to the group. "Along with us three, Bruno will also join, so keep that in mind."

A murmur filled the room, eyebrows raised, and some faces showed open skepticism. Fenna felt the eyes on her, some critical, others acknowledging. Her heart pounded in her chest, but she showed no sign of it. Her shoulders remained straight, her voice firm.

From the murmuring, Gunda suddenly called out: "And what happens now?" All heads turned toward her, and she flushed red with embarrassment. Gunda could feel the heat rising in her cheeks, and her heart pounded so loudly it echoed in her ears. She lowered her gaze and nearly disappeared behind her wild brown hair, which fell like a curtain in front of her face. Her hands trembled slightly as she tried to make herself as small as possible, her hazel eyes staring at the ground.

With a touch of gentleness, Fenna responded, "We'll stick to the plan Raban laid out… with a few changes." She took a deep breath, fully aware of the weight of her decision. The word "mutiny" had been a frequent guest in her mind that day. "The attacks on the patrols will be handled by the old shadows; I won't risk any of your lives for that." Some faces dropped in disbelief, a spoon clattered to the ground, while others suddenly broke into smiles.

"When it comes to the daylight attack — Arik will scout out which patrol we'll attack and then, with a few others, secure the retreat. We'll assign roles once the time comes." She gathered her courage for her next words. Her hands trembled, something Diemo and Romilda, who were seated on either side of her, noticed. Each of them grabbed one of her hands and held on.

Fenna first looked to her left, where Romilda sat. She saw determination. Then, she looked to her right and saw confidence. One last deep breath, you can do this, she thought to herself. "My first order to you is: We take care of ourselves first, then the old shadows, then everyone else. Do you understand?" The noise in the room vanished. Fenna's authority as the leader of the young shadows — a position she had held for over four years — became clearer in that moment. She, and no one else, was responsible for the young shadows.

Fenna felt a wave of power build up inside her, as if the responsibility she now carried both weighed her down and lifted her up. Her eyes glowed as she looked around at the young shadows, her lips pressed together, as if she was trying to regain full control of her nerves.

She began to fill the room with her presence. She had broken with the old system.

In the days that followed, Raban and Fenna clashed more often, and only reluctantly did he send the old shadows out alone at night to harass the patrols. The fact that an open fight with the consecrated ones was not yet planned was the only reason he stuck to the plan. Raban felt his patience fraying every time Fenna voiced her own opinion firmly and contradicted him. Her resolve and defiance angered him more than he was willing to admit.

Fenna, on the other hand, felt the fire of anger burning inside her, but she forced herself to stay calm, determined to hold her ground and give the young shadows a voice. The divide between the old shadows and young shadows became increasingly visible — both during the morning exercises, which were now held separately, and in the common room, where cliques began to form.

Despite the conflict brewing within the complex, they stuck to their plan. For three days, they caused unrest in the city, and on the fourth day at noon, all the fighters gathered in the meeting room. Bruno, Arik, and another healer were also present.

"How wonderful that we can all be in one room again," Raban grumbled as he began his address. He was far from happy with how things were unfolding, and his hopes rested on the successful execution of the plan to mend some of the fractures that had formed.

Tension filled the room, the flames of the torches crackled softly, and the silence between Raban's words felt heavy. It was as if each breath became more difficult, as if the air itself was burdened by an unseen weight. "I'll get straight to the point: Diemo and Arik, you'll head north — Romilda and Hatto, you'll head west. We won't proceed like we do during the usual raids; instead, you'll walk back and forth along the route until you spot the right patrol. And don't forget" — Raban gave Fenna a cold glare — "you'll regroup at the starting point after each round. Is that clear, Fenna?" He didn't even try to hide his disdain for her.

"Of course, my dear Raban," Fenna responded sweetly, unfazed by his energy. "And how about the assignments for the confrontation?" "Thank you for asking. Arik, Bruno, Gunda, Hatto — you'll secure the retreat and only engage if necessary. Ostara, you'll keep watch for reinforcements. Fenna and I will launch the attack from two sides. The rest of you will strike once we have their attention." Everyone in the room was focused, no one dared to whisper, for too much was at stake — and no one wanted to be on the receiving end of Raban's foul mood. "We meet at the south stairs in five minutes. Let's move!"

They all left the old camp simultaneously. The shed, to which the stairs led and which served only as a pass-through during raids, was bursting at the seams. Aside from the rustling of clothing and the wind whistling through the cracks, not a sound could be heard. Without waiting for a signal, Hatto, Romilda, Diemo, and Arik shifted into the shadow world. Those who remained in the shed remained silent the entire time, minimizing the risk of drawing attention too soon.

The silence was so thick it felt tangible, broken only by the faint trembling of hands stuffed into pockets and the soft footsteps of those fighting against the cold. Each heartbeat seemed louder than the wind whistling through the cracks as they waited for the moment to act. Then came a knock. No one knew how much time had passed. Raban cracked the door open and spoke quietly, "Are we ready?" Another knock answered him. Then the remaining shadow-walkers shifted worlds and saw the four who had scouted the patrols.

"We've spotted two patrols, both about ten minutes away from us," Diemo reported. "Each patrol has eight consecrated ones and four additional city guards — and each one has one of Arik's… targets." Raban had to think for a moment about which patrol to attack before making a decision: "We're heading north." His voice was firm and steady. "Retreat will be through the north stairs. If necessary, go through the harbor district. Move out!"

They locked the stairs and the shed behind them and set off. The snow still lay several centimeters thick, betraying their footsteps. What had been manageable at night could easily become their downfall during the day — but they were well aware of the risk. All the shadow-walkers weaved through passing groups of city dwellers, along houses and through alleyways. After just seven minutes, they spotted the patrol headed their way.

Arik and his group leapt onto two opposing rooftops. Hatto and Bruno took one side, Gunda and Arik the other. Ostara chose the highest point in the area and let her Second Skin manifest, growing two wings from it. Gunda and Arik stared at her in astonishment, having never seen this sight before. It was a welcome distraction from the nerves that had settled deep within both of them, and from their racing hearts as they prepared for the looming danger. "Get to the ridge of the house!" Hatto called over to them. "You'll have a better view of the area." He then ran up the eaves and perched himself at the top. "And no flirting, please — it'll only be distracting."

Gunda and Arik were embarrassed — and united in their desire to shove Hatto off the roof. Once they reached the ridge, they sat back-to-back, keeping both the side alley and the upcoming battle in sight. Neither said a word, leaving an awkward silence between them. Arik could feel Gunda's back against his, and for a brief moment, he felt a sense of comfort. But the cold of the roof and the looming threat quickly erased that feeling. Gunda struggled to steady her trembling hands, her eyes darting nervously down the side alley, while her heart raced wildly in her chest.

The other shadow-walkers took their positions. A particularly long alley lay before them, and groups of seven crouched on the roof's edge, ready to leap down at any moment. Arik watched as everyone activated their Second Skin and drew their weapons. He nudged Gunda with his elbow. "We should get ready too," he said shortly, letting the shadows flow over his skin. Without a word of agreement, Gunda followed his lead.

CHAPTER 30

In pairs, the guards and consecrated ones marched through the alleyway. There was just enough space to pass by them on either side. The narrow alley smelled of freshly emptied chamber pots and old smoke, the air damp and cool. Worn cobblestones covered the ground, cracked and uneven, making every step a challenge for the consecrated ones. The city guards, however, knew every feature of the streets and alleys by muscle memory, walking lightly. Dust and mortar occasionally fell from the walls of the houses, loosened by the pounding of heavy boots on the cobblestones.

Light orbs hovered over several of the consecrated ones, which Raban had expected, prompting him to signal the group to move higher up on the roof. Then, he leaped down a few meters behind the patrol and waited for Fenna. He and his two round shields, about 40 centimeters in diameter and made of solid oak, were completely cloaked in shadow. Sometimes Raban regretted that while the shadows could cover him, his round belly still protruded like a hill.

In this moment, Raban felt a familiar tingling of tension in his fingers. It was a sensation he hadn't experienced in a long time — a strange mix of fear and anticipation. He knew he couldn't afford any mistakes — not now, not with so many eyes on him. His heart beat faster as he thought about what was at stake: their freedom, their lives, and the remaining trust of the young shadows, if it wasn't already too late. He needed to show that they could still lead, that he could still lead.

On the other side, Fenna jumped down, keeping her distance at first to maintain the element of surprise. She let out two loud shouts and effortlessly shifted into her golem form, towering over the narrow street. Her head nearly reached the eaves of the roof. The contours were sharp, the shadows forming muscles ready to sprint at any moment. The shadow-walkers from Tarsk laid a fine web of shadows over the alley. It was thin enough to let light through, making it impossible to detect from the watchtowers. Even the consecrated ones didn't notice that the noose was tightening around them.

Raban initiated the attack. In the 15 meters he had for his charge, he gained enough momentum and shifted back into the normal world. Staying in the shadow realm didn't make sense this close to the light orbs. The noise of his fast steps became audible again, first alerting the city guards. They turned around, raising their spears and shields in a defensive stance. But it was too late. The last thing they saw that evening was a massive shadow with two shields and a bulging belly, leaping toward them.

He had aimed for the gap between them, holding his shields at an angle. The shields struck the guards' helmets, knocking them out instantly. The four consecrated ones at the back turned on the spot, summoning batons of light and forming a trapezoid formation to cover the entire width of the alley. They hesitated, waiting to see if the shadow would attack them. One of the consecrated ones in the rear row raised his right arm straight up and shot a signal flare into the air. His eyes were fixed on his opponent, so he didn't notice that the flare barely made it three meters before being caught and neutralized by the shadow web.

On the other side, Fenna charged forward. Halfway there — just after Raban had knocked the guards into the land of dreams and headaches — she also shifted out of the shadow realm. The two city guards and their four consecrated ones had already come to a halt, trying to assess the situation. They had exactly half a second to do so — the time it took Fenna to cover the remaining seven meters between them.

She barreled through the guards, feeling the impact reverberate through her massive golem body as she crashed into her opponents. Her arms and legs vibrated from the force of the collision. The guards were lifted off their feet, flung into the consecrated ones behind them. The consecrated ones were hit head-on, causing them to lose their balance. One of the consecrated ones in the third row conjured a massive wall of light, which his front-line comrades crashed into before collapsing to the ground.

His comrade beside him summoned a series of light rods from the wall to stop the golem — and to his delight, it worked. The rods drove deep into the golem, halting its movement. Triumphant, the consecrated one tried to extend the rods even further. A searing pain shot through Fenna's chest as one of the light rods pierced her body, and she could taste the metallic tang of blood in her mouth. Her breathing became ragged and labored as her body adjusted to the stabbing pain beneath her ribs.

At the same time, eight more shadows descended from the rooftops, rushing at the remaining consecrated ones, who had paid no attention to their flanks. Two of these shadows rushed to Fenna's aid, destroying the rods. She collapsed to her knees and reverted back to her normal form. She was not yet lying down, but she knelt, breathing heavily; as she coughed, she noticed blood splattering onto the ground. The two shadows that had helped her quickly dragged her into the shadow realm and carried her to a nearby courtyard. Bruno, who had been watching the scene closely, landed beside them and began examining Fenna's wounds. He sent one of the shadow-walkers back to the main group while the other stood guard at the entrance.

When Bruno saw the blood on Fenna's mouth and the wound on her side, his heart skipped a beat. He knew Fenna as one of the strongest among them, and the thought that she had been injured sent a pang through him. "Damn it, Fenna, this is the worst time to get hurt," he muttered under his breath. In a weak voice, Fenna responded, "Is there ever a good time for that, Hatto?" She coughed again, this time accompanied by more blood.

His hands trembled slightly as he prepared the bandages. He knew Fenna was strong — stronger than most — but in that moment, he felt helpless. 'What if she dies?' he thought. 'What if I can't treat her in time?' He took a deep breath, pushed his doubts aside, and focused on what he needed to do. Next to him, the second healer, one of the shadow-walkers from Tarsk and a man of Raban's age, appeared. He placed a reassuring hand on Bruno's shoulder, exuding confidence. "We've got this, youngster. If you let me, I'll show you how." Bruno looked up into the weathered face and nodded. "Alright, let's do this…."

Within a minute, they had torn through the patrol. The consecrated ones had been unable to adapt to the fight and form a defensive line. They were too few in number and had not expected such a targeted attack. All eight consecrated ones lay unconscious on the ground, gathered up by the shadow-walkers. Hatto had gone down to help, ensuring that each consecrated one could be carried by two shadow-walkers. On the rooftops, Arik resumed his watch, with Gunda on the opposite side, scanning for any more patrols.

Raban stepped over the consecrated ones and positioned himself at the far end of the alley. Breathing steadily, he closed his eyes. At first, nothing happened. Then, some began to notice a fog rolling in — a black mist that engulfed the alley, radiating a presence that warned everything and everyone to stay out. "Retreat!" Raban bellowed, stomping forward, the mist — extending about 50 meters around him — following his every step.

The black mist that trailed Raban felt cold and damp, like a living, breathing cloud that consumed everything in its path. The sound of their hurried footsteps echoed dully in the narrow alleys, accompanied by the soft crunch of snow beneath their boots and the wind howling through the tight passages. The townspeople who saw or touched this cloud were gripped with fear and fled.

On the rooftops, Arik and Gunda nodded to each other. Carefully, they ran along the ridges, always on the lookout for consecrated ones and obstacles. It was estimated to be about 400 meters to the north stairs, and the likelihood of encountering another patrol was slim. Due to the attacks of recent nights, patrol numbers had tripled — so only one-third of the usual patrol count was out. One of them circled the marketplace, while the other two patrolled the outer city districts counterclockwise.

As far as they could tell, the attack had gone unnoticed. Neither Arik and Gunda at the front nor Romilda and Diemo, securing the rear of the retreat, spotted any more consecrated ones. Ostara regularly flew her rounds, keeping an eye on the other consecrated groups, which she could identify from a distance by their light orbs.

The smell of cold stone and damp earth filled the air as they reached the safety of the complex via the North Stairway. Their bodies were soaked with sweat, and the cold bit into their skin. Their muscles burned from exertion, and their lungs ached from the cold air. Yet in that moment, the feeling of relief was so intense that it overshadowed everything else. Raban entered the stairway last and sealed the exit. He had been informed during the retreat that Fenna had been injured and that two healers were tending to her. He sent word to the healers to take the South Stairway if they were to stay longer. At that moment, he knew that at least three people — Fenna and the healers — were still near the site of the attack. Hopefully, they'd make it back soon, he thought.

They had remained hidden in the complex for 20 years without being discovered, and the events of this day should not change that. Raban was filled with pride. The attack and the preparations had been a complete success. In his thoughts, he silently gave credit to Jelto for the strategy, which had allowed them to avoid almost all unpleasant surprises beforehand. He grumbled quietly into his beard, "Shame you couldn't see this, sister."

Some time later, Arik found himself with one of the older healers in one of the quarters. The room was stuffy, filled with the smell of herbs, blood, and sweat — no one knew why, as the quarter had been completely empty until half an hour ago. The torches cast flickering shadows on the walls, dancing like ghostly figures. Six of the eight beds were occupied by fighters who had been involved in the attack.

Under the healer's guidance, Arik cleaned the wounds and applied a green paste to the bruises the fighters had sustained. Gunda and another fighter suffered from hypothermia and were given hot nettle tea. None of the injured uttered sounds of pain; instead, they swallowed it down. A part of Arik wanted to tend more to Gunda, but there was no time for that.

"Arik, I need you over here," called the older healer to him. "Coming right away, Lioba," he replied to Ricke's younger sister. It wasn't convenient for him at that moment, as he was just about to prepare more tea for the injured. But he had quickly learned in the past few days that Lioba was quite strict in her work and did not tolerate any backtalk. In this regard, she had much in common with her sister. If her build had been as robust as Ricke's, they would have been almost identical.

As instructed, he walked over to Lioba, who didn't wait for him to fully arrive. "You know how to stitch wounds, from what I understand, right?" she asked pointedly, not noticing the skeptical look he gave in response. "At the boarding school, I could only practice on the deceased, so why — " Not waiting for his reply, she handed him a needle and thread. "Get to it, then." He hesitated, much to her displeasure. "Or are you going to wait until he bleeds out?"

The young shadow-walker in the bed gulped at those words, and uncertainty crept into every fiber of his being. "Don't make such a fuss!" Lioba snapped at him — it was her way of offering comfort and reassurance. "It would take days for you to lose enough blood anyway. Two stitches should do it. Do you want a bite stick?" As she asked, she waved a thick piece of wood in front of his face, and her gesture made it clear that she wasn't joking. The shadow-walker took the piece of wood, ready to sink his teeth into it.

"Good choice," she affirmed in the same brusque manner. "It tastes just like the food we get here every day." Arik cleared his throat indignantly, as he had been one of those responsible for cooking until recently. "Let's hope Arik handles the needle better than the cooking spoon." She ignored Arik's displeasure and pushed him to get on with stitching the wound. "If you take any longer, the wound might heal itself."

Arik prepared for the first stitch in the young man's left arm. The shadow-walker flinched and let out a brief sound of pain. Neither the needle nor the thread were particularly thin, but they would have to do for this purpose. The shadow-walker bit down on the piece of wood and signaled to Arik that he should try again. The needle pierced the skin, emerging at the edge of the cut, before plunging back into the flesh.

As Arik stitched the wound, a familiar unease settled in his stomach. He had practiced this movement hundreds of times — but always on still, lifeless bodies. Now, a living, breathing young shadow-walker lay before him, in pain. "Just two stitches, just two little stitches, you can do this," he repeated to himself in his head as he pulled the thread through. But his hands trembled, and for a moment, he feared the needle might betray him. "Just one more push, and the thread will be fully through." He executed the motion and heard the wounded man groan.

After pulling the thread through far enough, Arik tied a double knot. "One down, only one more to go." The look on the wounded man's face spoke volumes. It hurt, and he was pleading for Arik to hurry. Arik took a deep breath and made the second stitch. Drawing on what he had learned from the first stitch, he managed to make the process a little more tolerable. When he pulled the second knot tight, the shadow-walker's body relaxed, and he sank back into the bed.

He removed the piece of wood from his mouth and breathed steadily. Lioba poured alcohol over the wound, and the young man's eyes widened once more as the burning sensation seared his skin like flames. "You'd better avoid torches or open flames for the next hour. Looks like your arm will heal just fine." In her usual caring manner, Lioba reached into a small jar that held another type of paste. "Open wide — this helps with healing!" she barked, smearing the paste onto his tongue. He grimaced as the bitter taste hit his taste buds.

The door opened. Bruno and another healer carried Fenna in and laid her on a bed. She was pale and appeared to be suffering from hypothermia. Her gray linen shirt was torn at the left side of her stomach, revealing a clearly visible wound. The air was thick with tension, and the expressions of everyone in the room betrayed their concern. Lioba hurried over to Fenna and smeared the same paste onto her tongue. Barely conscious, Fenna managed to swallow it with great effort before falling asleep.

Turning to Arik, Bruno called out, "Arik, heat some water!"

CHAPTER 31

Despite the success of the previous day, a heavy atmosphere lingered in the complex that evening. Tension ran high—Fenna was injured and would need weeks to recover, eight consecrated ones were being guarded in an improvised prison, and the trust in Teto's and Raban's leadership had continued to suffer. The young shadows and old shadows quickly reverted to forming their cliques, and even the allocation of quarters shifted accordingly.

The next morning dawned, and Raban began his usual morning round through the complex.

"EVERYONE UP!" Raban's voice echoed through the stone corridors as it did every morning, though it sounded gruffer than usual. Only in the hallway outside the improvised infirmary did he refrain from waking the injured. He could have sworn he'd heard some grumbling from the young shadows' quarters.

Slowly but steadily, everyone crawled out of bed and made their way to the washrooms and latrines. Occasionally, to their dismay, some shadow-walkers had to wait in line before they could relieve themselves. Raban decided to cancel the morning exercises and instead joined Tialda's group in the common room. The thought crossed his mind that they had been somewhat neglected in the chaos of the past few days.

"Good morning, everyone," he grumbled as he sat down with them. Confused looks and whispers accompanied him at the table. Since they had joined the shadow-walkers, they had mostly taken on roles as providers and craftsmen, feeling quite comfortable in those duties. Nonetheless, they hadn't been spared from the daily exercises, though they endured them without complaint.

"How are you all doing?"

Raban had been the one to first establish contact with Tialda, and thus, with the rest of the group at the table. He was their natural point of trust. Tialda's father was the first to reply.

"Morning, Raban. I think we're doing pretty well, right?" He glanced at his group, who nodded in agreement. "Yeah, we're fine. We've noticed how tense things have been around here the past few days." Tialda's father didn't mince words and got straight to the point. "We've decided to stay out of it as much as possible and just focus on our tasks. If that's alright with you."

This unexpected answer left Raban momentarily perplexed, forcing him to gather his thoughts. The noise in the common room, the scent of various foods, and the diminishing fresh air made this task particularly challenging. But after a minute, Raban managed to focus, and he was sure he had seen a few fleeting grins on the faces of the group.

"No, that's not a problem," Raban rumbled, relief in his voice. "If everything is fine, aside from this… situation, I'm actually glad to hear it. But I do have one question for you." All eyes were on him now, expectant, even pausing their eating.

"Who among you feels ready to start searching for shadowstones?"

Several hands shot up.

At the other end of the common room, Arik was sitting with some young shadows. "How are the wounded?" Alvar asked, his face clouded with concern — like everyone else's. "The first ones should be able to leave the infirmary by tonight, it seems," Arik replied calmly. "Gunda and the old shadow have mostly recovered from the hypothermia, and the others with injuries are improving. One of them seems to have a broken foot, though — he won't be able to walk for quite some time." In his mind, he went over the conditions of those in the infirmary.

"The young shadow from Tarsk with the cut wound will need a few more days… and Fenna…" He lowered his head to the table, staring thoughtfully into his cup, and sighed. "It'll take weeks for her wound to heal. Whoever got her wasn't an amateur. He must have been as strong as she is." His thoughts drifted to memories. "During training at the boarding school, we occasionally saw battle-hardened veterans among the Executors. They easily had four or five uneven oval stones and usually guarded the monasteries…"

Everyone at the table sat with jaws dropped — some, like Hatto, even let their porridge dribble from their mouths. It was the combination of what Arik was saying and how casually he said it that left them speechless. As if it were the most natural thing in the world for him to talk about Executors this way.

"I'd like to know if Raban expected the monastery guards to be ordered into the city. The monasteries are too important for their defenses to be neglected." He looked up and realized why he had been able to speak so undisturbed. Unfazed, he continued: "All administration is run from there, which is why every city has one. And that's also where the Church of Light keeps its knowledge. Haven't you heard this before?"

Everyone shook their heads. It was easy to forget that Arik had been trained as an Extractor for four years. He continued dryly, "I'm glad we managed to capture veterans, though.

They carry special tools that I'll need shortly." A broad, smug grin spread across his face. "Without scrapers and dissection knives, the procedure would have been quite uncomfortable. Mainly for the consecrated ones, that is."

A cold shiver ran down the others' spines, unease spreading among them. Arik's demeanor in that moment was unsettling, something they couldn't quite grasp. It felt much like the incident in the assembly room. Deep down, they sensed that part of Arik's humanity was no longer there. Goosebumps formed on their skin, though they couldn't explain why. With the words, "I have to go now, I'm expected," Arik left the common room without looking back at them.

He stepped into the dim corridor, feeling the cold, damp air envelop him. The sound of his footsteps echoed off the stone walls, accompanied by a soft, cheerful whistling. But his heart beat faster, a strange tingling sensation spread through his fingertips. Something inside him was simmering, an excited flicker that he could barely suppress. His eyes were fixed on the end of the corridor, where the improvised prison lay. As he drew nearer, he saw two guards already stationed at the door. Their tense posture was clear, though Arik's cheerful whistling made the tension fade slightly — only for fear to fill the gap.

They opened the door for him. At first glance, the room looked like any other quarters — just like the one next door where he slept. But this room smelled of sweat, blood, and fear — the prisoners were all injured. Simple, flickering torches hung between the beds on the walls, casting long shadows that turned the faces of the consecrated into eerie half-darkness. A mix of fear and desperation filled the air. The consecrated ones squirmed in their chains, eyes wide with terror as Arik approached.

Teto and Jelto stood in the center of the room, arms crossed, their gazes sharp and unyielding. Before they could speak, Arik took the opportunity for a jab: "Looking around this place, I must say, I've always thought our quarters had a bit of a dungeon feel. Nice to see that confirmed like this."

Teto's palms tensed, and he had to restrain himself from losing control. Arik wore the most insolent grin on his face, as if he had just won a particularly amusing game. Jelto's jaw clenched, his fists balled, and the veins at his temples pulsed visibly.

In a friendly, almost playful tone, Arik continued, "Good to see you both. I always enjoy having an audience." Teto placed a hand on Jelto's shoulder, stopping him from flying off the handle. It was Teto who intended to read Arik the riot act.

"Sit down, Arik!" Teto said quietly, but his voice carried a dangerous undertone, like the cracking of ice under heavy weight. 'Not now,' Teto thought. 'Not here.'

Arik thought briefly, "He's not yelling, he's speaking calmly. That's never a good sign." Teto gestured to the chair at the table between the two pillars in the middle of the room, but Arik waved him off. "I prefer to stand, but I'll need the chair in a minute." He had no intention of bowing to Teto and stared directly into his eyes — then launched his counterattack.

"If you're here to cut me down a notch, save it. I've already told Raban everything that needs saying. I'm here now to extract the stones."

His gaze intensified, and everyone could feel the determination in Arik's voice. A dark aura seemed to emanate from him, though this time, it wasn't from his power-stone. His stare captivated Teto and Jelto, who showed no reaction.

"You wanted me to do this, so I will. You never asked me if I was ready — you just assumed."

The air crackled, and the room suddenly felt cold — this was the calm before the storm. Another piece of shadow peeled away from the lightstone. His eyes turned pitch black, preparing for a conflict.

"That's why I've decided that neither you nor Raban can give me orders anymore." Dust fell from the walls.

He was only moments away from fully unleashing the lightstone. His shadowstone spoke to him in his mind: "I Am Ready. But You Won't Be Able To Hold Out Long Against Them." "I know," Arik confirmed. "But I won't make it easy for them."

"Leave this room immediately. I'd like to get started with your task." They continued staring at each other. For minutes. Teto finally admitted to himself that, no matter what he decided — there was no chance of victory. If he lost Arik, in any way, he would lose more than just a man — he would lose a strategic advantage. Without a word, he stomped out of the room, Jelto following him. His hands shook, ready to destroy an entire district — Jelto would have gladly helped. The door slammed behind them.

Arik walked through the room, looking at all the consecrated ones lying in their beds. Two of them had lost control during the confrontation between Arik and Teto. Their robes were partly wet. One of these was Alexander. Pure fear gripped him as he realized that the familiar voice arguing with Teto had been Arik's.

"Well, well, calm down, will you? You're scaring the others," he said, addressing all the other consecrated ones.

"My dear guests, I apologize for the earlier inconvenience." His voice dripped with mock sincerity; he was savoring the moment. The door opened, and six young shadows entered: Diemo, Romilda, Ostara, Hatto, Bruno, and Alvar. They all looked as though a storm had swept over them.

"Make yourselves comfortable; we'll be starting soon. And if you've just run into Teto, I've just put him in his place."

"We noticed," Alvar commented, and Bruno added, "We just hope the complex is still standing afterward."

"I'm not worried about that," Arik reassured them. "Now, let's get to business. Dear consecrated ones, I'd like to thank you for attending in such large numbers today. Allow me to introduce myself: My name is Arik, and until three months ago, I was a consecrated one just like you."

He let the words sink in, and another consecrated one lost control of his bladder.

"To be precise, I was an Extractor — until the moment Executor Alexander here…" He walked over to Alexander's bed and made a gesture indicating him. "…along with two others, implanted a shadowstone in me. Which is why today, an unlight-walker will be removing your stones. Who would like to go first?"

Pure terror had seized the consecrated ones. They writhed in their beds, trying to plead for mercy through their gags. For the shadow-walkers present, Arik's behavior was something they wouldn't forget anytime soon. But none of them were surprised, as they were all aware of his reasons.

Arik felt the adrenaline rushing through his veins. Every passing second felt like a small eternity. The consecrated ones breathed heavily, their eyes following his every move. Slowly, almost leisurely, Arik turned to Alexander, his footsteps echoing loudly through the room. 'You'll have to look at me first,' he thought, his grin widening.

"Calm down," he said to the other consecrated ones, his voice dripping with false kindness. "We'll begin shortly."

There was no longer any reason not to start with Alexander, as his fear had already reached its peak. Arik swiftly went to the center of the room, grabbed one of the chairs and the small leather set on the table, and sat down next to Alexander's bed.

"Well, aren't you happy to see me again?" It started as a soft chuckle, which quickly grew into a manic laugh. When he regained his composure, he wiped the tears from his eyes. "It's ironic, really. You wanted to kill me, and now I'm the one showing you how it's done correctly." Alexander squirmed, but Arik reached for the scissors in the leather set and cut through his robe from the top down, stopping at chest level.

"Could you come over here and hold him down?" Arik called out to the room. "I don't want the blood to spray everywhere." Another consecrated one soiled their robe, but Arik was too focused on Alexander to notice.

"You're welcome to watch and learn. We have a consecrated one here for each of you," he added, gesturing for them to come closer. They moved hesitantly, fear gripping them as well. His behavior unsettled not only the consecrated ones.

They stood around him, Hatto and Diemo pressing Alexander down. Arik returned the scissors to the leather set and pulled out the finely crafted scalpel. He held it up, watching the torchlight reflect off the blade. His hands didn't tremble, and his breathing was steady.

"You know, Alex, I no longer care why you did it. You're airheads, and I'm doing the world a favor by sending each of you to the afterlife." He felt no more nerves, no more restlessness, no fear, and no hatred — just calm.

For a few moments, he inspected the stone in Alexander's chest. A web of shadow lay over it, suppressing its energies. It was an uneven oval one, just like his own, fused with the skin. There was no gap between the stone and the skin; the transition was seamless. Then, he placed the scalpel at the top of the stone.

"Extractor Arik will now begin the ceremony!" The words escaped him before he could stop them. Over the years, the procedure had been drilled into him, and the Magisters had their ways of ensuring it was permanently ingrained. Arik paused for a moment, realizing what he had just said. He closed his eyes, taking a deep breath until the moment of stagnation passed. The young shadows around him flinched at his words, but they dared not disturb the ceremony.

He pressed the scalpel along the edge of the stone, applying pressure. Blood began to flow, and the white robe gradually turned red. It took a minute to complete the circle. Alexander screamed the entire time, but the gag muffled the sound enough for Arik not to be bothered. With his left hand, Arik reached back into the leather set to retrieve the next tool. To keep the scalpel within reach, he stabbed it into Alexander's thigh. A long, dull groan escaped Alexander. Arik had always regretted that the extraction could only be performed on the living. The Magisters had repeatedly assured him that every Extractor would get used to it in time — a prospect that hadn't made it any easier for Arik back then.

The tool in his hand was called a "scraper." It was most similar to a wooden spoon — except it was metal, its edges were sharp, and it had a deeper curve. "This might pinch a little," he muttered, half-concentrated. He slowly maneuvered the scraper under the stone until the resistance became too strong. He had to repeat the process several times from all sides until the connection was reduced to a thick, tough thread of tissue.

He used the scraper to leverage the stone enough to grip it with his left hand. A sharp tug was all it took to expose the tissue, ready to be severed. In the meantime, Alexander seemed to have lost consciousness. Arik pulled the scalpel from Alexander's thigh, causing blood to flow from the wound. He placed the blade beneath the stone and slowly cut through the remaining tissue.

"See? We're done."

A fleeting glance passed over Alexander's eyes. They all watched as the life drained from them, disappearing entirely once the stone was fully removed. The procedure was over. Arik wiped the knife and scraper on the unstained parts of the robe and returned them to the leather set. Then he held the stone in his hand, watching as the blood gradually beaded and dripped away from it.

Then he stared at Alexander. It was done. He was calm.

Without looking at anyone else, he spoke to the room. His vision blurred as tears began to form. "Have you ever wondered what happened in the assembly room?" It wasn't a question for which he expected an answer. The young shadows around him were puzzled by what Arik was getting at.

"For three months, I worked hard to become a shadow-walker, to be accepted as I am, to leave my time in the Church behind."

A pause followed. His mind was blank as he voiced what had been weighing on him for days.

"And then… they just decided it. They wanted to use me as what I had renounced, what I had wanted to leave behind. Without involving me in the decision."

The last piece of shadow peeled away from his lightstone.

"Even the removal of the power-stone no longer feels right… it was taken from me."

Tears rolled down his cheeks.

Then he brought the lightstone closer to his own. They connected through the linen shirt. His eyes widened, and light burst from his eyes and mouth.

"Now, Little One!"

Arik channeled the energies through his body, directing the shadow toward the light, merging them together. The bright light became unlight and enveloped him. He didn't hear the others' screams. In the unlight, he was undisturbed; they couldn't stop him. He took off his linen shirt.

His eyes were closed; he had all the time in the world. He continued directing the energies, the voice of the shadowstone guiding him. Slowly, the scars extending from his navel began to recede. Moments later, when all the scars had disappeared, the shadowstone sank into Arik. Shortly afterward, the lightstone changed color as it merged with the shadowstone. The unlight faded.

He opened his eyes slowly; he didn't know how much time had passed. Nearly all the fighters had gathered in the room, surrounding him. His gaze sought out Teto; he stared back in disbelief, pointing at Arik's chest. Arik looked down and saw the evenly shaped rod-like stone now embedded there. It was unlight.

Then he looked back at Teto, his eyes filled with unlight as he spoke.

"My life, my body, my decision." The words flew through the room like knives, finding their mark. "And anyone who wants to witness the next extraction can stay; the rest, please leave this room immediately."

CHAPTER 32

The air crackled with tension. Some of the people stepped back, while others stood motionless, seemingly holding their breath. Arik felt the flicker of the Unlight on his skin, the gentle pulsing of energy flowing through his body. The faces around him showed a mixture of fear and fascination. For many, this was a new situation, and they tried to remain calm as long as their leaders did.

For a moment, it felt as though time had stopped. Teto finally relaxed his posture, and slowly, the shadow-walkers began to move. Some left, their gazes unsure, almost shy. Others stepped closer to Arik, curious and eager to see what would happen next.

No one in the room doubted that Arik had full control over his power stone. With the exception of Teto and Jelto, everyone gathered around Arik and the bed of the next Executor, who was next in line. The room became crowded, and Romilda called out, "Move everything to the assembly room and make sure there's enough light." Arik quickly added, "Could someone please bring me a numbing salve? And get the other shadow-walkers — Lioba will definitely want to see what's happening."

The two leaders, along with Raban, stood motionless, unable to fully grasp what was going on. Shadow-walkers scurried about, moving between rooms as Arik gathered his tools and walked directly toward Jelto, who stood there with a stony expression. His eyes were dark and watchful, always scanning for threats or weaknesses. In this situation, he saw Arik as a threat, someone with the power to break the bond between him and his group.

"Jelto?"

"Arik?"

Both knew this wasn't a conversation — it was more like a battle. The air crackled, as if lightning could strike at any moment. Arik smiled slyly, knowing his goal wasn't to defeat Jelto, but to win him over.

"I imagine you've also seen loved ones and comrades have their stones removed," Arik said calmly, with no trace of sarcasm or cynicism. Jelto thought to himself, "What is he trying to say?"

"There are still a few leather kits over there. Feel free to take one, and I'll show you how it's done." Jelto couldn't detect any ulterior motive in Arik's offer. It was genuine. Then, Arik walked past him and left the room. Jelto stood frozen for several minutes, staring at the ground as memories played in his mind. A single tear, reflecting years of unspoken pain and loss, slid slowly down his cheek. Slowly, he stepped toward the table and gathered the remaining leather kits. Raban and Teto followed him in silence.

In the next room, nearly all the shadow-walkers from the complex had gathered. Arik was preparing the next consecrated one, who yawned as the numbing salve quickly took effect. He lay on the bed, his robe already removed, and his four stones exposed for everyone to see.

A bench was placed on the other side of the bed. Arik invited Jelto and Lioba to sit down. "Glad you could join us. Please, take a seat. Anyone else want to join?" Several shadow-walkers, both young and old, from Aregelia and Tarsk, raised their hands. Bruno gestured toward a particular old shadow from Tarsk, who had helped him with Fenna's injury. Arik looked around and saw Ostara had raised her hand as well.

"You there," he said, pointing to the Tarsker, who responded in a high voice, "You can call me Giso." "Giso, come on over, and you too, Ostara." After waiting for them to sit next to Jelto and Lioba, he continued, "If we capture more consecrated ones, more of you will get to practice, but for today, these four will do."

The others who had raised their hands lowered them again. A low murmur filled the room, with some sounding disappointed at not being chosen, while others were surprised and skeptical that Arik was even willing to teach this secret procedure. "If I could ask for some quiet…" Arik said cautiously, but his voice didn't cut through the noise. So, for this reason, someone yelled, "QUIET, DAMMIT!"

It was Raban, standing near the entrance with his arms crossed, watching the events unfold with growing contemplation. Over the past few days, he had often tried to process everything that had happened and question his own decisions — an unfamiliar and uncomfortable exercise for someone who rarely doubted himself. The moment Arik made the offer to Jelto, Raban understood the significance. Now, seeing the four shadow-walkers sitting in front of the bed, he felt validated. Arik was — whether knowingly or not — creating a shared experience, one that transcended previous group divisions and helped forge a common identity.

Raban had made up his mind: he would help Teto come to the same conclusion so they could both support Arik in fostering a sense of unity. Hope began to rise within him — the hope that the fractures within the group could be healed — and he was ready to hand over leadership to the younger generation and apologize to Arik.

As Arik set the scalpel to the skin, a soft, metallic sound echoed through the stone walls. The smell of blood and cold sweat hung heavy in the room, mixed with the bitter scent of the numbing salve. Dozens of eyes were on him. Raban and Teto exchanged glances, as if silently communicating. Arik proceeded methodically, pausing frequently to explain each step. Ten minutes later, he had removed the first power stone and placed it in a bowl of clear liquid normally used by the healers to clean wounds.

Next, he handed the scalpel to Lioba. Her decades of experience as a healer showed as she expertly handled the scalpel. To everyone's amazement, she worked quickly while maintaining her usual caring demeanor — something she only did when she was completely confident in what she was doing. Eight minutes later, she had successfully removed the stone and placed it in the bowl.

Giso was up next. Some shadow-walkers noticed how Lioba tried to discreetly observe him. Giso seemed to have an exceptional talent with the scalpel, perhaps even surpassing Lioba. Her face showed curiosity and admiration as she watched his steady hand, making precise cuts with every move. At one point, he noticed her gaze and looked directly into her eyes. It was the first time the shadow-walkers had ever seen Lioba blush without blood being involved.

Ostara and Jelto hesitated over who should handle the next stone. Why Jelto let Ostara go first was unclear, but no one had the inclination to question it. With trembling hands, she tried to make the first cut but couldn't bring herself to do it. Arik called Bruno over. "Ostara, is it alright if Bruno guides your hand?" she nodded shyly, and Bruno stepped behind her.

Ostara felt Bruno's cool hand on hers. The trembling in her fingers lessened, but her heartbeat remained irregular, pounding wildly in her chest. His firm grip steadied her, but her knees still felt weak, as if they might give way at any moment. She felt uncomfortable performing the procedure in front of so many people.

Together, they took fifteen minutes to remove the power stone from the shoulder. When they finally succeeded, she lifted her head. Arik and the others smiled at her, offering pride and encouragement. She tried to fight it, but the emotion was too strong, and tears welled up. They were tears of relief and release. To shift attention away from her and give her a moment to collect herself, Arik signaled to Bruno, who gently led Ostara out of the room.

They had now removed the last power stone from this consecrated one. His eyes were already closed as he took his final breath. "You three, come with me, we need to prepare the next one," Arik said to the trio he had instructed. Together, they returned to the adjoining room. Arik selected the next consecrated one, applying numbing salve to his neck and face. "Jelto, Giso, can you help carry him?"

They lifted the bed, sweat beading on their foreheads. Lioba and Arik assisted where they could, grabbing the sides of the bed to help. "Did the Church starve all of you like this?" Lioba teased. "He's as skinny as the last one." "We're lucky the patrol didn't consist of Magisters," Arik responded playfully. "Otherwise, we'd need two more people in here." They nearly dropped the bed as they couldn't stifle their laughter. Even Jelto, uncharacteristically, cracked a smile.

Back in the assembly room, they prepared the next consecrated one further. First, they undressed him, then counted his power stones — he had three in total. "So, Jelto, does any stone catch your eye?" Arik asked, handing him a leather kit. Jelto felt the heat rise in his face as he took the scalpel in hand. His fingers trembled slightly, but he forced himself to grip the blade steadily.

Breathing calmly, his hands no longer shaking, Jelto began the first incision. He was skilled with many weapons, and he treated the scalpel as such. It wasn't pretty, but Jelto did well and completed the task just as quickly as Ostara had. A fifth stone was placed in the bowl, and Jelto sat on the bench, frozen — only his lips trembled slightly, and he clenched his teeth to hold back the rising emotions.

A single tear ran down his cheek, a rare display of emotion. The shadow-walkers from Tarsk stood in stunned silence, unable to believe what they were witnessing. In all the years they had known him, their leader had never shown this kind of emotion. Giso wrapped an arm around Jelto's shoulders, clearly struggling to maintain his own composure. "Lioba, could you handle the other two?" Arik asked the old healer. "Of course. But do you have to stick around?" she responded in her usual strict tone but gave him a wink, understanding what was on his mind. "I just want to make sure you don't make any mistakes," Arik replied with a grin, adding, "Jelto, Giso, feel free to stretch your legs in the meantime."

Silently, both stood up and left the room, followed by a few old shadows from Tarsk.

It took some time, but Ostara, Jelto, and Giso returned and removed the next power stones. Arik continued to prepare the consecrated ones, helping here and there — often with Bruno's assistance — with the removal process. Every shadow-walker stayed until the very end, occasionally checking in the infirmary to ensure everything was in order.

That day, they removed a total of twenty-one irregularly oval shaped power stones. Arik was the one who gathered them all.

He had a basket brought to him, carefully placed the stones inside, and then stepped toward Teto. An unspoken truce hung in the air as he spoke: "Here, you have your power stones." His voice was neutral, devoid of hostility. "May I offer you some advice?" he added.

A wave of skepticism crossed Teto's face, his eyebrows furrowing as he weighed Arik's words. "Advice?" he repeated slowly, as though examining each word carefully.

"You might have noticed that all the stones are of the same quality — and that's no coincidence. The Church has found a way to ensure this," Arik explained calmly. Jelto, who had noticed Arik approaching Teto, felt something important was about to happen and stepped closer to listen.

"Why are you telling me this?" Teto asked, his voice guarded. "Each monastery should possess the same knowledge — the same goes the one near the city. If you wait a bit before distributing the stones, I can infiltrate the monastery and retrieve the scroll," Arik explained. "Some of the consecrated ones from the monastery have already been called to assist the patrols. We can use that to our advantage."

Jelto stepped closer, glancing briefly at Arik as if trying to gauge his reaction. "If we place the bodies of the prisoners in the marketplace, we could provoke the Church into withdrawing even more consecrated ones — both from the monastery and from Sydrik," he suggested in a calm tone. This was his way of showing Arik that he had earned his respect and that he supported the plan. "We'll need more people to handle the supply routes, which means pulling some of our forces here. What do you think, Teto?"

Teto nodded slowly. "I trust your experience, Jelto. We should also send ravens to the other cities, reporting that we've captured the stones. That should be convincing enough to get them to send us reinforcements." He took a deep breath, as though he had come to a difficult decision, and finally turned back to Arik.

"Arik, if you're really going to do this, then let me stand by your side."

CHAPTER 33

None of the shadow-walkers expected the rifts that had formed to heal instantly. Trust needed to be rebuilt, and such an endeavor required time — but the first bridge had been constructed, and more were being built. One of these bridges was the cooperation between Lioba and Giso. Together, they ran the infirmary like a well-oiled machine, spending — much to Fenna's dismay — far too much time in mutual admiration. To both of their surprise, they managed to initiate a lively exchange on healing arts and other matters.

"If they keep this up, I'll voluntarily walk into another patrol," Fenna said in frustration as Arik and Bruno sat down beside her bed to apply a fresh layer of healing ointment. Arik began by removing the previous day's ointment and asked absentmindedly, "As a golem or in your current form?"

"The latter is definitely an option," Fenna replied, "or I could just ask you to remove my stones."

"You wouldn't want that," Arik responded, taking the herb-scented healing salve from Bruno and applying it to Fenna's wound. "Once I've restrained you, I'll let Lioba and Giso handle the rest. Without anesthesia, in case you were wondering."

Fenna rolled her eyes in disbelief. "How bad is it?" she asked Arik and Bruno. Bruno answered, "So far, no sign of infection, and the stitches are holding." He smiled at her and continued, "You won't be ready for the morning exercises anytime soon, but with a little help, you should be able to move around the complex. If you're feeling up to it, you can even sleep in your own room again."

Fenna didn't need time to think about this. "Arik, will you take me there?" she asked sweetly, allowing him to help her up. "Believe me, I'm looking forward to a room without the constant smell of herbs."

Bruno hurried to a corner of the infirmary and returned with a staff. "Alvar made this for you," he said proudly, presenting her with a finely decorated oak staff, carved with a notch at chest height. The staff was slightly taller than Fenna, but it fit perfectly in her hand. Fenna pulled herself up with effort, her fingers gripping the staff tightly. Then, without a glance back, she dashed out of the room at a surprising speed, as if she were escaping.

Both shadow-walkers kept an eye on her, but they couldn't quite recall how Fenna had gone from the bed to the door so quickly. Hastily, they followed her and caught up halfway. "Arik, did you give her the wrong salve?" Bruno's words sounded slightly breathless as they nearly had to sprint to keep up with Fenna. Arik answered in the same tone, "Not that I know of. It's the same stuff as yesterday." They managed to escort her the rest of the way — and within minutes, they found themselves back in her quarters.

Relieved, Fenna collapsed onto her bed, closed her eyes, and savored the moment. Arik closed the door behind them; as if on cue, Fenna's voice shot through the room: "What do you think — when will Teto give his blessing for Arik to begin the infiltration of the monastery? And why does he have to be involved at all?" Her disapproval was unmistakable.

Bruno took the firestones and lit one of the room's torches. It had become second nature for them to rely on their night vision in the dark, so it rarely bothered them when they entered an unlit room.

"For one thing, he's a good fighter, and having him around when I stir up the hornet's nest definitely won't hurt me," Arik explained to Fenna. "And for another, it helps us become a community again. Not the same one we were before, but a new one that fits the current situation." Their eyes met, locking in an intense stare. Arik heard Bruno draw a breath as if to say something. His index finger shot up, making it clear Bruno should hold his tongue.

Frustration built up in his mind, so Arik decided to vent it through his words. "You know, I'm only 17, and in the past few days, I've felt like I'm the only adult in this entire complex. It's like I'm standing on the shoulders of a giant, forced to fix the mistakes and stupid decisions of those who are supposed to know what they're doing." Arik tried to calm his pulse, knowing that if he didn't, he'd have trouble with his unlightstone. Unlike his shadowstone, he found it much harder to control. He also waited for the moment when he could communicate with it again.

"I'm not saying everything has to go back to the way it was, but please — just swallow your pride, Fenna. And if you need an apology or whatever from someone, then talk to them." He closed his eyes and slowed his breathing. This matter was upsetting him too much. "There are so many other things I'd rather focus on… maybe even someone special I'd like to get to know better."

Sensing an opportunity, Bruno jumped in: "And that would be Gunda…" The name was delivered with perfect timing, so Arik couldn't react quickly enough. "Exactly, Gunda." The moment the name left his mouth, Arik realized he'd slipped. 'Damn,' he thought, 'did Hatto tell the others?' Trying to play it cool, he steered the conversation back under control. "Save your comments — this stays in the room."

As Fenna and Bruno grinned like cats with cream and he heard the stifled giggles that undermined his authority, he suddenly felt a soft but noticeable touch on his back. A chill ran down his spine, but he forced himself to remain composed. His eyes instinctively closed, and he sent a wave of his shadowstone energy through the room. Two seconds later, a clear image of the room formed in his mind, everything inside clearly visible in his inner vision. Someone had snuck into the room and was hiding in the shadow realm. Since there was no immediate threat from this presence, Arik decided to keep the secret to himself.

"Arik… alright," Fenna conceded. "You… probably aren't wrong. I'll handle it myself — and sooner rather than later." She looked down, slightly ashamed. "But please take Diemo, Romilda, and Ostara with you. And Giso, just in case." Arik nodded in agreement. "Don't take it personally, but I'd like to enjoy some peace and quiet now." They said their goodbyes and left the room.

Arik left the door open a moment longer than necessary, his gaze fixed on it to hide the fact that his eyes had turned completely black. "You go on ahead. I have something to take care of," he said, keeping his head positioned so Bruno couldn't see his eyes. His fingers trembled slightly, and a surge of nervousness shot through him, but he forced himself to stay calm and not let it show.

Everyone in the complex had their duties — and though Arik worked hard to foster group unity, he still wanted to keep some freedoms for himself. One of those freedoms was that not everyone needed to know where he was or what he was doing at all times. After closing the door, Arik sent another wave of energy to get a picture of the hallway.

"I get it, just don't use all the leaves again and leave some for the rest of us," Bruno replied dryly, giving him a wink before heading back toward the infirmary. His footsteps gradually grew quieter, fading into the general background noise of the complex's bustling activity. Then Arik slipped into the shadow world.

"Is this your first time?" His voice was calm, though he still couldn't see who was hiding in this realm. When no answer came, he turned around to survey the hallway. Standing in the middle of the hall was Gunda — and even in this shadowy dimension, her face blushed bright red, contrasting sharply with the dark surroundings. She stared at the ground, clearly nervous about what might happen next.

Arik was secretly grateful that he'd recently learned how to mask his own nervousness and project confidence — even though his heart was pounding in his chest, and he wished he could disappear. Ignoring his nerves, he said, "Come with me."

They turned left into one of the main corridors and followed it until they had to turn right. Sounds of strenuous work echoed from the workshop nine meters ahead — Alvar had left the door open and seemed to be planing an especially tough piece of wood. Arik and Gunda exchanged puzzled glances and wordlessly decided to ignore it. Just before the workshop was one of the armories. Since the hallway was empty, Arik led Gunda inside and closed the door behind them.

The armory was dimly lit and smelled strongly of leather, cold iron, and the sour remnants of sweat, which the ventilation system hadn't yet cleared from the air. They remained in the shadow realm, saying nothing. Arik's heart raced wildly, and it felt like an eternity had passed. "This is only the second time I've done this," Gunda whispered so quietly that Arik had to strain to hear her. "It... it... I'm sorry. Are you mad at me?"

He stood directly in front of her, and their eyes met. She nervously played with her long, curly brown hair that tumbled over her shoulders, slightly wild. Her anxiety was palpable, now that he had caught her, and she hoped he wouldn't push her away. "No," Arik finally said. "We're both not exactly great at this, are we?"

He then stepped closer to her, his eyes locked on hers. As they stood close, the difference in height became apparent — her head barely reached his chin. When he placed his right hand around her, she smiled, though shyly. Unsure of what was appropriate in this moment, Arik decided to take a chance and kissed her.

CHAPTER 34

In the early afternoon, Arik was in the large training room. It had become routine for him to practice combat techniques and train his powers daily with Romilda and Diemo. Ostara, Gunda, and Hatto were also in the room, all busy fighting one-on-one duels. With a skilled strike, Diemo managed to hit Arik at an unprotected spot with his staff, knocking him off balance. He then followed up with a blow aimed at Arik's legs. Arik couldn't recover in time and was swept off his feet. The impact was hard, but nothing he hadn't been through many times before.

"Concentrate, Arik. What's going on with you today?" Diemo asked, irritated, his voice sharp. "Is something distracting you or what?" Gunda blushed, and her opponent, Romilda, noticed immediately, grinning slyly as she quickly pieced together what was happening. Panicked, Gunda pressed her finger to her lips, silently pleading with Romilda not to tell anyone. Romilda giggled quietly, mischief written all over her face. "I'd like to know too," she teased in a low voice, "Care to enlighten us?" Like Gunda and Romilda, Ostara and Hatto stopped their fighting and turned their attention to Arik, who was still lying on the floor.

Closing his eyes, Arik disappeared into the unlight realm, instantly getting back on his feet. With his combat staff in hand, he silently sprinted behind Diemo, preparing to strike. Two meters from him, he reappeared, ready to attack. Their staffs clashed, the sound of their collision echoing through the training room. Diemo had anticipated that Arik would try this and was able to block the strike in time. "That's none of your business," Arik hissed through clenched teeth. In Hatto's mind, the pieces began to fall into place, and he burst out laughing.

Between fits of laughter, Hatto managed to speak. "Oh, come on… there's nothing… to be ashamed of…" Ostara looked at Hatto, confused, and he gestured toward Gunda with his eyes. "We're just… happy for you…" After those words, he gasped for air and continued laughing. Only Diemo seemed oblivious to what was going on. "Can someone please explain what's happening?" A hint of uncertainty and frustration crept into his voice. Before it could take over, Romilda came to his rescue: "Diemo, sweetheart, it seems Arik, like you, has someone he really cares about." She playfully nudged him and kissed his cheek.

"That's no reason to be distracted. Can I ask who it is?" The loud laughter that filled the room after his question baffled him. Even Arik couldn't help but laugh, and Gunda blushed even deeper. Romilda nudged Diemo again. "Oh, darling, I'll tell you later."

The door opened. The wood creaked softly before the door handle hit the stone wall with a loud thud. Teto and Giso entered; the latter quietly closed the door behind them. They looked serious, and the lighthearted atmosphere in the training room came to an abrupt end. Everyone in the room focused on their leader, their expressions filled with curiosity and uncertainty. "Good, you're all here, saves me from searching for you," Teto began without preamble. "This doesn't directly concern all of you, but that doesn't matter right now."

"Sit down. We have a lot to discuss. Please," Teto instructed them, waiting until everyone had taken a seat. Three wooden benches were arranged in a circle, so everyone could see each other. Gunda sat down next to Arik and leaned against him.

Arik returned her affection, putting his arm around her. He was slightly surprised that she showed her affection so openly, as she was usually more reserved.

Curious, Teto asked, "Did I say something funny, or why are some of you grinning?"

"No, Teto," Romilda replied, "It's not you. Please, continue." Teto shook off his momentary uncertainty and refocused. "To put it bluntly: the situation has changed. We're infiltrating the monastery tonight." They listened intently, eager to hear what had led him to this decision.

"After we left the bodies of the consecrated ones at the marketplace, two things happened. First: as far as we can tell, 40 consecrated ones were pulled from Sydrik and stationed here in Aregelia. Another eight consecrated ones from the monastery were assigned to the city guard." He paused briefly to ensure they were all following. "This morning, three carts, four soldiers, and eight consecrated ones set off south from Aregelia. Our squad, lying in wait behind the first village, ambushed them. We've sustained some injuries, some severe."

Arik and the others held their breath. The raid on the patrol had already come at a cost, and they hoped this time there would only be injuries. Gunda put her arm around Arik and pulled him close. Most of those in the squad were from Tarsk. Seeing their concerned looks, Teto tried to reassure them. "I've already sent Lioba, Bruno, and a few others to take care of them and bring all the injured here."

Not everyone relaxed, but Teto moved on to the more positive news. "The squad was successful. They captured three carts of supplies and took eight consecrated ones as prisoners. They'll be brought here under the cover of darkness. Arik?"

"Yes?" Arik responded with a raised eyebrow.

"How many consecrated ones are typically housed in a monastery?" Teto continued, and Arik began to suspect where this was going.

"Whenever I had the chance in the past four years, I tried to count. There were always around 20 Executors, a handful of Extractors and Explorers, and about five or six Magisters." Arik looked at Teto questioningly and continued his train of thought, assuming he was on the right track: "There should be about 15 people left in the monastery. The Magisters pose the greatest threat. From the hill near the monastery, we should be able to assess the situation a bit."

Clearly impressed, Teto confirmed, "Yes, that's exactly what I was getting at. Thanks for already figuring it out. It won't get any better than tonight — especially since they'll be focused on the southern part of the city." Taking a deep breath, he continued, "Jelto left the soldiers alive. If they act as he expects, they'll return to Aregelia and report the attack to their superiors."

"Tonight's mission will be different from the recent raid. Arik, you'll have to infiltrate the monastery alone. We'll stay outside and create a distraction." Teto was nearing the conclusion of his explanation. "We wouldn't be of much help to you inside — you're the only one who knows the place." He paused briefly again, seeming to struggle with something that was clearly uncomfortable for him. "After consulting with Fenna, it's best if a few shadow-walkers accompany us. She might have already mentioned this to you." Arik nodded. "Diemo, Romilda, Ostara, and Giso will be the ones. We'll set off tonight and meet in the common room. Is that okay with everyone?" No one objected; they all nodded. "Alright, see you tonight, and try not to get into too much trouble."

At that point, they ended the training as Giso asked them to help prepare the infirmary. Bandages needed to be rolled, salves mixed, and water heated on the fire to sterilize scalpels and needles. They bustled around eagerly, noticing Teto directing several supply workers and fighters to the south tunnel to assist those returning.

Then came the moment when screams echoed from the tunnel, and panic filled the complex. Four shadow-walkers were unable to walk, and three others made it only with the help of their comrades. They were all in bad shape, but Lioba and the other healers had already brought the worst injuries under control in the harshest conditions. They were quickly taken to the infirmary to prevent hypothermia.

The fighters who only had scratches or were unharmed were taken to their quarters to warm up. Busy suppliers brought hot root soup and tea, and even some extra blankets were fetched from storage. Everyone in the complex helped where they could, but those who caught a glimpse of the wounds quickly realized that four of the fighters would be out of action for the coming weeks and months.

Gunda, in particular, was deeply affected by seeing the people she had grown close to over the years in such a state. She stood motionless in the middle of the infirmary, her gaze blurring. Her friends screamed in pain as Giso, Lioba, Bruno, and Arik did their best with scalpels and needles. After Arik had finished stitching up one of the lighter wounds, he noticed Gunda. "She needs to get out of here," the thought forced its way into his mind. Through the chaos, he saw the dark, messy hair falling into someone's forehead. "Alvar!" Arik shouted across the room.

He quickly made his way to Gunda, sensing that something inside her was on the verge of breaking. He pulled her into an embrace; her breathing was shallow and rapid as tears ran down her cheeks in thick drops. Her gaze was vacant, as though she no longer perceived the world around her. By now, Alvar stood beside him, understanding the situation. "Don't worry, I'll take her to the common room and stay with her." Arik escorted the two out of the room and gave Gunda a desperate kiss on her forehead. There was no time for grand gestures; all he could do was silently urge her, "Please fight it… fight, please!" For these were the moments when a powerstone bearer could lose control — and the stone would take over.

Back in the infirmary, Arik immediately jumped in to help Bruno, who was in the process of relocating a shadow-walker's dislocated shoulder. A loud pop was followed by a sharp scream, and then it was over. In the midst of the chaos, Jelto and Gunder suddenly appeared in the room. "Get in line, Jelto," Giso called over to him, visibly stressed, "we're still up to our necks here." "It's nothing major. It takes more than a handful of consecrated ones and soldiers to take me down," Jelto laughed heartily. "I just want to make sure my guys and girls are okay. They fought really well. You should've seen what Gunder here pulled off, right Gunder?" Jelto gave Gunder a hearty slap on the back.

Gunder collapsed.

Everyone looked up, and for a moment, there was silence. Then chaos erupted again. Diemo rushed over and, together with Jelto, lifted Gunder onto the last available bed. They took off his robe, revealing large bruises in shades of violet and green spreading across his ribs and shoulders. "I was already wondering how he managed to handle all of that," Jelto admitted, now visibly shaken by the sight. "He took on two consecrated ones by himself. With badges on their shoulders. Right before they were about to wipe the floor with our weaker fighters."

"Arik, Bruno, take over immediately!" Giso ordered, grabbing a fresh scalpel and rushing over to Gunder. "This is bad. I need a bowl and the numbing salve. Now!" He leaned over Gunder, who had lost consciousness. "We'll patch you up," Giso muttered reassuringly to himself. His hands were steady, as were his heart and breath. To bolster his courage, he thought, "Fifteen years ago, you saw this more often. This is no different. Damn Paladins." He then made the first cut with the scalpel.

At some point — no one could say exactly when — things had calmed down again. Like the others, Arik headed to the washroom to clean himself. Blood and sweat clung to him everywhere. At first, he kept his linen shirt on; he hadn't thought to take it off before pouring water over himself. The cold water cut through the fatigue, clearing his mind for a moment, but the dirt and blood clung stubbornly to his skin, refusing to wash away. He quickly finished and hurried to the common room.

A warm, stuffy air greeted him. He looked for Alvar and Gunda but only found the former sitting with Diemo and Romilda. He hadn't gotten far when Romilda spotted him, stood up, and approached him with a plate in hand. "Come with me," she said as kindly as possible. Together, they walked a short distance until they reached the quarters of the junior officers. The day had clearly taken its toll on her, Arik thought as he glanced at Romilda's face. "She's in my room. We managed to calm her down and then put her to bed."

"She'll be alright," she said to him, trying to smile, though she failed. Her lips trembled. Word had spread that Gunder had collapsed. Many were shaken, and morale had taken a hit.

"Gunder will be alright too. Giso has already saved our second leader," Arik said, sounding exhausted, his reserves of optimism nearly depleted. "But it will take time."

"I know," Romilda admitted quietly, then handed him the plate. "Please eat something and then get some rest." She opened the door for him. "You can sleep here. We'll wake you later."

With a "Thanks for everything," Arik entered Romilda's room. It was dark, but he adjusted his eyes. Gunda seemed to be fast asleep. He ate a few dried fruits and some of the bread he had been given. Finally, he lay down beside Gunda on the bed and fell asleep immediately.

Late that evening, there was a knock on the door. "Arik, wake up!" Teto shouted from outside. Groggy, Arik took a moment to wake up fully and realize that he was staring into Gunda's hazel eyes. Weak torchlight crept in from under the door. She had snuggled up to him, their noses almost touching. As he felt her closeness, the rest of the world seemed to disappear. Her warmth and the gentle rise and fall of her chest calmed him. She radiated joy that he was here with her and kissed him.

"Please, Arik, don't go. Stay here."

"I'll be back, I promise."

CHAPTER 35

The sky was clear, the air icy, and the snow under their boots crunched loudly in the still night. The wind had completely died down, and among the bare, barely swaying branches of the trees lining the road, the stars glittered. Only the moonlight illuminated their path, casting long, distorted shadows across the trail. The northern trade road lay deserted, and the gates of Aregelia had long been closed. They had, however, left the city effortlessly. Not a word had been spoken between them.

"We still have seven kilometers ahead of us, so let's pick up the pace," Teto finally said, pulling his coat tighter around himself. The cold bit sharply at the air, and their breath turned into small clouds of mist before their faces. "Any questions about the plan?"

Arik was the first to respond. "Just before the monastery, we'll go up the hill, Diemo helps me get inside, and you distract the guards while I head to the library. We'll meet back at the hill." His voice sounded tired, as though he'd repeated the plan too many times.

"And if something goes wrong?" Teto pressed on. His voice was stern but calm — he knew that every little mistake could cost them their lives.

"Then we flee into the woods and later return to the hill. We've been over this ten times already…" Arik replied, irritated, rubbing the back of his neck. The tension weighed heavily on him.

"If necessary, we'll go over it a hundred times," Teto interrupted sharply. "Also, remember where we're hiding the provisions. Otherwise, we'll have another problem later. Understood?"

"Yes, Teto," came the unified response from Diemo, Romilda, Ostara, Arik, and Giso.

The rest of the journey continued in silent step. Each was lost in their own thoughts, focused on what was to come. Even as they passed the village where Arik had grown up, not a word was spoken. For Arik, it had been a long time since he had called this place "his" village. His parents were dead, his sister had disappeared after her consecration, and no one in the village had wanted him or Bero back at the time.

The latter was the main reason why, over four years ago, they had stayed at the boarding school and become consecrated ones. Everything that had happened since — the suffering, the battles, the loss — could have been avoided if they had returned to the village back then. But there was nothing he could change now. That thought had become colder to him than the winter air surrounding him. The last tie had been severed when Bero had the misfortune of meeting Teto.

Now, this place meant nothing to him. It was just a shadow of his past, and even that shadow was fading. "Maybe..." a quiet thought tiptoed through his mind, "... we could burn down one of the huts on the way back to warm up."

Shortly after leaving the village, the wind and snow set in — like an icy messenger warning them to turn back. The wind whipped at their faces, the snow thickened, and visibility diminished. They pushed against it, now struggling to move forward. Teto shouted something into the wind: "Gather around me!" They obeyed, moving closer together.

Standing tightly together, Teto focused for a moment, directing the energies within his body to the right places. A dome of shadows suddenly spread out from him, enveloping all six shadow-walkers. It wasn't as large as the one he had used when fighting Arik, but that wasn't necessary — as long as it kept out the wind and snow. Giso whistled in admiration. "A shadow dome. It's been a while since I've seen that technique. You don't happen to have a firestone to warm us up as well, do you?"

Teto couldn't help but grin; the thought was understandable. "Just rub your hands together faster, Giso," he teased back.

For half an hour, Teto maintained the shadow dome, allowing the group to reach the turnoff toward the monastery. Breathing heavily, he finally said, "If I'm going to be of any use later, I'll have to drop it now." He dissolved the shadow dome, and immediately the wind and snow lashed at them again. But now it came from the side, affecting them less. Teto pulled out a few dried fruits from his provision pouch and ate them to keep up his strength.

After another kilometer, they reached the forest, which sheltered them from the howling wind and allowed them to move faster. In the distance, through the trees, they saw the lights — it lay still, almost lurking, before them. Their target was near. They climbed the hill. Only about 200 meters separated them from the monastery. "There's a spring over there," Arik said, pointing west. "We should refill our water skins." He then led them to the water.

Between a few stones, a stream trickled down the northern slope of the hill, passing the monastery before curving westward. The basin from which the water flowed was large enough to dip their skins in, but the water was icy, and their hands froze. Still, they were fortunate it hadn't frozen over yet. They also decided to stash their provisions near a nearby tree, making it easier to find later.

"Alright," Teto finally concluded, sifting through his thoughts. "Let's get started. If my memory serves me right, the right side is where the old training camp was." He pointed toward the lights visible through the trees to their right. There was no need to be particularly quiet, as they were far enough from the monastery, and no patrols were expected. "You mean where the stables are?" Arik asked.

"Exactly. Over there are the stables, the forge, and the washhouse. Everything's still the same as when I was here," Teto continued. "But the buildings on the other side... I didn't know those. They must be new."

"That's where the library and the 'training rooms' are located," Arik added, a sense of unease creeping in at the memory. "The building seemed new to me too, but like the rest of the complex, there's a two-meter-high wall around it."

"Diemo, you'll go with Arik and make sure the wall isn't a problem," Teto's voice was calm but razor-sharp — the tone of a leader who brooked no disagreement. He had thought through the plan precisely, and any deviation could be deadly. Diemo and Arik nodded, fully aware of their task.

Then Teto addressed the next shadow-walker: "Ostara?"

"I know, I'll be up in the trees again." Her response seemed slightly irritated, as her abilities often relegated her to the role of a scout — but to her surprise, today was different.

"You'll fly over the monastery, create a distraction from the other side, and give the signal when it's time." Teto grinned broadly. "Then you can get back to the trees. But please, fly in a wide arc toward the hill."

Ostara couldn't suppress a wide grin, her hands nervously fidgeting with her belt as she realized the weight of her new role. "Alright, I'll do it," she said, her voice trembling slightly, filled with both excitement and tension. Her eyes sparkled with anticipation, though her breath carried a hint of anxiety. Teto then continued with the final assignments.

"Giso, you stay up here." The wind howled softly through the trees. "If any consecrated ones come up the hill, ambush them. Stay silent, stay invisible. And if they see you…" Teto's gaze bore into Giso. "Send them to the other side." Giso nodded, his eyes fixed on the monastery. Direct confrontations weren't his strength — but he had plenty of experience with ambushes, and he was grateful for this assignment.

"Romilda, you're with me. We'll head to the gatehouse." This was the last assignment, and Teto felt the need to clarify something. "And please avoid introducing me as your father again. Last time, that almost went south." Everyone present heard Romilda giggle quietly. Seeing the curious looks directed at him, Teto added, "She pulled that stunt on the way to Tarsk with four consecrated ones and nearly threw me off my game. Now, move out!"

Their paths diverged, and Arik led Diemo down the slope to the northwest. Back then, he had spent a lot of time in these woods, as Thomas, Michael, and Alexander couldn't find him here when they were on monastery duty. He knew the hidden paths and always managed to outmaneuver them; once, he had nearly succeeded in losing them in the forest.

It only took a few minutes for them to reach the wall. Both shifted into the shadow realm, and Arik gathered energy in his legs. After his stone had briefly taken control two months ago, Arik realized that the jumping technique he had used then was something he still needed to master. He shot upwards, stopping just as he could glimpse part of the courtyard over the wall.

The monastery's parade ground, which lay before the new main building, was snow-covered and empty. Not even old footprints were visible. There wasn't a soul in sight. Arik doubted Teto's plan. Wouldn't it be better to avoid any commotion and sneak into the monastery unnoticed? But he admitted it was too late for such thoughts, and now they could only wait for Ostara's signal. What signal was Ostara even supposed to give?

Minutes passed. The wind howled through the trees, cutting through any stillness that dared to settle. Only the hooting of owls provided a brief respite for the two waiting figures. Then it came—a sound that froze the blood in their veins. High-pitched and shrill, it echoed over the treetops and across the monastery. Startled, Arik looked down at Diemo. "Was that...?" He didn't dare finish the sentence.

"Yes, that was Ostara," Diemo confirmed, and some color drained from Arik's face.

"Well, here we go." Diemo stood before the wall, moving his fingers like a puppeteer. A portal opened before him, and he stepped through. Arik, still perched on his stilts, shot upwards again, leapt over the slanted wall's bricks, and landed next to the portal's exit and Diemo. They exchanged a glance.

"I'll need your portal again soon, so don't be upset that I just jumped," Arik began to explain. "But first, we need to get to that vegetable garden over there." They sprinted off, leaving deep footprints in the snow.

It was about 100 meters they had to run. The snow slowed them down considerably, but after 15 seconds, they reached the edge of the vegetable garden. In the distance, from Ostara's location, came sounds. The sharp crack of wood splitting broke the silence, followed by a long, ominous creak.

Seconds later, a dull thud echoed through the trees, accompanied by the shattering sound of tiles breaking.

Arik blinked in disbelief and turned to Diemo. 'That... that wasn't a tree, was it?' His voice betrayed that he had a hard time imagining anything else. "Sounded like it." Diemo's response was dry, showing that he wasn't surprised. "When it matters, she rarely does things halfway."

Noise was now also coming from the direction of the gatehouse. Windows shattered; the dull thud of projectiles striking clay, mortar, and massive stones reverberated. The first voices rose in the courtyard, sounding disoriented, half-asleep. Amid the confusion, one voice stood out — commanding, authoritative, uncompromising. A voice that could organize a henhouse in under a minute. Because it could — and because it had plenty of practice. Magister Helder.

"Magister Helder is here." A shiver ran down Arik's spine as bitter memories of Helder resurfaced. The way he had tormented him for being late to class because of a prank pulled by the three boneheads. Disobedience, weakness, excuses — none of that had any place in Helder's world, and he made sure everyone knew it. More than once, Bero had taken the fall for Arik — and the ten lashes they got for not completely digging the latrine trench were the least of what could have happened.

Finally, Arik added, "Next time, we'll come here with everyone... and level this cursed place to the ground!" The fury in Arik's voice was unmistakable, and a familiar pang shot through his chest as memories of the brutal punishments and Helder's coldness resurfaced. But he quickly calmed down. It was just a brief flare-up. The desire for revenge and the hatred that had fueled him for so long had packed up and left some time ago. But the urge to seize opportunities when they arose had not.

"Stay focused, Arik. Helder wasn't exactly a beacon of good memories during my time either." Diemo seemed concerned that the magister's appearance might lead to hasty or reckless actions. He placed a firm, steady hand on Arik's shoulder, as if offering him support. "Let's get inside before we run into him." With a smooth motion, Diemo gathered the shadows until a pulsating portal formed in the air, ready to take them to the other side — and they stepped through.

CHAPTER 36

"What exactly are we looking for in here?" Diemo's voice was barely more than a whisper. The large room, along whose outer wall they stood, seemed to emit an unknown aura that extended its influence even into the shadow realm — forcing everyone to speak softly. But even that, it seemed, disturbed the oppressive silence in the library. The rows of shelves stretched from one end of the darkness to the other, resembling silent guardians of knowledge long forgotten. The room was empty, yet it felt as though the books themselves whispered, as if the centuries-old dust on their spines commented on their footsteps. The coldness of the shelves seeped through the air, while the chaos outside faded like a distant memory.

Arik didn't respond immediately. He had to focus intensely, using his night vision to get an overview. His lips moved, forming thoughts, but he didn't voice them. Then he closed his eyes, diving deep into his memory. Somewhere, buried in his recollections of the Magisters and their cryptic remarks, there had to be a clue about where they should search. He had often tried to catch the phrases and side comments they carelessly let slip. Had they ever mentioned the storage of the scrolls?

"It's got to be here somewhere..." Arik finally murmured. His gaze wandered aimlessly over the dusty shelves, but his mind was racing. "The Magisters... they never said much about the exact storage, but it must be in a special section. A scroll that describes the process of how these damned power stones can be fused together." Without looking at Diemo, he added, "Outside of the human body, I mean."

Diemo stepped a few paces forward, his eyes scanning the book spines. The air was heavy with dust, wrapping around them like an invisible veil. "And we're just supposed to search... all this?" He gestured vaguely at the shelves, which seemed to stretch into infinity. "Isn't there supposed to be a restricted section?"

"No... the Magisters don't make that kind of distinction. To outsiders, the entire library is forbidden," Arik said, slowly walking down an aisle. "The Magisters don't like disorder." He paused, frowning, trying once more to remember. "Everything's got a system... there must be a section that deals specifically with power stones."

The silence stretched as they searched. Time lost its meaning, the chaos outside becoming just a distant thought. Suddenly, Arik heard Diemo's voice call out: "I found something!" Arik sprinted over to him. Luckily, it was a small section not far from their entry point. To their left, they discovered several scrolls, neatly lined up. "I'll take it from here," Arik said as he began to sift through the rows. "This could take a while, given how many there are." He glanced at Diemo. "You stand guard. The distraction outside won't last forever."

Before Diemo could even find and take a position, a flash of light illuminated the room, yanking both of them out of the shadow realm. For a few moments, they were both blinded and deafened; the shelves had shielded them from worse. Like a small sun, a large bright orb hovered overhead. It pulsed, bathing the library in a bright light. Both knew instinctively that this was no novice's doing.

"Shadow-walkers in the monastery library?" Magister Helder's voice, typically dry and monotone, now carried a hint of surprise. "We truly live in interesting times... indeed, indeed." Neither Arik nor Diemo knew how much Helder had seen. In the shelter of the shelves, Diemo sprinted back to Arik as the Magister continued speaking: "If you're unfamiliar with the orb above you — that's a shadow ban, completely negating your powers. So, reveal yourself and give me one good reason why I shouldn't hand you over to the Extractors!"

Quietly, Arik turned to Diemo. "Find a corner as far away from the light orb as possible, somewhere in the shadows." His mind raced, searching for an escape plan. "He's only seen one of us, so make sure you get out! I'll distract him as long as I can." Diemo understood Arik's plan and nodded. As long as Helder didn't know Arik still had his unlight powers, they weren't entirely doomed.

"I…" Arik hesitated, searching for the right words. "I…" Another brief pause. "I… wanted to speak with you, Magister Helder." The Magister's footsteps echoed through the library, as did those of the people accompanying him. Arik noticed something odd about the way they walked. Helder strode almost elegantly down the aisle, while the others moved almost… clumsily. Laughter and cackling could be heard as well. Helder had brought two Executors, and Arik knew exactly who they were. He needed to keep a cool head; only then could he make the best of the situation.

"Why would a shadow-walker want to speak with me?" Helder sounded curious and excited, as if this situation were entirely new to him. "I can't quite fathom that." By now, Arik had recovered from the flash of light. He effortlessly shifted into the unlight and moved in the opposite direction of Helder's approach. The unlight dampened the brightness of the large light orb, which was soothing to Arik at this moment. Several rows later, he reappeared, knowing he couldn't keep this up forever.

"Have you recently wondered why one of the city patrols was found ambushed and without their stones on the market square?" It was both a distraction and a provocation. This way, Helder wouldn't ask why Arik hadn't approached him directly, instead of tearing half the monastery apart with others. Helder responded coolly and analytically. "Indeed. That did raise a few questions." He pivoted on his heels and slowly walked down the aisle in the direction from which Arik's voice had come. Arik could hear the Executors combing through the rows. "Since you know about the stones, I assume you were involved."

"Good observation, Magister," Arik admitted without hesitation, disappearing into the unlight again, seeking a new position. "There are curious coincidences, shadow-walker," Helder purred, speaking softly. "A little over three months ago, a young Extractor disappeared shortly after his consecration. Three of the Executors in his cohort claimed he had bragged to them about turning his back on the church, now that he had a power stone and all the necessary knowledge." The Magister paused, and Arik reappeared at the other end of the library.

"We searched for the consecrated one for two weeks, and during that time, one of the Explorers vanished. Then, recently, the attacks on the patrols began; and we discovered that the stones of the consecrated ones were removed. You didn't happen to cross paths with that Extractor, did you?" It was a rhetorical question, and Helder was on the verge of piecing together the full picture.

Since Arik hadn't heard any fighting sounds from Diemo's direction, he assumed Diemo had managed to escape. The relief was mixed with frustration, however — the mission itself had failed. The scrolls seemed out of reach, and there wasn't enough time to go through them all. A bitter taste filled his mouth. What would Teto say?

Then one of the Executors turned into the aisle where Arik stood. His face contorted in disbelief when he saw Arik. "That… that… can't be," Michael stammered, "we killed you." He stood frozen, unable to comprehend what was happening. The entire time in the library, he had felt a nagging familiarity with that voice, and now he stared at someone who couldn't possibly be standing before him. When Arik disappeared before his eyes again, panic began to set in. "A… ghost…" Michael continued to stammer, his face drained of all color.

It was the perfect moment. Michael was like a rabbit frozen before a snake. Unable to perceive the unlight, his mind concocted a false explanation. Arik didn't have much time as he remained in the unlight. Crafting weapons from unlight wasn't something he had mastered yet, but it was enough for a simple, sharp knife — Diemo's teachings paying off. The blade wasn't even ten centimeters long. It was quite similar to the shadow weapons, yet it felt different. It felt right. The opportunity was there. He struck.

"Wrong guess," Arik hissed between his teeth as he emerged from the unlight and plunged the blade into Michael's stomach. It slid through the soft flesh like butter. Arik twisted it, feeling a brief moment of resistance before the first blood flowed. He pulled it out and delivered a kick to Michael's chest. Michael staggered back, still wearing a look of disbelief, before toppling over. There was no time for celebration, so Arik kept a cool head, already considering retreat.

There Arik stood in the aisle, blood splattered on his hand, still gripping the knife. "Well, that was unexpected," he muttered to himself in surprise. His breathing was steady, as was his hand. "What now?" he murmured, closing his eyes to better sense the movements of his enemies. He came to a realization: "The mission can't be salvaged. Maybe… I'll finish something else while I still have the chance."

In a loud voice, Arik called out for Helder — he should know who was responsible for the current situation. "The Church of Light was supposed to be my home, Magister. That was my intention for years." The statement, loaded with all the emotions of the past, shot out of Arik's mouth, echoing through the library. It sounded like a justification. "But you never stopped children from beating other children. Eventually, it was bound to escalate." He gathered all his strength and focus to avoid screaming. "The three Executors fed you a lie because they were the ones who nearly killed me!"

A loud, horrified scream—Thomas had realized who the intruder was. He charged into the aisle, only to see Michael lying on the ground. A second scream followed. Thomas knelt beside his fallen comrade and closed his eyes. With vengeance burning in his eyes, he slowly turned his head toward Arik. "How dare you, whipping boy?"

Fury ignited within him, driving him forward. In his eyes, a lowly existence had committed the ultimate sin — not only injuring but killing an Executor. Foam formed at his mouth as he sprang to his feet and charged at Arik. Meanwhile, he conjured two spiked clubs. Arik barely parried the first blow with his knife, but the second hit him, tearing a gash across his forehead. Arik went down, adrenaline surging through his body, his thoughts racing. "Just a few more moments, and I'll be ready again," he told himself.

Thomas loomed over the fallen Arik, his head blocking the giant orb still illuminating the room. "Magister, I've got him — I've got the traitor," he shouted triumphantly, turning back to Arik, his grin wide, ready to taunt the beaten foe. "Any last words, weakling?"

Arik struggled to sit up and then yelled through the library: "Helder, the three implanted me with a shadowstone." Immediately, he took another hit from Thomas' weapon but managed to retreat far enough that it only grazed his nose before he went down again. "I am the masterpiece of your failure, Magister!" Then Arik began to laugh uncontrollably.

Thomas raised his weapon again, ready to deliver the final blow, but he didn't get the chance. A staff of light pierced his chest from behind. Disbelieving, Thomas looked down, his face a mask of shock. Blood started to flow, thick and dark, as Helder dissolved the staff with a curt motion. Thomas twitched once before collapsing lifelessly. "Pathetic." Helder stepped over Thomas' lifeless body, his face twisted in disgust as he looked down at the young Executor.

Helder looked down, his mouth twitching slightly as if he felt a fleeting moment of satisfaction. "One mistake has been erased, now for the second." His voice had returned to the strict, monotone tone that Arik knew and had long feared — a tone that hinted at the harsh discipline that had hardened Arik over time. But now, Arik lay on the floor, laughing uncontrollably, and Helder gazed down at him like an insect he was about to crush.

There wasn't a moment when Arik had felt fear. Not even as Helder stood directly over him, his face showing no mercy. Arik hadn't just managed to surprise Helder and take down Michael, his second tormentor — no, he had sealed Thomas' fate with just two sentences. For Magister Helder tolerated no failure and punished everyone accordingly — a fact that Arik had now used to his advantage.

"Were you also the one who removed the stones from the consecrated ones?" Helder asked as Arik, still deeply amused, grinned up at him. "Of course, Magister, of course. Did you enjoy my work?" Helder's stony expression didn't change a bit. For him, this was merely about filling in a few blanks. "Yes, I could see the talent on display. Some cuts weren't quite clean, though." Disappointment laced his voice.

"That was probably the work of the others who took over," Arik said. The game he was playing was more than deadly — and he was savoring every second of it. Especially when he could see the smallest muscles in Helder's face twitch, revealing more about his emotions than words ever could. "Alexander was the first whose stone was removed. I took it and fused it with myself."

Helder's fingers tightened into a fist almost imperceptibly as Arik spoke. For a brief moment, his breathing changed — heavier, more uneven. Yet his expression remained neutral as he slowly and deliberately replied, "Interesting... very interesting." Only the flicker in his eyes betrayed the storm brewing beneath the surface.

"But explain one thing to me, Arik: What is the end goal of all this?" Helder paused briefly to organize his thoughts. "Although... it doesn't matter what the end goal is. Perhaps you and your little gang of ruffians will manage to stir up more trouble for a while; maybe you'll take over one of the many cities again — but is it worth it?" Helder wasn't expecting a response, and he was even prepared to suppress one.

They locked eyes, staring at each other intensely. Arik had stopped laughing by now. Helder continued, his voice calm but threatening: "You know, the Church of Light isn't some great evil that needs to be stopped. From the very beginning, 50 years ago, the goal was to end the constant conflicts between cities and realms, so that peace could finally reign." Helder's left eyelid twitched, and Arik recognized the sign. It was the tiny movement of a man who was barely containing himself. The slight tremble in Helder's lips revealed the suppressed rage boiling within him. "Every city can voluntarily join the Church's empire and accept its leadership. So much unnecessary bloodshed and suffering could have been prevented."

A long pause followed, allowing Arik to absorb the words. What the Magister explained wasn't entirely off base; many of the cities that the Church had taken over over time had remained conflict-free for decades and developed into major trading hubs. "That's why don't take it personally, Arik, that I now have to put an end to your existence." Helder's words carried regret — and a strange form of respect that Arik had never heard from him in all those eight years. For Arik had deeply impressed him for the first time.

"That's fine, Magister," Arik finally replied. He had been ready to switch to unlight again for several minutes but preferred to toy with the Magister a little longer. A bright light shot from Helder's fingers as he raised his hand. Arik dove to the side, the light sizzling past him, leaving a burning streak on the floor. Helder advanced calmly, as if the swift movement of his opponent didn't concern him in the slightest. "You won't escape me so easily, shadow-walker."

"Don't tell me, Magister, that you carry a firestone." Grinning, Arik got back up, "That would surely violate the Light's purity doctrine you've always preached." Helder didn't take the bait. A surge of pure energy rushed toward Arik as Helder, with a smooth motion of his hand, formed a wave of light. Arik leaped back, feeling the heat brush against his skin as the energy narrowly missed him. The ground beneath his feet sparked where the forces collided. Arik could see the power in Helder's eyes — but he was ready to push it to the limit.

"I'll take that as a yes." It was time to go. Arik knew he wouldn't survive a prolonged fight with Helder. "Then you've been very, very naughty, Magister." One last jab. "At least now I don't have to feel bad anymore for filling up your apple juice with something else. Consider it punishment." Arik grinned at Helder one last time and saw the next wave coming toward him. Quickly, he switched to unlight.

He escaped, making his way out of the library. From a distance, he couldn't hear whether the Magister was cursing or screaming in fury — and at that moment, he didn't care. Arik fled through the cloister, searching for the nearest exit he could find. After just two minutes, he had to end his stay in the unlight and switch back to the normal world. That's when he reappeared before a group of Extractors who had sought shelter in the monastery from Teto's distraction maneuvers. Realizing his mistake, Arik bolted, and behind him, the shouting began. "Unlight-walker!" the cries echoed loudly and repeatedly.

Feeling the burning gaze of the Extractors on his back, Arik raced through the halls. Every step echoed like a thunderclap in his ears. The shouting behind him grew louder — everyone not engaged in the distractions seemed to be chasing him. The footsteps grew faster — they were closing in. Moments later, he found a portal that led outside. Returning over the wall wasn't an option; the use of unlight had drained him too much to immediately use his shadow abilities again. His only option was the gatehouse. More footsteps and shouting echoed behind him. Like a growing herd, they chased him, ready to trample him — especially the Executors, who could count higher than five.

Arik neared the gatehouse. He would have loved to stop and admire the beauty of Teto and Romilda's handiwork — the perfectly executed destruction and chaos they had wrought. But his pursuers wouldn't allow it. He swiftly climbed over the debris lining the way, but he missed the last piece and fell flat on his stomach into the snow and mud. The cold snow burned against his skin, and the icy water soaked through his clothes. His pursuers drew nearer. The sound of boots crunching through snow and rubble echoed in his wake.

Arik struggled to his feet, his legs feeling like lead. He pulled up the hood of his cloak to shield himself from the elements and then limped forward, each step painful, but he had no choice. The footsteps behind him grew louder, ever louder. He felt adrenaline surging through his veins, the pain in his legs drowned out by the sudden rush of energy.

He kept running. Stumbling. The snow clung to his boots. He almost fell again. But he couldn't stop. The pain in his legs and the cold in his bones grew more intense, but he couldn't give up. The cries of his pursuers reached his ears, "Unlight-walker!" and he heard the clinking of weapons, growing closer and closer. His heart raced.

Arik looked up at the hill ahead. That was his goal. If he could just make it a few more meters, he could disappear into the trees. He had to hold on. Limping slightly, he kept running, his lungs burning, but he kept going until the pain in his legs became a dull throb. The hill was not far now.

CHAPTER 37

- 6 -

The events on the hill unfolded differently than Arik had expected. The idea that he could be knocked out in the Unlight realm was something he had never imagined. Wasn't he supposed to be the only Unlight-walker around?

He regained consciousness, a gray veil draped over everything around him. "Had he not left the Unlight?" That was the first question that came to mind. "How long was I unconscious, and who…?"

"Hello, Arik. Long time no see," came a raspy voice from behind him, followed by a brief chuckle.

Vanadis.

Vanadis?

Slowly, Arik turned around. Before he could even see her, the question struck him: "What in the world is she doing here?" Something about her was different; he noticed it immediately. Her hair was tied back, her gaze focused. "Was she wearing some sort of uniform?" She had a thin leather armor over a beige tunic, with straps and buckles everywhere. Arik scanned her from head to toe. Thick, black woolen pants with metal leg guards, and well-padded high leather boots. "If I didn't know any better, I'd say she looks like a soldier or at least a guard." But then again, did he know better?

"Are you going to plant roots here? The others are already waiting for us!" Her voice carried both determination and authority. "Follow me!" she finally commanded and walked westward, past the supply bags, deeper into the dense undergrowth.

Though his limp had disappeared thanks to his power stone, he still had to be careful not to slip on the stones and brush scattered across the ground. Falls in the Unlight could hurt just as much as in the shadow world or reality.

She didn't look back to see if he was following. "I know what you were about to do just now. Not every time will someone be there to stop you from doing something foolish." Her words were strict, her attention focused on the path ahead. "You could have died — weren't you aware of that?"

"Really? You don't say!" Arik threw the sarcasm back at her. "With so many limitless options right in front of me, naturally, I would gladly choose one that would lead to my death."

Vanadis simmered. She had never liked sarcasm — except her own, of course, used to mock others. She felt something about Arik that made her want to bite the bullet, and it stung her pride. She wasn't quite at the point where she wanted to flay him alive, but for now, she came to a conclusion: "Let him be; I'll deal with him once this is over."

"I've worked hard over the last few months to build something with all of you. Do you think I'd just throw it all away at the first sign of resistance? You would have known that if you hadn't vanished! Where in the world did you go? Did you leave because you were scared or something?"

Vanadis could tolerate many accusations, and most of them were even true. But there were some things that enraged her, making her ready to crush anyone who dared throw them at her. Cowardice was one of them.

She abruptly stopped. The wind ceased, and the animals fell eerily silent. He'd done it—she turned around, one of her eyelids twitching uncontrollably. "What did you just say?"

"You heard me, smoke crow."

"Say that again… and you'll regret it."

Simmering turned to boiling. Arik noticed the trees around them seemed to pull away from her — but his brain told him that couldn't be possible. His eyes must have been playing tricks on him. He managed to stay calm. He was going to set boundaries, and nothing was going to stop him.

"What are you going to do? Kill me? My knees are shaking with fear."

"Oh, trust me, I'll find something fitting for you if you don't take that back."

"No chance, you crazy old lunatic hag."

"TAKE IT BACK!"

In the blink of an eye, the boiling had become a volcano, ready to erupt at any moment. Were there actual cracks forming beneath his feet, or was it just his imagination?

"No. And if you've got a problem with that — there's a horde of consecrated ones back there you can take it out on." Arik stayed still. Just a few minutes ago, he had been ready to give up his humanity, to let the stone take over. Vanadis couldn't intimidate him anymore in that state of mind. If she tried anything, he'd pick up right where he'd been so rudely interrupted before.

Her entire body twitched uncontrollably.

"Keep going a few more steps, and you'll find the others. I left something back there." With those words, she left the

Unlight, and Arik followed suit. With one last, narrowed-eyed glare in his direction, Vanadis melted into the shadows. She headed in the direction of the consecrated ones. Why did he feel like he had just unleashed a merciless storm on his enemies?

- 5 -

He stopped briefly and paused. He let go of the protection of light and shadow that had surrounded him. Had he gone too far in provoking her like that? Didn't she deserve to be confronted? Why did she have to react so aggressively? How had Teto endured her for twenty years?

Shaking his head and dismissing his thoughts, he continued on his path. Beyond the dense needle wall of a fir tree, a snowy clearing opened up. Only a small, snow-free circle about three meters in diameter stood out. The entire group was there… and more. Besides the ones he had set out with, there was a young woman about Ostara's age and Fenna's size, along with an older man of Diemo's build. They wore the same type of clothing as Vanadis. Arik's suspicion that it might be some sort of uniform solidified. The young woman winked at him when their eyes met. She seemed familiar, but he couldn't yet place her.

Smiling faces greeted him. Some of his companions looked a bit worse for wear. Small wounds were visible, but Giso had already tended to them. Diemo and Teto appeared unharmed, and no one was in critical condition. Romilda rushed toward him and hugged him warmly. Her hair was disheveled, dried blood clung to her face.

"Where did you go? We were worried about you. Did Vanadis lead you here?" The relief Romilda felt at that moment spilled out in a flood of questions. "Where is Vanadis anyway?"

Romilda had pulled him into the melted circle of snow. Arik could feel the warmth there. He took off his wet linen shirt, and Diemo immediately wrapped his own coat around him. "Thank you, Diemo." Arik snuggled into the warm coat, a blessing for his frozen limbs, and he could feel his fingers again. The older man from Sydrik picked up his linen shirt and held it in the air. Steam rose from it within seconds as it dried.

Meanwhile, Arik answered Romilda's question: "I think she's about to tear into the mob of consecrated ones." The joy and relief in their faces gave way to concern and skepticism. The unspoken question hung in the air — Arik already knew what it was. "I accused her of cowardice for leaving us."

For those who had known Vanadis for years, their emotions quickly shifted again. Panic and fear surged in Teto, Romilda, Diemo, and Ostara. In the distance, they heard a roar.

It was bone-chilling. Flocks of ravens took flight from the trees, seeking a safe place. What they heard was different from Ostara's earlier screams that night. It was more akin to deep thunder and rumbling, like a storm that suddenly erupts, bringing destruction. Another roar echoed, followed by panicked screams. The consecrated ones were fleeing for their lives.

Teto stepped up behind Arik and placed a hand on his shoulder.

"There was a reason the Church made an example of the power stone bearers after the fall of Aregelia. They let the beast slip away, the one that wiped out an entire power stone corps. She was partly responsible for ensuring no more cities fell. The 'example' they made was nothing but revenge for that."

His hands trembled uncontrollably as the words slowly sank into his consciousness. The trembling spread to his legs. It wasn't just fear, but a dark premonition — that what he had set in motion could no longer be stopped. If Vanadis sought revenge for the things he had thrown at her, something worse than death awaited him. He was now sure of that. Meanwhile, he had put his linen shirt back on and handed his pants, which were warm and dry within moments, back. Yet the shaking didn't cease, though Arik knew it wasn't due to the cold.

"What is she even doing here, Teto?" Arik asked his leader. As long as Vanadis was in a rage, he wanted to stay as far away from her as possible.

"Our actions in Aregelia forced the Church of Light to pull forces from the siege in Sydrik. The city is a key part of their supply route, and they need to defend it." Teto rubbed his temples as he explained. "Vanadis and the other four are here to help us liberate the city."

"The other four? I've only counted two so far," Arik remarked, prompting Teto to explain further.

"They arrived at the old camp about half an hour after we left. Two others stayed behind, and Vanadis followed us with those two." He gestured to the pair in uniform. "But we'll get to that later. Diemo told me you were interrupted during the search, and you covered his retreat."

"I'm sorry, Teto. There was no way to retrieve the scroll," Arik said, sounding deeply regretful. "One of the Magisters appeared suddenly, as if he knew we were there. I can't explain how else Helder could have immediately cast a shadow ban."

The pressure from Teto's hand on Arik's shoulder increased, as if to reassure him. He spoke with a firm, kind voice, "We should never underestimate our enemies. The Church's empire is vast for a reason. It's not your fault that the Magister showed up — he was just clever enough to see through the distraction."

Teto took a breath and patted Arik three times on the shoulder. By then, Diemo, Romilda, Ostara, and Giso had joined them. "We'll manage. The important thing is we all made it out, more or less in one piece. Don't you agree?"

A weight lifted from Arik's shoulders as Teto spoke those words. It was true, the Magister had surprised many students over the years with his cunning. It didn't shock Arik that they had been outsmarted by him. "Yes…" Arik responded, slightly unsure after a brief pause, "…I nearly didn't make it. I took a risk, but I had to."

One of Teto's eyebrows rose as curiosity stirred among the others, urging Arik to continue. "Michael and Thomas were the Executors accompanying Helder."

Only Giso and the fighters from Sydrik remained unaffected. Arik continued slowly, unsure of how best to express himself. "Michael… I killed him." Gasps escaped the others. They were astonished that Arik had managed to defeat an Executor. "And… Thomas… he's the one who wounded me, and he was impaled by the Magister."

The group fell into disbelief. A Magister turning on his own subordinates? Romilda finally asked the question on everyone's mind: "Why? Why would he do that?"

Arik stood motionless in the cold. He felt neither shame nor regret when asked this question. He had long known he could exploit the weaknesses of others, but never had he used that knowledge for something like this. "I told him the truth." His voice was calm, emotionless. "That I am his masterpiece of failure because he let students like those three torment me. And that it was they who had implanted the shadowstone in me."

The young woman from Sydrik chimed in, continuing the explanation dryly. "Helder tolerates neither failure nor betrayal. So, the punishment was justified in his eyes. I'm impressed, little brother."

All heads turned toward her at once. Each person mouthed the word "little brother," trying to piece it together. Only Arik began to connect the dots in his mind. "Ilvy?"

They embraced each other tightly, tears streaming down their cheeks as they held each other. They hadn't seen each other in over five years.

- 3 -

It took a while before they let go of each other. A thousand questions raced through Arik's mind, and he wanted to ask them all at once. But his body seemed to have reached the limit of its endurance, and the emotional impact of this reunion weighed heavily on him. Despite the joy of seeing his sister again, he was utterly exhausted — both physically and mentally. Tears mixed with the dirt and blood on his face, and his legs still felt shaky.

In the distance, Vanadis continued her rampage, and the panicked screams of the consecrated ones grew fainter and fewer. The sounds of battle and chaos seemed to fade into the background for a moment as he looked at his sister. Her presence felt surreal, and it took all his remaining strength not to collapse.

"How… what…" Arik stammered, completely overwhelmed by the unexpected family reunion. His voice was shaky, his head throbbing with questions he couldn't even properly formulate. He felt drained, as if his last reserves of energy were slowly ebbing away. Emotionally exhausted, he tried to smile, but the smile felt weak and empty.

His sister had a mischievous smile on her lips and seemed genuinely happy. She noticed her brother's exhaustion and gently placed a hand on his arm, as if to transfer her calm to him. She tied her light brown curls into a ponytail and wiped the tears from her blue-gray eyes. "Maybe Teto should explain — he has a better overview than I do."

The group was still processing the revelations Arik had made just minutes earlier. Diemo, Romilda, and Ostara stared in disbelief at Arik and his sister. They noticed the exhaustion on Arik's face, but no one dared to say anything.

Teto didn't look particularly happy to take on the task, but reluctantly, he began to speak. "Alright. This will soon be known anyway." Despite his reluctance, he spoke calmly and composedly, though an occasional snort revealed his tension. He glanced briefly at Arik, whose shaky breathing betrayed his weakness. "To get straight to the point: Vanadis has been regularly abducting students like Arik's sister from the boarding school and bringing them to the southern lands for the past 13 years."

Silence spread. Occasionally, a distant scream could still be heard. "It's those who stay longer than four years at the boarding school," Teto continued. He hesitated briefly, struggling to maintain his composure, and swallowed hard before continuing, "She…" He had to pause again to control his voice. "She lost both her children shortly after they were consecrated. Their first mission led them to the southern wildlands, and they never returned."

Arik felt a wave of sorrow and sympathy rise within him. But his exhaustion left him no time to fully process the weight of this revelation. He felt the world around him pulling together like a veil, and his head dipped slightly. Still, he forced himself to stay alert — he needed to hear what else Teto had to say.

Teto paused for a moment, his eyes clouded with memories. "Three years before that, her husband — our former leader — also died, and since then, Vanadis hasn't been the same. Together with Raban, she has made it her mission to smuggle as many children as possible to Sydrik to save them from the Church of Light."

- 2 -

Arik heard the words, but they seemed to pass through a fog. His shoulders sagged, and he realized he was barely able to stand. The screams had stopped. The only sound left was something moving slowly and heavily through the thicket of trees. The cold wind carried the scent of damp leaves and blood, and their muscles tensed instinctively. The hair on the back of their necks stood on end as the smell grew thicker.

Teto summoned several shadow spheres, which now orbited his wrist. Romilda and Diemo cautiously moved forward, their eyes sharp and alert. Without a word, they formed their Second Skin from shadows, ready to attack at the slightest provocation.

The rustling grew louder, and through the underbrush, crawling and gasping, a consecrated one emerged. It was impossible to discern the color of his cord at first glance, but the state of the man made it clear that he was no longer a threat. Blood streamed down his forehead, and one of his shoulders hung limply. He clawed his way forward on all fours like a wounded animal, his breath labored as he raised his head with a pleading look. "Please... help... me," he rasped, his voice barely more than a whisper. Then he collapsed, his trembling hand outstretched towards them, hoping they were allies.

Teto examined the consecrated one. For a moment, there was silence, broken only by the distant creaking of trees in the wind and the faint wheezing of the man. Romilda and Diemo exchanged a brief, uncertain glance.

"We leave him," Teto decided, his voice cold and detached. "If he's still breathing later, we'll collect him and remove his stones."

A brief hesitation rippled through the group as they regarded the lifeless body. But then Diemo nodded, his eyes hard. "Understood."

"Diemo, Romilda, take the lead. Everyone else, stay ready for battle. Giso, make sure Arik doesn't collapse."

In pairs and full of tension, they continued their path. The darkness around them seemed to grow heavier. The trail led them deeper into the forest, the cold biting into their skin, but they encountered no other consecrated ones. After a few minutes, they reached the clearing where their supply bags and the spring were located.

Before them unfolded a horrific sight. The place, once peaceful, was now filled with an eerie stillness. The metallic scent of blood hung thick in the air, mingling with the dampness of the forest. Ten or eleven consecrated ones — by their count — lay scattered in bizarre positions, as if they had been thrown around like dolls.

A head grotesquely stuck in the hollow of a tree far too small. Another body dangled upside down in the branches of a tree, blood dripping from the limbs. In the hollow where the spring water pooled, another consecrated one lay submerged — the water darkened, its reflection shattered.

Most of them weren't on the ground but trapped in the branches, as though the forest itself had devoured them. And in the center of it all stood Vanadis. Like an artist admiring her work. She appeared calm, serene, in stark contrast to her earlier fury. A sense of peace radiated from her now.

Everyone in the group felt it — and it unsettled them deeply. A cold shiver ran down their spines, and several gasped for air as nausea rose within them. In that moment, Arik, and perhaps everyone there, silently swore never to provoke Vanadis again. No matter what came.

"Glad you finally made it. Unfortunately, there's no one left. Can someone crack my back?" she called over to the group, waving in the hope Teto had brought one of the healers. Giso stepped forward cautiously, his movements careful, as if a wrong step might spell his end.

"You can come closer," she grinned at him. "You're one of the shadow-walkers from Tarsk, aren't you?"

"Yes, I'm Giso." His steps quickened slightly, and he positioned himself behind her. With a quick jerk and a loud crack, he adjusted her back. Vanadis' eyes widened noticeably. "Right there," she groaned, pain etched in her voice. "Thanks. I'm a bit rusty, and age doesn't help either."

"Glad to help." Giso showed no sign of his unease. Even in the battle for Tarsk, he had been spared such a sight.

Meanwhile, the older Sydriker had pulled the consecrated one from the spring. "He's done for," he noted gruffly, turning the lifeless body onto its back. The water began to clear, the blood washing away. The wind and snow picked up again. Diemo, Romilda, and Ostara gathered the remaining supplies and passed them to the others. The snow under their feet started to melt as the warmth from the spring spread once more.

They took the moment to regain their strength, consuming what food they had left. No one dared challenge Vanadis for her portion — an advantage she clearly enjoyed. As Arik scanned the surroundings, something caught his attention.

"I don't see Magister Helder anywhere," he said, his voice laced with concern. The Magister was a formidable enemy.

"He wasn't part of that uncoordinated mess from before," Vanadis replied dryly. Scratching his head, Teto added, "If I'm not mistaken…" He paused briefly, his eyes seemingly following a hyperactive fly, "… he's the last one left. I expect he's waiting down at the monastery. So, let's go pay him a visit."

After a few more minutes of resting, they set off again, following the narrow path down the hill. Everyone stayed on high alert, ready to respond to any ambush. As they moved forward, they discussed their tactics, the tension growing with each step closer to the monastery.

- 1 -

It felt like an eternity had passed since Arik had fled through this gatehouse — and once again, there was no time to admire the destruction his comrades had wrought. He climbed carefully over the debris lining the path, cautious not to fall again. He approached the courtyard before the library. The entire area was deserted, the wind and snow cutting into his face as he searched for the Magister.

"HELDER!" Arik shouted as he stood in the courtyard. "YOUR LACKEYS WERE NO CHALLENGE FOR ME. PREPARE FOR YOUR END, YOU LITTLE LIGHT WRETCH!"

His words echoed across the courtyard, bouncing off the walls. Nothing happened. Arik strained to perceive even the smallest change. The last bit of energy he could muster was poured into his awareness. His body screamed for sleep and rest. In the distance, he heard the snapping of branches and twigs creaking under the increasingly fierce wind.

His instincts urged him to take a few steps back to avoid being surprised by the wall. Then it happened. The cloister courtyard of the library began to glow. Hundreds, no, thousands of light spheres shot into the sky, scattering in all directions. They lit everything up like tiny suns. The snowstorm stopped abruptly, replaced by falling raindrops. The spheres descended as quickly as they had risen. Suddenly, a portal opened beneath Arik, and he vanished into it. No sooner had the light spheres touched the ground than they exploded, leaving scorched marks behind. In an instant, the courtyard had transformed into a ruined battlefield.

About 200 meters away in the forest, Arik fell out of the portal and landed in the snow. The branches cracked as his feet hit the ground. The portal closed. The group witnessed Helder plowing the field with his light spheres. When it was over, Arik looked toward the wall, where Diemo stood. In one fluid motion, Diemo spread his arms toward both Arik and the field, creating a new portal. "Alright, round two." Arik took a moment to gather himself and then stepped through.

It was always a strange sensation for Arik to enter the portal, and he still struggled to get used to it. The slight pulling was uncomfortable, as was the air growing thicker around him. The faster the portal was traversed, the more unpleasant the experience became. He had hated it when Diemo had made him fall through the portal loop again and again, leaving him disoriented.

Once again, he stood in the courtyard, and Diemo closed the large black portal behind him. Arik took a deep breath, ready to prod the bear. "IS THAT ALL YOU'VE GOT, HELDER? IS YOUR POWER ONLY FIT FOR CHEAP TRICKS?"

This time, he knew the Magister was in the library, and he focused all his attention in that direction.

After about a minute, Helder emerged from the library doors. He looked almost harmless — a small, hunched old man with thinning hair in a beige robe. As snow fell in thick flakes and the wind raged, he walked toward Arik. Calm and unhurried, as if he had all the time in the world. Nothing, not even the forces of nature, seemed to touch him.

With each step, the light around him shimmered, forming into armor — not just a shield, but a warning. The light didn't flicker; it burned steadily, like an eternal flame that knew no fear of threat. Helder didn't find the process necessary, but it was part of the protocol. "These children," he thought, "they still don't understand what true power is."

Arik waited for the right moment. He wanted Helder to make the first move. When they were only fifty meters apart, the Magister stopped and locked eyes with Arik. The air around them seemed to thicken, as if the wind had suddenly held its breath. Nothing stirred. The silence pressed against their ears.

As he had done before in the library, Helder made a sweeping gesture with his hand, creating a wave of light that surged toward Arik. To Arik's surprise, it wasn't as large as earlier that evening. The wave stood two meters high and spread quickly. Still, it posed no real threat to Arik, as Diemo reliably handled his retreat. Diemo had trained tirelessly, perfecting his techniques up to this point. The wave crashed against the wall and dissipated.

- 0 -

Arik was now in relative safety, while the Magister stood on the battlefield. Even as Helder approached Arik, Teto, Romilda, and Diemo were preparing for battle, each donning their shadow armor. Teto, sitting beside Romilda on the wall next to Diemo, gave the command: "Diemo, now." Everything needed to function like clockwork, or the plan would fall apart.

About a meter in front of Romilda, thirteen small portals opened, no bigger than a fist in diameter. Romilda stood up. She could see how, around Helder and behind his line of sight, the exits of the portals appeared. From each portal, one of her shadow hairs shot out, targeting Helder, who was still scanning the battlefield for Arik. Eight tendrils wrapped around Helder's arms, lower legs, thighs, and neck, while the other five converged, aiming to pierce his back armor. Romilda felt her shadow tendrils digging into the light armor. The resistance was strong. Her head pounded, her muscles tensed as she gathered her strength. "Just a little more… just a little more…" But the tendrils stalled, stuck.

They had surprised him and immobilized him completely. Teto didn't hesitate, leaping from the wall. He had about 75, maybe 80 meters to cover to reach the Magister. Hundreds of his shadow spheres formed around him, and with a sweeping motion of his right arm, they surged toward Helder. Darkness and surprise were the advantages the shadow-walkers held. The enemy needed as little time as possible to orient himself or launch a counterattack.

Dozens of spheres found their mark, pelting Helder relentlessly. But he held his ground. Where the shadow spheres struck the armor, the light grew thinner and weaker. After just a few hits, holes began to form, which Helder couldn't close fast enough. At first, the impacts felt like dull blows, but as the armor gave way, he felt them directly — as if someone had punched him in the gut with full force.

"I've almost got you," Teto thought as he closed in on Helder. His muscles burned, each step took more effort, and his breath became labored. Then it happened. The Magister exploded with a sudden burst of light, sending a three-meter-wide shockwave in all directions. The portals and shadow tendrils disintegrated in an instant, and all remaining shadow spheres evaporated harmlessly. Helder stood there, panting, blood trickling from the corner of his mouth.

Without wasting a second, he crossed his arms over his head and swung them outward. A massive orb formed in front of him. Arik and the others recognized it immediately — a shadow ban — and it was five times the size of the one in the library. The ban spread across the entire courtyard, lighting up the surrounding forest. The brightness was blinding, causing the darkness to flicker and making Teto's shadow armor waver, almost on the verge of disintegrating. The atmosphere crackled with energy, and Teto felt the ban pushing against his own power.

Helder couldn't be allowed to gain the upper hand here. Instantly, a wall of shadow erupted from Teto's body — this time directed outward. The wall collided with the shadow ban. Both the Magister and Teto poured every ounce of their strength into maintaining their abilities. His muscles trembled from the effort, and the pressure on his body was unbearable. For both of them, it felt like an eternity as light and shadow battled for dominance. To gain the advantage, Helder funneled the energy from his light armor into the shadow ban, forcing Teto to his knees.

Then something hit Helder from behind. A rapid series of coordinated strikes sent the Magister crashing to the ground, pain shooting through his body. Diemo had used the distraction, running along the wall to position himself behind the Magister, waiting for the right moment — and it came when Helder dissolved his armor.

Helder couldn't process it fast enough. His entire focus had been on Teto, and he had completely neglected to guard his flanks — a mistake that sealed his fate. He hadn't been in active combat for a long time, and his body was far from battle-ready, his muscle memory long gone. They had provoked him and lured him into a trap.

With a diving tackle, Diemo knocked the Magister down and hammered into him with the creed that Gunder drilled into every shadow-walker daily: "Skills aren't the foundation of martial arts — they're just an extension."

They had done it. Helder lay unconscious on the battlefield.

Exhausted, Teto collapsed. Giso rushed over to tend to him. Relief was visible on everyone's faces. Arik, barely able to stand, was being supported. Diemo stood over the defeated Magister, breathing heavily. They all knew how close it had been, and the weight of victory made the last few minutes feel like an eternity.

They had taken the monastery.

Epilogue

They didn't have much time to secure the treasures of the monastery. They estimated two, maybe three days at most, before the garrison from Aregelia would send a patrol to investigate why the monastery had gone silent.

Together with Giso, Arik set to work removing as many lightstones as possible. Vanadis and Diemo had left at first light to search for survivors and bring them to the monastery. Apart from Helder, only three others had survived the night. The Magister was now chained up in one of the training rooms within the library building. The first light of dawn streamed through the windows, falling directly on him. Arik's hands were dirty and still trembling from exhaustion; he hadn't gotten much sleep. Time was working against them.

"We need to hurry," Giso muttered as he prepared the Magister for the extraction. "If they find us here, there'll be no mercy."

Arik nodded silently. He could feel the weight of responsibility on his shoulders. Every lightstone they could secure meant more power in the hands of the shadow-walkers — and less for the Church of Light. But thoughts of power and strategy felt hollow. The battle had taken its toll, both physically and mentally.

"Have you thought about what comes next?" Giso asked as he removed another stone. His voice was calm, but Arik could sense the tension beneath it. It wasn't a question he wanted to face right now. He was just relieved he didn't have to perform the procedure himself.

Arik sighed deeply, wiping the dirt from his forehead, staring blankly for a moment. "Vanadis was sent to help with the city's capture, but I don't know if things will get any easier from here." He paused, closing his eyes. "The Church will send Paladins and fortify Aregelia once they find this looted monastery. We're on the brink of an open rebellion."

He let out a long sigh.

"Can you manage here alone?" Arik asked.

"Don't worry about it."

"I still need to find the scroll. I didn't get to it yesterday."

"It's fine, Arik. Reinforcements will be here soon."

Reinforcements. More shadow-walkers, who could help transport the medical supplies and secured stones from the camp. Hopefully, he'd see Gunda again. Vanadis had mentioned before bed that Bero was at the old camp as well, but Arik had been too drained to react.

Standing in the doorway, Arik turned once more, his gaze falling on Helder. A weary smile tugged at his lips as he reflected on the events of the past few days.

His tormentors were gone; his long-lost sister had resurfaced, and his presumed-dead best friend would soon be at his side again. Gunda... thinking of her brought him a strange sense of peace. She was someone he could trust, someone who understood him without many words. When they spent time together, the harshness of the world seemed to fade, if only for a moment. She was important to him, more than he could express right now.

A sense of contentment washed over him, and Arik simply let it be.

Milton Keynes UK
Ingram Content Group UK Ltd.
UKHW041944131124
451149UK00005B/510